MW00698567

THE
LOGGERHEAD
MURDERS

Georgia Ann Mullen

Copyright © 2019 Georgia Ann Mullen
www.georgiamullen.com

All Rights Reserved

This book is a work of fiction. Places, events and situations
in this book are purely fictional and any resemblance to
actual persons, living or dead, is coincidental.

First published by KDP

ISBN: 9781072670346

Printed in the United States of America

To the volunteers who dedicate their summers to finding sea turtle nests, protecting them, and guiding hatchlings to the sea.

**Other Books
by Georgia Ann Mullen**

The Canal Tales Series

A Shocking & Unnatural Incident

Wixumlee Is My Salvation

Stolen

Table of Contents

CHAPTER ONE

If you asked me, these people were more than a tad wacky. While I relaxed to the sound of shushing waves and pondered the slice of moon overhead, my friend Hannah peered across a short, black plastic fence, squinted at the sand, and willed each grain to move, or so it seemed from the set of her jaw. A few of her friends had their rear ends sunk in beach chairs, but others paced nervously. Even those sneaking peaks at their phones cast rhythmic glances at the sea turtle nest that, in their collective opinion—expressed repeatedly throughout the evening—was taking way too long to hatch. Now Hannah, nest mother for this patch of fertile sand, was talking about sitting through the night. Really? Sea turtle eggs have been hatching on this North Carolina beach for a hundred million years and, until the last ten years, with zero help from humans. They can handle it.

"You really want to stay overnight?" I whispered, trying not to sound incredulous. I couldn't insult Hannah. She'd been kind and supportive, inviting me to Goose Inlet after my husband's violent death, finding me a cottage to rent, introducing me to her friends, trying to pull me out of what she called depression but what I knew was raw anger—stirred into well-cooked guilt.

"You really want to stay all night?" I repeated, knowing I owed Hannah much more.

Hannah had rescued me after my husband, Aidan Finn, was killed in a laboratory accident on Mother's Day. A day he should have been home with his family. His 86-year-old mom, his widowed sister, and his wife— me, mother of his children. Instead he'd gone into his lab at Research Triangle Park and never come out. I was baffled why Aidan would visit his laboratory on a Sunday, something he'd never done before. I still hadn't received an official explanation for the explosion at Tillson Pharmaceutical. What had gone wrong? The company was mum. Aidan couldn't explain it either. Aidan was dead.

"Definitely staying," Hannah replied, digging her toes in the sand. "This nest is a week late. These babies could boil any minute."

I sunk deeper into my chair. Hannah wasn't talking about poached eggs nor did *boil* have anything to do with turtle soup, a dish I'd eaten at Bookbinders in Philadelphia before it closed. To be accurate it was snapper, not loggerhead, but still. It was a culinary venture I'd never admit in present company. No, boil described the anticipated exit of a hundred-plus tiny sea turtles from the sandy nursery that had sheltered them for the last two months.

"But there's no depression," I countered. "Isn't that the first sign?"

In turtle talk, *depression* had nothing to do with mood, although the sight of a small indentation in the sand set turtle people tittering. A depression usually meant activity in the nest and that a hatch was imminent.

"I've sat at nests without a depression, gone home, and found turtle tracks the next morning," Hannah said, scowling. "I'm not going to miss the first nest of the season."

I swallowed a sigh.

"You can go, Abby. No shame in being tired."

Depressed, in the human sense, is what she meant. Because I didn't throw things, cuss, or spit meanness, Hannah thought I'd breezed through the early phases of grief—ignored denial, skated past anger, quickly bargained—and landed solidly in depression, with no hint of acceptance in sight. During woozy talks over bottles of Rioja, Hannah had urged me to climb out of this hole, but truthfully, I didn't want to climb out. For some reason the anger felt right. And anger tempered guilt, if just barely.

Hannah's diagnosis wasn't totally off base. I did slip quickly past the first stage of grief. There was no point denying, since what was left of Aidan was barely identifiable. The explosion was being investigated, of course. A chemistry lab doesn't blow up without attracting the attention of the Chemical Safety Board. Tillson, proud of its rigorous safety management system, was cooperating fully. Just not with me. My questions, good ones from an experienced journalist, weren't answered. All I got was a tight-lipped sentence from his former research director that, "We'll determine what went wrong." *What went wrong* was a pitiful description of the catastrophe that had shattered our family. Any explanation the CSB came up with would be inadequate.

My husband was dead and, despite my grief, I couldn't shake the feeling it was his fault. After shock and disbelief, I sank into fury. And remained stuck.

Around eleven o'clock, nest sitters began folding their chairs, collecting water bottles, tucking phones into cargo pockets. Some had to work the next day. The people who stayed late, besides the supremely committed, were seniors who could still drive in the dark. Tonight, only one man remained along with Hannah and me. I'd met London James at a sea turtle fundraiser soon after coming to Goose Inlet. He'd made a great show of putting his name down early on the most expensive items in the silent auction, but never returned after higher bids were placed. A loose-limbed man who stood too close, he had sniffed around me like a retriever puppy, but I'd refused to give him a solitary pat. Even if I'd been single, instead of recently widowed, I would have stepped away from London James.

I hunkered down in my beach chair, wrapped myself in a blanket to ward off sand flies, and watched London play with his smartphone. After a few minutes he stopped announcing every planet and satellite that passed through his night sky program and began whispering to Hannah. Hannah Hunt, at forty-five, was still a hot ticket and, as far as I could figure, the only reason London hung around the nest. Hannah was tall, square shouldered, and still within her recommended body mass. Still worked at the Montessori school. Still sang karaoke— what she lacked in musicality, she made up in volume. Still consumed by the Goose Inlet Sea Turtle Project, of which she was founder and chief honcho. Besides all that, Hannah was gentle, gracious, yeah, superhuman. So

London James stuck around, pretending to be wrapped up in sea turtles, when I knew damn well he was more interested in wrapping up Hannah. Never trust a man with an inverted name.

"Abby! Look!" Hannah, crouched on hands and knees, peered over the plastic fence.

"What?"

"Turtles!"

Finally. I crawled to the nest and squeezed my eyes into slits. "I don't see anything."

It was pitch dark on the beach and no flashlights or lanterns were allowed to distract the hatchlings from taking their appropriate path to the ocean. Less than a quarter moon cast tepid light across the large square of staked-out sand Hannah called Nest One.

I leaned close to the fence, straining to see anything resembling a tiny turtle.

"Is that a head?"

"Yes," Hannah whispered. "The scout's making his move. See, his front flippers are out." A few seconds later Scout dragged his potato-chip-size body all the way out of the nest and sat motionless, head pointed toward the sea.

No one said a word. We waited in the dark. And waited. Scout didn't move a flipper, but sand seemed to be flicking elsewhere about the depression.

I strained my eyes to see. "What's that wet spot?"

Hannah nudged my shoulder. "You mean dark spot. It's a turtle. Partially out."

So it wasn't my imagination. Baby turtles were in motion, flippers tossing grains of sand. Slowly, the dark spot spread, a couple more hatchlings crawled to the surface, but none exhibited any zeal to charge toward the sea.

"How long is the leader going to sit there?" The dude hadn't moved in ten minutes.

"When the scout's ready, he'll go. Then they'll all go. One hundred eighteen eggs in this nest. The boil will be spectacular."

We waited. I hugged my stomach. Sitting the last few days at the nest, I'd been nonchalant, but now my skin tingled. In all the years I'd know Hannah, I'd never seen a sea turtle nest hatch. We Finns did not take seaside vacations, because Aidan didn't enjoy the beach. He cringed at the grind of sand between his toes. The ocean's "odor" made him queasy. I didn't hold it against him because his dislike was a learned response. I'd once heard his mother describe the marshes around Savannah as "putrid." Besides, Aidan had many good qualities to make up for being anti-ocean. He was a loving family man, and for years we pursued weeks-long vacations in the western part of the state. The woods, hiking trails, and clear, cold mountain lakes were stimulating, but I still longed for our children, Derek and Kate, to experience an honored American tradition, a seaside vacation. To achieve some balance, I'd brought them to the coast for a couple weekends each summer, but our timing never coincided with a turtle hatch.

A chill crept across my shoulders. Stop, Abby. You said you didn't hold it against him. And Aidan can't defend himself.

I sat back on my heels. I was on the beach now and, while I wasn't consumed by sea turtle frenzy like Hannah and her posse, I was ready to guide these hatchlings to the ocean. I wouldn't let Hannah down. Not after all she'd done for me. But the baby turtles continued to take their sweet time, and my mind resumed its wander.

Two months before the explosion killed Aidan, I'd snagged the features editor position at *Carolina* magazine. I'd been a freelance writer when the kids were little, but once they entered school I wrote features full-time, mostly good news accounts. I wasn't one to chase bad news. Digging up dirt was not for me. I'd picked print journalism because the sight of a gaggle of TV reporters chasing a public figure down the sidewalk and shoving a microphone in his face reminded me of a flock of seagulls attacking a toddler waving a hotdog. It turned my stomach. Kind of like Aidan's reaction to suntan oil. Instead, I enjoyed bringing people's talents to light, and there were so many regular folks with astonishing gifts and abilities. The receptionist at Derek's former middle school sang like an opera diva. An accountant at Tillson built experimental airplanes. These people deserved recognition, and I was thrilled to give it to them.

The features editor job came with a comfortable salary but kept me in the office more than I liked. So each month I farmed out most stories to a stable of writers but kept one for myself. I'd had two productive, rewarding months as editor before tragedy struck.

A week after Aidan's death, my boss found me sitting beside his grave in the cemetery. We'd cremated what was left of Aidan's body and buried it, so we would have a place to visit in his memory.

"I came by your house. Kate said she didn't know where you were."

"So, you thought to look here?"

He lifted his shoulders in a "where else?" gesture. We sat together in silence before he said, "Come to work, Abby."

Work? What was that? Nothing. Not important. But he pressed, saying it would be good for me. I went back to the office, but nothing was the same. Nothing was good. Or important. I fumbled at my desk and at my phone and computer. My office walls closed in like the sides of a trash compactor. Anger, guilt and grief wrestled for control, and I had to dash down the stairwells, burst through the exterior door, and lope around the building until the vigorous activity strangely calmed my racing heart. Why all this surging emotion? One, I was furious at Aidan for sneaking off and never coming back. Two, I felt guilty for looking up divorce lawyers three days earlier.

That's all I did. Looked them up. Well, I put a few in my Favorites. I wasn't unhappy with Aidan. I loved him. But I suspected he was up to something and keeping me out of it. For a good four months he'd seemed preoccupied, less interested in me and the kids, and often not in his lab when I called. Sometimes he left for a meeting after dinner. After it happened a few times I stopped thinking "work" and started thinking "working girl." Or rather girlfriend, an outlet I'd never suspected Aidan of seeking in our twenty-three years of marriage. I'd certainly never had a boyfriend. I'd thought about it. What woman didn't? But I'd never acted. Had Aidan acted out a fantasy? I'd let my imagination wander. And so it happened that I was alone one Friday evening and, after ordering three pairs of capris from Land's End and sipping two glasses of wine, I googled "divorce lawyers" and found a few who could be helpful should I decide to pursue a drastic change in my lifestyle. I doubted I would pursue a drastic change. I wasn't a risk taker. But I thought about it.

Hannah shifted. "Are they moving?" I asked. When she shook her head, my daydream continued.

Running around the building didn't help for long. I forgot to return phone calls, misplaced tracking schedules, lost photographs. Deleted a freshly edited story. The main thing I'd been good at, organization, eluded me. I spent long stretches of valuable time staring at a computer desktop collage of jpgs, manuscript files and mislabeled folders, one foot tapping a monotonous rhythm, the same questions circulating through my mind. Why had he gone into the lab on a family holiday? Why did his lab explode? Why couldn't I get answers?

While sympathetic, *Carolina*'s executive editor lost patience. "Take some time off, Abby," he ordered. He didn't need to add that I was making a mess of things. The whole office had been inconvenienced by what he called my "confusion."

"When should I return?" I eyed him warily, bolstered by survival instinct. He mumbled something that sounded like, "You'll know when you're ready." When I asked if he would hold my job, he growled, "Take the summer off. Rest," and guided me out of his office. I could taste my relief. Gone was my responsibility for things that just weren't important.

Hannah came to my rescue, inviting me to Goose Inlet with instructions to meditate and walk the beach. Anger would melt in the summer heat, grief would mellow into longing, and I'd be my strong, productive self again. If my scorching anger would only melt. And my guilt over those three saved divorce lawyers would vanish.

"Too bad the rest of the volunteers will miss this," Hannah said, breaking into my reverie.

Yes, unfortunate for those who sat for hours then missed the hatch. But their absence gave me a front-row seat. Hannah had given me a binder full of information detailing everything I needed to know about loggerhead turtles. I'd begun reading half-heartedly but became captivated by the biology and important contributions these ancient sea creatures made to ocean health. When Hannah said a poaching culture still existed among some of the oldest native Goose Inlet families, I was appalled.

Beside me, Hannah inhaled sharply. Without warning, the scout took off at breakneck turtle speed toward the water. I watched my friend. Her face was as open as the moon. Eyes wide. Mouth slack. Shoulders forward. Expecting the best. Hannah had said that she and two volunteers, LuAnn and Bianca, had moved this first nest from in front of a lifeguard stand to its present place near a dune. One hundred eighteen eggs had been gently dug up and placed in a new nest, the exact size and shape of the original, in this safer location.

I glanced at London, who'd jumped to his feet and appeared mesmerized by the urgency of this first baby turtle, its tiny face scuffed with sand, heading down the long trench that would lead him safely to the water. One out. One hundred seventeen to go.

A smile spread across my face. All Hannah's yapping about turtles and nesting and due dates. It was coming to a head with this first nest of the season. My ambivalence about sitting quietly in the sand for hours washed out to sea. I quivered with a mix of anxiety and awe. I was about to participate in a natural wonder. Cripes, Abby, you are so fickle.

"Scout's gone," Hannah whispered. "Here they come."

What the dark of night had conjured in my mind as a wet spot quickly separated, and three more hatchlings charged down the dark trench. A fifth turtle poked its head and front flippers out of the hole and scrabbled awkwardly, unable to get a grip on the edge. I felt the urge to cherry-pick it with finger and thumb and set it gently on the sand. Encourage it with a gentle pat on its tiny quarter-size shell. But touching hatchlings was a no-no, so I clenched my eager fingers into fists until the baby's front flippers secured enough traction to claw out of the hole. Without pausing, it took off after its nest mates, never looking back.

I scooted as close as possible and gripped my lower lip with my teeth. Here comes the much-touted boil. I'd seen this phenomenon in videos and it was astonishing. To see it in person, well, I had to admit I was jumping in my skin. I stood up and clutched a wooden stake for support. Soon a platoon of turtles would bubble out of the nest, trample carelessly over each other, and march down the sixty-foot trench Hannah and her team had dug to the ocean.

With a lump in my throat, I watched the sunken spot in the sand. And watched. And watched.

"Is that it?" I whispered. Five?

"Of course not." Hannah shifted on her knees and stared after the fifth turtle crawling steadily down the trench. With surprising speed, it had already reached midpoint.

London stood at the bottom of the ditch. "Four in the water," he said in monotone.

"One more's coming. Make sure he gets in the ocean," Hannah called softly, "and doesn't wash back on a wave."

I slipped close beside her. After several long minutes, I couldn't stop myself from asking, "Five turtles? That's all?"

"No!" Hannah replied, her voice tight. "I moved this nest and counted the eggs. I put one hundred eighteen turtle eggs down there." She sat back in the sand. "Sometimes this happens. A few turtles come out but the rest take longer."

Hannah was the expert. She'd founded the sea turtle project with friends who wanted to help this threatened species. She'd organized teams of volunteers to supervise the nests and carried out proactive measures. The project offered turtle talks at the local museum to educate volunteers and the public. She even got town police to warn off bored teenagers and drunken tourists who got their kicks riding the backs of mama turtles that crawled onto the beach at night to lay their eggs. Hannah had done a fine job educating both visitors and residents about the need to protect endangered sea turtles. How could some Inlet natives still think sea turtle eggs made tasty omelets?

"I'm staying tonight," Hannah said, adding quickly, "Abby, you don't have to."

London dragged his beach chair beside her. "I'll keep you company."

I watched my friend slump onto a blanket and knew she was troubled. Hannah had shared stories about her many experiences with turtle hatches. Sometimes the nest hatched in pieces. A couple dozen one evening, the rest late at night or, on rare occasions, even the next night. But five measly turtles? That wasn't normal.

I squatted beside her. "More will come. Give it time." God, Abs, can you sound more condescending? Hannah barely nodded. I folded my beach chair, found my sandals, and walked through deep sand to the parking lot.

I unlocked my new beach cruiser, a whim purchase based on it being purple and on sale, and pedaled home. As my feet made routine rotations, I wondered just how bad a friend I was. A good friend, a genuine friend would have kept Hannah company on the beach. But, tonight's thrill had flared and fizzled. Even though it was a slow year for nests by Goose Inlet standards, if I missed this hatch, there'd be another. Two nests had been laid early in May before I got here. Two more the first week of June. Half of July was over and that meant no new nests had been found in more than a month. Volunteers wondered aloud why mama loggerheads had given up on Goose Inlet. The sea turtle patrol drove the entire length of the beach every morning but returned with nothing new to report. No one had a clue why mama turtles had stopped scoring the beach with their tractor-tread flippers. Stopped scooping sand. Stopped dropping eggs. A count of four nests was at the low end of the spectrum, but nesting season lasted till the end of August. At least that's how long turtle people patrolled.

I pedaled through the quiet streets, telling myself that I'd sit with Hannah tomorrow night when the rest of

Nest One hatched. Unless the little critters crawled out tonight, like she hoped. And I hoped they would, because what could have happened to one hundred-thirteen turtle eggs? Hannah's comment about a poaching culture in the Inlet tainted my thoughts, but I pushed that nastiness aside. Besides, London stayed. He didn't strike me as a beach person, but Hannah said he'd rented an oceanfront house at the beginning of nesting season and made the trip every weekend from Raleigh. Today, he'd arrived at sundown and when he wasn't chatting up Hannah or plotting the stars, texted nearly non-stop. Hannah said he was a sales rep for a pharmaceutical start-up. Today he must have come right from work, because he still wore dress slacks and a button-down shirt. That attire in itself did not put him out of place, but I found it odd that, while volunteers doffed their flip-flops as soon as they reached the nest, or sooner, London never took off his wingtips.

* * *

No turtles crawled out of Nest One Saturday night. And none Sunday night. On Monday morning I stood beside Hannah, staring down at the tiny depression that had yielded five baby loggerheads.

"I talked to Will," Hannah said, squeezing the fingers of one hand with the other. "I told him about our poor hatch on Friday." Will Brown was North Carolina's sea turtle project biologist. If Hannah wanted to move a nest or do anything outside protocol, she needed Will's approval.

"I know nests have been late in the past," she continued. "Some we sat for fourteen, sixteen days.

Those were usually late September and October nests. But we had five live babies hatch at a decent time, sixty-eight days after nesting, then nothing." She kicked the sand with her bare foot.

"Do you think somebody maybe—?"

"Will told me to dig tonight," Hannah said hurriedly. "Treat it like a normal excavation three days after a hatch." She looked at me expectantly.

"I'll be here, Hannah." I threw an arm across her shoulders, "It'll be okay."

CHAPTER TWO

At seven o'clock Monday evening, a covey of volunteers and tourists crowded around Nest One. I was surprised to see London James, who obviously had not returned as usual to Raleigh Sunday night.

"I hope you find live babies," I told Hannah. At least a few. If it turned up one hundred-thirteen unhatched eggs, or unfertilized eggs, or damaged eggs or whatever, Hannah would be crushed. Over the weekend she'd nibbled her lips raw and, never giving up on a hatch, had guarded the nest all Sunday night. Dark circles rimmed her eyes. What a lousy start to the season. Off to the side, volunteers clustered, mumbling about the Inlet's odd first nest.

"Damn strange. I lived on this beach my whole life. Never heard of a nest with just five damn eggs," Dutch Magnus, a big-bellied man in cutoff jeans, said. He sported a twisted, pointed, dreadlocked beard that stuck out horizontally from his chin like a misplaced unicorn horn. Dutch had hung out at Nest One a few times but wasn't a member of the team. Loud and garrulous, he'd spent at least an hour this evening chatting up tourists, explaining turtle behavior and answering questions with authority. Hannah said he owned the Big Bang fireworks store on the South Carolina border, but left running of it to a friend and spent most of his time at the weather-beaten Goose Inlet beach house his family had owned for generations. Referred to in town as Dutch's Digs, it squatted like an old gray toad a couple lots down from my rental cottage.

"You, too, Joop." Dutch elbowed his companion. "Your family's been here longer than mine. What kind of a nest got only five damn eggs?"

Joop Dahl hitched up his board shorts to better show off his eighty-four-year-old knees. His wide feet were scarred and callused from close to a century of walking barefoot. "Shoot, I remember hundreds of them little turtles crawling all over the sand. We use to play with 'em. Make 'em run races for us."

"Christ, Joop. Pipe down." Dutch glanced over his shoulder. "Miss Hannah's already in a blue mood. She hear that she'll run you off the beach."

"Naw, she won't. Me and her's tight." Joop held up one hand and attempted to entwine two arthritic fingers in the universal *tight* symbol. He gave up and flipped his skinny, gray ponytail over his shoulder. "She told me I'm one of her greatest historical assets."

I knew Hannah had made great effort with Dutch and Joop to bring them into the turtle fold and consequently educate their scores of relatives. In the early years both men, whose ancestors, Hannah said, had settled this stretch of North Carolina sand in the early 1800s, would torment volunteers with stories about being sent to the beach by their grannies to dig up turtle eggs for grandpa's breakfast. Dutch, when he got a little drink in him, was especially offensive. Hannah said that when she reproached them, they claimed to be telling ghost stories.

Smart woman, she took the sting out of their tales by turning them into instructive lectures. She asked Joop to give a short history talk at the start of each season's orientation meeting. With this outlet, he no longer had to boast about the turtle conquests of his youth. He was even on the turtle patrol, driving the four-wheeler once a week at six a.m. up and down the length of Goose Inlet, looking for nests laid overnight. With his decades of experience, he was the project's best spotter of the tractor-like tracks leading out of the ocean and back, the number one indication of a newly laid turtle nest.

I liked Joop. Dutch, ten years his junior, was a bit sketchier. He shared patrol duty with Joop but spent each afternoon at the Chubby Fish, swilling down dark beer. I knew this from volunteers' gossip, and also because he kept me informed. Whenever I asked, "How's your day going, Dutch?" he'd huff, "Just left the Chubby Fish," as if exiting a global conclave.

I watched a family approach the excavation. The dark-haired girl looked about seven and tiptoed up to the nest, hands clasped beneath her chin, trying to peek past the grownups. Her brother, a gangly boy of maybe ten, hopped over the trench and back, dodging his mother's hand as she tried to catch and settle him. I vaguely recalled the trio sitting with volunteers for one, maybe two, evenings but never staying late. Today, a tall, muscular man with close-cropped, light brown hair walked up from the shoreline and joined the family near the excavation site.

"Benito!" he said, as the boy poised to jump. Benito came and stood beside his mother. The girl slipped her hand into the hand of the man I guessed was her father, although he didn't have the rest of the family's dark coloring.

"Let's do it," Hannah announced with a two-beat hand clap. The black plastic fence had been taken down, rolled up, and stacked off to the side. Hannah knelt in front of the slight depression that still marked the nest. With both hands gloved, she began to slowly scoop away sand. LuAnn Sheetz, the lank-haired, mid-forties volunteer who had helped move the nest more than two months ago, knelt beside her, solemn-faced and silent.

LuAnn's boyfriend had disappeared a week ago in what appeared to be a boating accident. Dutch Magnus had laughed about "that clumsy fool Randy Boone" falling out of his fishing boat. Other volunteers were sympathetic, consoling LuAnn and, while not promising Randy's safe return, maintaining that he'd be found soon. Hannah said LuAnn called the Coast Guard daily to see if they'd found his body. I watched the woman's pinched face and wondered how close she was to bursting into tears.

Hannah had given LuAnn the task of tallying up everything gleaned from the nest. Pieces of shell. Maybe some eggs that didn't hatch. Hannah said an accurate count was required in her report to Will Brown, who in turn maintained meticulous records for the state. LuAnn had first refused, but Hannah, perhaps thinking the activity comforting, had coaxed her to participate.

I picked up a plastic pail with an inch of water-covered sand in the bottom. Here Hannah would place live turtles rescued from the nest. If they were healthy, they'd crawl to the ocean, marking this beach as home. If they were female, and survived twenty-five to thirty years at sea, they would return to lay eggs on the Carolina coast. Maybe even on this same beach. The state required Hannah to remove one egg from each sea turtle nest immediately after it was found, so that the egg's DNA could be recorded and biologists could track where turtles nested and which hatchlings were related.

Twelve inches down, Hannah hit wet sand. Her scooping became slower and more laborious. Soon she was lying on her stomach, scraping handfuls of cement-like sand, concentrating on digging directly below the exit hole. In a few more minutes, she'd clawed out an eighteen-inch depth.

"Here's one!" She handed the remains of one hatched turtle egg to LuAnn who set it down gently. Dig, dig, dig. "Here's the second one." She handed over another dull white, rubbery mass. Scraps of the third, fourth and fifth eggs followed.

Hannah dug deeper, without result. No eggs, hatched shells, or live baby turtles. She rotated her body and start digging at an angle.

"Sometimes they take a twisty route to the top," she said, scooping until she'd made a tunnel on the diagonal. "The actual nest could be off to the side."

Bianca, another long-time volunteer and LuAnn's co-worker at a local coffee shop, started digging in a different direction. Soon they made a cavity two-feet wide and two-feet deep, but did not find a single turtle egg, shell remnant, or live baby.

Bianca sat back on her heels, face twisted. "How many eggs did we move?"

"One hundred eighteen," Hannah mumbled, just loud enough for me to hear. "They're down here. Gotta be." She continued to reach deep inside the hole, making another venture off to the side, digging beneath the dune.

After a few minutes, Bianca said, "Stop, Hannah." She laid a hand on my friend's shoulder. "The nest is empty."

Hannah grunted. "Wait. I—I've got something." Hand still deep within the hole, she turned her head, a bright smile lighting her face. "I feel feet wiggling! It's a live one!" With one arm, she boosted herself into a sitting position and held out her hand. Then, with a yelp and a gag, threw its contents into my plastic pail. I stared into the bucket.

Inside, three human toes—painted red—dangled from a thin strip of skin.

CHAPTER THREE

Hands on hips, Goose Inlet Police Detective Erik Magnus stared at the red toes lolling in the plastic pail and ignored the man talking loudly beside him, his uncle Dutch. How the two could be related, I could not fathom. Hannah had said they were joined by blood and that the detective was a disappointment to his uncle, who had raised him to be—well, to not be a cop. There was some family resemblance. The detective—I figured him for mid-forties—had his family's height and bulk but had not yet developed the Magnus paunch. I hoped he wouldn't. He was strikingly handsome with a salt and pepper goatee and mustache, dark brows, and eyes that lingered, as if he were thinking things over. His wavy black hair was pulled back in a short ponytail which contrasted, not unpleasantly, with his dress slacks, sports coat and tie. Despite his formal attire, he didn't look out of place on the beach. Perhaps because he'd taken off his dress shoes and socks and stood chucking one heel into the sand as he pondered the red toes.

The man staring into the big hole in the sand was marine biologist Will Brown. He was a lean guy with sinewy arms and legs muscled from surfing. Hannah had praised his physical and mental attributes to me over a bottle of Malbec and had hinted she wouldn't kick him out of bed for eating crackers, even though he was a good ten years younger than she. With his blond buzz cut, T-shirt, khaki shorts and bare feet, he looked barely out of his teens, but Will Brown was far from a kid. He had a master's degree in marine biology and had started in the state's environmental department as an intern before being hand-picked to head the sea turtle project.

Two police officers had encircled the excavation site with yellow tape, patiently nudging Dutch, Joop, and a flock of volunteers and tourists outside the ring. The man that I'd presumed last evening was Benito's father stood off by himself, hands in his pockets. A couple yards behind him stood another man wearing a uniform-style work shirt and boots. Dark hair curled out along the rim of his baseball cap. He didn't look familiar, but my acquaintances in Goose Inlet were limited to Hannah's friends and turtle people. Obviously, not everyone fell into those categories.

"Erik! Erik!" Dutch called. "Damn it, Erik. I'm talking to you."

"You should have called us right away, Hannah," Magnus said, turning his broad back on his uncle.

She slumped. "I know but—I called Will—he couldn't make it till morning." Her voice trailed off. "He left before dawn to get here," she offered, as if to placate the detective.

It was now eight o'clock Tuesday morning.

"We stayed all night. Me. Bianca. Dutch and Joop." Hannah glanced around. "Abby, too. Nobody tampered with the nest," she said, perhaps by way of apology. She gripped her elbows. "Or what should have been a nest."

"What should have been a nest is now a crime scene. It was a crime scene last night, too. You should have called the police." Magnus would not give an inch.

Hannah looked off to the side and sunk a canine into her already raw lip. "So, what do we do now?"

"Well, we could dig up the other nests and see if we find the rest of the body."

"Absolutely not!" Will Brown bounded away from the nest, eyebrows drawn low, mouth puckered. Hannah grabbed his arm, as much to steady herself, I thought, as to stop him from coming nose to nose with Magnus.

"Relax," Detective Magnus said firmly. "That was a joke."

"A lousy one," the biologist snapped.

Chatter beyond the yellow tape stopped. Everyone watched Magnus, then Brown, then Magnus again. Hannah patted the project director's arm and whispered something I couldn't hear. Brown's shoulders sagged. He ran a hand through his short hair. The detective looked Brown up and down, then looped his thumbs inside his belt and turned back to the nest.

A volunteer named Fala called from behind the yellow tape. "We're not just all about the turtles, Erik. It's terrible someone's been mutilated like this. We're sickened. Every one of us." Ignoring the comment, Magnus wrote something down in a small notebook he'd retrieved from his shirt pocket.

Brown straightened his back. "But catching the mutilator is your job, Detective," he said with an edge in his voice. "My priority— Hannah's, the volunteers—our priority is protecting the turtle nests."

"Someone stole one hundred thirteen sea turtle eggs, Erik." Hannah choked on the words. "And stuck those toes in their place. To laugh at us."

I squinted at Hannah. True, there had to be a connection between the toes and missing sea turtle eggs, but I couldn't fathom where laughter fit in with something so disgusting.

In an imitation of Will Brown, Hannah shot a hand through her own short, brown hair. "You don't even know if the toes are real." Her voice rose to a squeak on the last word.

Good point. I did think what appeared to be toes—pinky, ring and middle—looked a bit plastic. Especially painted red all over. Not just the nails.

"They look real to me," Magnus replied. He nodded at a man tripping through the deep sand toward us. "But here's the man to answer the question. Doc Bailey."

"Sorry I'm late. Another gang murder in the city." Doctor Bob Bailey—I'd seen the medical examiner's photo in the newspaper—slipped on latex gloves. "So, what do we have?"

He reached into the plastic bucket and pulled out the flexible mass of what at least some of us suspected was human flesh. Turned it over. Wiggled the appendages. To my horror, "This Little Piggy" coursed through my head.

"Well, they're real. Human. With a bad pedicure." Bailey dropped them into a clear evidence bag.

"Any guess on how long they've been buried?" Magnus asked.

"Erik, you know I don't guess. Decomp isn't too bad, maybe because of this nail polish, or whatever it is, coating them. It's holding the skin together. But I'm not saying anything till I do my exam." Bailey lifted the bag to eye level. "Damn strange, though, that red polish. Or paint. Or, whatever."

Hannah covered her mouth with her hand and looked away.

"Today's July 19," Magnus said. "So, this nest was laid, when, Hannah? Early May?" The detective knew his turtle stuff.

"May 9. Last Friday it was a week past its hatch date," she replied.

Bianca ducked under the yellow tape and sidled over to the group. "We moved this nest, Erik."

The detective's head jerked up. "Who moved it? When?"

LuAnn Sheetz, who'd been gazing out at the ocean from her post beside the excavated nest, dropped onto the sand, brows scrunched tightly together. Last evening when Hannah had pulled the red toes out of the hole, LuAnn had scrambled away on hands and knees and puked behind a trash can. Who could blame her? Your friend reaches into a nest and feels something wiggling, thinks it's a sweet little baby turtle, but it ends up being three human toes. It's a wonder the whole gang of us didn't heave. And on top of it, one hundred thirteen turtle eggs had vanished. Like Hannah, LuAnn was taking the loss personally.

"The turtle project!" Bianca snapped, her bush of silver hair vibrating like a sheaf of wires. "Who else would move it?"

Magnus's jaw set. "I want to know who actually moved this nest. I want a name."

Bianca counted out on her fingers. "Hannah, LuAnn, and I moved it. Early in the morning. Right after Joop found it on patrol. It was in a bad place."

"We moved it away from foot traffic," Hannah mumbled.

"And I personally counted one hundred and eighteen eggs left, after the one we had to give to Will." Bianca said. "Only five hatched. So what are you going to do about that, detective?" She crossed her pudgy arms. "Somebody stole those eggs." Her glance bounced among the volunteers, locals and tourists standing outside the police tape. "Poachers!"

A collective gasp burst from the crowd. It was the first time the "P" word had been said out loud.

"My priority is the person who was attached to those toes." Magnus jerked his head toward the bag Doc Bailey held.

"You can't assume he's dead," Bianca argued. "Maybe he sliced 'em off with a weed whacker."

Magnus rolled his eyes but before he could respond, Doc Bailey asked, "Did a fox get 'em? The eggs, not the toes. I know foxes can be trouble."

"We never saw ripped shells scattered around the top of the nest, showing fox predation," Hannah replied, coming out of her trance. "We had netting over this nest like the others, specifically to keep foxes and dogs out. There it is." She pointed to a tangle of orange plastic netting tossed against the dune. "Foxes didn't get one egg, let alone one hundred and thirteen."

Magnus walked away from the nest and stared out at the glassy ocean. Was he thinking the same thing I was? Mainly, what a way to wreck a beautiful morning. The breeze was gentle and salt-scented. I could barely hear the waves washing the sand. After a couple minutes, the detective returned, rubbing the back of his neck.

"It's obvious we have two crimes here. Number one, a dismembered body." He didn't say, but in my head I heard *possible murder*. "Number two, poaching of sea turtle eggs."

"A federal crime," Hannah declared. "A crime against a protected, endangered species."

Magnus held up his hands. In my head, I heard *save the sermon*.

"Will you solve both crimes, detective?" LuAnn asked. Everyone looked at LuAnn as if she'd popped up out of the sand.

Magnus shook his head slowly. "Missing eggs aren't my priority."

"What about the SBI?" Joop shouted from behind the yellow tape.

"Don't be an idiot." Dutch nudged him. "All the state bureau of investigation cares about is busting meth labs and telemarketing swindles."

Will Brown narrowed his eyes. "NOAA and Fish & Wildlife will look into it." Like Hannah, Brown had turned quiet, almost meditative.

"Good. Give 'em a call," Magnus said. "They should know somebody poached your eggs." He ducked his head and a corner of his mouth lifted.

The detective walked a short distance, turned and scrutinized each person standing around the excavation hole, then the volunteers huddled behind the crime scene tape. Does he suspect one of the turtle people of placing those toes beneath the nest? Why on earth would someone do that? Anyone, let alone a turtle person. When his dark gaze settled on me, my skin prickled. Cripes, what a look. He can make a person feel guilty even when she's not.

Magnus walked back to Hannah, thumbing his chin. "I'll talk to the chief. He might be able to beef up the night patrols. If we can spare the manpower. In the meantime, I'll have my men dig out that hole. Just to make sure the rest of the body isn't in it."

A look of panic crossed Hannah's face.

"They'll go easy. Small shovels." Magnus said. "You can supervise." He watched her closely. "You're pretty sure there aren't any eggs or live turtles in there, right?"

Hannah rubbed her brow, as if soothing a headache. Finally, she answered. "I'm sure, Erik." Big sigh. "I'm sure."

The volunteers watched Detective Magnus pick up his shoes and socks and stride toward the beach access. Were they thinking the same things I was? A maiming and possible murder. Poaching on a beach with good turtle PR. The crimes were a billboard flashing "Big Trouble in Goose Inlet."

CHAPTER FOUR

I'd never seen Hannah so down. Red eyes. Droopy mouth. My friend was hurting. Yet Bianca's demand that Detective Magnus find the turtle egg poacher, while barely glancing at the three lonely toes stuffed inside Doc Bailey's evidence bag, irritated the hell out of me. And I had the sick feeling Hannah shared Bianca's mindset. True, if the eggs had been poached someone had committed a federal crime. Doing anything to harm or hinder endangered sea turtles was a felony. I wasn't sure if lopping off someone's toes registered as serious in the law books, but it certainly ranked high in the moral code.

As minutes passed, watching Hannah sift sand through her fingers, my irritation dwindled. While Bianca was close to the edge, Hannah was not callous. Hannah had a special relationship with loggerhead turtles. She knew and loved everything about them. Nobody knew who owned those toes. The toes weren't personal.

After the officers finished their search, I lured Hannah to my cottage for coffee. Lily Pad was a small, one-story house a couple blocks from the Inlet's only stop light. While wind and salt water had wrinkled neighboring houses, my cottage boasted a new coat of turquoise paint and bright white workable shutters. In the living room, a space large enough to accommodate a six-foot sofa and two upholstered chairs, a wide picture window welcomed a winsome view of the beach. Behind the sofa, a round, scarred table surrounded by a gaggle of mismatched chairs waited patiently for dinner. I hadn't cooked much in the small galley kitchen, preferring to toss seasoned meats onto a wobbly grill that sat on a cracked concrete patio. Protein and a salad made up most of my meals. If I ever decided to break into a cooking frenzy, I'd be accommodated by a surprising length of counter space, always a good thing.

Behind the living room and kitchen two square bedrooms overlooked a sandy back yard anchored by dollar weed. Most neighboring bungalows settled in overgrown jungles of wax myrtle, oleander and Indian hawthorn, but Lily Pad's shrubs were trimmed and healthy. A small front lawn separated it from Pinfish Lane, a narrow, one-way street dividing the cottages from a stretch of low dunes that merged into the beach. The cottage's best feature, however, was a long, wide porch across the front. So far, that's where I'd spent most of my time. Reading. Watching. Wondering if I'd ever recover from or learn the reason for Aidan's death.

"I understand your anguish," I said, setting down a carafe alongside cups, sugar and milk. "You put ten years into this project. Educating the locals. The tourists. But someone still might have poached turtle eggs in Goose Inlet. Do you have any idea who would do that?" I filled two cups with rich Sumatra, deciding not to comment on the lack of concern over the owner of the toes. I hadn't heard much beyond "ughs" and "ohs," and some low grade gagging as volunteers crowded around the plastic pail. Hopefully, after they thought about it a while, turtle people would cease to reflect Miss Bianca's lack of sympathy.

Hannah reached for the sugar bowl. "I hate to say it, but my best guess? One of the old families." She stirred two teaspoons of sugar into her cup. "It was, and may still be, part of their culture. We stopped them from running baby turtle races but—" Her sigh could have matched the exhaust from a hot air balloon.

I set my cup down with a thump. "Are you saying Joop or Dutch got a hankering for turtle egg omelets and couldn't stop themselves from digging up a nest? And eating one hundred and thirteen eggs for breakfast?" I laughed but shrank inside when Hannah's lids lowered.

"Sorry." I hid behind my coffee cup. "Just trying to wrap my head around this. The world has billions of chickens. Why do people have to steal eggs from an endangered animal? Chicken eggs aren't good enough?"

"Chicken eggs aren't erotic."

"Huh?"

"In some cultures, sea turtle eggs are prized as an aphrodisiac."

I leaned back in my chair. "Like rhino horn?" Everyone knew those animals were poached to provide men, particularly in Asia, a little boost, at least psychologically. "You're talking way beyond omelets."

"And aphrodisiacs go way beyond rhino horn." Hannah rested her forearms on the table. "You've never heard of tiger penis soup?"

I swallowed hard.

"Or deer dick wine?" Hannah stretched across the table. "In China, athletes drink deer dick wine to heal injuries *and* boost sexual performance." An unnerving elaboration that made me queasy.

"Next time we eat Thai, remind me to skip the plum wine, just in case."

"It's all a bunch of crap." Hannah slapped the table top. "There's no evidence this guzzling does anything to keep a phallus from flopping."

I swallowed a chuckle. "It's a placebo."

"That's no excuse to murder animals. Some of them are almost extinct! Sperm whales, sharks, tigers, bulls, seals, rhinos, seahorses, blowfish. Sea turtles!"

Hannah does her homework. She'd been a high school biology teacher for years in Raleigh. Which might explain her attraction to Will Brown. She and I were close friends in college, Hannah helping me through a trying time in my life. A few years after graduation, we developed an interest in gardening that took us to nurseries and garden shows around the country. Our friendship was tested only slightly—and only jokingly—when Hannah moved to Goose Inlet and I admitted being jealous of her living by the ocean. Five years ago she left her job as the Inlet's middle school science teacher and took a position with the local Montessori, saying she wanted to teach children how to respect nature when they were little and easier to influence. And more playful. In her view, more loving.

"Sex isn't the only incentive," Hannah said. "Turtle eggs are healthier than chicken eggs, lots of protein, and taste better, according to those who've tasted them. Dutch and Joop were keen on pointing that out to me when I first met them. Ugh! The arguments we had. First over their violations against sea turtles. Then over the obnoxious stories they told project volunteers, just to get a rise out of them."

"How'd you meet those guys?" I occasionally saw Joop at Briny Bill's, the local grocery. He and Dutch had bantered through a disjointed range of topics the few times they sat Nest One. Hannah suggested more than once that they take their loud discussions farther down the beach.

She poured herself another cup of coffee. "It was hard to avoid them. I met Dutch when he trampled me coming out of the Chubby Fish. Damn near broke my foot. I met Joop on the beach." She raised her face to the ceiling and closed her eyes. "He was sitting in the lotus position, eyes sealed, smoking a cigarette." She pantomimed placing and removing a cig, once, twice, three times. "At least two other spent smokes were stuck in the sand. I told him the beach wasn't his personal ashtray, and he better put those butts in the trash can when he was done."

"What did he say?"

She opened her eyes. "He told me to butt out."

Hannah considered the beach an extension of her home, which meant she wanted it clean. She still took a three-mile amble along the shoreline every morning, picking up trash. She claimed that if the sunrise was beautiful, she glowed all day. Sometimes she invited me to join her. On the mornings she didn't, I was content to lie in bed, think about Aidan, and slip through a sluice of anger, guilt and gloom. My feelings shifted each day and sometimes each moment. One minute I was frustrated, the next remorseful, the next brokenhearted. I'd lost my husband. Forever. And I didn't know why.

On that fateful Mother's Day, we'd brunched at a café known for stuffed French toast and gourmet Eggs Benedict. It had been a joyful meal. Warm spring sunshine filtered through the gauze curtains. Kate and Derek turned off their phones and engaged their grandmother and aunt in playful conversation. Aidan took one call just as breakfast was being served then turned his phone off, too. Afterward, we took a stroll through the arboretum, not too long, because his mother couldn't walk far. I expected we would take Mom and Sis home, then spend the afternoon playing board games before our kids headed back to their own digs. But Aidan had driven us home and announced he needed to stop at the lab to check a chemical reaction. I thought he was joking. Aidan never did that. He was a hard-working scientist but not obsessed. He didn't work evenings or weekends. My mind jumped to his mysterious evening meetings, and I followed him to the car. When I offered to come along for the ride, he insisted he had to go alone and, after a quick kiss, off he went. Never to return. I was still waiting, with less and less patience, to learn what had blown away my husband of more than two decades. And why.

"Abby." Hannah touched my arm.

"Huh?"

"I lost you."

I blinked a couple times. "The placebo—?"

Hannah shook her head. "I was telling you how I met Joop. I really got to know him a few mornings later when I saw a man digging in the sand with his hands. I walked up behind him and saw the hole was deep. He was so busy, he didn't hear me. He pulled out a rubbery white egg and put it in a bucket. Then he dug out another. And another. When I asked if those were sea turtle eggs—I knew they were—he jumped. He stared at me a moment but went right back digging. I knew sea turtles were endangered—loggerheads have been on the list since '78—and what he was doing—digging up their eggs—was a crime."

"You told him so?"

"Of course I did!" Hannah reached into a bowl of fruit on the table and pulled out a banana. "He ignored me. I swear, if there'd been a hunk of driftwood handy, I'd have conked him on the head." Her nose wrinkled as if smelling something stinky. "We're friends now, but the memory still makes me angry."

"Do you think Joop—?"

Hannah tugged a long strip of peel off her banana. "Stole the eggs?" She shook her head. "I just can't grasp how he could. He's an odd duck, but he's been a volunteer for years. Patrols every Wednesday."

"What about Dutch?" I asked. Dutch lived in one of the most ramshackle cottages along the ocean. Vines, none of the pretty blooming kind, strangled the tilting front porch. Sand, weeds, and oyster shells made a patchwork quilt of his front yard. What I called neglect, Dutch called local charm.

"He's in the project, too," I said, "but, I don't know, breakfasts like grandma used to make? Old customs die hard. Or, maybe one of them," I fluttered my eyelashes, "has a girlfriend and maybe on a whim—"

"Those two old codgers!" Hannah snorted and wiped banana off her lip.

"Exactly! Those two old codgers. You're the one who brought up the aphrodisiac stuff. What do they do—swallow the eggs raw?"

Hannah chewed her banana. Frown lines scored her forehead. "Both those clans, the Dahls and the Magnuses, are huge."

I scratched the back of my neck. "I dunno. Two large, native clans. Maybe those families have been poaching their breakfast and enhancing their sexual performance for a couple hundred years."

Hannah handed me the banana peel for my compost pail. I didn't have a garden like at home, but still couldn't bring myself to throw valuable nutrients into the garbage can. I had a small compost pile in a corner of the backyard. Hannah could have any homemade fertilizer I managed to produce by the end of summer.

We refilled our coffee cups and sipped quietly. One hundred thirteen sea turtle eggs had disappeared from Goose Inlet's first nest of the season and been replaced by three human toes. We'd reasoned out some viable motives for the egg loss. We had nothing to explain the snipped digits.

CHAPTER FIVE

I found a quiet place on the beach, away from tourist blankets and umbrellas, and opened a paperback. After Hannah's poaching lecture, I needed to fill my head with visions of something other than turtle omelets washed down with penis wine. I was two chapters into a zany Stephanie Plum escapade when a plastic ball rolled against my feet.

Several yards away, a man playing with a little boy looked my way then trotted over to retrieve the ball. "Sorry," he said with a small grin and tilt of his head. I returned his smile, lifted a casual hand, and resumed reading.

A short time later, I heard a gentle, "Excuse me." I looked up and realized my book had collapsed on my chest and that the man with the ball had returned.

"I'm sorry," he said. "I wasn't sure if you were sleeping, but I had to ask. I'm Tanner Banks. Are you Abby Finn?" His voice dropped a notch. "Aidan's wife?"

I blinked, my mouth instantly dry. "I am."

In the bright sunshine Tanner Banks looked to be the color of an over-baked chocolate chip cookie. He was tall and, although he bore a Yuppie name and an American accent, his distinct cheekbones, straight, shiny dark hair, and large, almond-shaped eyes convinced me he'd been blessed with a United Nations heritage. He was slender but his sleeveless T-shirt showed off rounded biceps and hard-earned pectoral muscle. This attractive man with the beautiful smile sat down beside me in the sand.

I swallowed hard. "How—did you know Aidan?" Had I met Tanner Banks before? With his distinctive looks, he should have been hard to forget. "Do I know you?"

"We met briefly. At a Christmas party a few years ago. I worked in the same building as your husband, different department. We ate lunch together sometimes. Until I quit."

I nodded, trying to recall if Aidan had ever mentioned him.

Tanner looked off to the side and back. "I heard about his—accident. I'm sorry. Aidan was a great guy."

We sat silently until I swallowed the lump in my throat. "You quit?" I asked, squeaking out the word. "You left your job and moved here?"

Tanner's face brightened. "I dumped sales a year ago and followed my passion. Now I have a small business as a kayak guide. Tours. Day trips." He made a small volcano in the sand. "I hadn't seen Aidan in months, so I was glad when he showed up. I was surprised he was down here in winter though."

A jolt of surprise bumped my knees together. My lips forced themselves into a puckered, "What?"

"Glad I got to see him. On the beach."

I looked out at the water and back. "You saw Aidan in Goose Inlet?" A chill pressed against my arms, freezing the nerves beneath my skin. "When?"

"Oh," Tanner scratched his chin. "After Christmas. Maybe late January. Said he was just down for the day. Looked surprised to see me. We hadn't kept in touch after I left. I was glad to catch him."

I hugged my arms, wondering if a long-sleeved shirt was in my beach bag. Aidan, the man who disliked beaches, had been in Goose Inlet? Did Hannah know this?

"And I see London James has a house here now. Comes down on weekends."

It took me a moment to ask, "You know London from—?"

"Raleigh. He was friends with a co-worker of Aidan's. Mark—something."

I sank back in my chair. "It is a small world."

Tanner knew London and London knew Aidan's co-worker, Mark-something. I'd have thought less of the coincidence if I didn't harbor an odd aversion to London James. I rubbed at the goosebumps on my arms.

"I'm sorry. Did I upset you? I have water." Tanner pulled a reusable bottle out of his backpack and handed it to me, at the same time watching the little boy retrieve the ball from water's edge.

I tried to speak twice before managing, "I'm good. Just thinking." Pressure built behind my eyes. Aidan had two Marks as lab partners. And another Mark, a golfing buddy, floated somewhere in the large company.

"Mark Simons?"

"Hmmm. I don't think so."

"Mark Jeffers?"

Tanner shook his head. "This guy liked to monkey around in a home lab in his garage. Aidan said the guy made him nervous."

"Marc Diamond?"

"That's him!" Tanner snapped his fingers and smiled. The little boy came up, and Tanner gave him a drink of water.

Aidan had been wary of Marc Diamond, who shared his hood. Inside the hood was where chemists conducted their most noxious experiments. Fumes were carried out of the hood by an exhaust system so they wouldn't sicken, contaminate, or possibly kill the scientists. Aidan considered Marc reckless. He was sloppy in the lab and boasted about tinkering with compounds in his home laboratory, something Aidan would never contemplate creating. Aidan also suspected Marc pilfered chemicals from their work storage room for use in his playhouse. Aidan had considered turning him in but Marc had five kids and a stay-at-home wife. I had argued that five children were five reasons to turn him in, but Aidan balked. "I'll ruin his career. Hurt his family," he'd said.

"The four of us had lunch together a few times," Tanner said, breaking into my thoughts.

Realizing my shoulders were bunched around my ears, I dropped them to relieve tension in my neck. Tanner called to the boy who'd kicked the ball toward a dune and run after it.

"Spur of the moment thing," he continued, turning back to me. "I'd come over to get Aidan, and Marc would be waiting for London, so we'd join forces." Tanner shrugged like it was no big deal.

To most people, it would not have been. I, however, was struck by the fact that London James, who knew Aidan's lab partner Marc, and whom Aidan had lunched with more than once, was now living part time in Goose Inlet. That in itself was not profound. The fact that London had not mentioned knowing my dead husband—after being introduced to me by Hannah, acting interested in a cloying way, and sitting several evenings beside me at Nest One—it was strange. And rude. Even stranger was my sand-hating husband being in Goose Inlet alone in winter.

I didn't realize I'd fallen silent until Tanner stood. "I just wanted to say hello. And that Aidan was," he smiled gently, "a great guy."

"I miss him," I replied softly. As Tanner and the little boy kicked the ball along the shoreline, he looked back at me once over his shoulder. "I miss him," I repeated, but only in my head.

CHAPTER SIX

I caught up to Hannah on the beach. "Did you know Aidan was here in Goose Inlet last winter?"

Hannah stopped walking. "No."

"You didn't see him? It was after New Year's. A man just told me he saw Aidan on the beach in late January." I looked Hannah square in the face. "You'd tell me the truth, wouldn't you?"

"Of course I'd tell you the truth. God!" She started walking but I grabbed her arm and jerked her to a stop.

"He was here alone," I said. "I was not with him."

"I wasn't with him either." Hannah's voice ratcheted up a notch. "I didn't see him on the beach or anyplace in town. He's not a beach person. Why would he come here?"

I released Hannah's arm and headed in the direction of my cottage.

"Abby! Wait!"

I was not a regular walker, but I could move when I had to. Or wanted to. And right now I wanted to move. I cut across the sand, took the first available access, and once on solid pavement jogged the rest of the way home.

I was sitting on my porch when Hannah came up the steps. Without a word, she went into the kitchen, brought out a glass of water, and dropped into an Adirondack chair.

"What's gotten into you, Abs?"

"Oh, nothing! I just found out my sand-hating husband, who deprived his family of ocean vacations, came to Goose Inlet—a beach town—alone. I tried for twenty years to get him down here for a long weekend, without success, and he came *alone*? In *winter*? And never told me?"

"I think you're making too much of this." Hannah drank down her water.

We sat a good five minutes without talking. Five minutes was a long time when it involved silence.

"Do you think Aidan came to see me?" Hannah finally asked.

My teeth clamped down hard on my tongue. Hannah and Aidan had a history. Minor, but it was there. They'd dated twice before she introduced him to me in the university library. I'd quivered when she said he was a grad student. The previous year, a grad student had abandoned me pregnant, and I was gun shy. But then Hannah invited Aidan to our apartment for dinner. While we cooked, he played with Derek, who at three months old smiled like an angel. I was shocked when he changed the baby's diaper and grateful when he offered to babysit during midterms. After Christmas, he began spending more and more time at our apartment and not just to play with my baby. When I graduated, we married.

Hannah never married. She'd had two serious relationships that didn't pan out. She also had numerous, inconsequential boyfriends, often several at the same time, and joked about carrying a little black book.

As for Aidan, he was a rarity. A good-looking guy, oblivious to admiring glances. Or so I'd thought until last spring when he began his evening meetings and absences from the lab. He stopped sharing details about his day, and now there was this thing about being at the beach in winter. He'd come to the Inlet instead of going to work. Did he really have a girlfriend? Or was he into something else? Something illegal. Good Lord, Abby! You're wondering if your husband was involved in something illegal. Seriously? But why come here for one day? What did he do here?

"Abby, Aidan and I dated briefly in college, but that was our only romantic encounter—ever. And it wasn't really that romantic. Aidan wasn't my type. He was too—too—"

"Ordinary?"

Hannah sighed. "Stable. A stable man was good for you. You needed it. I needed something different."

"Hey, you like what you like and need. All I want to know is why my husband came here and didn't tell me. It's pestering me. Like a bug bite. That's just not Aidan."

Hannah squeezed my knee. "I wish I had an answer for you."

We sat quietly until I rested my hand atop hers. "I'm not suspicious. More confused."

She nodded sympathetically. "Who told you Aidan was at the beach?"

"A man named Tanner Banks."

"I know Tanner. Some friends and I kayaked with him a couple times. Don't know a lot about him, but he seems a nice guy. Cute, too." She winked. "How does he know Aidan?"

"He worked at Tillson. In sales. They ate lunch together sometimes." I scooted forward in my chair. "But the odd thing is, Tanner said Aidan knew London James." Mister Text-the-Night-Away. "Is that not crazy?" I chewed the inside of my cheek. "Maybe Aidan came down here to see London." I looked at Hannah for confirmation.

She shook her head. "London said he didn't get his house till spring." Hannah went inside and came back with water-filled glasses. "It's just coincidence, Abby. What do they say about the six degrees of Kevin Bacon?"

"Huh. More like the six degrees of Aidan Finn."

CHAPTER SEVEN

"You're sunburned," Hannah said, placing my bottle of pinot grigio in a tub of ice on her patio. That Hannah had invited a few friends to an impromptu dinner party was a good sign she wasn't consumed with worry over possible poaching. I felt a bit unsettled to see London James mulling oranges and cherries for Hannah's favorite drink, the old fashioned. Two turtle volunteers, Jill and Fala, sat in colorful plastic patio chairs around an unlit fire pit.

"I fell asleep on the beach," I said, lightly touching the hot skin below my collarbone.

Hannah showed me her best teacher's scowl. "Without sunscreen."

"It was nearly empty of tourists." I knew Hannah's smirk was a comment on my not thinking I fell into that category. "I saw an egret. Thought they only hung around the marsh."

"An egret? The great or the snowy?" London asked, surprising me that he knew there was a difference. Maybe he wasn't a total city slicker. Or maybe he'd been educating himself to impress Hannah. And why hadn't he told me he knew Aidan?

"The snowy egret. With the yellow feet," I replied. I knew my egrets, too, thanks to a book on coastal flora and fauna. "I'd like to go out in the marsh sometime. Rent a kayak. Do any of you paddle?"

London handed me an old fashioned. "I'm not fond of boats."

"Not even big boats? Like cruise ships?" Hannah asked, as she snapped the bottoms off a pile of fresh asparagus.

"Umm." London waggled his head back and forth before shaking it firmly. "No."

"I've been out a few times," Jill said. "Tanner Banks takes us into the bays."

"He's the guy does the travel tours?" Fala asked. "New to the Inlet?"

Jill nodded. "He arrived two seasons ago. Nice man. Cute, too."

I told them I'd met him yesterday on the beach.

"Tanner's a man following his dream. I can identify with that," Hannah said, smiling big. "And if you want to buy a kayak, Tanner can help you pick a good one." She rolled asparagus around in olive oil, sea salt and oregano. "These will go on after the salmon. Does everyone like it blackened? I can do it other ways. Preferences?"

Everyone opted for blackened. Hannah dredged five pieces of salmon in a homemade mix, then sat down while the flavors steeped.

"I invited Tanner tonight, but he couldn't make it," She took a long sip of her drink. "By the way, London, I saw you and Tanner arguing on the beach today. You're not the reason he didn't come, are you?" She raised her eyebrows questioningly, but London was silent.

Hannah sat up in her chair. "Seriously? You were arguing?" She put a hand to her chest. "I was joking."

"We were discussing something," London said, his eyes hard as pebbles.

"I didn't mean to pry."

London walked to the potting bench Hannah used as a bar. "Anyone for another round?" Fala and Jill held out their glasses.

Jaw stiff as a brick, London mulled more fruit and sugar, poured in whiskey and a little ginger ale, as Hannah liked it, and gave the drinks a stir. I was startled when he handed me a glass with an imperious, "Abby!"

For Hannah's party, London had relaxed his costume considerably from the button-down, wing-tipped attire he'd worn to the turtle nest. Tonight he wore leather huarache sandals, tan shorts, and a tasteful Hawaiian shirt.

I set my second drink on a side table and watched Hannah lay salmon filets on the grill. She glanced once or twice at London, who sipped his cocktail and stared at the wood-stocked fire pit.

Soon we sat down at a round metal table laid with rattan place mats and ocean blue plates. The salmon was juicy, the asparagus crisp. Conversation was light, while everyone concentrated on Hannah's delightful concoction of flavors. After we polished off most of a sticky, chewy, flavor-bursting blackberry cobbler, Hannah lit the fire pit. The smoke kept mosquitoes away and the fire, settling into embers, provided cozy ambience. Hannah brought out a tray of cognac and cordials.

I had drunk two old fashioneds, two glasses of white wine with dinner, and now opted for a small glass of Grand Marnier. The sweet orange liqueur slid down my throat and took the sting out of my sunburn, although truthfully, the whiskey and wine had done that hours ago. I was feeling comfortable and content until I remembered I was a widow too soon and too violently and that London James, sitting across the patio from me, had known my husband and still hadn't mentioned it. My mellowness drifted away, taking with it the lid that held my irritation in check.

"So, London," I began, ignoring the corner of my brain that said don't spoil Hannah's party. "I understand you knew my husband."

"I did." He propped his feet on a low stool and crossed his ankles. The soles of his sandals were clean and smooth.

"How is it—why is it—you haven't told me?" I took a dainty sip of Grand Marnier. "I mean, that would just be a polite thing to do, wouldn't it?" Acknowledgement of acquaintanceship in the least, to say nothing about condolence for Aidan's death. Even total strangers offered condolences.

London snatched the cognac bottle and poured two fingers worth into his snifter. He quickly drank half. "I don't know, Abigail." His second swallow finished the liquor. "Somehow it seemed awkward. I didn't know your husband well. Met him only a couple times."

"Through Marc Diamond," I said. "Aidan's lab partner." London's face darkened. I wondered if that was why he and Tanner argued. Tanner had told him about meeting me and talking about their lunches together.

Why would that cause an argument? And it had been a squabble, according to Hannah.

London grabbed the cognac again and filled his glass past the halfway point. "I wasn't there often. I stayed away. Aidan made me uncomfortable."

I coughed on my liqueur, making my nose burn. "Aidan? He was the most pleasant man on the planet."

London shook his head. "There was just something—I hate to say this—but Aidan—"

When he winced, my blood bubbled.

"I'd come into the lab looking for Marc, and Aidan would block whatever he was doing on his computer. Click off a website. Odd behavior."

My temper rose so fast and so high my eyebrows felt singed. "Maybe he didn't want you snooping at his research. You work for a different company, don't you?" My cordial glass rang when I set it down on the metal table.

London tossed out his hand. "And then when I saw him in town talking to that Hispanic woman's husband—"

The roots of my hair tingled, and I jolted in my chair. "What? What Hispanic woman? What husband?" From the corner of my eye I caught Fala wriggling in her seat.

"You've had too much to drink," Hannah said, swiping London's snifter. "You, too, Abby. This conversation has gotten out of hand."

"Time for us to go," Jill said, scooting to the edge of her chair. Fala popped out of hers like a prairie dog from a hole and hurried across the patio.

"Everybody stop!" I kicked the stool out from under London's feet, surprising even myself. Standing practically on his toes, I demanded he explain about Aidan and *that Hispanic woman's husband.* "What the hell are you talking about?"

A smirk tweaked London's lips. "I saw them together. Here on the beach." He held out his hands, palms up. "And now the turtle eggs are missing,"

"Oh, come on, London." Hannah picked up the tray of cordials. "No one seriously believes Alegria or her husband are responsible for poaching turtle eggs in Goose Inlet."

"A lot of people—" Fala began. "Well, some folks are pointing fingers at her at least."

"Her who? Who the hell is Alegria?" I demanded.

"You saw her, Abby. At Nest One's excavation," Fala explained. "Pilar's mother."

I had no idea who Pilar was and said so.

"The little girl with her mother. Benito's mom."

Oh, Benito. The trench jumper. The sound of his father's voice rang in my ear, as I recalled a tall, solid man with sandy hair and a complexion darkened by the sun rather than genetics. Three-quarters of the family looked south of the border, making Mr. Muscle *that Hispanic woman's husband.*

I felt my face contort into something nasty. "You are implying my husband had something to do with stealing our turtle eggs?"

"Oh, Abby. He doesn't mean that." Hannah said, her voice strained.

"Well, he said Aidan talked to *that Hispanic woman's husband,* and Fala said people suspect this Alegria of poaching." I leaned over and clutched the arms of London's chair.

"And you're saying *my husband* was part of that? You are one crazy bastard!" I lifted the arms of London's chair, flipping him over backwards into a hydrangea bush. I wished it had been the fire pit.

CHAPTER EIGHT

"This will be short. I don't have much time. Busy, busy, busy," Marc Diamond said, as we arranged lunch items on a square table in Tillson's cafeteria.

I'd called Marc at eight this morning and was transferred to his voicemail. My message was pleasant but insistent. I needed to talk to him. When he didn't respond, I called again and left a second message, this one a bit edgier, saying I needed to speak with him today, it was important, and couldn't wait.

I didn't really know Marc Diamond. I'd spoken to him casually at holiday parties and picnics. He and Aidan weren't close friends, but I was his deceased lab partner's wife and he should have the courtesy to return my call. When he did, around ten o'clock, I suggested meeting in the company cafeteria. With co-workers present, I figured he'd be on good behavior, less likely to storm out or slink away, although I wasn't quite sure why he'd do either.

"How are you holding up?" Marc asked, lifting up the bun to peek at his burger.

I leaned forward. "How much time do you have?" I was a tad prickly after a two-and-a-half blast down the highway, the last thirty minutes through Research Triangle traffic.

"For lunch?" He still hadn't looked at me.

"For the truth." Marc's casual query about my emotional state after losing my husband in an explosion in this very building, and in the lab they shared, did not soothe my emotions.

Marc picked up a knife, cut his half-pound burger in quarters, and gnashed down on one dripping chunk. After three chews and a swallow, he met my gaze.

"So, you're doing okay?"

I considered thumping his nose to shock him into some semblance of sensitivity but instead asked, "Is there anything new with the investigation?"

"Into what?"

"The explosion! I called your research director several times to see if CSB learned the cause of the accident, but he just said it was under investigation."

Though ferocious, the explosion had been contained to the bench where Aidan was supposedly standing and to his immediate surroundings. There had been no fire to threaten the building. The scientists who had labored with Aidan, including Diamond, had been disbursed to other work spaces. What was left of the lab was barred to everyone except CSB and SBI.

Marc shook his head. "I haven't heard anything."

"Does it always take this long?" Before he could ask "to do what?" I added, "To determine the cause of a laboratory explosion."

Marc talked around the drink straw in his mouth. "Honestly, Abby, I don't know. Never had my lab explode before."

Your lab. The one you rip off for chemicals. Well, Aidan wasn't positive about that.

"If you hear anything, please tell me."

"Absolutely." Marc ran his finger along the bottom of his plate, scooping up runny burger cheese. He swirled the gooey finger in his mouth then wiped his hand somewhere beneath the table.

I sighed and looked around the room. The security guard who'd admitted me into the building stood in the doorway. Our eyes met, he nodded slightly, then walked to the counter and poured a cup of coffee. As he exited the cafeteria, he glanced at Marc and the pleasant look that usually graced his face dimmed.

"Is that all you want to know?" Marc asked, picking up another chunk of sandwich.

I pushed aside my salad plate. "I'm spending the summer in a little beach town and just found out my husband visited there last January and never told me."

He snorted. "I don't tell my wife every move I make."

I expelled a puff of air. "Aidan didn't want to go anywhere near the ocean, so it's ridiculous he'd visit Goose Inlet." Marc picked up his soda glass, tucked the straw between his lips, and sucked up half his cola. "Then I learned a part-time Inlet resident, a man named London James, is a friend of yours and that you, London, and another coworker had lunch with Aidan. More than once."

Marc swallowed his latest burger bite. "I have lunch with a lot of people."

"Not the point! I've spent time with London on the beach. Why didn't he tell me he knew my dead husband? It's strange. Callus. Bordering on offensive. Why wouldn't—?"

He cut me off. "I'm sorry, but I don't know why Aidan didn't share his day trips and lunch dates with you." He picked up a half-dozen French fries and bit off the ends. "And I'm not in London's head either."

I shivered. The air conditioning felt set on 60. I pulled my salad back and dug around for olives. Marc was right. How would he know what went on in Aidan and London's heads? But, come to think of it, Marc had not offered personal condolences for my husband's dramatic death either. His name had been on the sympathy card from Tillson, but, good grief, he'd shared a lab with Aidan for years. Didn't that merit a few words of personal comfort? A phone call? I'd been asked, "How are you holding up?" more than once, but Marc's query sounded lame. When I looked up he was staring at me.

"Aidan and I were lab mates," he said, "but we didn't pal around." Marc's hand jerked suddenly and his glass tipped over, spilling cola into my salad. Instead of apologizing, he barked in a harsh whisper. "He came to my house! Uninvited. Showed up waving my lab book, saying I hadn't signed my notes and they were due the next day. Bullshit! I could have signed them at work in the morning."

His outburst shocked me. I stared as he made a sloppy attempt to soak up his spilled drink with a fist-full of napkins.

"We were lab mates, that's all," Marc repeated, breathing deeply, as if trying to settle himself. "Aidan was friendlier with a guy in sales."

"Tanner Banks?" I dipped a finger into my water glass and dabbed at cola spots on my blouse.

Marc shrugged. "Some Asian guy. Or a mix. Left Tillson a while ago."

I bit my tongue to avoid challenging the Asian-mix comment. "Tanner lives in Goose Inlet now." I counted to five before adding, "Your buddy London comes every weekend."

"The Inlet's a sweet little town," Marc said, almost to himself.

My eyebrows jerked in surprise. But of course, Marc knew about the beach town. Residents of the interior made frequent trips to the shore. He had a large family, and a beach vacation was dirt cheap compared to a Disney trip.

"You've been there?"

"My grandparents had a house—" He clamped his mouth shut.

"You went there as a kid?" I leaned forward. Marc was about my age. "That was—when? The '70s. You were a teenager in the '80s."

Marc collected his utensils. Balled up the soaked napkins and dropped them on his plate. His mouth worked, opening and shutting like a just-hooked fish, but he didn't answer. His steel-legged chair screeched on the concrete floor when he pushed it back. He picked up his tray and looked toward the exit.

"So you know Goose Inlet."

"Everybody knows Goose Inlet, for Christ sake." He flexed his neck, as if twisting out a kink.

"And you vacationed there as a kid?" Something inside me pressed for an answer. "Marc?"

Without answering or saying goodbye, Diamond threw the remains of his lunch into a trash container and hurried out of the cafeteria.

If his grandparents had a house, he came regularly and probably had friends. I sat a minute wondering who in Goose Inlet played with Marc Diamond as a child. He was a lot younger than Joop or Dutch, but Erik Magnus might be close in age. There were hundreds of other Inlet natives. I didn't know everyone in town. Not even close.

I collected my purse and took the elevator down to the main entrance.

"Sorry about your husband, Mrs. Finn," the security guard said softly, opening the door to let me exit. "I counted on Dr. Finn for a cheerful word." He paused and his eyes narrowed slightly. "Most of the time." His gaze shifted to the ground and back. I took it as a sign of compassion rather than discomfort.

"Thank you Mr. Ramsey," I replied.

"Oh, just call me Wade, ma'am," he said quickly and grinned. He was a young man, late twenties, with a strong physique. A former marine sergeant attending community college with a dream of running his own security company someday, according to Aidan.

"I liked Dr. Finn a lot." Wade touched my elbow lightly as I passed through the door.

The steamy outside air hit me like a punch. I hurried toward the parking garage, eager for the comfort of my car's AC. The abrupt switch from brilliant sunshine to shady garage blinded me, and I nearly ran into Aidan's former research director, a portly guy with fuzz poking up around his ears like rounded horns. After Marc Diamond's exasperating conversation, I was now, face to face with the man who repeatedly ducked my request for information about my husband's death.

With no control over my tongue, I blurted, "Marc Diamond is stealing chemicals. Aidan said so." Immediately, I felt like a fool. Abigail Finn, gossip monger.

The director flinched. "I can't—can't discuss," he sputtered, slicing a finger through the air. Just as quickly, he reached for my hand. "I wish you the best, Abby. And the kids, too." He looked past me toward the main entrance, as if judging his ability to sprint to the door. "You're doing well? Derek and—?"

"Kate. We're fine." I was shocked by my outburst, but embarrassment dissolved quickly. I pulled back my hand. "And we'd be much better if we knew why our husband and father was blown up in his own laboratory."

Was the equipment defective? Had he mixed up the wrong stuff? Was there a leak somewhere? Was it his own mistake? I needed to know.

Hunching his shoulders, the director licked his lips. "I can't discuss the explosion or anything else associated with the investigation." He shook himself, as if in reprimand, and exited the parking garage in double time.

I stared after him. Wade Ramsey stood outside the building, watching us. He waved the director through the doorway, but remained a few moments gazing in my direction. Then he nodded slightly and re-entered the building.

The guard's behavior struck me as compassionate. The research director's need to remain silent about *anything else associated with the investigation* increased my stress.

CHAPTER NINE

I needed something to quiet my mood on the drive home, so I talked to Derek on my hands-free. He was at work so the conversation was short, but he assured me he would move Kate into her dorm when fall semester started. Thankfully, Aidan and I had invested in college funds. Tuition, room and board for Kate's next two years were covered.

I had offered to help with the move, but Derek insisted they could handle it. I was a little disappointed, and also a little worried I wasn't being a good mom, but, truthfully, not too let down. The thought of climbing multiple sets of stairs with boxes and bags and suitcases and all the paraphernalia a modern female college student *needed* made my knees tremble. I'd helped move Derek for four years and Kate for two. Of course Aidan had been with us, hauling the heavy stuff, balancing the awkward stuff. Afterward we went out to dinner before sharing last hugs and kisses.

Is that why I backed off helping Kate this time? Because Aidan would not be there? Did I want to preserve that happy family memory intact? Whole. Solid. Not missing a major foundation block.

Kate and I had Skyped recently, chatting about her last days as an au pair on Cape Cod and her excitement over starting new classes and seeing old friends. I'd wanted to keep my daughter close after tragedy struck last spring, but Kate insisted she had an obligation to fulfill. She couldn't leave that family hanging, she said. Derek later told me his sister wanted out of the Raleigh area where the family had been complete, at least for a little while.

Kate and I had talked about Aidan and how badly we missed him. I told her nothing about the strange string of coincidences I'd uncovered. I didn't understand them myself. Why burden my daughter? Likewise, I'd said nothing to Derek.

We'd all see each other in a few weeks. There would be hugging and more tears. Skype was good. Phones were good. I thanked Mother Universe for the advanced electronic communications that made keeping in touch with my children easy. But only human arms could truly embrace.

As I pulled into Lily Pad's driveway, my phone dinged: *Good to see you, Mrs F. If you have questions, text or call. Be glad to help.*

It was from Wade Ramsey, the security guard. Why did he have my phone number? Besides offering condolences for the loss of my husband, a man who'd been kind to him, what more could Wade Ramsey do for me?

CHAPTER TEN

"You sure it's safe?" I scanned the exterior of a hot pink, cement-block building. "Have you checked with the health department? Lately?"

"Stop!" Hannah nudged my shoulder. "Are you still grouchy about your argument with London?"

It was two days later, and I remained furious with London James and not the least bit sorry for attacking him, however out of character my behavior had been. But I'd put on a smile when Hannah invited me to breakfast.

"Aunt Biddy's is a Goose Inlet landmark," Hannah said with some heat. "Been here sixty years. Everyone loves it. Natives and tourists both."

"Calm down. I'm kidding." And hungry. I stepped into Aunt Biddy's Diner and was knocked back by the clamor. People chattered, forks dropped, chairs scraped, mugs clunked onto tabletops. There were nearly constant calls for "Peggy!"

"Just grab whatever table's available," the server, a bird-boned woman of at least seventy years, called above the din as she bobbed past on thick-soled sneakers, carrying plates piled with blueberry waffles.

Hannah pointed at a table cluttered with flatware, coffee cups, juice glasses, egg-smeared plates and crumpled paper napkins. Four plastic chairs pushed away from the mess as if embarrassed by it. I looked around for a booth. I disliked sitting at tables, especially those smack in the middle of a noisy eatery. From a large, round table in the corner, Dutch Magnus, his belly magnified by a gaudy Hawaiian shirt, waved and hooted.

"Are you inviting us to join you?" Hannah asked, placing a hand on Dutch's shoulder.

"Sure. Just got here. Haven't ordered." Dutch elbowed Joop to slide over.

"You're colorful today," Hannah said.

Dutch's shirt was bright yellow with orange, blue, red and green balls swirling bottom to top as if caught in waterspouts. I'd seen them at the beach store for ten bucks. A real deal. I considered putting on my sunglasses.

"Hey, girly." Joop's gnarled hand pulled me down next to him. His white whiskers poked north, south, east and west, and his long ponytail looked slept in. "You as nuts about sea turtles as Hannah is?"

"Nobody could be as nuts about sea turtles as Hannah," I replied. "But I like the turtle people and enjoy sitting on the beach after dark." The waitress set down menus and four cups of coffee.

Dutch cleared his throat. "What you in the mood for, darlin'? Food-wise."

I picked up my coffee cup. "I was thinking of an omelet."

Joop clapped his hands. "Well, honey, you came to the right place. Aunt Biddy's has the best turtle egg omelet in coastal Carolina."

"Don't even start." Hannah wagged her finger an inch from Joop's nose. Considering London's accusation against Aidan, I wasn't in the mood for comments, joking or otherwise, about omelets made from poached sea turtle eggs.

"That's what I'm ordering," the old man insisted. "You can't beat Aunt Biddy's turtle egg omelet." His putty-colored tongue slid across his lips. "How 'bout you, Dutch?"

Dutch waved dismissively. "Aunt Biddy's good, but my granny made the best turtle egg omelet, hands down."

"If you guys keep this up, we're leaving," Hannah said with a scowl that warned she wasn't kidding. She turned to me. "Trying to rile me. Think it's funny." She poked Dutch's shoulder. "You know I don't like talk like that. And neither does Abby." Right. Neither does Abby. Especially now, with the general consensus being that the first nest of the season had been poached.

Joop leaned back and placed spindly arms over the back of the booth. As if he hadn't heard Hannah, he intoned in a storyteller voice, "My granddaddy wanted turtle steak and soup every Sunday. Did his own hunting for eggs and meat. Had a friend who butchered the critters for him."

Hannah leaned forward but before she could speak, Joop wagged his own finger. "Now don't get down on me, girl. I'm just educating your friend. Like we do at the history center."

"I've learned a few things at Hannah's lectures," I said. Hoping to take the wind out of his sail, I listed on my fingers. "Females wait till they're thirty before mating."

"Honestly," Hanna murmured. "Doesn't that just sound like a smart policy?"

Thinking back to my own college experience, I nodded. "They lay three to five nests each season, some more. Hatchlings take about a six hundred-mile glide on the Gulf Stream and jump off just past Bermuda, someplace I've never been. When they get to the Sargasso Sea they feast for years on sea plants and small sea creatures. Then they hop back on the Gulf Stream and ride all the way to England, down the coast of Africa, and back to the Caribbean. Quite a trip." I looked around the table. Dutch was staring at me like I had a hatchling on my lip. "One last thing. Loggerheads grow from two little inches into three-foot-long adults and weigh at least two hundred fifty pounds. Often more."

Joop patted my hand in a grandfatherly way. "If you think that's the last thing, honey, you're strung out on hooch. Listen to me. There's lots more."

"I've watched a bunch of videos, too," I added quickly. "Loggerheads' jaws can crush whelk and conch. And a naturalist recorded one hundred species of animals and plants living on one single loggerhead turtle."

"You're like a goddamn talking Britannica," Dutch drawled.

"You know what's terrible though?" I pushed my coffee cup aside. "Hundreds of thousands of sea turtles—not just loggerheads but all types—are caught accidentally every year in shrimp and fishing nets. The poor things drown. Turtles spend a lot of time in the water, but they still need to reach the surface to breathe."

"Yeah, but more fishermen are using special equipment that let them escape those nets," Joop said, craning his neck, searching for a waitress. "I'll give you this, you know a lot a book learning. Or Worldly Web learning." He pointed a crooked finger at me. "But you don't know squat about history."

"You need to hear it from an expert." Dutch pressed his belly into the table edge. His stiff, twisted beard, a good four inches long, jutted out like a sword.

Joop raised his voice. "And the expert is me."

Hannah opened her mouth then sighed. "Okay. Educate her." She leaned toward me. "Unless you don't want to hear their grizzly tales."

"They ain't grizzly, for crissake!" Joop shifted in his seat. "Didn't you hear me say it's history? It was the culture back then. People ate those eggs and loved every swallow."

"For some it was business." Dutch jumped into a story about how he packed as many eggs as he could find in a burlap bag, walked to the Coast Guard Station, and took the boat to Little Bay. "Folks there bought my eggs for a dime a dozen."

"They weren't *your* eggs," Hannah growled.

"Mama had me put the money in a jar, and it went to buy school supplies. Sometimes even school clothes." He nodded sharply at Hannah, who stared at her menu, as if not listening.

I could tell by the spark in Dutch's eye that he was just getting warmed up. Truthfully, I didn't mind hearing these stories. Like Joop said, they were part of local history. But it appeared Joop had been elbowed out of the telling.

Now Dutch was saying that when his daddy was a kid, a restaurant staked lookouts on the beach. When a mama turtle came up to lay her eggs, a couple guys would flip her over. "She couldn't do shit about it," Dutch said, his voice distinctly lacking the remorse I expected from a member of the sea turtle patrol.

My gaze went to Hannah involuntarily, and I didn't ask if they killed the turtle right there on the beach.

"Don't worry about your friend." Joop waved his hands as if calming down a crowd. "She's heard all this before." Dutch opened his mouth but Joop slapped the table top. "Pipe down and let me tell my stories."

"Then tell her the one about Madam Turtle," Dutch said.

Peggy came over and, to my relief, the men ordered biscuits and gravy. Hannah chose oatmeal, and I opted for French toast. Next to an omelet, my tongue tingled for Eggs Benedict, but after being threatened with the Madam Turtle story, I couldn't face two poached eggs staring at me like big tearful turtle eyes. At least French toast disguised the eggs.

"Madam Turtle," Joop began, laying his forearms on the table, "was about five hundred years old and missing her right hind foot."

"How do you know she was five hundred years old?" I asked. His tale was off to a ridiculous start. Joop might be right about the turtle missing a foot, but Hannah's instruction had taught me that an extremely healthy, extremely lucky sea turtle might—might—make it to one hundred years. Loggerheads who made it to adulthood died somewhere around age fifty-seven.

Joop's lips worked. "Well, I ain't certain, but that's what's been passed down. It's what you call folklore." He took a sip of coffee. "And I said *about* five hundred."

He picked up his knife and fingered the serrated side. "*About.*"

"She got it," Dutch barked. "Get on with it."

Joop claimed his approximately five hundred-year-old turtle thought the light on the boardwalk was the moon and crawled over the dune to get to it. "It was the early 1920s. The Yellow Birds were playing some sweet tunes, and Madam Turtle was enticed by the golden strains."

Having given up on Bach and Mozart, I presumed. Hannah, too, rolled her eyes. I was surprised she could sit through this diatribe. Yet the basic story, however embellished, fascinated me. *Carolina* magazine ran a regular history feature, but I couldn't remember seeing a story on twentieth century sea turtle egg poaching. But then, in the early 1900s digging up sea turtle eggs wasn't against the law.

Joop told how his daddy and another guy got a bunch of tourists to help drag the Madam up to the pavilion. "She was the centerpiece of the evening. Folks couldn't get enough of her."

"They disturbed her from laying her nest!" Hannah hissed.

"They just wanted to show off a five hundred-pound turtle."

"So she was five hundred years old *and* five hundred pounds?" I asked, screwing up one corner of my mouth. If I was writing this story, those *facts* would be checked before being printed in *Carolina.*

Joop, his ponytail lying across his shoulder like old braided hemp, stared at me a good five seconds before continuing. "Story was she laid about a dozen eggs before getting hauled up for display."

"And she most likely had a good ninety left in her," Hannah grumbled.

"They turned her loose after a while," Joop said, his voice curling into a whine. "She went back in the Atlantic. Probably came back later to drop her load."

"Which your ancestors promptly dug up and cracked into a frying pan." Hannah leaned back to allow the waitress to set down our plates.

"Now don't be nasty." Joop picked up his fork and began shoveling biscuits and gravy.

"I got a picture of me at a year old, sitting on the back of a turtle." Dutch reached toward his back pocket.

"Please, let this be the last turtle murder story." Hannah sprinkled brown sugar on her oatmeal then poked around in a plastic basket for butter.

"Last one. Promise. It's all part of Abby's education." Dutch dug out his wallet, pulled out a faded, black and white snapshot from behind a sheet of cracked, opaque plastic, and passed it around. I scrunched my eyes to make out a pair of hands holding a bald, bug-eyed, pug-nosed baby atop a turtle shell.

"One of the big-time fishermen, Bobby Roy was his name, had his truck on the beach the night before that picture got took."

"Bobby Roy was some kind of cousin of mine," Joop said, wiping gravy off his chin.

Dutch forked up a mound of dripping biscuit, stuffed it in his mouth, chewed twice, and swallowed. He said Bobby Roy and his buddies were hanging around, relaxing, when a big—big—sea turtle crawled up, took a look, saw folks on the beach, and tried to turn around and go back to the ocean.

"Bobby Roy, smart thinker that he was, jumped in his truck and pulled in front of her, blocking her way." Dutch's chin thrust his pointy beard forward to punctuate his remark. "Then him and his boys, quick as a lick, flipped that critter over. She weren't going nowhere."

Dutch leaned close to the table, bug-eyed like his baby picture. "And wouldn't you know this guy's luck, a second turtle come flopping out the water. Bobby Roy revved up the truck, maneuvered like a pro, and blocked that one, too. They flipped that turtle, yes they did."

He forked in a couple more mouthfuls of soggy biscuit. "Both turtles got loaded into the truck and it was quite a feast the next day." Dutch grinned and nodded at each member of his audience. There was silence around the table. Even waitress Peggy stood stiff as a telephone pole, coffee pot in hand.

"And that's when you got your picture taken?" I asked. "At the *feast*?"

"Yeah," Dutch replied. "Atop the turtle shell. It was empty, but what the hell. Still a turtle shell." He held out his coffee cup for a refill.

"Bobby Roy made himself tables from those shells." Joop wiped up the last of his sausage gravy with his finger. "Or maybe he made two chairs."

CHAPTER ELEVEN

"That was hard on you." I took Hannah's arm as we walked to the beach. Having paid our share, we left Dutch and Joop haggling over the rest of the breakfast bill. Something about who'd ordered prune juice and double bacon. "Those guys don't know when to shut up. We should have left."

Hannah ran her hand across some oleander. "I thought about it. But Joop's right. I let him tell one or two stories at orientation. It gets volunteers riled and enthusiastic about protecting sea turtles."

"Well, if you'd gotten up to leave, I'd have been right behind you."

Hannah squeezed my fingers. "That would have wound them up even more. They'd follow us out and start an argument about which animals are okay to eat and which aren't."

I thought a moment. "You mean that thing about people getting upset about dolphins getting caught in fishing nets—"

"—but no one cares a lick about the tuna. That's exactly what Dutch throws up to me. And why is it okay to eat cows, pigs and chickens but not whales, tigers and dogs?"

I kicked off my flip-flops at the beach access. "But Dutch and Joop are in the project, and from what I see, quite active. Even getting up before dawn to patrol."

Hannah shrugged. "They tell those stories to rattle my chain. It's their personalities. They think it's funny."

"It's not funny." I felt slightly two-faced, since I really did enjoy the turtle tales from a historical point of view. And listening to them told with spirit and energy had taken my mind off that jerk London. And Aidan, who I missed most in the morning. Both of us had begun work at nine and, being early risers, we always had time for breakfast with lots of freshly ground coffee. I hated eating breakfast alone now, and rather than do so, had taken to skipping what experts insisted was the most important meal of the day. Missing Aidan and missing breakfast went hand in hand.

"Don't let those guys bother you, Abby. Most volunteers tolerate them. New volunteers, like you, learn quickly to ignore them. They're just two old farts with big mouths. Original beach bums. This is their town. They were born here. So were their great-great-great-great-grandparents, and maybe a few more greats before that. You and I are transplants. They barely tolerate us living in their world."

We walked through sand still cool beneath the early morning sun.

"Their town," I repeated thoughtfully, as we splashed through puddles left by low tide. "How'd it get its name? Goose Inlet. I haven't seen one goose since I got here."

Hannah skipped around a scattering of sharp-looking shells. "Good story. One of Joop's clan, the Dahls, tried to raise geese on some land north of the beach when this area was barely populated, a few centuries back."

"Back when the Madame was just a teenager."

Hannah snorted. "Right." She kicked up some water. "Anyway, a monster hurricane came by and tore out the inlet right in front of that Dahl farm. So people called it Goose Inlet."

"Reasonable, I guess." I added this piece of local history to my memory bank. Maybe I'd do a story on Goose Inlet when I returned to *Carolina*.

"Funny thing is, that hurricane blew away all the geese. They couldn't find one survivor."

That made the tale even better.

"But the name stuck." I stooped to pick up a pink shell.

"That's the story," Hannah said. "Or, as Joop would say, it's what you call folklore."

A hundred years from now would Nest One be a blip in Goose Inlet folklore, with tourists listening to Joop's great-grandson tell the tale about the summer one hundred thirteen loggerhead eggs went missing and three human toes were found in their place?

CHAPTER TWELVE

I thought about Aidan all through an early supper—what was he doing in Goose Inlet in January?—and hoped a walk on the beach would quiet my anxiety. Heading north, I decided to check out Nest Two. *My* turtle nest.

When Hannah adopted it for me as a birthday gift, I'd been amused and plainly thankful that I wasn't the actual nest mother. What a pain to have to organize a team, dig a trench, wrestle with the plastic fencing. I dreaded the thought of policing tourists, outwitting foxes, or camping out all night when the little dudes refused to hatch. Real nest mother duty had been snapped up by Jill, a passionate New England transplant. As honorary nest mom, I was content to receive a certificate and a purple sea turtle project T-shirt.

I looked casually at the large square of blocked-off sand that marked the nest. And looked again. Closer. Very close. Huh! Is that a depression? As the thought left my head, the sand dropped another half-inch.

"Holy Christmas!" What felt like an ice water injection raced up one arm and down the other. I looked around but didn't see anyone I knew. It was five o'clock. Sea gulls careened back and forth, squawking and laughing. All the turtle mumbo-jumbo I'd heard from volunteers rattled through my brain. Gloves. Rake. Broom. Team.

I fumbled with my phone. Jill, Jill, Jill. She answered on the second ring. "We've got turtles!" I shrieked. "Just below the surface. And gulls! Lots of sea gulls. Circling! Hungry! Get here fast!"

Ten minutes later Jill, Hannah and five volunteers arrived with plastic pails, a rake, and a box of latex gloves.

"Let's hope these babies wait till the sun goes down," Jill said. "Gulls will be gone then."

I leaned over the fence, peering at a not-so-tiny hole. "I see flippers wiggling down there. What if they come out now?" I asked in the standard turtle nest whisper.

"Let's hope they wiggle a while before the scout makes his move," Hannah said softly. "Could take an hour, sometimes more, before they boil. But if they come early, we're ready. We'll put the babies in pails and release them after dark. Gulls won't get a single one."

"I'm glad you're confident." My hands actually trembled.

"I'm glad you checked your adopted nest." Jill gave me a hug.

Two volunteers raked and smoothed the trench, extending it all the way to the hard-packed sand near the water. Two others checked the fence, packing more sand at the bottom to anchor the black plastic and block any holes. Jill passed out a latex glove to each volunteer and some to tourists who'd wandered over to see what the bustle was all about. She waved to a woman plowing through deep sand and gave her and her children each a glove.

"Here, Pilar," Jill said quietly to the little girl, who wore an ear-to-ear grin. "The babies are coming soon. We have the bottom of the fence buried in sand, so turtles shouldn't be able to sneak through. But if you see one try to climb out or dig its way out, please guide it back gently with the back of your hand toward the bottom of the trench."

Jill looked at me with raised brows then back at the girl then back at me, in a signal harking back to the argument at Hannah's house. I got it. The Hispanic woman's daughter, Pilar. The Hispanic woman herself spread a blanket several yards from the nest, perhaps, I wondered, in preparation for her husband's arrival?

"Can we pick them up?" the girl's brother asked in a voice far from a whisper. I thought he looked a little too eager and not in a positive way like his sister.

"No, Benito," Jill said. "Please don't pick up the turtles. It's important their flippers touch this sand all the way to the ocean."

The boy shrugged, and I decided to keep one eye on the turtles and another on Benito. That little trench jumper wasn't going to pilfer one of my turtles. As I looked around for the kids' father, I noticed the curly haired man in the baseball cap who'd been at Nest One's excavation standing near the bottom of the trench, hands on hips, looking out to sea. Hannah walked down and offered him a glove, but he waved her off.

"How many babies do you expect?" Alegria asked quietly.

"We don't really know," Jill replied. She walked to the blanket. "This nest was laid in a good place, so we didn't have to move it. Which means we couldn't count the eggs. I'll be happy if there's a hundred. That's a nice round number."

Jill walked back and took up position at the top of the nest. I squatted on the side and stared at the depression, although I really wanted to stare at Alegria, the Hispanic woman with a husband who, according to London James, knew my dead husband, Aidan Finn.

"Now it's time to be quiet." Jill motioned Pilar and Benito on each side of her and held a finger to her lips. Volunteers and tourists, each with one gloved hand, lined both sides of the trench, eyes focused like lasers on the nest.

Sixty minutes later we still waited.

"This is like my first labor." I whispered to Hannah. "Tweak, tweak then wait. Tweak, tweak then wait. What's holding them up?"

"Same thing that held up Derek. When he was ready to come, he came. Same with baby turtles."

"Well, it's dark now. No worries about snacking sea gulls."

Jill's hand shot up and the group snapped to attention. When a head and flippers poked out of the nest, Benito, who'd been lying on his stomach, jerked to his knees and pointed.

Ten minutes later two hatchlings pulled themselves out of the hole. From nose to toes, the babies were the requisite two inches long. One would fit in the palm of my hand. The three baby turtles rested several minutes, then charged toward the ocean. Then came the boil. Baby turtles, heedless of their nest-mates' heads and toes, scrambled over each other in manic haste. The moon, nature's lantern, was not high in the sky, yet the hatchlings formed a wedge and paraded like a well-trained army to the sea. I watched, mesmerized.

And much too quickly it was over. "Is that all?" I asked, getting a déjà vu-all-over-again feeling in my stomach.

"What's the count, Hannah?" Jill asked, as she watched the hole.

"Fifteen," she replied, dully.

Well, that was better than five, but far cry from a nice, round one hundred.

"More will come. This happens sometimes," Jill said, sounding much like Hannah with the first nest.

From the look on my friend's face, I didn't think so. Hannah sank in the sand, her right hand clutching the roots of her hair. LuAnn, Dutch and the other volunteers returned after making sure all the hatchlings made it into the water.

"Well, they're off to the Sargasso," Dutch said. "Where's the rest?"

"Let's wait," Jill said. She swept away the prints the baby turtles had made in the trench, then dug her rump into the sand and pulled her knees up to her chin.

This was my adopted nest, but I was torn between the emotional need to escort scores of hatchlings safely to the sea and my intellectual conviction that, with a hundred million years of experience, these ancient reptiles could handle birth on their own. For Hannah's sake, I settled in the sand next to my friend. In the black night, I barely made out the huddled shape of London James on the other side of the trench. Pushing away my anger, I rested my forehead on my knees and closed my eyes.

At midnight, Jill told her team to go home. She and the diehards—Hannah, Bianca, and this time me—hunkered near the nest and whispered our worries until two a.m., when we finally gave in to sleep. The next morning we awoke before dawn, brushed sand off our faces, and checked for baby turtle tracks, but the sand was clean.

CHAPTER THIRTEEN

Three days later, I joined an especially large group of volunteers and tourists gathered around the meager depression Nest Two had left in the sand. The story had spread like oil from a broken tanker about the unusually small hatch. Although the "P" word wasn't vocalized, volunteers' faces asked the same question. Who stole the eggs? There were no suspects or clues or any reason to believe the eggs had been poached from Nest One, except for the bald fact that there was no sign of one hundred thirteen eggs from a determined clutch of one hundred-eighteen. And now, Nest Two had offered up only fifteen turtles from Jill's estimated one hundred.

At seven o'clock, Jill knelt and scooped sand away from the slight depression that marked the turtles' exit. Eighteen inches down she came up with a rubbery, white shell and handed it to a morose LuAnn, who'd been asked again to assist with the count. After retrieving remnants of ten turtle eggs, Jill moved aside and invited me, as honorary nest mother, to dig for the rest.

I was touched. I knew how dedicated nest parents were. How attached they became to their nests. Even mothers—most Inlet nest parents were women—who'd had nests every year were giddy at hatch and excavation times. So for Jill to move aside, especially at this questionable nest, to allow me to touch the hatched shells or unfertilized eggs or live baby turtles caught in the sand was a special kindness.

I passed the rubbery remains of five turtle shells to LuAnn. Some were complete masses, others I pieced together with remnants, but in all came up with a good count. Fifteen shells from fifteen live turtles that volunteers had guided safely to the sea. What I didn't find were the other eighty-five eggs from the hypothetical nice, round one hundred.

"Fifteen?" Hannah choked on the word. "Keep digging, Abby! Jill! Dig! There have to be more. Find them."

We bent over the already large hole. "A clutch of fifteen isn't normal or acceptable for a loggerhead nest," Jill mumbled. "Not this time of the year. Maybe in November."

"What happens in November?" I flopped onto my stomach to extend my reach as the cavity got deeper.

"The sand's colder. There might be over-wash. Heavy rain. That affects the eggs and we might get a partial hatch. Or no hatch at all. It's sad but not unexpected. Dig to the left," Jill said. "I'll go to the right." She clawed at the wet sand. "But in July? What the hell's going on?"

"Dig straight down," Hannah ordered. "Abby. Dig down. Directly below where the depression was."

Jill and I exchanged looks, but I steeled my fingers against the hard-pack and scraped at the cement-like grit. For Hannah's sake, I'll just keep digging down, down, down, till I reach—

"Here's something," I whispered to Jill. I dug my fingers around what I hoped was a turtle egg. It was round and thick.

It was not a turtle egg. LuAnn gawked at the lump in my hand, filled her lungs with steamy ocean air and let out a shriek similar to the red-tailed hawk scream I'd heard at a raptor fair in Raleigh. Only shriller. With a gasp, I flung the chunk wildly and watched it land near a crowd of tourists. I needed a giant glass of wine. Better yet, had I replaced that bottle of Jack?

"What was that?" Hannah shouted. But I couldn't answer. She ran up to the pack of tourists clustered in the sand, yelped, and fumbled for her phone. Dropped it in the sand, picked it up, pounded it against her thigh, and punched one number.

"Get me Detective Magnus. Now!" she shouted before sinking like a shipwreck in the sand. Jill said something quietly. "Yes, I'll call Will Brown!" Hannah's arm shook as she held the phone to her ear.

The detective arrived quickly, dressed casually, in slacks and a golf shirt, as if he'd come from the Cabana Bar down the road. Hannah, hunched over, rocking in the sand, raised an arm and pointed. Magnus stalked over to the dune and stared at the two-tone glob floating in a pail. Someone, I had no idea who that clear-headed person was, had rescued it from the sand.

"What part of the body did you uncover this time?" he asked sullenly. Hannah lifted her head enough to cast a dark look. Magnus pulled out his phone, and I heard him send for Doc Bailey and two more police officers, even though, or maybe because, Dutch and Joop had assumed the duty of crowd control.

I plopped next to Hannah. London James squatted nearby, texting. Yeah, spread the news. More body parts found under sea turtle nest in Goose Inlet.

The medical examiner arrived, pulled the blob out of the pail, and passed it gently from hand to hand. "Somebody cut out part of a tattoo," I heard him tell the detective quietly. "From a very fleshy part of the body."

I thought so, too. I'd steeled my stomach and taken a better look. Yellow and green swirls formed some sort of design, although I couldn't tell what it was or if it implied writing.

"Thigh?" Magnus asked.

Bailey scrunched up his nose. Shook his head. "Not my first guess—oops, that's right, I don't guess."

I was pretty sure I'd pitched what looked like a tattooed hunk of human butt as far as I could.

Bailey fished around in a pocket and came out with an evidence bag. "It's in pretty good shape," he said. "Whatever this red stuff is, it inhibited decomp. At the lab, I'll be able to determine if the toes and tattoo chunk are from the same victim."

In response to LuAnn's gasp, he added, "I say 'victim' but that doesn't mean the person's dead." LuAnn dropped onto the sand. Other volunteers stood around, hands covering mouths, too stunned to speak.

"How many nests do you have on this beach?" Bailey asked. Before Hannah could answer, he waggled his head. "Just wonder how many more trips I'll need to make before I assemble a complete human body." Did anyone else see his lips twitch as he headed back to the street? Perhaps a warped sense of humor came with the job.

***

I plopped down on my bed and reviewed the past hour. Detective Magnus had stood in the living room of Hannah's cottage, a long, narrow, ochre and turquoise cement block structure dating back to World War II, and asked if she suspected another poaching. Hannah said she would be more positive if she'd moved the nest and counted the eggs, but since she didn't do that, nobody did, she could only speculate. Magnus replied that speculation played a big role in finding the truth.

I'd been a bit ticked off that now he seemed more concerned about poaching than a mutilated victim. "With Nest One, you were all about the toes. Understandably," I'd said, "Now here we come up with a chunk of somebody's butt—"

"The ME didn't confirm that," Magnus said in a cautionary tone.

"I had the first good look at it. To say nothing of the privilege of handling it," I replied.

Hannah had asked if the detective was making a connection between a mutilated body and poaching. Magnus tapped his palm with his notebook, and stated that connections were even more useful than speculation.

I'd insisted there had to be a connection. Toes and a piece of rear end were buried deep inside empty turtle nests. Hannah declared that somebody had removed Nest One's eggs and put the toes in their place to laugh at us. Now here was Nest Two and the culprit was laughing even harder.

A group of volunteers had followed us to Hannah's cottage and milled about on the porch. Snatches of dialogue, dominated by the words "poach, poached, poacher and poaching," drifted through the screen door. I'd recognized Bianca's strident voice and Jill's more inquisitive tone. I heard Dutch say, "Randy Boone" and get hushed. I'd peeked out the front window but didn't see LuAnn.

Annoyingly, London James had followed us inside and dropped his long body onto Hannah's sofa as if he belonged there. I was surprised when he informed Detective Magnus that it was past midnight, that Hannah was exhausted, and could he continue this questioning tomorrow? Even Hannah's head swiveled when London said, "I'll bring her down to your office, if you like."

"I can get to Erik's office myself," she'd snapped. London had raised his hands in self-defense and retreated to the porch. As I lay heavily on my bed, I had a hazy recollection of his gaze following the flying tattoo in a twenty-foot arc from my hand to the sand.

With a small smile, Magnus had tucked his notebook and pen into his golf shirt pocket, where it stuck up like a small billboard. "Eight a.m. tomorrow will be fine. Get me a good start on my day." He'd said it with a Carolina twang that reminded me that he was a southerner and member of the Magnus clan. Detective Erik Magnus was an Inlet native who might have grown up eating sea turtle egg omelets.

CHAPTER FOURTEEN

"What did you talk about?" I took the cups from Hannah's hands and set them on the wicker table on Lily Pad's front porch. I'd called her phone twice to get the scoop on her early morning chat with Detective Magnus, but the calls went right to voicemail. Now, in late morning, she was at my door with iced coffee and a bag of flash-dried snap peas.

"He wanted to know how a piece of human flesh could end up buried under a nest of turtle eggs that had not been moved." Hannah grunted. "Like I would know." She popped the lid off her coffee and took a sip. Slowly turning the cup round and round, she gazed toward the ocean. After several moments, I tried the old penny-for-your-thoughts query.

Hannah pursed her lips and looked me in the eyes. "I'm thinking about you doing a little investigative reporting."

"What!"

"Find out who's poaching our sea turtle eggs. See if it's connected to these horrible mutilations."

"No, no, no." I shook my head so hard my hair slapped my cheeks. "That's not my kind of writing. I write *good news* stories."

Hannah smirked. "Oh, come on! I've seen you pouring over those twenty-page *New Yorker* exposes. Your nose is two inches from the print."

"Only if I'm not wearing my glasses."

She pointed a snap pea at me. "You gulp down those stories like tapioca pudding. And you always have five more questions you think the writer should have asked. You love that stuff. You can investigate the poaching on our beach and write about it for the Inlet weekly. Better yet, the city paper. And I bet Raleigh's *News & Observer* would print it."

I shook my head.

"Why not?" Hannah crunched a handful of dried peas. "It could be a series. First report on the poaching—"

"There were stories on the poaching after both nest excavations." I pointed to the local paper lying on the porch floor.

"A few paragraphs! I'm talking in-depth articles. After writing about the poaching, you can do a history story. Quote Joop Dahl, for Christ's sake. I don't care. But make people aware—"

"You've done a great job of making people aware, Hannah."

"Obviously not!" She jumped up and stalked across the porch, eyes welling with tears. "This is killing me! Don't you care? Don't you want to help?" She threw herself into her chair. "You're always flaunting your curiosity gene. Use it!"

I took a minute, trying to figure out an unemotional rebuttal.

"You're a good reporter," Hannah said quietly, giving me an opening.

"I'm a good listener. People tell me things. I don't snoop." I was a good editor because I recognized the need for investigative stories, and I assigned them to aggressive reporters. "I don't have to dig, pry, wheedle, or threaten to get the stories I like to write."

"The *safe* stories."

I flinched at Hannah's mocking tone.

"I thought you'd jump at the opportunity, Abby. I'm not just looking for publicity about poaching. For God's sake, somebody has been chopped up, very possibly murdered in the process, and you have to be stupid to think it has nothing to do with the poaching. They're obviously connected."

"I agree. And so must Detective Magnus." We were silent for a moment. "But Hannah, I'm coping with my husband's violent death. Do you really think I want to get tied up in a mutilation story?" Hannah's face softened. "I admire reporters who can do those things, but I'm not a chills and thrills kind of gal. I don't ride roller coasters. I'm not a risk taker." Not anymore. As a college student, I'd taken one big risk and lost. Twenty-three years later I toyed with a second risk, divorce, and lost my husband to a freakish, explosive death. The universe slapped my face for even thinking such a thing.

Hannah stared at the floor. She knew me better than anyone. Did she believe me? I noted her twisted mouth and clenched fists. Nope, not convinced.

"Besides, I'm here for R&R, remember? I bollixed up my job at the magazine. Was damn lucky they didn't fire me. What makes you think I can pull it together to investigate a poaching scheme—with accompanying mutilation—and write some big expose?"

I believed what I said, but was exasperated because Hannah was right. I'd been a *New Yorker* subscriber for decades. Read it cover to cover and was secretly envious of reporters who probed private places without guilt. Women who delved into complex mysteries and solved impossible riddles. I had a big time nosy gene but lacked the pushy one. Or should I just be honest and admit I lacked courage? The high-paid investigative reporters befriended police and criminals in equal measure. They peeked in people's windows. Bugged their cars. Invaded their financial records. Toured their garbage. Pilfered their mailboxes. Hacked their computers. Intimidated their friends. Antagonized their attorneys. They eavesdropped on conversations. They could read upside down. And they didn't care if they got caught snooping. They were never embarrassed. Could I do that? No.

And since I was being honest, at least with myself, I acknowledged a timid streak going back to childhood when I'd been labeled shy. In my youthful mind, I'd had a healthy wariness of strangers that should have been commended. But here I was all grown up and still timid about poking my nose in other people's business when their business needed challenging.

"Poking into poaching is risky, Hannah." I aimed for a quiet, reasonable tone. "You know I don't take risks." She didn't reply. "I took one risk and you know what happened."

She answered without looking at me. "Derek."

"Correct." I'd been a college junior and thought I'd met the man of my dreams. What the hell did I know? The second time I met the blue-eyed, curly haired graduate student in astronomy on the flat roof of his apartment building, I let him introduce me to the cosmos. I'd come to college a virgin and was embarrassed by it. Too many of my dorm mates told titillating stories from way back in high school. I had none. Until I shocked them with news that I was pregnant. And they all backed away, as if it was catching.

The grad student received his master's degree and blasted off to work at an observatory in New Mexico. Derek was born three weeks before the start of my senior year. He was a beautiful baby with a charming coo and I loved him instantly. But do I need to say that working, going to school, and raising a baby exhausted me body, mind and soul? My family helped. So did friends. Hannah even arranged her course schedule to watch Derek while I attended class.

But the challenge nearly beat me. I had taken a big risk and made a tiny baby. My one big blast of bravado had backfired. I went back to being my safe self, and to make a long story short, got stuck on good news.

I collected our coffee cups and went inside, coming out quickly with a pitcher of sangria and tall glasses. "It's noon," I said, in answer to Hannah's raised eyebrows. "And we live at the beach." I poured the fruity wine and handed her a glass. Orange and lemon slices floated on top. From the porch, we could see *that Hispanic woman* kicking a ball around the sand with her kids.

"Maybe we should invite Alegria for a glass of sangria," I suggested, admiring the burgundy-colored liquid in my glass.

Hannah looked at me cross-eyed. "Why? Because she's Latina? Would you invite her if we were drinking beer?" Obviously, she was still irritated with me.

"She brings her kids to the nests." I set my glass down and sat up to get a better view of the beach. "But no one talks to her much."

"She's the woman with the husband London said Aidan met on the beach," Hannah replied grimly.

"I figured that out, Hannah."

"Which is why you want to meet her. Not because you think she's lonely."

"You're starting to sound mean."

We stared at the ocean and sipped our wine.

"So to get back on subject," Hannah said in a gentler tone. "Alegria's Costa Rican."

"I figured somewhere in Central America."

Hannah pulled the pulp off an orange slice with her teeth and tossed the peel into a flower bed I'd planted with zinnias of all colors and sizes. "It's organic. I simply bypassed your compost pail," she said in response to my frown. "But Alegria, it's just—some turtle people talk."

"Fala! She piped up with the poaching accusation pretty fast at your party. I'd had a few drinks and a lot of that talk didn't make sense—"

"You were drunk, Abby."

"—and had a hard time putting their comments together, but I wasn't wrong about London accusing Aidan of being a poacher."

"He didn't call him that."

"I wasn't that drunk. London James strongly implied by saying Aidan had met with Alegria's husband on the beach and because Alegria is Hispanic—a misnomer, she's Latina like you say—and is from Costa Rica—that Aidan was responsible for turtles eggs being stolen from Goose Inlet. Right?"

Hannah thought a moment. "Maybe not responsible. But involved somehow."

"Involved somehow. Still not acceptable. Still a damn lie!"

Breathing heavily, I poured more sangria and hoped the steady action would calm my building temper. "Tell me about Costa Rica. Why do people suspect Alegria of poaching?"

"There are pictures on the Internet," Hannah said. "People carrying bags of sea turtle eggs off Costa Rican beaches. Some people believe anything they see without checking it out."

"Who's stealing the eggs?"

"See, that's what I mean. Those 'poachers' are actually taking part in a conservation program. But people don't believe it." Hannah finished the last of the snap peas and crumpled the empty bag. "And they extend their suspicion to that family." She nodded toward the ball kickers.

"Seriously? Our volunteers really believe Alegria stole our turtle eggs?"

"Some are hinting. Erik asked me about it—well, not about Alegria specifically. But about the money in poaching. Fala's cousin was in Costa Rica last year. He took a scooter into the countryside and found roadside stands selling turtle eggs for two dollars each. That's just the local market—grocery stores, restaurants, bars."

Benito kicked the ball deep into the dunes and chased after it. We could hear his mother calling to him, "No one's allowed up there. Come down."

"Even with the conservation project on some beaches, poaching is out of control in Costa Rica,"

Hannah continued. "It's an epidemic. Statistics are shocking. Some beaches lose ninety-five to one hundred percent of their eggs."

"Good grief!" I jerked my arm, sloshing wine out of my glass.

"The beaches are being raped by gangs of criminals. Smugglers who supply Latin America and Asia."

"They ship eggs from Costa Rica to Asia? How?"

"Plane probably. A ship would take too long and the eggs would most likely spoil."

"Must be expensive. Seems hardly worth it."

"Oh, but it is." Hannah twirled her finger in her glass and fished out a strawberry. "Turtle eggs go for one hundred to three hundred bucks each in Asia. That's U.S. dollars, honey. Big money."

"For one stinking egg?" My eyes widened. "And if they went by boat they would be stinking by the time they got to China or Argentina."

"It's a mess down there. Violence is increasing. One Costa Rican gang even killed a young conservationist. Turtle egg smuggling is getting as serious down there as drug smuggling."

I leaned forward. "And people are gossiping that Alegria is part of a turtle egg smuggling operation here in Goose Inlet?"

Hannah refilled our glasses. "They're mumbling. You know how people are."

CHAPTER FIFTEEN

After Hannah left, I took a bike ride down to the ferry launch. On the ride back, still filled with nervous energy, I decided to walk the beach. A debate was going on in my head about whether or not to jump into investigative journalism—and I couldn't believe I was debating the issue. Hannah was getting to me. Maybe that was a good thing.

I coasted into the public access lot near my cottage just as Alegria and her kids started up the wooden ramp that would take them across the dune. On the spur of the moment, I called, "Hey! Wait up."

Pilar wore a pink sea turtle project shirt and had already kicked off her sandals. "Mama, wait." She pointed at me locking up my bike and waving to attract their attention.

"I'll walk with you." I grabbed my water bottle and hurried to the ramp.

Alegria's black eyes opened wide, then she smiled. "That would be pleasant." Benito pushed past his sister and raced ahead, whooping at the gulls.

The beach was crowded, even though it was getting toward suppertime. I recognized turtle people mixed in with tourists and Goose Inlet locals. Fala and Hannah appeared to be holding an impromptu turtle talk with a group from the hotel.

We walked up in time to hear Fala say, "We're sociable, but nest sitting isn't a party gathering. If it's too noisy, the turtles won't come out."

"Are they scared of noise?" Benito asked, holding his hands around his mouth as if ready to shout.

"Lots of activity and sound makes the turtles think there's a predator up here," Fala replied. "Something big that wants to eat them."

"Like what?" Pilar asked, a tiny tremor in her voice.

"An alligator!" Benito shouted, before Alegria shushed him.

"More like a sea gull or a fox," Fala said. "Or a dog. Sometimes people let their dogs run loose at night on the beach. That's not good for turtle nests. But alligators, Benito, aren't usually found here on the sand, although it has happened. Right, Hannah?"

"Only found a gator on the beach once," she replied. "Don't ask me how he wandered up here or from where, but I came across him one morning watching the sunrise." A wave of comments, some astonished, others skeptical, rose and fell quickly.

Alegria walked toward the shoreline, explaining that the children liked to splash in the water. She opened her beach chair and sat down facing the ocean. I dropped onto the sand, close enough for the waves to cool my hot feet. The motion soothed my nerves, and the waves' rhythmic pulse muffled conversation.

"Your husband doesn't like to sit the nests?" I asked.

Alegria stopped rummaging in her tote bag and glanced at me, eyebrows raised. I explained that I'd seen her a few times with her kids, but him only once or twice. I hoped it didn't sound like I was keeping tabs on the man. I was just making conversation. Right?

She pulled a box of animal crackers from her bag and handed it to Benito, telling him to share with his sister and not drop the empty box on the sand. She turned to me. "My husband is interested in the sea turtles, but can't always come." Alegria paused. "I told him about the great losses." She mouthed, "Poaching."

"It has everybody pretty upset," I said, accepting an animal cracker from Pilar. I couldn't stop myself from asking, "You're from Costa Rica?"

"The children are U.S. citizens," she replied quickly and looked me in the eye, as if expecting a challenge. "My husband is American. I am studying for the test to become a citizen."

"That's great." I watched a tiny crab toss sand out of its dime-size hole. "I've always heard good things about Costa Rica." It was true, except for the smuggling and poaching, and I'd just heard about that. Hannah's turtle talk broke up and a handful of people brought chairs down to the water.

Alegria's eyes brightened and she asked if I'd been there. I told how Aidan had bit the bullet and taken me to Drake Bay on the Pacific coast for our twentieth wedding anniversary. It was beautiful but remote. "What part of the country are you from?"

Alegria opened her mouth to speak, then paused as if collecting her thoughts. "I am from the north. On the

Caribbean side. Limón," she said, her tone cloaking the city's name so that I barely heard her. She looked out at the water.

"Do sea turtles nest there?" According to Hannah they were all over Costa Rican beaches and easy poaching prey.

"Many." She leaned toward me and almost whispered. "But they are not pampered as they are here." She didn't sound sarcastic. Just matter of fact. "There are a lot more turtles laying nests in Costa Rica. Some beaches have thousands of nests."

"Thousands?" If Goose Inlet scored a dozen nests a season, Hannah was elated. "I can see why they're not pampered. How could you find thousands of nest mothers?" I laughed softly. "Your country has a good reputation for eco-friendly resorts. That's why we went there."

"We are conservation-minded. Our economy depends on it."

"Really?"

We twisted around at the harshly spoken word to see LuAnn Sheetz standing behind Alegria's chair.

"Hi, LuAnn," I said.

With two long strides she positioned herself in front of us.

"You've heard about Ostional Beach, haven't you?" she asked, her tone sharp as a shark's tooth. "You've seen the photos. People carrying off trash-size bags of turtle eggs on their backs?" LuAnn's cheeks blotched red and her breath came in short huffs. "It's an attack on nature. Goddamn poachers!"

People sitting nearby stopped chatting. Two bikinied teenagers walking past elbowed each other and snickered.

I didn't know what to say. Hannah and I had talked about this only hours ago, although Hannah had not mentioned this particular beach—Ostional.

"But that is deceiving," Alegria said.

"Deceiving my ass." LuAnn charged past Alegria's chair, causing her to flinch, and headed toward the dune. She glared over her shoulder, brows pinched, mouth puckered, as if scrunching up her face to hold back something rotten.

"Wait. Let me explain to you." Alegria started to rise but sat back down. "She must know the truth. The pictures do not tell the real story." Her gaze coasted among the suspicious faces turned her way. "Everyone should know the truth."

Uncomfortable with the stares, I looked down and made small muddy mounds of wet sand. Alegria was Costa Rican. Big deal. Did gossipers like LuAnn seriously think a woman from the land of thousands of nests had poached their handful of precious turtle eggs? I looked over at Alegria gently tapping her chin with her fingertips.

I scooted closer. "So, what's the truth?"

Alegria sighed, and it wasn't until then that I realized she had been holding her breath. She told me about a conservation program the government started thirty years ago to help the turtle called Olive Ridley. "That beach—Ostional—is only about a mile long," she said, "but hundreds of thousands of turtles—"

"Wait—hundreds of thousands*?"*

"Hundreds of thousands of Olive Ridleys swim to it. They lay something like ten million eggs."

"That's impossible!"

Alegria shook her head, said it was true, and that it happened twice a year. They called it the *arribada*—an arrival. I screwed holes in the wet sand with my heels. With ten million eggs lying around, was it criminal to ask Mother Nature to spare a few omelets?

When Alegria called the *arribada* a disaster, several people pulled their chairs closer to listen. She explained how most of the eggs in the first nests got trampled by mother turtles that arrived later. The beach became filled with broken, rotting eggs and turned into a soupy mess.

"It wasn't healthy for other eggs laid late in the season," she said, adding that only a few eggs survived. Conservationists said one, maybe two percent, hatched and finally convinced the government to let people form a cooperative to harvest the early eggs from the first *arribada*. Unfortunately, thanks to the Internet, people all over the world saw bags and bags of sea turtle eggs being carted away and became frantic.

"But the picture they see—think they see—is a lie," Alegria said. "It's a conservation program, not poaching. The eggs from the second *arribada*, they leave alone."

I drew my eyebrows low. "What do they do with thousands of collected eggs?"

Alegria cast an uncomfortable glance at the people around us, some of them project volunteers, and said almost apologetically, "The eggs are a delicacy. Bars and restaurants buy them. People love to eat them."

I nodded. "Better taste, packed with protein."

"Please don't blame these people," she said in a stronger tone. "Taking eggs on Ostional is legal. People do it to make money. And it helps the turtles." When I did not reply, Alegria held out her hands, palms up. "Eating turtle eggs is a way of life." When she didn't say more, some of her audience drifted away.

"I don't know," I said, after a pause. "Can bars and restaurants absorb thousands, millions of eggs?"

Alegria's gaze flickered to the waves washing the shoreline, then across to the volunteers seated in a tight circle nearby, absorbed in conversation. She admitted that, because the animals are protected, there was a huge black market for turtle eggs in Latin America and that real poaching goes on all over Costa Rica.

"And not just eggs. Turtle meat is very sweet." She turned almost pleading eyes on me. "The poachers, their lives are hard. They live in huts without water or electricity."

She wants me to sympathize with native people bringing in a little extra money. I did. But Hannah talked about big smuggling operations. Criminal activity. Gangs.

My phone dinged. Wade Ramsey: *Heard management is doing a serious inventory of chemicals taken from lab storage in last six months. Even those Dr. Finn used.* My stomach tensed. Was the research director taking my accusation against Marc Diamond seriously, or was everyone under suspicion?

CHAPTER SIXTEEN

The next evening on the beach, I sat a stone's throw from LuAnn Sheetz, curled up on a blanket. She'd landed looking like she'd washed up after a hurricane. She hadn't acknowledge me, just rolled out her blanket, and fallen asleep.

"Hey!" Dutch called, raising both arms in a rock concert wave. I made a shh-shape with my lips and pointed. "Sleeping. Rough day." Despite my irritation with her recent outburst at Alegria, I sympathized with her foot-dragging gait and up-all-night face.

"That's LuAnn," Dutch replied. "Rough day. Tough life."

I picked up my chair and they followed, plopping into their own low-slung beach chairs at the waterline. Earlier in the day, I'd run into Fala at the grocery, mentioned LuAnn's misery at the nests, and been treated to a mini biography. I learned LuAnn's mother was in assisted living in Raleigh, that her meds were pricey, she took a lot of them, and LuAnn was always jumping through hoops with an online pharmacy. Fala seemed to have the scoop on all things "Sheetz," and having the curiosity gene, I listened carefully. I hadn't made an effort to be friendly with LuAnn in the nearly two months I'd been in Goose Inlet. She hadn't made an effort either. She had friends and didn't seem excited about making new ones. Her boyfriend was missing, and her glum reserve at the first two turtle nests had been a billboard declaring, "Stand back!"

"The old lady's just got Social Security," Dutch said, when I mentioned LuAnn's problem sorting out her mother's meds, "so LuAnn helps out."

My parents had died when my kids were small. Derek and Kate were young adults now, he working with his own apartment, she a college junior, but I still helped with their expenses and spent holidays with them. How would I cope if my parents were alive and struggling with old age ailments? Would I have time to drive them to the doctor, deal with prescription screw-ups, and evaluate assisted living arrangements? While working a demanding full-time job?

"And on top of managing her mother's situation, she's worried sick about her missing boyfriend," I said. "No sign of him." All I got from Joop and Dutch in response were grunts. "Was he a fisherman?"

The men exchanged looks. "Well, he fished," Dutch said. "Fishin' didn't make Randy Boone a fisherman."

"Sounds like you don't think much of him." This was not gossip. This was learning what made Inlet residents tick. They were an odd bunch. A conglomeration of natives, snowbirds, new transplants, old transplants. Coastal Carolina was a hodge-podge that defied generalization. How did one define a local?

"Randy was okay," Joop said, pulling a water bottle out of a knapsack. "It was really only Dutch had a problem with him."

Dutch kicked up a spray of sand. "You'd be pissed, too, if his mutts drove you crazy."

I turned toward him. "What happened?" Both men looked out at the ocean. "Come on, Dutch, what happened between you and Randy?" This was about as pushy as I got.

Dutch pouted a moment then leaned forward, telling how Randy moved to the Inlet three years ago and took the empty cottage next door to him. "I knew from day one we was gonna have problems. He had these two little yappers. I called 'em Dumb and Dumber."

"See, if you didn't call his pups names, Randy probably wouldn't have taken a dislike to you." Joop wrapped his scraggly ponytail around his finger.

I waited, curiosity bubbling. Dutch said one dog looked like a Doberman but was the size of a rat terrier. The other he labeled a Pom-York-Chi.

I raised my eyebrows. "Pomeranian—"

"Pomeranian-Yorkie-Chihuahua." Dutch's head sunk into his shoulders. He looked ready to bite.

"You could tell that?" I tried to picture this designer dog.

"Hell no! But those three are the yappiest dogs on the planet. I looked it up online at three a.m. when they woke me up—again. Who lets their dogs out at three in the morning?"

"You do if they gotta piss," Joop offered.

"And that's my point." Dutch said, taking a swig from his water bottle. "You let 'em out. You let 'em in.

You don't let 'em out, go back to bed and let them argh-argh-ARGH for ninety minutes. I speak enough dog to know argh-argh-ARGH means, 'Open the goddamn door and let me in!'" Dutch lurched to the edge of his beach chair and the back flipped up and smacked his head.

I folded in my lips to keep from smiling. "Did you think to talk to him about it?"

"Talk to that idiot?"

"Or call animal control?"

"Shit, they don't do nothin'," he snapped. "I did something. I showed 'em." Dutch's face split with an evil jack-o-lantern grin. He leaned over until our shoulders touched. "I had fireworks left over from New Year's."

"Oh, no."

"Oh, yeah. Sure enough, next day, four a.m., the argh-argh-ARGH starts up. And I'd had enough. I put my flip-flops on —"

"Hope you put your pants on," Joop mumbled loud enough for me to hear.

"—got the crackers and my old lighter. Dumb and Dumber flipped into high gear soon as I opened the back door. I walked back and forth along the fence—"

"See, you antagonized those dogs," Joop said, tugging on his ponytail.

"Shit, I wanted those moronic mutts as hysterical as I could get 'em."

I noticed that people sitting near us had tuned into Dutch's story, wide-eyed and slack jawed.

"I even kicked the fence a couple times. Those hounds exploded. And that's when I lit the crackers and tossed 'em over the fence." Dutch sat back cackling, his thick Magnus shoulders quaking. "BANG! BOOM! BOMB! They was Wolf Packs and they blew!"

A mom and dad with three little ones cast frosty looks at Dutch as they packed up beach toys and moved away.

"Those dogs went crazy. Yelping and whining. Their argh-argh-ARGH turned to ieee-ieee-IEEE." Dutch threw his head back and laughed, his twisted, pointy beard stabbing the air.

My family had owned dogs when I was a kid and I loved them dearly. Aidan and I had taught our children to be gentle and treat their puppies with respect. Still, I wasn't sure I'd have been patient if Randy's barking dogs woke me repeatedly in the wee hours of the morning. My impatience would not, however, have resulted in tossed firecrackers.

"He's leaving something out." Joop told how Randy came flying out of the house calling for his dogs.

"He shoulda been calling for them earlier," Dutch growled through a snarling lip.

"Randy said you turned tail and scuttled home." Joop crossed his arms and looked down his nose at his friend.

"Secondhand bullshit!"

"Were the dogs hurt?" I asked.

"Randy took them to the vet when they started peeing in the house," Joop said. "Vet decided they had psychological trauma."

I waited a bit before asking, "Did the barking stop?"

Both men stared at the sand. Finally the words squeezed out from between Dutch's tight lips. "Not till Randy disappeared and LuAnn took the yappers to her place."

***

I lit a candle and settled into a wicker chair with a glass of wine on Lily Pad's front porch. The evening had been informative but unsettling. After the men left and LuAnn woke up, she surprised me by striking up a quiet conversation in which she appeared several personalities removed from the harpy who'd shouted at Alegria about Costa Rican poachers. She'd even accepted my invitation to lunch tomorrow. She shared how her mother's situation wore her down, mentally and physically. She didn't mention her missing boyfriend, but I knew LuAnn was obsessed with finding out what happened to Randy or at least finding his body. I could identify with that. LuAnn struck me as a complex personality struggling to stand amidst chaos. How did one cope with constant turmoil? One tragedy had struck my life and nearly done me in. LuAnn's life seemed to be a lesson in endurance.

I'd wanted to know more about Randy Boone and, before they left, Dutch and Joop eagerly filled me in. Randy, I learned, came from a county across the river that people born into rarely left. I knew a man who'd taught school there and who had described the area as "like the Third World. Primitive and underdeveloped." I'd written a magazine story on the county and found it bucolic and charming. Two attributes I missed living in the traffic-jammed Triangle.

Joop had wondered if Randy moved to better himself, but Dutch snickered that, "Randy couldn't do much to better himself."

Both men had talked in volume more suitable to the Chubby Fish, and I'd wondered if there was something other than water in their plastic bottles. I hoped that LuAnn, huddled on her blanket not that far away, was truly asleep. I'd knock silly anyone who spoke unkindly about Aidan. As proof, I'd knocked London into a flower bed.

Thinking about these strong personalities gave me the idea that Aidan might have been having a difficult time with someone at Tillson Pharmaceutical. As agreeable as he was, not everyone got along with all their coworkers all the time. Dispositions and egos sometimes clashed. But Aidan's tools, along with beakers and flasks, were reason and logic. The possibility of anyone not getting along with a diplomat such as my husband seemed far-fetched, but, be realistic, Abs, it is possible someone might not have liked Aidan. Or not liked something he'd done. A strong pressure settled against my heart. The pressure turned into a squeeze. But not like him enough to kill him? I thought about Wade Ramsey's message about Tillson inventorying the use of chemicals from the lab's storage closet. It sure sounded as if not only Marc Diamond was suspect.

I pulled my thoughts back to Dutch and Joop, who'd said he found Randy's jon boat in one of the bays, sans Randy. When I'd asked if the authorities suspected foul play, Joop said there wasn't blood in the boat. Randy simply had vanished. Aidan had pretty much vanished, too. Chills raced up and down my arms. It happened so frequently lately, I considered it my personal air conditioning.

"Anything coulda happened," Dutch declared. "If he didn't disappear on purpose or jump over the side, hell, there's a heart attack, a stroke. Randy was working on sixty. About fifteen years older than LuAnn." He shrugged. "Some freak accident and—oops, Randy goes overboard." He rolled his shoulders, as if working out a kink. "Any way it happened, Randy's gone."

I thought he seemed awfully certain. "You're sure it was Randy's boat?" I'd asked.

"It had *My LuAnn* painted on the bow. Nobody else would admit to that," Dutch had snorted and poked Joop's arm.

I'd scowled and declared him devoid of compassion, for dogs and people, and sarcastic to boot. He'd shrugged and turned his attention to Alegria's husband, jumping with his daughter in the waves. "Now that's who my nephew should be looking at for poaching," he'd said. "His wife's Costa Rican and he works at the port."

"Are you the one who started that ugly rumor?" I snapped.

"I wonder if she's legal," Dutch drawled, twirling his spiky beard.

"Now you're starting more gossip?" I felt my temperature rise.

When father and daughter joined the rest of the family, Alegria whispered in her husband's ear, and he'd glanced at LuAnn on the blanket.

"Those citizen papers don't come cheap," Dutch had replied sagely.

CHAPTER SEVENTEEN

The next day I knocked at the door of a brick ranch house five blocks from the beach. A frenzied, high-pitched racket and the frantic scraping of sharp nails on wood preceded its opening.

"Shut the hell up!" LuAnn shouted at two small dogs that snarled and snapped around her ankles. Randy's mini-Dob and designer Pom-York-Chi yapped and darted and clawed at the door, which bore fresh wounds from recent assaults.

"Shut up!" LuAnn swept at the dogs with her bare foot. They slid back a yard but ran around in circles *argh-argh-arghing*. "Goddam yappers." LuAnn scrutinized me, as if searching for the reason I'd disrupted her day.

I scanned her billowy nightshirt with a pouty-mouthed mermaid on the front. "We're going to lunch," I prompted.

"I didn't forget. Just—lost track of time." LuAnn's sun-scorched hair stuck up on one side like a tidal wave. She sighed, as if resigned. "Come on in. Those mutts don't bite."

The door screamed for oil when I opened it and gave Dumb and Dumber an excuse to ramp up the volume. Stepping around the animals, I entered a small foyer that spilled into a living room crammed with painfully outdated furniture. A half-dozen faded, upholstered chairs and ring-scarred tables bumped into each other like old pals at a reunion. Junk mail stacked up on a coffee table, its glass top grimy with spills. Greasy takeout containers lay topsy-turvy on the dusty wood floor. The odor of stale beer wafted past my nose as the door closed. I wasn't a nitpicking housekeeper, but I hoped LuAnn didn't invite me to sit.

"Have a seat." LuAnn waved toward an orange sofa pushed flat against one wall. "Take me a minute to throw on some clothes." She dragged her feet down a short corridor and disappeared into the last room on the right. The dogs followed.

I blew out a long breath. This is what I got for being sympathetic. LuAnn's exhaustion after a trying day in Raleigh and the men's derogatory comments about her lost boyfriend had tugged at my heart. I felt guilty about ignoring Hannah's repeated suggestion that I befriend LuAnn, and since we'd had a surprisingly pleasant chat, I'd invited her to lunch. As it turned out, she either hadn't remembered the invitation or had thought so little of the offer that she hadn't gotten out of her nighty.

I mentally kicked myself for getting suckered in, but caught myself in time to prevent serious bruising. Don't forget, Abby dear, how jagged emotions slashed you head to toe immediately after Aidan's death. In the first few weeks I'd felt gutted. Shattered. Outraged at being cheated out of a continuing life with a husband I loved. I leaned against the doorjamb and felt a pall pass through me, a dimming similar to a cloud drifting slowly before the sun. Three months were barely a blink in the scale of grieving. I was nowhere near healed and doubted I ever would be. I looked at a clock on the wall.

"LuAnn?" I took two steps down the hallway. "Are you ready?"

I walked down the hall, glancing at walls covered with framed photos, wondering if LuAnn's Inlet ancestors went back as far as Joop and Dutch's. I peeked into the bedroom. LuAnn, still wearing her nightshirt, sat on a bed that looked like it hadn't been made in weeks. A faded floral bedspread was jammed down under the footboard. A pillow lay on the floor. Another rested on dingy, twisted sheets. The room's musty odor told me gray was not their original color. Frantic barking came from inside a closet. I knocked on the wall gently, but LuAnn, eyes glued to a photograph in her hand, did not respond.

"Is that—?"

She turned the picture over on her knee and placed a hand atop it. "Randy."

I stepped into the room. "How long has it been?"

"Over two weeks."

I considered sitting next to her on the bed, but nothing in the woman's body language was welcoming. I took a deep breath. "I lost my husband—"

"I know! I know you did!" LuAnn jumped up and stuck the photo in a mirror frame above a chest of drawers. "I don't want to talk about dead men, okay?"

I jerked back as if punched. "Fine with me." I retreated to the doorway, my early reluctance to befriend

LuAnn flooding my system. "Look, you're not in the mood for companionship, so I'll go." I turned and came face to face with a large portrait of a rough-faced man in a fisherman's cap wearing the same scowl as LuAnn's. Definitely blood-related.

"Wait!" she stumbled after me. "I—I just don't feel like going out. Maybe we could order something and bring it back here."

I turned from the portrait. LuAnn's face had crinkled like a dried apple. Her watery eyes and twitching mouth sent sympathy swirling through me again. Right. Who wanted to talk about dead men?

"Sorry I'm in a lousy mood." LuAnn sunk onto the floor, her nightshirt billowing like a downed parachute. "Didn't get much sleep—I didn't sleep well last night."

I remembered sleepless nights. May and June were full of them. "I'll get us a couple fish dinners from the Seahorse. How's that?"

LuAnn wrinkled her nose. "Actually, I like the Sloppy Parrot's better. With extra tartar. Phone number's on the fridge."

I returned twenty minutes later with two fish dinners and a quart of diet soda. The little yappers were nowhere to be heard, LuAnn had changed into a tank top and shorts, and the tidal wave on her head had collapsed, hopefully under the weight of a shower.

"That smells good." She sounded revived, if not cheerful, and led me outside into an overgrown yard.

Overgrown? Jungle was more accurate. Two huge pines anchored the yard and beneath them several trees and a legion of shrubs fought for space and air. I recognized river birch, redbud and dogwood. The red berries of yaupon holly stood out against a line of disease-ravaged pittosporum. One of my favorite trees, the red buckeye, would have been handsome if it hadn't been covered, like everything else in the yard, with a thick layer of pine needles.

"Someone did a lot of work in this yard." I silently added *at one time*. I had a large garden in Chapel Hill. A lawn service was maintaining the grass, but my flower gardens would go *au natural* until I returned home. Hopefully, they wouldn't look this bad.

LuAnn unwrapped her fish dinner and popped a hush puppy into her mouth. "My grandparents did the work." She forked up some coleslaw. "And their grandparents." She rubbed a series of hush puppies in honey butter and chewed them up.

"Your great-great grandparents lived in this house?" I cocked my head. "It's not that old."

"The land's been ours for a couple hundred years. My family owned a lot of this island, way back. The great-greats had a different house on this spot. Gram and Gramps tore it down and built the core of this place. Mom and Dad added on. I haven't done anything to it."

No kidding. I broke off a piece of fish and relished its sweetness while watching a platoon of bees attack Spanish lavender.

"Nest Six was laid last night," I said. Bianca had told me this morning at the coffee shop that she and Hannah had been lucky enough to see the mom laying. Bianca also said LuAnn failed to come to work this morning. I'd replied that she might still be physically exhausted after yesterday's round trip to Raleigh and mentally fatigued over the uproar with her mother's meds. If that were true, her weariness could also explain her disinterest in our lunch date. The possibility sparked a twinge of guilt for my irritation over her greeting me at the door in her nightgown.

"Do you know who's lined up as nest mom?" I asked. LuAnn shook her head. "Bianca didn't know either, but she said they didn't have to move the nest. It was laid in a good place with perfect tracks leading up to it and going back into the ocean. Very visible."

LuAnn picked up a French fry. Nibble, nibble, nibble. Gone.

I took a bite of fish and looked up to find her staring at me.

"What?" I sipped soda and struggled through the compulsory bubbles. "Something on your mind?"

LuAnn sucked in a cheek and held it a few seconds before letting it go with a pop. "I was wondering how well you know that—*Latina*."

Her emphasis on the last word set my nerves skipping. I swallowed a big bite of fish and managed to choke out, "Alegria?"

LuAnn tossed her head, as if the name wasn't important.

I coughed a couple times. Swallowed more soda. Finally the fish went down. "I know she spends a lot of time on the beach and brings her kids to the nests. We both know she's from Costa Rica." And you bitched her out for it.

LuAnn scraped the last shreds of coleslaw out of a paper cup. "Do you know where in Costa Rica she's from?"

"Some place called Limón. On the east coast. I had a nice conversation with her."

"Bet she didn't tell you about Moín Beach. Near Limón."

I shook my head. "Never heard of it."

"Well, it's a gangster's paradise. And do you know what gangsters do? They kill." LuAnn picked up a plastic knife and sawed through her crispy fish. Shards of crunchy breading popped about the paper plate. "And the goons who control Moín Beach—the sea turtle poaching thugs—killed a guy—"

I raised my fork in acknowledgement. "A conservationist. Hannah told me."

LuAnn pushed her plate aside. "I bet the Latina didn't admit to it."

No, Alegria had not mentioned the death.

"She didn't tell you how they kidnapped him and four women. Tied him up. Dragged him through the sand. Left him to die on the beach." LuAnn held her knife in a clenched fist and pounded the picnic table. "She didn't tell you he was twenty-six years old."

I eyed the knife, plastic though it was.

"And now she brings her husband."

I raised my eyebrows. "*Brings* him?" I didn't understand what she meant. "Alegria's husband doesn't sit at the nests with her and the kids." I searched my memory. "Maybe once."

"But he came to the excavations! Snooping around."

"Snooping?" I dimly remembered him at Nest One's excavation. Was he at Nest Two? "He came to the beach with his family. What's the big deal?"

"Why is he here?" she demanded.

I gathered the dregs of our fish dinners and stuffed them in the takeout bag. "LuAnn, he lives here. And all sorts of people come to excavations. Volunteers. Locals. Even tourists. Why shouldn't he?"

"Do you know anything about him?"

"I don't even know his name." I hadn't thought to ask Alegria and she hadn't mentioned it.

"Jason Stone."

I nodded. "He's American. So are the children."

"But do you know what her name is?" Before I could answer, she spit out, "*Villalobos.*"

"She kept her maiden name. Most Latin American women do." As a child growing up in a town outside Boston, I'd had several Brazilian neighbors. Most of the adult women had surnames different from their Brazilian husbands. It was a cultural thing.

LuAnn acted as if she hadn't heard me. "Do you know what that means?"

"Her name?"

"*Vil—la—lo—bos,*" LuAnn repeated with enough attitude to make me want to slap her. "Get it?"

I checked the time on my phone.

"Town—of—wolves." LuAnn loomed over the table like a predator.

"Oh, come on. That's a literal—is that even accurate?" And who cares anyway.

"That's what Limón is. A town of wolves. A town of killers."

"Wolves always get a bum rap." Wolves and snakes. They both had important jobs in the web of life but most humans cringed at the sight of them. Some killed them indiscriminately.

"Town of *wolves.* Town of *poachers.*"

"LuAnn, you're going off the deep end."

"And now they're here. In our quiet little beach town."

"You're saying Alegria Villalobos stole turtle eggs from our nests? Why would she do that?"

"For money! And you know the clincher?"

I refused to guess.

"Her American husband, Mister Jason Stone, works at the port. So those sea turtle eggs were long gone within hours of her snatching them." LuAnn crossed her arms and grinned. I thought her canines were unusually long.

I held back telling her she was looney as a drunken monkey. "You're implying—"

"Declaring."

"I gotta go. Thanks for lunch." Thanks for lunch? I paid for it. The screen door slammed behind me as I hurried from the backyard into the house. From behind a bedroom door, Dumb and Dumber's sharp *argh-argh-arghs* assaulted me the length of the hall. I was tempted to fling the greasy takeout bags into LuAnn's festering dump in the living room, but pitched them into the first trash container I saw on the street. Which was where I wanted to chuck LuAnn Sheetz.

CHAPTER EIGHTEEN

I walked home along the beach, hoping the waves' hush-hush would quiet my emotional bedlam. That LuAnn was something. The woman played the sympathy card—*my boyfriend, my mother*—then lashed out at Alegria and her husband with spiteful, unsubstantiated accusations. Well, that was my first and last attempt at friendship with LuAnn Sheetz. I wasn't that hard up for companionship that I had to bear someone shouting claptrap and trying to bully me into denouncing a woman based on her last name, for cripes' sake.

Hannah can fix her up with someone more in tune with her way of thinking. Like that other rumor monger London James! My irritation skipped from LuAnn to London, and it hit me again that we'd moved in the same circle for two months and he hadn't told me he knew Aidan. When he finally admitted the association, it was with the caveat that Aidan was a bad man. Well, Aidan wasn't the saint I thought he was. He snuck around and kept secrets. But was he doing something illegal or was he being naughty? Was he having an affair or was he committing a felony? It was hard for me to imagine either.

Secrecy was a recent addition to Aidan's character. I could understand his behavior if he needed to protect his family. But from what? We did not dwell in destructive environments or mingle with perilous people. We lived safe, quiet, pleasant lives. We'd lived the good life.

So stop this destructive mind-wandering, Abby, and remember the good times. Negative thoughts won't ease your anger or your guilt. And there'd been many good times. Hundreds. All those Christmases when the kids tumbled downstairs and giggled over piles of presents under gaily decorated trees. Countless hikes up rocky slopes beneath tall, fragrant pines. Whole days swimming in clear mountain lakes. Had I really missed the beach? Be honest, Abs. Not that much. Aidan had made each mountain vacation a treasury of memories. Snapping camp fires. Charred hot dogs. Gooey S'mores. He'd taught his children the names of plants and trees. Pointed out the black bear browsing for berries, while hoisting both kids into his arms and backing slowly and quietly down the trail. We'd relaxed in the daily pleasantries of shared meals and movie nights. We'd sat together, proud parents, at school band concerts and screamed our throats raw at soccer matches. I'd never gone alone. Aidan was always there. Ready with praise. Always sincere. He was a good parent. A good man. In my heart, Aidan's most winning trait was that he had never—never—made a distinction between Derek and Kate. When strangers told Aidan that Derek looked like him, he smiled and thanked them.

London James popped back into my head, terribly uninvited. You're going to run into that guy all summer,

Abby, so get over it. Forget he knew Aidan because that only puts you in a lousy mood and you don't want bad thoughts about your husband. Cherish the happy times because Aidan can't make more.

"Hello, there."

I looked up from the sand, not realizing I'd been walking with my head down. Tanner Banks walked toward me. I hadn't seen Tanner since the day he'd landed that bombshell on me about seeing Aidan in Goose Inlet.

"Where's your son?" When he didn't answer, I added, "The little boy you played with on the beach?"

"Oh!" He smiled. "That's my neighbor's boy. His mom was called into the hospital. Short-staffed. I offered to watch him. He's a high-energy kid. Wears me out."

We strode a few paces in silence. I wondered if I should mention the argument Hannah witnessed between him and London. Did the fact that they both knew Aidan make it my business? Probably not.

"Haven't seen you on the beach. Busy with your touring trade?"

He grinned wide. "It's a good, healthy busy." He paused. "Hey, do you kayak?" Tanner nodded, as if willing me to say yes.

"I have. Often and I love it. Mountain lakes are my specialty. Don't own a boat, though."

He waved a hand casually. "I have lots of boats. Paddles. Life jackets. The wind and tides are good tomorrow morning. How about going out on the water with me?"

An odd Puritanical hang-up, probably inherited from my Boston ancestors, wafted through me. Was it appropriate to venture out on the water with a man I'd met once, briefly, and two months after my husband's death? I did a quick analysis.

One, the old *Gone With the Wind*-black dress-year-of-mourning was a century or more out of fashion. Two, Hannah and Jill knew Tanner and had paddled with him. Three, if neither propriety nor safety were valid excuses, the pertinent question was whether or not I wanted to be on the water with anyone at all. Sadness, anger, guilt—emotions that had become common, but not comfortable, companions—washed over me,

I shook my head. "I don't think so."

Tanner picked up a shell and tossed it back into the water. "Do you have something better to do than be out in fresh air, listening to a blue heron caw?" he asked with a grin. He certainly was a smiley dude. "Have you heard one? They're beautiful birds but let out an astonishingly harsh croak."

I laughed. "I have heard a blue heron." I squinted and looked up into his eyes, which, under the brim of his baseball cap, resembled puddles of fudge. "Is anyone else going?" A group excursion would be fun.

"Oh, you want references?" He chuckled pleasantly. "Well, there's your friend Hannah. I've gone out with LuAnn occasionally and Randy, before the accident. All my touring customers return to land safely. I've even been on the water with Dutch and Joop. And if I didn't dump those two overboard after five minutes, you know you're safe with me."

His playfulness was refreshing, and I noticed that his smile always reached his eyes.

I wiggled my toes in the shallow water. A quiet paddle might offer a chance to find out more about

London. As much as I wanted to forget the London James-Aidan Finn connection, it nagged like a hangnail.

"I know we've just met. It's not a date, Abby," Tanner said quietly. "Just a chance to enjoy nature." He pumped his arms. "Get a little exercise." In the sunshine, his soft brown eyes appeared to melt around the edges. He fluttered his fingers and added, "No strings," in a stage whisper.

I laughed nervously, embarrassing myself. I was being silly. And slightly arrogant to think this handsome man with an exotic heritage would be interested in me. "Sounds good. Where should I meet you?"

"There's a tiny beach on the ICW off Willet Street. You can park there."

Goose Inlet was smack on the Intracoastal Waterway, a 3,000-mile inland water course that ran along the Atlantic and Gulf coasts from New Jersey to Texas. It was made up of a conglomeration of natural inlets, saltwater rivers, bays, sounds and artificial canals. While I was still a freelancer, one of the editors at *Carolina* had taken the leap and retired early. She'd bought a thirty-six-foot Cape George Cutter and sailed up and down the ICW for twelve years, always wintering in warm, sunny climes.

Tanner thumbed his phone. "Checking the tide and wind. Yep, nine o'clock looks good." He glanced up. "Too early?"

"I'm up before seven with my first cup of coffee."

"I'll bring all the equipment. Wear a hat and water shoes if you have them. Oh, sorry, you've done this before." He ducked his head in a charming way.

"It bears reminding." We'd been walking slowly

along the shoreline. I stopped and pointed at Lily Pad's red metal roof above the low dune. "That's my house."

"See you tomorrow at nine." He tipped his cap theatrically.

I watched Tanner Banks stride through the surf, his footprints lasting barely a second before swishing away.

CHAPTER NINETEEN

Being out on the water with Tanner Bank was nearly the highpoint of my day. Watching one hundred fifty-six baby sea turtles erupt from Nest Three in a jaw-dropping boil that left all who witnessed it exhilarated to the point of dancing took first place. After escorting the hatchlings to the sea, laughing, cheering turtle people packed into the Sloppy Parrot, shouting out the night's highlights as they ordered cold brews and savory snacks.

"One of the biggest nests in Goose Inlet history!"

"No poaching this time!"

And no unearthed toes or tattooed butts, I thought. As friends and I slid into a booth, my phone dinged. Wade Ramsey: *Rumor buzzing. Chemicals taken from lab storage signed out under Dr. Finn's name.*

I typed back quickly: *Of course he used chemicals. He worked there.*

Wade: *These chemicals not used by Dr. Finn in Tillson experiments.*

I dropped my phone on the table, and my good mood crashed along with it. So what did Aidan do with those chemicals?

"One hundred fifty-six live ones!" a volunteer yelled from the bar area.

"Rest of you guys will have a hard time beating that," Fala called to parents of the remaining nests. I forced my attention back to my tablemates. Hannah was loud and giddy after two glasses of merlot, the bartender having filled them to the top in honor of the successful hatch. I grinned back at her and tried to ignore the cold chill gripping the back of my neck.

A few feet from where I sat, someone set a draft beer in front of LuAnn. One mug already stood empty on the table she shared with women I recognized as hard-core turtle people. LuAnn drank down half of her new mug, pulled out a photo, and smiled broadly. It was a rare smile for somber LuAnn, and a bit surprising since Randy was still missing. My heart hopped immediately to Aidan, who hadn't been found either. I swallowed the last of my wine and ordered another. Some of Aidan had been found, identifiable by DNA. I expected most of my husband had been carried up through the exhaust system that cleaned the air Tillson coughed into the atmosphere. I stared up at the Parrot's glittering ceiling, where glow-in-the-dark stars had been stuck. My wine arrived, and I took a good swallow. If some of Aidan was floating in the cosmos, I liked to think it was his soul, squeaky clean. Good lord, Abby, drunk already? I sighed, regretfully. No, not yet.

I watched LuAnn's friends scoot close, rub her shoulders, whisper in her ear. Everyone needs good friends. Triangle friends had enclosed me in a protective cocoon for days after Aidan's volatile demise, keeping reporters and TV cameras away. *Carolina's* freelancers had phoned and sent cards. Staff members brought meals, drinks, paper plates.

And then there was Hannah. "Come to Goose Inlet. I'll take care of you," she'd said. And I did.

Three men squeezed through the narrow space next to our booth. I got a quick look at Jason Stone as they boosted themselves onto a high-top table. I should talk to that man. Find out if Aidan spoke to him on the beach like London claimed. How would Alegria's husband react to London's insinuation? *And now the turtle eggs are missing.* When Stone slid off his chair and walked to the popcorn machine, I followed.

"Alegria missed a great hatch," I said, surprising him enough that he bumped his head on the popper's narrow opening. "Sorry to startle you."

"Alegria—uh, no. Too late a night for the kids," he said, eyes narrowing slightly.

I raised a hand. "You don't know me. I've talked to your wife at the nests." He nodded slightly. "I might have seen you there once or twice." He continued to stare, as if anticipating more than small talk.

"Look," I said, motioning him to the side of the popcorn machine. He glanced at his friends. The men had their backs to us.

"I'll get—right to it," I said stumbling over the words. "Someone told me he saw my husband talking to you on the beach last January."

"I talk to a lot of people on the beach," he drawled with a lopsided grin. I waited. "Last January?" He scratched his head. "If he was a tourist, I'm not likely to remember him."

"He wasn't a tourist. He was just *here*." How stupid does that sound?

"Gosh, ma'am." He bent closer and grinned big. "I'm no private eye."

"It's strange that he was here," I persisted, shuffling my feet. "I mean, my husband hates the beach. Never comes here. Or to any beach. But this guy said he was in Goose Inlet last winter. If you knew my husband—"

"What's his name?"

"—you'd know how crazy that is."

I slapped my forehead. "Ugh. Sorry. His name is—was—Aidan Finn."

He shook his head slowly, as if giving it some thought. "Don't know that name."

"Medium height and weight. Dark wavy hair. Wire-rimmed glasses." Yeah, that narrows it down.

Tanner Banks, wearing cargo shorts and a tank top, and looking languidly Hawaiian, cruised past with a mug of amber draft. He glanced from me to Stone but kept moving. This morning on the water, we'd talked about celebrating with large orders of hot chicken wings if Nest Three hatched successfully. Right now my stomach didn't feel up to fiery fatty food.

"You don't remember talking to him?" I held Jason Stone's eyes, willing him to remember. To change his mind. To admit it. Because Aidan *had* been in Goose Inlet. Tanner talked to him. The question was, had Aidan talked to *that Hispanic woman's husband*. The man I stared at right now. And what did they talk about? I tapped my open palm with an empty popcorn bowl. Waiting.

Stone leaned an arm against the wall and looked down at me. "I'm sorry. If I had more to go on—if you knew what we talked about—"

"Of course I don't know what you talked about! I didn't even know he was here till—" I dove the bowl into the popper and drew it out quickly, scattering kernels on the floor. "Never mind." This was the worst interview I'd ever conducted. Totally inept. Probably because I'm shit faced. Or close to it. The bowl wobbled in my hand, more popcorn bouncing onto the floor.

Stone swept the kernels away with his foot. "Sorry, ma'am." He stretched to push at a piece of popcorn almost out of reach. "No man introduced himself to me as Aidan Finn on the beach last winter."

I clutched the bowl with both hands. "No, I'm sorry. Sorry I snapped. Sorry to bother you. The guy must be mistaken." London probably made the whole thing up. Jackass.

I returned to my empty booth on shaky legs. Tanner slid in, too.

"Hungry?" he asked. "I ordered two dozen wings."

Strong male laughter drew my attention to the high-top table, where Stone sat with his companions, our strange tête-à-tête forgotten.

I faced Tanner across the table. "Wings?" Pull yourself together, Abby. "How hot?"

His bared his teeth to indicate hotter-than-hell hot.

I pulled several sheets off the table's paper towel roll, hoping Tanner didn't notice my trembling hands. "Perfect. Don't like 'em wimpy."

"You put something on that burn?" he asked, nodding at my red shoulders. I'd applied sunscreen at home, but we ended up paddling for five hours, and I was having such a great time that reapplying something to hold off the sunshine was furthest from my mind.

"Lots of aloe." I ordered a mug of dark beer, which always went better with wings, in my opinion. "Thank you for a fabulous time on the water, Tanner."

"You already thanked me. Multiple times."

I leaned back. "I felt loose, relaxed, truly free paddling through those bays. And I haven't felt that way in months." I changed my mind. Paddling had been the highlight of my day. Not even seeing one hundred fifty-six baby loggerheads scampering safely to the sea had touched me as deeply as had the smooth, glassy estuary at high tide. The clear, blue endless sky. The kingfisher skimming the water. The constant, light, cooling breeze. We'd paddled to the large barrier island that bordered the inlet, eaten lunch, then walked across to the ocean side where brown pelicans, my favorite sea birds, dashed headfirst into the water to catch their own meals.

Tanner took a long drink and tried to hide a burp. "Sorry. I burp when I'm happy. And I'm happy drinking good beer." He paused. "And I'm happy I gave you an enjoyable day on the water." Exhaling deeply, he nodded at the men a couple tables away. "You know Jason Stone?"

"Not really."

"You looked uncomfortable talking to him just now."

I shrugged. "Was nothing."

He tapped my hand gently with one finger. "Everything okay?"

I pulled off more paper towels and folded them into triangles. "Fine."

Liar, liar pants on fire. Not only was there the Aidan-Stone conundrum, thanks to the security guard's last text there was Aidan's name written on chemical theft. I glanced around the room, seeking a diversion. I pointed my chin. "Look at Hannah. She's a different woman."

Hannah had been glum since Nest One's pitiful hatch. She'd hosted the dinner party and had managed a cheerful face and conversation. At least until I'd tossed London James into the flower bed. I'd been surprised by my own strength. Maybe I'd channeled the same power that helped ninety-pound mothers lift trucks off five-year-olds. Not that London weighted as much as a Ford 150. He'd lain in the hydrangea branches, stunned, but his face flamed Crayola red. I'd left quickly, apologizing to no one. Tonight, after a fruitful hatch, Hannah seemed her old self, laughing and joking. Still, I knew poaching would remain on my friend's mind until the villain was caught.

"I hope the poaching's over," Tanner said, as if the word had been printed on my forehead. "Wonder if we'll ever find out who did it. And who that poor soul was who lost his body parts."

"And what the connection is between the two," I offered. A man came by and asked for Tanner's business card, saying he had family visiting and they all liked to paddle.

"Hannah hasn't heard anything, positive or negative, from Will Brown," I continued after the man left. "She said she's at the bottom of the totem pole when it comes to getting information."

Hannah had told me that NOAA, the North Oceanic and Atmospheric Administration, was offering up to $1,000 for information leading to the arrest and/or conviction of persons poaching endangered sea turtles, but that was way the heck over in the northwest Pacific, near Guam and the Northern Marianas Islands.

Still, it felt good to know something was being done somewhere in the world. Hannah said a poacher could get up to a twenty-five thousand dollar penalty. Fines could add up to a hundred grand. "And the creep can go to jail for a year," she'd declared. When I complimented her on the research, she said she didn't need to be an investigative reporter to dig it up. Ouch. I hadn't appreciated the gibe and wondered peevishly if Hannah had researched the amount of jail time a mutilator got for cutting off someone's toes and a chunk of tattooed butt.

A server set two baskets of wings on our table. The tang of hot sauce made customers in the next booth turn their heads and inhale. Tanner ordered more beer.

"What's he doing here?" I tucked a paper towel under my chin and nodded toward London James, standing near the back deck. "It's Tuesday. He only comes for the weekend."

Tanner picked up a wing and quickly dropped it back into the basket. "Hannah said he just started a two-week vacation."

"She didn't tell me that." I set a sizzling wing onto a small plate.

Tanner snorted. "Do you think she would?" Tanner had admitted during our paddle that he'd heard through the grapevine—my guess from chatty Fala—that I'd sent London flying.

I ducked my head. I'd been drunk and lost my temper. And embarrassed my friend. If anything, my dumping London out of his chair was a good demonstration of my anger, not my depression. For a brief moment I considered confronting him with Stone's denial that he'd talked to Aidan, but the dolt would probably say something else foul and my mood would take an even sharper turn for the worse.

London left the deck and ambled around the Parrot, wearing what my dad used to call a "shit-eatin' grin"—

whatever that meant. When he strolled past our booth I noticed his flip-flops. The man's gone native. He nodded to Tanner and continued a circuitous route to LuAnn's table, coming up behind her. Whatever he whispered in her ear made LuAnn palm the photo to her breast. After raising a jaunty finger in salute to her friends, he sauntered away.

That was the first one-on-one I'd noticed between LuAnn Sheetz and London James, but I'd had no reason to keep tabs on them. LuAnn was a hard-working turtle volunteer. London was a big city bozo. He still didn't interact with anyone at the nests except Hannah. I wondered again if there was something going on between them. Hannah hadn't shown any indication of taking my attack on London personally, which is what I'd expect if they were bed mates. She'd been more concerned about the hydrangea bush. And wouldn't she share something like that with me? Of course she would.

"Don't you like the wings?" Tanner asked.

I raised a fragrant piece and pulled the chicken off with my teeth. "They're good. Just the right heat."

I polished off two more and was sucking sauce off my fingers when Detective Erik Magnus walked into the Sloppy Parrot. He wore flowered board shorts and a sleeveless T-shirt that proclaimed "I Got My Crabs from Dirty Dick's." Most of Magnus's hair had pulled out of his topknot and curled around his neck. A sheen of sweat on his face and shoulders marked recent outdoor activity. Volleyball? The Parrot hosted league play in a side lot.

As if he'd been waiting, Dutch appeared from the shadows and pushed a mug of dark beer into his nephew's hand. The detective nodded thanks and scanned the bar. His gaze settled on Stone, who, like the men with him, wore work clothes and heavy boots. One of them reminded me of the man in the baseball cap I'd seen at the nests.

Magnus's gaze shifted to LuAnn, who'd just been served a plate of food. Dutch was bent down, talking in her ear, his pose sympathetic. This struck me as strange, since he hadn't expressed much compassion for LuAnn losing her boyfriend or for Randy probably losing his life. After giving LuAnn three pats on the shoulder, Dutch ambled over to Stone's table and the four men conversed several minutes in a joking manner, Dutch catching Erik's eye in the process.

What was that old coot up to? Consoling LuAnn. Chatting up Stone. Making sure the detective saw it all. By now Dutch had probably shared his opinion about who was poaching Goose Inlet turtle nests with his nephew. I recalled his remark that Stone might be trying to buy citizenship papers for his wife. It was a sinister accusation. A charge I was sure Dutch made up just to stir the pot. Some people enjoyed doing that.

I was feeling the unease I sometimes got researching a story that warned me people were not being honest. Strangely enough, this even happened with good news. Even though I believed Tanner about talking to Aidan on the beach, I texted Wade Ramsey: *Do you know if Aidan missed any days of work last winter? After Christmas?*

The answer came back quickly: *Just one. In January. It was my birthday and the office gave me a cake. I took a piece to Dr. Finn but he wasn't in so I wrapped it up and left it on his desk.*

Confirmation. Aidan came to Goose Inlet. My phone dinged again: *Was gonna leave a piece for guy who lunches with Dr. Diamond, since he shows up a lot, but DD said skip it. Guy wasn't coming in that day.*

A sick feeling washed over me like a following sea. It couldn't be coincidence that Aidan and London both missed work the same day and turned up at the same beach. More likely, London had followed Aidan—why?—and seen him talking to Jason Stone. So Stone was lying. London had accused Aidan of acting suspiciously in his lab, hiding his computer work. Quickly clicking off websites. What kind of websites? Why did London care? Dutch suspected Stone was our poacher. Was Aidan browsing poaching sites? *And now the turtle eggs are missing.*

I scrolled up to Wade's earlier text: *Rumor buzzing. Chemicals taken from lab storage signed out under Dr. Finn's name.* What was the connection between chemicals and turtle eggs?

CHAPTER TWENTY

I strolled to Briny Bill's after an early morning beach walk and saw London James talking quietly to LuAnn Sheetz on the sidewalk. LuAnn stared at the ground, took a step right then left then back again, as if hoping to step around him. If London was attempting to console her over Randy, she didn't act comforted.

Twenty minutes later, I was behind London in the grocery line juggling coffee, cheese and cans of tuna fish.

"Haven't seen you at Nest Four," I said, staring at the back of his head while a customer argued with the cashier over a coupon in the store's flyer. "What's keeping you off the beach?"

"Busy with work," he replied, not bothering to turn around.

"Aren't you on vacation?"

He moved up a step and mumbled something about "keeping up with current projects."

He didn't grouse at me for assaulting him at Hanna's dinner party, and I didn't apologize. I'm not prone to violent acts. I've never struck someone. My action had been in defense of Aidan and felt justified. Now, a tiny part of me suffered a niggly bit of doubt. Why had Jason Stone lied about talking to Aidan?

***

That night, Nest Four expelled ninety-eight eager hatchlings into the black night ocean, and nest-sitters rejoiced. LuAnn sat in the shallow water and wept as each baby turtle flip-flopped its way to the salty sea. I marveled at the woman's bottomless reservoir of tears. She cried over Randy. She cried over turtles. She cried when a nest turned up empty. She cried when a nest boiled with scores of live babies. I couldn't pinpoint exactly what tonight's waterworks were for, but they did make me wonder, somewhat guiltily, if I grieved enough for Aidan. Or was LuAnn Sheetz simply an Oscar-worthy drama queen?

CHAPTER TWENTY-ONE

The trip was to be an all-day affair while Tanner mapped a new kayak tour. He'd invited Hannah and me, but she had to interview a new teacher for Montessori, which would begin in a month. The trek would be hot due to calm winds, but Tanner promised I'd see lots of birds, maybe dolphins in the bays. This time we would put in at the wildlife ramp and cross the ICW, because Tanner would be starting his tour from that launch, where there was lots of parking for customer cars and his trailer loaded with a dozen boats.

I had a healthy respect for the ICW. The other day I'd seen some kayakers get trapped in the middle with big boats pounding along on a few hundred horsepower that threw a hell of a wake and could slam a small boat broadside. Small motor boats dodged around like gnats. And then there were those noisy jet skis. Hannah had told me to be vigilant.

"Crossing the ICW isn't like strolling along on a mountain lake. Look both ways, like crossing a street," she'd said. "If no boats are coming, you go. Fast. Haul ass. But if you get stuck with a big wake, just point your bow into the waves. You'll be okay." Just okay?

Now, here I was at the wildlife ramp, zipping into one of the bulky lifejackets Tanner provided for his customers. The vest-style was hot and cumbersome. The fanny pack style stand-up paddle boarders wore looked much more comfortable. Maybe I'd get one if I bought my own boat.

"I'm glad we're doing this on a Tuesday," I said,

"Way calmer than a weekend," Tanner agreed. "Middle of the week is when boat owners work to support their water habits." He smiled big, adding, "And I used to be one of them."

"Now you pick your play days and your work days." I pushed and snapped the two halves of my paddle together. "Hannah said crossing the ICW is like crossing the shipping channel. Look both ways and go like hell."

"Couldn't say it better myself." He paused. "But I hope the first time you cross the shipping channel you won't do it alone."

I shook my head firmly. That was a big risk I definitely would not take. "I've been told today will be much different than paddling a mountain lake. What about current and tide? And wind?" Like I knew what I was talking about.

"I don't go out unless I know what to expect from Mother Nature," Tanner said. "Today we won't be fighting the elements. It'll be a long, easy paddle. You might call it uneventful."

"Nothing wrong with that," I said, and we laughed.

He dropped a small cooler into his front hatch then attached a GPS to the coaming along the front of his cockpit. "If all goes well, I'll map a tour of the bays all the way to Salt Island."

"Will we have time to swim?" I asked, already anticipating a dip. The calendar was on its second dog day of August and the thermometer on Lily Pad's porch had registered 86 at eight a.m.

"Definitely. I brought crab salad."

"Cucumbers, cherry tomatoes and string cheese."

"Perfect accompaniments," Tanner said. "It's two hours before high tide, so we have several good hours before we notice the drop."

I really should start paying attention to tides. Knowing when to expect high or low was important for paddling and also for walking the beach, low tide being easier on the ankles. Goose Inlet was on the cusp of the low country, but its beach wasn't long and level like the ones in South Carolina or Georgia. Instead it sloped away from the high-tide mark.

We climbed into our boats and crossed the Intracoastal uneventfully. Paddled past the handsome gazebo a homeowner had built on the ledge overlooking the marsh and took the first turn into the bays.

"We have good water," Tanner said. "Creeks will be wide. We'll ride above the oyster beds." He winked at me.

Oyster beds. I'd gotten stuck on one during my first venture with Tanner. I'd been paddling along, gazing across the marsh, relishing the sunshine, smug that I wasn't squinting under fluorescent lights inside an office, when I heard a loud scrape and felt a tug that brought me to an abrupt stop. My jaw dropped when I saw I'd floated onto a wide oyster bed whose sharp shells had grabbed my boat like Velcro. My first attempts to dislodge the boat resulted in screeching sounds that warned me to stay put. Tanner had paddled up, apologizing for getting involved trying to identify a plant growing along the shore, and letting me wander.

"Not your fault," I'd said. What an idiot! Gawking at water birds and ruining Tanner's touring kayak.

He told me to push off with my paddle, but I was afraid of poking a hole and pictured the boat sinking and myself hanging on to a line while Tanner towed me back across the ICW. He said to forget the boat, push and scoot, so I pushed and scooted. After much cringing and cussing, I slid off the oyster bed and sat still in deep water a good two minutes to make sure the boat wasn't leaking. Back at the launch, we'd turned it over, and I'd groaned at the sight of its corrugated, cardboard-like bottom. I offered to pay for the repair, but Tanner said with a smile, "It's fixable. I'll write it off."

Today, we followed meandering creeks that wound through the marsh like old city pathways. Streets in the heart of Boston, where I had relatives, followed the same paths cows had plodded four centuries ago, or so the story went. What paved these creeks? Schools of fish? Troops of terrapins? Armies of alligators?

"See that long bridge?" Tanner interrupted my reverie. "That's private beach access for people living in the condo complex. Pelican Pier."

"It goes all the way to the ocean?" The distance looked close to a half-mile. "That's a long walk."

"Bianca lives there," Tanner said. "Has a beautiful view of the estuary."

I saw that the creek we paddled flowed under the bridge. "Can we make it through?" With approaching high tide, there didn't seem to be much space between the boat and the walkway.

Tanner nodded and led the way between pilings. I was relieved to see the bridge a good foot above my head. We came out into a small cove lined with trees and scrubby shrubs.

I let my boat glide to the center of the cove. "These water lilies are beautiful." The yellow flowers, half-open above the surface, were scattered among heart-shaped leaves.

Tanner coasted up. "That's spatterdock—cow lily. Water lilies are fresh water plants. And that's sea lettuce. It also grows in brackish water."

Below the surface, the sea lettuce billowed with the grace of underwater sails. A Great Blue Heron poked about in the shallows, its long, S-shaped neck stretching and retracting. I grinned when it came up with a fish. The spatterdock spread across the water, undulating like a magic carpet. I was taken with the scent of still water, mud, grass. In contrast, a light rose fragrance drifted out from the condos' common garden.

"This is the most peaceful place," I said. "A place to bring a book, float and read." There was no chance of drifting out of this secluded cove, situated far from the waterway and hedged by the saltmarsh cordgrass Tanner called spartina. I watched a Green-backed Heron land on a fallen tree. Funny how, with its short neck and football body, it didn't remotely resemble its long-legged, long-necked cousin, the elegant Great Blue. I was attracted by an egret that sailed in from the marsh. It landed in a corner of the cove but took off immediately, its hoarse, rattling call sounding much like a New Year's Eve party horn.

"Great Egret," Tanner said.

"I recognized its black feet and yellow bill. But what's that?" I pointed into the corner the egret had deserted abruptly. "See those purple flashes?"

Tanner took off his sunglasses and squinted for a better look. I dipped my paddle in the water and set off slowly across the cove, Tanner one stroke behind. We reached a jangle of dead tree limbs, decaying sea grass, bird feathers, and a clutch of plastic bottles and beer cans.

Tanner shaded his eyes. "A jacket? Windbreaker, looks like. Purple stripes."

I paddled farther into the debris. The white jacket was streaked with mud but didn't look worn.

"Damn, I hate this trash." Tanner picked the bottles and cans out of the water and dropped them into a mesh bag he kept in his boat for just that purpose. He reached out his paddle and scooped at a fast food box. "Carry in. Carry out. That should be the law. Not eat, drink and puke in the ocean." His voice sharpened with the first angry edge I'd heard from Tanner Banks in the wild.

Wishing to help, I forced my kayak between the half-submerged branches closer to the floating jacket. Pulling alongside the knots of sea grass surrounding the coat, I reached down and grabbed the bottom edge with my fingertips. When I pulled up, my boat tipped aggressively.

"Oh!" Palpitations tiptoed across my chest. I liked boats. I liked water. But nearly being jerked overboard took the fun out of both. "It's stuck on something."

Tanner fished out a plastic bag then coasted alongside me.

"I'll get it." His jaw was set and his lips drew a tight line across his mouth. "I know this probably flew out of a boat by accident, but I wish people were more careful storing their stuff."

He aimed his paddle at the bottom end of the jacket, floating an inch above the water. The paddle slide beneath the fabric, but when Tanner tried to lift the piece of clothing, the paddle stuck fast and his boat tipped far to the side.

"Dammit!" He managed to steady the boat, but the paddle was jerked from his hand.

"Careful!" A wave of apprehension washed over the back of my neck and tugged at the roots of my hair.

Tanner reached down and picked up the paddle end closest to him. The other side remained stuck beneath the jacket. He pushed the paddle forward. "Might be stuck on a rock. Or tree root. Maybe I can dislodge it." He moved the paddle back and forth, finally succeeding in pushing the far end through the top of the jacket. He turned it, hooked the coat and pulled. A human head popped out from beneath the decaying sea grass.

CHAPTER TWENTY-TWO

"Holy Christ!" Tanner lurched back.

My mouth opened with a squawk and my knees jerked, sending my boat bobbing. A choking squeal erupted from my throat. I jammed my paddle into a mass of downed branches and pushed off, sending the kayak skimming backwards into the middle of the cove. My heart ram-banged, and I grappled to loosen my lifejacket which seemed to have shrunk around my chest. Gulping air in noisy gasps, I leaned back in the boat, hoping to expand my lungs and slow my heartbeat. When I pulled myself upright, Tanner was sitting blanched-faced and motionless, so I didn't feel too guilty about scooting across the cove like a spooked water strider. When my breathing had slowed to short hiccups, I dipped my paddle in the water and stroked slowly up to Tanner's boat. Together we stared into the tangled debris.

"Holy hell, it *is* a body." It wasn't until I attempted speech that I noticed my tongue had been clenched between my teeth.

With the head freed, the rest of the frame had floated out slightly from its trap of downed branches.

I couldn't tell if it was a man or a woman. The hair was short and appeared light colored despite a coating of mud and rotten leaves. The legs weren't visible, perhaps still snagged on something underwater.

While the body floated almost gracefully, my nerves jitterbugged beneath my skin. "I can't stop shaking." I wasn't even embarrassed by the tremor in my voice.

"He must have fallen off the bridge and hit his head on a rock," Tanner said.

I looked closely. "I don't see any rocks unless they're underwater. Maybe he hit it on a piling. Although that would be an awfully awkward fall."

We studied the floating body, barely undulating in the quiet cove.

"He didn't have to fall into the water right here," Tanner said. "Could have been carried into the cove by the tide." He looked in all directions. "Although it's a tight area with all this sea grass closing in the opening under the bridge."

Tanner took the bandana from around his neck and wiped his face. "We have to call the police."

His comment shook something loose inside me. Something that surprised me. I heard myself say, "Let's see who it is first."

Tanner looked at me from the corner of his eye. "I thought you were still shaking. You want to identify the dead guy and maybe shake some more?"

I wasn't a risk taker, but my curiosity gene strained like a marlin against a hook. And there was no risk involved. The body wasn't going to jump into my boat and bite me. It was pretty well dead.

"Don't you want to know who it is?"

"We shouldn't tamper with him." Tanner held on to my boat, keeping me from drifting.

"We keep calling it *him*."

Tanner shrugged. "Kinda looks like a man's jacket."

"Women wear men's clothes. Jackets, sweatshirts." My initial fright had slipped several notches, and the body tugged at me like an impatient three-year-old. "Come on." I paddled as close as I could get and waved Tanner in.

He stared as if seeing me for the first time. Finally, with a head shake and loud sigh, he stroked to the opposite side. I used my paddle to swish away floating grass, revealing more of the jacket. And a deep gash in the blond head.

"Flip him over," I said. Tanner groaned. "Come on, you're stronger."

He hesitated. "We really should call Detective Magnus. Like, right now."

"Come on, Tanner!"

"It's tampering with a crime scene."

"Shoot, the body will roll back onto its stomach and no one will know the difference."

He dropped his head, mumbling. "Who are you?" I was beginning to wonder the same thing. We got into position and he slipped his paddle under one side of the body and lifted. It rose slightly but fell back into the water with barely a splash.

"Try again," I said. When Tanner slid his paddle under a second time, I pushed down on the other side with my paddle.

"Lift up now!"

Tanner raised the left side and the body turned slowly as if on a spit and settled onto its back.

147

"Holy shit," Tanner said softly.

I rested my paddle across my boat's cockpit. I didn't know all the people in Goose Inlet, but I knew London James.

CHAPTER TWENTY-THREE

Spattered mud clotted Doc Bailey's calves and rotting grass clung like varicose veins. He claimed he'd left his rubber boots on his back porch, having used them clamming over the weekend. The medical examiner looked put-upon when he clambered out of the water and stood barefoot on a strip of slick black mud beneath the bridge. As if London James had chosen this spot to die just to inconvenience him.

"You can't get the county to buy you an extra pair of boots?" Detective Magnus asked with a grin, coming up beside the ME. Magnus was also barefoot, pant legs rolled above his knees. Obviously he didn't have rubber boots either. I gave them both gold stars for dedication to duty. I wouldn't have stepped into that muck. Luckily, this wasn't an oyster bed.

Tanner and I sat in our boats, which a police officer named Kane had tied to a tree near the waterline. She had been first to arrive after Tanner called the Goose Inlet PD from his phone. While we waited for the big chief, he told me Officer Kane was a paddleboard instructor in her spare time and had talked to him about organizing tours similar to his kayak excursions. Kane—I was too shaken to ask if that was her first or last name—took up position on the bridge overlooking the body, her eyes never leaving the back of London James's head. It seemed unlikely, but I wondered if his was the first dead body she'd seen. At least a dead body floating in water, which I felt confident in assuming she'd always considered a happy space.

"You can hose off at my place," Bianca called down to Magnus and Bailey from the bridge. She was one of a crowd that included Pelican Pier residents, homeowners from neighboring Atlantia, a scattering of town dwellers, some open-mouthed tourists, and those habitual hangers-on, Dutch and Joop. LuAnn had walked up with them, but sat several yards away near the condominium garden. Through the sparse shrubs, I glimpsed her hunched shoulders, frizzled hair, and hand on the shirt pocket where her cherished photo of Randy resided. While Dutch and Joop hung over the rail, coaching the ME's assistants on the easiest way to haul London's body out of the muck, LuAnn stared into near space, her gaze drawn upward by the occasional squawk and swoop of a gull.

I didn't blame her. I'd shaken like a stand of sea oats in a thunderstorm until well after the police arrived. My nosy gene had compelled me to peek at the body floating beneath that jacket, but I truly didn't want it to be someone I knew. Not even the infuriating London James. What was he doing in this part of town? He didn't socialize. Didn't appear to have local friends. He seemed to hole up in his beach house and do what? Sleep? Read? Text? So, how did he end up here, in mucky water under a bridge at the far end of the Inlet? And with a two-inch gash in the back of his head.

"What do you think, Doc?" Magnus asked. "Accident?" He spoke softly, but his voice carried across the short stretch of water that separated Tanner and me from land.

"Won't know till I get him on the table," Bailey replied.

"You both knew the victim, right?" Magnus said, slightly louder, looking toward our boats.

I nodded. "He was sort of a turtle volunteer."

"Sort of?"

"He showed up at the nests. Mostly kept to himself."

Tanner offered no comment on London James. I kept quiet about Hannah seeing them arguing on the beach, which certainly qualified as hearsay. And there was no way in hell I'd volunteer that I'd attacked him at Hannah's house. Would it matter to Detective Magnus if he knew that London and Aidan were occasional lunch mates and both were dead? I didn't want it to matter. When Tanner didn't mention knowing London in Raleigh, I kept quiet.

Magnus rubbed the back of his neck and turned in a slow circle, scanning the marsh behind me. As he turned, his dark gaze floated across my boat, up the embankment to the bridge, where Officer Kane examined the railing. He watched her a moment, then scrutinized the shadowy water below the bridge. He continued to turn until he again faced the marsh that bled into the larger estuary. The spectators, who'd been shuffled off the bridge into the condominium parking lot, had gone silent.

"Can we go now?" Tanner asked, his voice breaking into the stillness. He repositioned his sunglasses and set his straw hat on his head. Magnus seemed to consider the request, then nodded for Officer Kane to untie our boats.

As we back-paddled, I saw Bianca wave energetically at the detective.

I looked for egrets and heron as we floated down the creek that returned us to the ICW, trying unsuccessfully to push the scum-coated body from my mind. I had not liked London James. I'd been mystified as well as insulted by his lack of empathy. And when he did acknowledge my husband, he'd accused him of suspicious—no, criminal—behavior with the barest, limpest, fabrication of proof. I had questions about Aidan's recent behavior and his violent death, but refused to believe he was involved in anything illegal. Still, in the deepest recesses of my soul, I hoped London's baseless accusation connecting Aidan and poachers died with him.

I moved slowly, my paddle barely making a sound, and considered how London had wound up lifeless in the muck. Slipping and falling between the rails seemed an awkward maneuver. An inebriated person might climb onto the railing, lose his balance, and fall headfirst into the water, but London didn't strike me as a sloppy drunk. Maybe he died somewhere else, as Tanner suggested, and was washed into the cove by the tide. Or, with a gash in his head that could have rooted a small house plant, it seemed possible someone had cracked London with something sharp and pushed him off the bridge. Who in quiet Goose Inlet would do that? And why? I contemplated the seven deadly sins. Lust. Gluttony. Greed, Pride. Sloth. Wrath. Envy. Any one of those could force a person to murder. Well, maybe not sloth or gluttony. Did an angry, greedy, jealous person kill London James? Or someone with something to protect?

I had not liked London, but one thing was certain. Someone else had liked him even less.

CHAPTER TWENTY-FOUR

After finding a dead body in his beloved estuary, Tanner had agreed a relaxing paddle plotting his next big tour was not in the works. I'd called Hannah immediately after returning home to tell her about London, and now I dialed her again.

"Detective Magnus just called. Told me to come in." I'd never been summoned to a police station before. As a freelancer and newspaper stringer covering the police and city government, I'd always been the one asking the questions.

The line was silent a moment. "Does he think you know something?" Hannah asked.

"I don't know what else I can offer. We told him everything this morning." Almost everything. I wondered if Tanner had been called, too, and spilled the beans about the argument and his Triangle connection.

My stomach crimped. Had Magnus discovered the tenuous connection between London and Aidan and decided to make a big deal about it? So they had a couple lunches together. People did that all the time and they didn't have to be best buddies. If asked, I'd be honest about lunch. But all that other bullshit—Aidan hiding his computer, meeting with Jason Stone—all that I'd keep to myself.

The Goose Inlet Police Department was housed in a square building attached to the town hall. An officer who'd accompanied Officer Kane on the bridge led me past two rows of empty desks to a back room. All out fighting crime, I hoped. Looking for a mutilator, a poacher, and now a murderer. Lots of work for a small town police department. The officer stuck his head through the open doorway. "Miss Abby's here," he said and retreated.

Detective Magnus rose, hand extended. "Thanks for coming in."

His large, broad hand encased mine, but I managed to give him my firm, confident, reporter's shake. We watched each other for a couple beats, before Magnus let go and waved for me to sit down.

"So, what caused the gash in London's head," I asked before the detective sunk into his high-backed chair.

Magnus huffed. "Usually I ask the questions." The chair creaked, protesting his weight.

"I did some crime reporting in the Triangle."

"Old habits die hard?"

I tossed out a hand to indicate *of course.*

Magnus stretched his legs beneath his desk. "Doc Bailey's calling London James's death a murder."

I blew out a slow breath. "The wound in his head–?"

"Something sharp."

"Somebody hit him?"

Magnus waggled his head.

"Someone attacked him on the bridge." For some reason, Dutch's pointy beard filled my mind's eye.

Magnus reached for a mug. "Would you like coffee? Officer Dan can bring you some."

"No, thanks." I waited while he took a drink. "An argument turned deadly? A push, he slipped, cracked his head on the way down."

The detective locked his hands behind his head. "I see you like to take control of an interview."

I rolled my eyes. "Can't help it." But, truly, I was surprised. I'd been doing good news for so long, I thought I'd forgotten the few bully tactics I'd honed.

Magnus rolled his hand in a circular motion. "Go on. I'm enjoying this."

I kept my mouth shut a moment then couldn't help asking with exasperation, "Did the blow kill him or did he drown? Were there signs he'd been pushed into the water?"

Magnus looked at me intently. "What kind of signs?"

I tossed out a hand, palm up. "Splinters on the body? Most likely his face and hands. His knees. Wood fibers on the jacket? Nail tears?"

He cocked his head but didn't answer.

I sighed and counted to five before asking, "Why am I here?"

Magnus tapped a pen on the edge of his desk. "You weren't fond of London James, were you?"

"I didn't care for him much."

"Flipping someone over backwards is a violent act."

"Who told you that?"

"Story is you got mad and knocked him over." Magnus's dark scrutiny did not let go. "Want to tell me why you were mad at him?"

"It was personal."

"Personal things become public when there's a murder."

My stomach tightened. It took me a moment to choke out, "Do you think I murdered him?"

When Magnus smiled, the roots of my hair tingled. I'd had an editor who smiled widest when he was furious. Magnus wasn't furious, but he'd gone from entertained to suspicious. Of me!

"He was acting like a jerk and I tipped him into a flowerbed." I tried to match the detective's stare but my gaze began to slip. "No big deal," I mumbled. "And he didn't run tattling to you. Accusing me of assault."

Magnus rested his chin on his knuckles. "So you admit you didn't like him."

"Not *liking* him is no reason to hit him on the head and throw him into the water." I was beginning to not like Erik Magnus. "It doesn't mean I hated him. That I'd kill him." After a pause, I added, "Aren't there people you don't like?" The detective didn't answer. "I had a reason to dump London into a flowerbed. I had no reason to kill him." I stood up. "May I leave?"

Magnus nodded toward the door. In the ladies room. I glared into the mirror above the sink. Goose Inlet's detective should be out hunting up a real suspect. One with a motive. And while he was at it, find out who buried the toes and tattooed butt chunk under the nests. I splashed cold water on my face. And find Randy Boone's body. How long has that man been missing? Almost a month. I massaged my temples, trying to calm myself. I was damn glad I hadn't mention London knowing Aidan. Where would Magnus run with that? The detective was shooting at the stars. Still, an unease I'd been trying to keep at bay elbowed its way to the front. Could there be a connection between London's death and Aidan's?

CHAPTER TWENTY-FIVE

The next day when volunteers gathered for Nest Four's excavation, chatter centered mostly on London James. His murder, reported as such in the news, left everyone baffled. No one had known enough about London alive to speculate on who wanted him dead. And who'd known him well enough to kill him? Certainly no one in Goose Inlet. He'd been a loner, lurking on the edge of the turtle group. A spectator not a participant. No one claimed him as a friend. Hannah had not invited him to her home for another grilled salmon dinner nor, she insisted, for anything else. Still, a murdered tourist naturally put the locals and other tourists on edge.

In contrast, Randy Boone, being LuAnn's boyfriend, was well known and missed by nearly everyone but Dutch. Volunteers grumbled that the police weren't doing enough to find him. Local fisherman kept their eyes open for his body and his gear. Leisure boaters went out in groups to scour the water in grid fashion but came back with nothing. Of course, the Coast Guard was on the lookout.

In addition to the murdered and missing men, no one had forgotten the shocking mutilations found under the turtle nests, which naturally kept poaching high in volunteers' minds. Both outrages remained unsolved.

These worrisome issues faded, at least temporarily, when Nest Four's mom dug up the remains of all ninety-eight hatched turtle eggs. Her team members danced to beach music only they could hear.

"See," Hannah said, climbing up from the sand and waving the clipboard on which she'd recorded the stats for state biologist Will Brown. "We're over that nasty patch. Two successful nests in a row. We're on a roll!"

Hannah whooped and hollered with the rest of the volunteers, but I saw clouds in my friend's eyes. "You're not convinced," I said over a slice of eggplant pizza at Guido's later that night.

"Not convinced of what?" Hannah replied, dipping her crust into a bowl of sauce.

I lowered my voice. "That the poaching is over. You don't think—"

"I don't know what to think." Hannah signaled the server for another glass of wine. "What am I supposed to think? If you know, tell me."

I set my glass down with more thump than I'd intended. "Of course I don't know what you think. I'm not the expert on turtles and poaching."

"Well, you could become an expert by doing a little investigative reporting."

I ignored the comment. "I know the odds aren't good."

So far seven nests had been laid, an extremely quiet season for the Inlet. Last year the beach had harbored fifteen. Hannah said as many as thirty-six nests had been laid one season. Of this year's prized seven, four had hatched. Of those four, two had been poached. Fifty percent! Bad odds. I knew it and Hannah did, too. I couldn't blame her for being touchy.

Hannah's wine arrived, and after taking a long sip she reached across the table for my hand. "Hey, sorry." Her mouth bent down at the corners. "You're right. I'm not convinced. Worse thing is, I can't stop it. We have an extra officer two nights a week, and some volunteers are patrolling on their own. But what happens if they catch someone? The poacher or poachers could be dangerous."

"Like that beach at Ostional."

Hannah pointed her pizza crust at me. "We don't really know what we're up against here. And I can't get any information from Will."

"Maybe someone's telling him to keep quiet." My phone dinged. I wasn't surprised to see Wade Ramsey's name, but his text confused me: *Management searched Dr. Finn's computer for anything about chemicals he signed for. Didn't find anything*

I dropped my pizza slice and texted back: *?????*

Wade: *They don't think he signed for them. His name on it but he didn't do it. Didn't take them.* Someone else signed out the chemicals under Aidan's name. It was done by computer, so handwriting wasn't an identifier.

I texted back *ok thanks* and stared out the restaurant window.

"What's that all about?" Hannah asked.

It took me a moment to answer. "Something about chemicals Aidan did or did not sign for. A security guard there sends me texts, but I wonder how much is gossip. I wish I'd get something pertinent about the explosion."

"Taking an awful long time to get answers," Hannah said quietly.

"I call Aidan's research director for an update from the CSB and get a big fat nothing." Even though I feared his texts were little more than rumor, I was glad to have Wade Ramsey on my side. Security guards stood around all day while people talked as if they were invisible. He might hear something valuable. I should have more faith.

"Everything in my life is hush-hush," I said irritably. "The explosion. The poaching. Why is everything so secret?"

Hannah held her glass to her lips but didn't drink. "Even when Will was down here when those first two nests were poached—" She lifted a shoulder. "It was almost like he wasn't even surprised."

I'd noticed that, too. I recalled Will staring down into the first excavated site, saying little. He should have been outraged like the rest of us. I popped a piece of sundried tomato into my mouth and chewed thoughtfully.

"He probably figures the natives got hungry and now their appetites are satisfied. It's over," Hannah said, affecting nonchalance. Could the problem really be just greedy locals? I didn't believe that and didn't think Hannah did either.

She twirled her wine glass carefully. "Nest Five should hatch soon. Then there's a big gap till Nest Six boils the end of September." She paused and lowered her voice. "They might already have been poached."

My stomach sunk. Hundreds of hatchlings could already have been lost.

CHAPTER TWENTY-SIX

"Good thing I'm not a cop, 'cause I haven't even a half-baked idea about who killed him and why," Tanner said quietly, as we paddled a creek in the estuary south of the beach.

"Some people are blaming 'a passing stranger'," I said. "But that seems unlikely to me."

Goose Inlet was a small beach town that people didn't really pass through by bus, train or car as they might a larger city or popular resort like Myrtle Beach. Tourists and vacationers came with a purpose. They rented cottages and stayed for a while to swim, fish, boat, listen to live music, and eat a lot of seafood.

"For one thing, London's wallet was still in his pocket when police dragged him out of the water," I continued. "Remember, we saw the detective pull it out and open it. A passing thief would have lifted that wallet, or a watch, or whatever looked valuable."

"A local killer might, too," Tanner said. "To make it look like a robbery."

True. But he didn't. We paddled a while in silence.

"Do you think other nests were poached? I mean, nests the patrol never found?" I was ready for a change of topic, but this one wasn't cheerful either. "What if there were more than the seven we know about?" I held my paddle out of the water. "What if a poacher found a nest, stole the eggs, and wiped out the mama's tracks before the patrollers found them?"

That ubiquitous chill climbed my spine and reached the crown of my head. Goose Inlet's latest nest, found three days ago, had been staked and covered with orange netting to discourage foxes and dogs from digging. But how secure was it from humans? Two of our nests, protected the same way, had been poached. And what if we hadn't found them all?

Tanner flicked a bug off his nose. "It's possible a poacher could find a nest before the patrol, but he'd have to hang around all night, waiting for a turtle to come up. We have a long beach. A turtle can crawl up anyplace to nest. More than one person would have to cover this large area."

A gang. A criminal gang. Like in Costa Rica where a band of criminal poachers killed a conservationist. This was probably uncharitable, but London James didn't strike me as a conservationist.

"It's painful to know we lost more than a hundred eggs." I said. "And that's not counting what we lost in Nest Two. Maybe another hundred." A dreadful count, even to my novice ears. "Sorry, but I just don't buy we're talking about a few omelets and a few—" Watch it, Abs, you're not talking to Hannah. "Maybe the eggs were shipped out of here."

Tanner stopped paddling and wiped his sunglasses on his T-shirt. I raised my paddle, too, and our boats floated with the current into a stand of tall sea grass.

"So, you're thinking major smuggling operation." He grinned at me, one eye closed to block the sun.

"Not major." I splashed cool water on my arms. "But Hannah said some Asian men will pay three hundred bucks for one turtle egg. I bet they don't care if it comes from a beach laid with thousands of eggs or a beach like ours with a half-dozen nests."

"That might be the first time I've heard you take this personally." Tanner replaced his sunglasses then dug in his dry bag and pulled out two sandwiches. "*Our* beach." He handed one to me. "I like that."

I unwrapped two pieces of wheat bread spread with peanut butter and layered with thin slices of ripe banana. I took a bite and nutty sweetness caressed my mouth.

When I didn't respond, he added, "Sounds like you're getting comfortable in Goose Inlet."

"It's an easy place to get comfortable." I took a swig of tepid water from my stainless steel bottle and decided it was time to buy an insulated one like Tanner's, even if I wasn't ready to buy my own boat.

"Think you'll stay?" His eyes were not visible but his voice held a touch of—interest?

Don't flatter yourself, Abby. Besides, you're the Widow Finn. Sometimes when I looked at Tanner, comfortable in his boat, I saw Aidan sitting there. Which was odd because my husband was even less a water man than a beach man. I kayaked mountain lakes with Kate and Derek, while he sat on the cabin porch reading spy novels. Still, I saw him everywhere and longed to have him back, doing things we both enjoyed. Talking about the things married people talked about. Kids. Work. Crazy relatives.

"You might get a good off-season rate on Lily Pad."

I balled up the plastic wrap and handed it back for Tanner to place in his bag. "My job's in Raleigh and being held with the understanding I'll return. I can't—"

He waved his hand. "Easy, easy. It's just a thought."

"And my kids are in the Triangle. Kate's still in college."

"And you want to be nearby."

"Well—" That was a dumb excuse. Thousands, millions, of kids went away to school. Left the state. Left the country. I couldn't fall back on Kate, an independent girl who came home for holidays and the occasional weekend. She would soon be overloaded with class work and searching for next summer's internship. Derek was a working man with an active lifestyle. I had my demanding job at the magazine. Even when Aiden was alive, we'd lived independent lives.

"I have to keep my job." I was twenty years from early retirement. "Don't know what I'd do for income in Goose Inlet." The local newspaper? I doubted the salary was half what I earned at *Carolina*. I shifted in my seat. My knees bumped the insides of my boat, once, twice, as if pulled by hidden strings. What's that about? I'd been calm in the kayak until Tanner brought up staying in Goose Inlet.

CHAPTER TWENTY-SEVEN

The three hours we spent paddling the bays slipped by like a pod of docile dolphins. In late afternoon, we sat in a booth at the Sloppy Parrot, hot, thirsty, and sticky from multiple layers of sunscreen. We'd chosen the Parrot because it recently won Best Wings for the second year in a row, which didn't tell us anything we didn't know.

"I'm going for super-hot this time," Tanner declared.

I laughed. "Aren't you hot enough?" I ducked my head, hoping he didn't think I was talking about anything but temperature. Tanner was hot in the biblical sense, but I, barely three months a widow, would throw myself off the Inlet pier before letting him think I noticed.

We ordered pints of amber ale and twelve-piece orders of wings, hot and super-hot. The beer didn't last long.

"Should have drunk water first." I caught a burp in my hand. Tanner alerted the server for water and more ambers.

Two men walked into the Parrot and ducked into a booth. One was Jason Stone. The other I'd seen before with Stone at the Parrot and a couple times at turtle gatherings. He'd looked on with interest but never got close enough to say hi. He was deeply tanned, shorter than Stone and wore a small, gold hoop in his left ear. His dusty jeans, scuffed boots, and black, sweat-stained work shirt comprised a uniform similar to Stone's. I noticed the port insignia on the arm of his shirt, marking them co-workers.

"Two Yuengling," Stone told the server. He glanced about the room, grazing our booth with no indication he recognized me.

Well, why should he? I'd spoken to him once. A disjointed, tipsy interrogation during which he'd good-naturedly denied speaking with my husband here last winter. According to Wade Ramsey, Aidan and London had missed work on the same day. London said he'd seen Aidan talking to Stone on the Inlet beach. Tanner unintentionally backed London up because he talked to Aidan in Goose Inlet and I believed him. So, who was lying? Stone or London?

Our sizzling wings arrived, heralded by the spicy aroma of Frank's Hot Sauce. We gave them a minute to cool, and I noticed that, while they appeared relaxed, Stone and his companion didn't exhibit the camaraderie I associated with, say, Dutch and Joop. Tanner must have noticed me staring.

"That's Tack Stanley. I played cornhole with him a couple times." Tanner swiped his finger through the sweat on his stein. "Works at the port."

"Yeah, I got that." I tapped my shoulder where an insignia would be. I scooped a chunk of bleu cheese with a wide stalk of celery.

Tanner dropped a few wings onto his plate and sucked the heat off his fingers. "Did you have a good time today?"

I gave him a sidelong glance. "You know I did."

"What did you like best?"

There was so much! "I liked when we pulled the boats onto the sand and cooled off in the water. I liked when the blue heron flew across my bow, and I could see individual feathers on its wings." Thrilling! I smiled across the table.

Tanner's eyes lit up. "I like it when you smile. When you're happy."

I dropped my head. Happiness was a touchy point. I felt guilty when I laughed. Sometimes even smiling left me remorseful. How could I be happy when Aidan was dead? It just didn't seem right. The morning after the explosion, I'd sat in my living room, thunderstruck, my leaden heart weighing so heavily that moving my hands and feet seemed impossible. When the sun shone, I glared out the window, hot tears sliding down my cheeks. How dare the sun shine! Not today! My husband had been blown away. A few hours later, when clouds crowded out the sun and doused my world wet, I'd nodded agreement. Yes. This was proper. It should rain.

"Since you enjoy kayaking so much," Tanner said, "there's something I must teach you."

I stopped spinning a chicken wing 'round and 'round on my plate. "What?"

"The wet exit."

"What's that?"

"How to reenter your boat when you fall out."

"Shouldn't that be called the wet entry? And anyway, I don't intend to fall out." I paused with a wing halfway to my mouth. "Okay, it could happen. But if I fall out, I'll push the boat to land and get back in."

"What if land isn't around?"

"You mean like if I'm in the middle of the ocean? I don't intend to ocean kayak." Not for a long time. Or never. Too risky.

Tanner leaned on the table. "You might fall out in the ICW. Or in a deep-water creek. Even if you can touch, it's not easy to get back in. What are you going to do?"

"Blow my whistle. Get help." Tanner had given me a whistle that emitted an ear-shattering shriek meant to attract boaters, fisherman, stand-up paddlers, anyone, in an emergency. I'd attached it to my PFD.

"You could do that," he said. "But what if no one else is around?"

"You told me not to paddle alone."

He looked me straight in the eyes. "Humor me, Abby. Even if someone is around, like me, you have to know how to get back into your boat."

I looked over at Stone and Stanley. The men appeared to be having a quiet conversation, as much intent on polishing off their popcorn as conversing.

"So, let's set a date," Tanner said. "I have a tour later this week, but I'm free tomorrow."

My eyes widened. "So soon?"

"Nine o'clock at Willet Beach?" When I hesitated, he added. "It's important, Abs."

"I know. But Dutch is taking me on sea turtle patrol tomorrow morning."

"That's at six a.m. You'll be done—"

"He wants to go to breakfast after. Says it's a tradition."

"How many hours do you intend to eat?"

I laughed, wondering how many hours I could spend one on one with Dutch Magnus. "Okay. Nine o'clock."

Tanner turned back to his wings. "Can't get enough of these," he said rolling a meaty piece in hot sauce.

He gnawed it to the bone and wiped his chin with a paper towel. That's when I noticed he was growing a beard. How had I missed that? Aidan had worn a beard. A carefully trimmed one that turned a tender gray over our two decades of marriage. Tanner's beard would be dark. I wondered how long he'd let it grow. Would it be ragged, fitting an outdoorsman? I liked beards. I'd loved Aidan and liked Tanner. They were similar in some ways. Tanner had Aidan's quiet manner. When we paddled, he spoke in an undertone.

"This water belongs to nature," he'd said on our first excursion. "We're guests here and must be polite."

Without a doubt, paddling the serene back bays marked my happiest times in Goose Inlet. I smiled to myself, thinking how I'd hesitated about going out on the water with him. How he'd patiently explained that men and women paddled together all the time and no one thought anything of it.

"We go out because we enjoy the water," he'd said. "I paddle with married women. Married men paddle with single women. It's not unusual—or suspect. Relax, Abby."

Today, it had taken merely five minutes, with the sun warming my skin and the spartina singing a sloughing lullaby, for me to relax. So, even though we'd been out three times in the last nine days, and he now was going to teach me a wet exit, I gently pushed away the thought that it was too much.

"Abby?" Tanner nudged my hand with the tip of his finger. "I asked if you'd consider buying your own boat."

I swiped a napkin over my mouth and took a sip of beer. If I bought a boat, who'd most likely be my paddling partner? Tanner Banks. Hannah paddled, as did other turtle people, so I would strike up other partnerships. But, truth was, I liked kayaking with Tanner. He identified every bird that flew by. He knew the name of the crab that clung to the marsh grass. He could tell the difference between a log and an alligator. Good to know. Tanner Banks was peaceful and easy to look at. But, good grief, my husband had been killed just three months ago and— and what? Here came that annoying unease again. Too often I felt as if I'd been tossed into the air and still hadn't come down. Most forms of enjoyment distressed me. Even eating a bowl of ice cream. I struggled to tame these discomforting thoughts.

"I'll think about it." Actually, I looked at boats online every time I came back from paddling and had bookmarked a few websites.

"I can take you over to Explore Outdoors," he offered. "Check out what's available. If you see one you like, they'll let you try it out first."

"Maybe." I dipped a carrot stick into bleu cheese dressing and took a bite. Aidan had loved to dip his wings in bleu cheese dressing. "Just to take the sting out," he said.

I glanced toward Stone and Stanley's booth and was surprised to see their conversation had become animated, though not loud. The men leaned over the table until their noses were inches apart. Stanley appeared to take control of the dialogue, because Stone suddenly pressed into the back of the bench and stopped talking.

Stanley's shoulders bunched up around his ears and his head looked locked in place. The port insignia on his left shoulder grabbed my attention, pulling together port and poaching and smuggling. A heat swelled in my stomach that had nothing to do with spicy chicken wings.

Maybe Stanley was Stone's supervisor at the port and caught him smuggling turtle eggs onto a ship. Turtle eggs his wife poached. I squeezed my eyes shut. Good God! I sounded like LuAnn!

Stone shook his head, mouthed what I thought was, "No!" then got up and stalked out of the Parrot. Stanley remained in the booth a few minutes, drumming his fingers on the table. I turned back to my lunch.

"Seems like a bit of disagreement between those gentlemen," Tanner whispered. When I looked back, Stanley was gone.

CHAPTER TWENTY-EIGHT

"It's awfully nice of Joop to give up his turn," I said, walking to the Bobcat. I categorized the two-seat, four-wheel drive utility vehicle used to patrol the beach for sea turtle tracks as somewhere between a Jeep Wrangler and a pumped up golf cart. Volunteers took the Bobcat out every morning from the beginning of May to the end of August. Today was August 5 and the sun not set to rise for another twenty-six minutes.

"Joop's been on hundreds of rides. And he knows it's gonna rain today." Dutch tossed me a towel. "Wipe your seat off. And get the other side of the windshield for me." I wiped at the mist but another coating quickly covered the windscreen.

I raised my eyes to towers of dark clouds stretching to the horizon. It was six a.m., the earliest I'd gotten up in months. A pretty sunrise would be a nice reward, but not likely to happen. I wasn't crazy about getting drenched but wouldn't pass up a chance to ride with the turtle patrol. I wondered if my lesson with Tanner would be canceled due to thunderstorms. I could hope.

"Do you think we'll find a nest?" I climbed in and buckled my seatbelt.

"First we find the tracks. Mamas like to nest during thunderstorms, and the one we had last night was a beauty. Weather's hanging around, too." Dutch cranked the ignition, loosened the handbrake and stepped on the accelerator. The Bobcat lurched forward as a flash of lightning lit the sky.

I knew the patrol was cancelled if the weather was bad or threatening. I put lightning on the danger list, but Dutch didn't stop the vehicle.

"Sit tight. We're going. I need a spotter. Ain't gonna let you chicken out."

"I won't chicken out," I said, wondering if Dutch was teasing. I never knew how to take his comments. Or Joop's. When I'd mentioned I had not kayaked in the river, Joop told me the river was home to ten thousand bull sharks and to not get out of my boat to swim, even near shore. Ten thousand? I'd gone back to Lily Pad, looked up bull sharks online, and gotten quite a story.

The bull shark, I learned, was aggressive and swam in warm, shallow water, either salt or fresh. It liked the coastline, hung out in estuaries—that one set me back— and swam up the Mississippi River as far as Illinois. Females went about eight feet long and could weigh a hefty two hundred ninety pounds. Males were shorter and a lot lighter. Of course, a few people claimed they saw or caught eleven- and even fourteen-footers. Someone even recorded a bull shark weighing six hundred ninety-four pounds, but that sounded like one of Dutch or Joop's stories. A bull shark's mouthful of teeth had a shocking one-thousand-three hundred-pound bite force, and it seemed like they didn't give a hoot what they chomped down on: bony fish, small sharks (including other bull sharks!), turtles, birds, dolphins. Land mammals that fell in the water. Starfish, stingrays, sea urchins, sand dollars, sea cucumbers—mmm, salad. And, the occasional human. So, the article said, stay out of murky water, where a bull shark could sneak up and do its bump and bite routine until its prey—you—were unable to flee. One last point: Bull sharks had virtually no tolerance for provocation. So if you saw one, leave it the hell alone.

The Bobcat rumbled over the short wooden ramp that led from the parking lot to the beach. It bounced and slid through deep sand toward a white pounding surf.

"What we're looking for are tractor-type tracks," Dutch said. He pointed to the left above the high tide line. "That's not them."

"They look fresh."

"Yeah, but those are police tracks. Town cops patrol at night." Dutch drove around a deep hole some enterprising vacationers had dug in the sand. "You're looking for two sets of tracks. One set coming in, another set going back to the water." He chuckled. "Looks like somebody drove a farm tractor up on the beach." He swiped a dirty baseball cap off the floor and plopped it on his head. "With our loggerheads, a set of tracks is about a yard wide. But you won't see a drag mark down the middle from her tail like some other sea turtles leave."

I pointed, but Dutch shook his head. "Trash truck."

"Big thing to look for—holes. We ask tourists to fill in holes they dig in the sand, but people don't listen." He swerved to the left. I looked out my side at a cavity at least two feet deep.

"A bitch we dropped a wheel in there," Dutch said. "Even worse a turtle falls in. Turtle can't back up, so there she be. Face down in the hole." Dutch grimaced. "Poor thing'd suffocate."

"Has that happened?" I asked, frowning. For all his teasing about turtle omelets, Dutch Magnus seemed genuinely sympathetic toward sea turtles.

"Not here."

I looked down at strands of seaweed that had been arranged to spell a female name. "Lisa" had gotten to the beach even earlier than we did. "How long is the route?"

"From here to the top of the inlet, about two miles. Then two miles back. It's a beauty of a ride if you catch a pretty sunrise." He eyed the black clouds. The mist had turned to drizzle, and I had to look around the windscreen to see the beach since the Bobcat didn't have wipers.

"Look at that." I stared down at two Styrofoam cups, complete with plastic lids and straws, set beside each other in the sand as if staged for a photo. A line of trash cans sat twenty feet away.

"We'll pick up trash on the way back," Dutch said, as he drove over a plastic water bottle.

Another flash lit the sky over the water, but I didn't hear thunder.

"Watch that ridge." Dutch pointed across me to a fourteen-inch drop that marked the beginning of hard-packed sand left exposed by low tide. "Look for where she tried to break through." She being a mama turtle with a load of eggs to lay.

We bumped along for a few minutes in silence, except for the growling noises coming from the Bobcat as it struggled through the sand.

"Not that I care, but I wonder who bumped off that prissy dude," Dutch said, pulling his cap down low on his forehead. The wind was picking up.

"You mean who killed London James?"

"He was the only prissy dude on the beach. And he's dead." Dutch swerved around a broken beach umbrella half buried in the sand.

"Should we pick that up?" I asked.

"On the way back. Gotta run the patrol. If we pick up everything along the way, we'll never get done. Patrol comes first." We bounced over some deep ruts.

"Turtle tracks?" I asked, but he shook his head. "You don't seem sad London's gone."

"Why should I be? Didn't know the man. He kept to himself. Ignored the rest of us. All except Hannah and now and then LuAnn."

The newspaper said London James's body had been shipped to Idaho. "Do you think there's a murderer walking around town?" I asked.

"I don't," Dutch replied emphatically. "There's some talk like that, but I don't believe a local killed him. Nobody knew that guy well enough or cared enough to whack him, for chrissake."

"Bianca thinks like you," I admitted. She'd shared her opinion the other morning while toasting my onion bagel and wiping up the large coffee LuAnn had spilled on the counter. "She thinks London was into something illegal and some criminal type, like the Mafia, bumped him off."

"Yeah, I heard her blab that, too. The Mafia in Goose Inlet?" Dutch snorted. "Mafia's small potatoes these day. But, hell, who knows. Anything's possible. I just know someone from the Inlet didn't do it."

He nudged me and, frowning, pointed to a row of piling fragments jutting up from the sand like broken teeth. "All that's left of my daddy's pier. We used to fish off it till Hurricane Hazel took it down. Cracked the pier off right in front of our store. Daddy made his living with a bait shop and the fishing pier. Store in front, house in the back, all set on pilings."

Dutch rubbed his morning stubble. "Ol' Lady Hazel was a bitch of a storm. Cat 4. Winds hit a hundred fifteen. Gusts to one-sixty. Seventeen foot surge."

"When was that?"

"October '54. Killed about a thousand in Haiti. Then landed right between the Carolinas. North Carolina lost nineteen. Took almost a hundred way up there in Canada."

"Were you here? Or did you evacuate?"

Dutch said he was twelve and remembered his daddy insisting the family was going to sit Hazel out. His mama, though, gave each kid a pillow case and said fill it up with clothes and food. Then she picked up her husband's whiskey bottle and told him to get his ass out the door.

"Mama said she wasn't gonna lose him and have to sell her tired old bones to feed eight kids." Dutch laughed. "Mama was a pistol." He inhaled quickly. "Would you look at that? Deer tracks going right down to the water."

"Deer drink salt water?"

Dutch's face contorted. "What's wrong with you? 'Course not. They go down there and swim. Takes the bugs off 'em."

"Like I'm supposed to know that." I scowled.

"Well, now you do." Dutch swerved right and left, trying to find a smooth route. "Are you looking for turtle tracks?"

"I'm looking." The drizzle had kicked up to the next level and my head was wet, but I kept my eyes roving left and right over the Bobcat's hood.

"Hazel even threw a whale up on the beach," Dutch said. I heard wonder in his voice that sixty years couldn't erase. "Down near the border. Dead animals everywhere. After it was over and we came back, I found a kitten crawling across a pile of junk blocking our front door. Little thing was covered with sand, its fur stiff and poking in points. Eyes like slits, crusted over with grit. Ears stuck out like a bat's."

Dutch stopped the Bobcat and thrust his head out the side.

"See something?" I asked.

He grunted. "Thought I saw tracks." He drove down into the hard-packed sand to go around a pile of beach chairs left out overnight. "See that? A mama turtle bumps into that pile, she turns around and goes back into the water. She'll give it a couple more tries, but if she can't settle on a place, she dumps her eggs in the ocean and all those babies die." Dutch's face twisted into a grimace.

He guided the Bobcat back up into deeper sand and continued with his hurricane saga. "Cottages were small back then, one floor things. Weren't nothing left of 'em. Looked like a giant stumbled down the street, knocking one house into another. Or he shook the houses like dice and rolled them across the sand. Wood and sand. That's what was left of my world after Hazel." Dutch stopped talking while the Bobcat bounced over a series of deep ruts. "Boats everywhere but in the water. Joop had a 32-foot yacht tipped on its nose in his front yard. Come clear over from the marina."

We approached a low picket fence that marked the entrance to the stretch of sand where four-wheel vehicles were allowed to park overnight. "Don't expect to find turtle tracks here," he said, "what with all the activity. Turtle be crazy to crawl up here. But wc look anyway."

Jeeps and trucks of every make and model lined up in clusters facing the ocean. Behind them, campers slept in igloo-shaped tents staked above the high tide line. BBQ grills, some charcoal, some propane, paired up with the tents. Collapsed lawn chairs scattered like playing cards.

"Over there's where you found your dead guy." Dutch tipped his head to the left.

I looked at steps marking the long bridge that crossed the cove where Tanner and I had found London James floating face down in marsh debris. "Have you heard anything from your nephew, the detective?"

Dutch snorted again. "Erik don't consult me about his murders."

"Nothing in the paper or on TV, except when it first happened." I bumped my shoulder against Dutch's playfully. "Thought you might have the inside scoop."

"Ha!" It was short and loud like a gunshot. "He won't admit it, but Erik don't know any more about who killed that guy than I do."

I braced myself as we bounced over a deep rut. The north beach was corrugated by giant SUV tires. "Do you think his death is tied to the poaching?"

"I know who's tied to the poaching. That Latina's husband. If he smuggled her into this country, he could just as easily be smuggling turtle eggs out."

"That is absolutely unfounded and ridiculous!"

Dutch shot his fist past my nose, pointing. "Look at that. Someone brought his own generator." Grinning, he nodded toward the dune. "And here's a private potty."

Men and women were starting to stick their heads out of tents. Others were already fishing. At the top of the inlet, a man threw a white net into the shallows, casting for bait.

"These campers are here overnight. Maybe one of them poached the turtle nests," I said testily.

"And maybe one of them killed the city slicker?" Dutch screwed up his face. "Maybe. This place don't sleep. Folks carry on all night. People in Pelican Pier always bitching about it." He snorted. "Bianca said she was standing on her balcony the night that guy got killed."

I recalled her waving to get Detective Magnus's attention at the cove. "Did she see anything? Hear something?"

Dutch shrugged. "She talked to Erik, not me." He steered around a smashed beach ball. "Guy was just a damn tourist. They come, we take their money, and they go. That James guy came and then he went. End of story."

"How can you be so callous?" I grumbled, even though I'd cared little for London.

Dutch whipped his head around. "Me callous? I wasn't the one who dumped him in the fire pit."

I groaned. "It was a flower bed."

The drizzle was now rain. Dutch pointed north. "Joop and I saw a doe and fawn swim across right there," he said, indicating the island across the inlet. He nodded at a father and son sitting in front of their tent eating breakfast. Although the setting was drastically different, they reminded me of the mornings Aidan cooked bacon and eggs on a camp stove outside our mountain cabin.

The rain turned heavy as we left the four-wheel drive area. I stared again at the long bridge over the cove. No leads on London's murder. No leads on the owner of the toes and tattooed butt. This didn't happen on TV crime shows. A dazzling flash of lightning backlit the ebony clouds, followed by gunshot thunder. Dutch pressed the accelerator to the floor and the Bobcat jumped in the sand. "Time to haul ass," he said.

Rain drove hard off the ocean. Dutch had his head thrust forward, watching the sand in front of him through a windshield that had become a wild map of rivulets. The Bobcat bucked over deep ruts. "This is like bronco riding," I yelled. Wind-driven sand stung my bare legs.

Dutch spun the wheel this way and that to avoid the worst furrows and holes. It dawned on me that I was taking a bit of a risk bouncing down the beach under a tower of thunderclouds and driving rain. "This is fun!"

"Fun for you!" he exclaimed. "I'm getting drenched."

Exposed to rain and wind coming off the ocean, the left arm of Dutch's long-sleeved shirt was soaked. Sitting to his right and blocked by his considerable breadth, I was barely damp, except for my head, which I continued to stick outside the Bobcat, searching for turtle tracks.

Dutch turned right onto the wooden ramp and jack-rabbited to the parking lot.

"We didn't pick up trash," I said.

"Next time. Weather sucks."

"We didn't find a nest," I added. "I was really hoping we would."

"Well, we all hope that, sweetheart, but it don't always happen." Dutch shut down the Bobcat. "We patrolled this beach every day for three months and how many nests did we find?"

"Seven so far."

"And that's enough! What would happen if we found one every day?" Dutch herded me toward my car. "What would we do with a hundred-twenty nests?" He cackled like he'd told an inside joke. "Come on. I'll let you buy me breakfast."

I stopped dead. "Only if you promise not to tell turtle omelet stories."

"Don't be a sissy." Dutch pointed across the road. "Look! There's Joop."

CHAPTER TWENTY-NINE

Two hours after turtle patrol ended and two minutes into my wet exit lesson, I clung to the side of a kayak, heart chugging, muscles quivering. The video I'd watched the night before made the process of getting back into a kayak after falling out look easy. All I had to do was flip my capsized boat right side up, push down on the stern, jump, get my chest onto the back of the boat, wriggle to the cockpit, sit down, and voila! I was in.

Step one was easy. I flipped the boat over on the first try. Step two, I couldn't accomplish in water waist deep with Tanner steadying the bow.

"It might be easier if I took this off," I said, reaching for the buckle on the belt pack PFD I'd bought recently. When inside my boat, the inflatable lifejacket was light and inconspicuous. Now, the bulging pack caught and stopped me from getting onto the stern. Or so I complained. Tanner and I debated over removing the PFD, but Tanner wouldn't budge. Since I always wore a lifejacket, I had to learn wet exit with it on. Annoyed, I pulled the tab and inflated the damn thing, thinking this might make the task easier.

I grasped the deck lines, pushed down, jumped, and threw myself onto the back of the boat. Well, not that last part. Tanner said to watch again. It was his fourth demonstration. Grab. Launch. Scoot, Straddle, Pull. Drop the butt. Legs in. Voila!

"Men have more upper body strength," I mumbled, hoping my feminist soul wouldn't slap me upside the head.

"You saw women demonstrate reentry in those videos." He turned the stern back toward me.

After three attempts and much gasping, groaning and grimacing, I managed to get my chest onto the stern. For some crazy reason, my struggle conjured an image of London James scrabbling in the cove, trying to climb the pilings. Concentrate, Abigail!

"Good! Hang your legs down for balance," Tanner instructed. "Keep your center of gravity over the boat's center of gravity. And over the earth's center of gravity."

Seriously? Planet Earth is involved? The boat wobbled, and tip! I was in the water. Come on, Earth, gimme a break. I leaned my head on the boat and caught my breath. My arms ached like they had when I'd tried to climb a rope in gym class. Decades ago. I didn't want to look like a weak, cussing klutz in front of Tanner Banks. So I stopped cussing.

"I'll give it one more try." I grasped the deck lines, pushed, pulled, jumped, and my chest landed on the boat. I hooked my fingers into the next row of deck lines, tugged forward. Tanner nodded encouragement. I tried to move my legs but my bare thighs, never my best feature bare or otherwise, stuck to the boat. I was wearing a tankini and loose swim shorts that rode up every time I moved my legs.

"This hurts!" My skin either pulled away from the boat like a plastic sticker peeling off a windshield, or stuck fast, preventing forward motion. "Ow!" The water, the pain. London's gashed head floated through my mind. I slipped off the boat, breathing hard. Faint black and blue marks already mottled the tender skin of my inner thighs and upper arms. That fast?

"Can we try something different? There's a way to hook your foot in the cockpit and pull yourself up. Is that the cowboy scramble?" I asked as piteously as possible.

Tanner looked at my bruises. "We could. Or we could go for a nice paddle and cowboy up another day."

I slapped the water with a flat hand. "I'm in, partner." I floated my kayak into knee-deep water and got in my usual way by straddling the boat and flopping my bottom into the seat. Pull in one leg. Pull in the other leg. *Voila!* And with minimal help from Earth's gravity.

I looked up at small clouds scattered like popcorn on a blue blanket and my weariness ebbed. Two oyster catchers flew by, their tuxedo coats and long, orange bills standing out against the sapphire sky.

"Do you think we'll ever find out who poached our turtle eggs?" I asked, adjusting my sunglasses. The corners of Tanner's mouth turned down. "Or who killed London?" He shrugged. We dipped our paddles in the ICW and stroked past the marina, into the estuary's maze of creeks and rivulets.

Nature was impossibly beautiful. And precious. How anyone could meddle with it, dirty it, wound it, extinguish it, was beyond my comprehension. How could anyone kill anything?

***

That evening, Hannah and I ordered New Castle Brown Ale from a server sporting short, blond pigtails. LuAnn ordered Bud Light. We'd seen her coming out of the hardware store and Hannah invited her to join us at Sardine.

"Hiring them younger and younger." I turned my chair to face the three square feet of space that would serve as a stage.

"No kidding," LuAnn replied. "When my mom went in the hospital the first time, one of the doctors reminded me of Doogie Howser." We laughed. Even LuAnn.

Hannah pulled out her credit card. "How was your ride with Dutch this morning? Sorry you didn't find a turtle nest. Did Dutch behave himself?"

"He was a gentleman. And most informative." I paused. "After we drove onto the four-wheel beach, it occurred to me that maybe one or some of those campers might have poached our nests." In response to Hannah's raised eyebrows, I added, "Only because they're on the beach overnight. And nobody patrols that area. Dutch said it's pretty wild up there."

"Last summer someone got stabbed," LuAnn said. "We stopped going." Her voice dropped. "Randy and me."

I quickly put together poaching and knives and whacked off body parts. "Or maybe one of the campers bumped off London James. That's one theory, right? That a local didn't do it. It was an out-of-towner."

"Don't have to be from out of town to camp." LuAnn took a long swallow of beer. "I just said me and Randy used to go up there."

"I'm sure Erik considered that," Hannah said. "He's been all over the Inlet asking questions."

"Bianca was on her balcony the night London was killed," I said. "I wonder if she heard anything. Talked to Erik about it."

LuAnn's happy level dropped several notches. She ran her hand up and down her beer bottle then stared at her fingers as if not knowing what to do with the wetness. Would it have been better if we had found Randy Boone instead of London James in that cove? LuAnn would have her boyfriend's ambiguous status settled by that fateful word "closure." Hannah was right. LuAnn and I had a lot in common. Neither of us had a body to mourn.

"Did you master the wet exit?" Hannah asked, opening a bag of pretzels. "Tanner taught me last summer."

"You can do that?" Maybe Hannah's height was an advantage. "I got as far as the stern." When I showed off my bruises, Hannah said to keep working on it. It was something every kayaker should know. So much for sympathy.

We moved our chairs so a barefoot boy with an acoustic guitar could pull his small amplifier next to his stool. He'd be singing folk songs his grandparents taught him, or so Joop had informed us at the door. Joop implied he was related to the boy, a distant cousin or nephew. Highly possible, since the Dahls, like the Magnuses, were related to most every native in Goose Inlet, including each other.

Joop bumped a plastic chair across the slatted wood floor to an empty space at our table. "I asked around. Consensus is Stevie's a distant uncle." Everyone chuckled. "Anyway, he works hard all week and plays music to relax."

I figured Stevie worked at BK or Mickey D's and would look cute riding a scooter with the pigtailed waitress. Joop said he was thirty, a CPA up for partnership in a big city firm, and engaged to an eye surgeon at Duke. Hannah handed her card to Pig Tails, told her to serve the CPA his favorite drink, and that we'd run a tab.

Sardine was the Inlet's smallest bar, the size of a modest bathroom. A short counter and five stools took up the inside space. Outside, large pots of reasonably live flowers, some net-draped pilings, and two murderous bug zappers surrounded a small deck. The joint was tiny. Sardine's motto, expressed in a sign behind the bar, was: "Bottoms Up. Now Get the Hell Out." It was a reasonable demand. Crammed around the bar, eight drinkers were packed like, well, sardines.

"LuAnn, I'm happy you came out tonight," Hannah said, clicking her beer mug against LuAnn's Bud. "I know you like music. Someone told me you sang as a kid."

LuAnn pressed her cold bottle against her forehead. "Sang with a band. Just around town. Couple gigs in the city."

"What kind of music?" I enjoyed everything except disco. I felt reasonably sure tonight's singer wouldn't burst into "Stayin' Alive" or "How Can You Mend a Broken Heart?" Good thing, too, because those songs would surely set LuAnn blubbering. Right now, she looked glum, but she seemed to have the waterworks under control.

"My brothers ran the band. Beach music." LuAnn shrugged. "It was okay." She stared into mid space for a moment, as if conjuring a memory. "I liked stronger stuff. I wanted to sing like Janis Joplin."

Hannah and I eyeballed each other.

LuAnn's lips perked up in the corners. "Yeah, me and—" But she clamped her mouth shut.

"You and a friend?" Hannah touched LuAnn's hand. "You wanted to sing Joplin?"

LuAnn screwed up her face. Tossed her head as if she didn't care.

"She was powerful, but not really your era," Hannah said.

LuAnn was definitely weathered, but I had a feeling she was younger than she looked. Her music, as mine, would have been more like hip-hop, punk and heavy metal. Maybe electronic stuff. Those guys who moved like robots. Janis Joplin was more down and dirty blues. Besides losing our men, LuAnn and I had another thing in common. I liked Joplin, too.

"Are you still in touch with that friend? It's not too late to form another band" Hannah said cheerfully. Steve was in the third stanza of "Puff the Magic Dragon," and Joop's crew was singing heartily. "

LuAnn seemed to shrink, "Nope. Don't want to be." She shook her head then sat up straight. "Hey! Can we get more beer here?" she shouted, making us jump.

CHAPTER THIRTY

I pushed my grocery cart around the corner and nearly collided with Bianca. "Hannah insists the best place to run into friends is Briny Bill's," I said. "Sorry."

"Not your fault," she replied. "I hate grocery shopping, so I rush through it. Came around that corner too fast." We pulled our carts to the side. "Did you hear about Nest Five?"

"What's up?"

"Fox predation." Bianca grimaced. "Some beach walkers noticed the orange netting disrupted and stopped to investigate. The sand looked dug up and there were animal footprints in the trench and on the dune behind the nest. Hannah confirmed the tracks. Bits of shell were scattered around, so the fox actually got in the nest."

"That nest is due to hatch any day."

"And it's big. We moved one hundred twenty-three eggs from the waterline. Hannah got permission from Will this morning to dig it up early to see how many the red devil got. Excavation's tonight. Seven o'clock. I'm going."

"Me, too." I paused for a garbled announcement over the PA system. Something about a car blocking the delivery door. "It's been quite a season, hasn't it?"

"The craziest in my time as a volunteer. Say, how long you staying in the Inlet?"

"I'll be part of the mass exodus. Going back to Chapel Hill after Labor Day."

Bianca's mouth turned down. "I'll miss you. Liked talking with you at the nests. Wish your experience wasn't skunked by poaching and murder." She scratched at what looked like a couple of old mosquito bites.

"Wonder if either will be solved before I leave."

"Been decades since someone got killed in this town." She shivered. "That James guy stuck out like a pickle in a peach pie. I said hi to him a couple times but didn't get more than a nod. Still, he didn't need to turn up dead. Poor guy."

"Did you see anything that night? Dutch told me you were on your balcony. Just wondered if you heard arguing or fighting."

Bianca dug around in her purse and came up with a piece of gum that she unwrapped and popped into her mouth. "Erik came by asking everyone at the Pelican his police questions. I wasn't the only one who saw people walking around in the rose garden and on the pier that night. And heck, that's not unusual. This is a beach town. Folks don't go to bed at eight o'clock."

"Did you recognize anyone?"

"Just the dead guy. He wasn't dead yet. Was coming from the garden. Just walking, kind of stumbling along. I figured he was drunk. It was late, past midnight."

"You didn't see anyone following him?"

"Nope. Wish I'd seen more. I just thought there goes another drunk. I went to bed. Told Erik the same thing."

Bianca rearranged the items in her cart. "And then there's Randy. I feel terrible about LuAnn losing him and not even having a body to bury. He was no prize, but he sure was crazy about her." She sighed deeply. "Two losses in one summer."

There was a moment of silence as a shopper reached between us for a jar of banana peppers.

"You're an Inlet native," I said. "Did you know LuAnn as a child?"

Bianca moved her cart so a man could snag a jar of yellow mustard. "We were friends in grade school but kind of went different directions after that. I wanted to go to community college. LuAnn leaned toward a different crowd."

"I was with her last night at Sardine. She said she sang with a band. Beach music."

"Her brothers dragged her into it, once they realized she had a decent voice."

"Did she sound like Joplin?" I asked.

Bianca jerked her shoulders back. "Janis Joplin?" I nodded. "I never heard anything like that come out of LuAnn Sheetz," Bianca replied with a smirk. "Of course, she never got a chance to really shout one out. Her brothers had her singing backup to "Sixty Minute Man" and "Ocean Boulevard.""

"How'd she handle that?"

"Hated it. Both the music and singing backup." Bianca screwed up her face. "If she had visions of belting out "Piece of My Heart," crooning "My Guy"—which was the only solo they gave her—must have been like singing with a mouthful of molasses."

Bianca held up a finger and looked up at the ceiling. "Wait." She chuckled. "LuAnn did have another song. Her brother Lester wanted her to do "I Need Your Lovin' Every Day" with him, but LuAnn said that was disgusting." Bianca poked my arm. "You know, singing a song like that with her brother."

I knew the song. It had limited lyrics but the potential to be sexy.

Bianca stared past me at the shelves of condiments then reached out and grabbed a large bottle of Sriracha. "The Sheetzes lived down the street from me. The band practiced in their backyard, and her folks didn't mind if kids came to listen. Lester wanted that song in the lineup, so LuAnn said she'd sing it with any guy in the band but him."

"Did she?"

"Oh—yeah. Sang it with a summer boy and did they tear it up! Her mama came flying out of the house and sent everybody home." Bianca flushed with laughter.

"LuAnn never sang with him on stage? That was the end of it?"

"Hell no. They sang that song on stage the next night, and LuAnn wasn't just singing backup. She was all over that tune *and* the summer boy. When they were done, every girl on the dance floor had creamed her pants."

We stared at each other with raised eyebrows. "Did anything come of it? Between him and LuAnn?" I asked.

Bianca leaned her head back. "What was that boy's name?" She dug her teeth into her upper lip. "His family had a cottage—an aunt or grandma. Lester heard him playing guitar on the porch. Before you knew it, the kid—

what'd they call him?— talked himself into the band. Played with them every summer, even into college." Bianca rolled her cart back and forth. "LuAnn said she'd leave the group if—what was his name?—couldn't play. Name was spelled wrong."

I leaned my elbows on my cart handle. "What did his name start with?"

"I'm thinking N or M." Bianca stared at the groceries in her cart. "Norm. Nick. Melvin. M—Marlin. Mmm—Marc!" She clapped her hands. "M-a-r-c. And his last name—LuAnn said she wanted to tie him to her finger and keep him forever. Like a diamond ring."

My whole body went still as a deer in headlights.

"Marc Diamond!" Bianca grinned like she'd won Jeopardy. "LuAnn was crazy about him."

It felt like all my blood rushed to my head. "How'd Marc feel about LuAnn?"

"Well, honey, pretty darn good, if the way he sang "I Need Your Lovin' Every Day" was any clue." And she wiggled her hips in a naughty way.

"Puppy love? Or more serious?"

"Serious on LuAnn's part."

I'd dumped out a box of puzzle pieces. LuAnn Sheetz and Marc Diamond. Aidan's lab partner was LuAnn's summer love. And Marc knew London James. And London knew Aidan. And London and Aidan were dead. And—so what? Something was missing. A whole lot of somethings were missing. Maybe all I had was a box of coincidence.

Bianca put on a sour face. "But, you know. Those summer boy things don't last. LuAnn was heart-broke when he married, as she put it, "that big-haired skank from Greensboro."

CHAPTER THIRTY-ONE

Word of a predator brought a larger than usual crowd to Nest Five's emergency excavation that evening. Gathered in a tight knot around the nest, tourists, locals and volunteers exchanged stories. It was obvious a Goose Inlet version of the old telephone game had flourished. A family of foxes had dug up and devoured *all* the eggs. A large dog was chased away as it clawed into the nest. A small child had scooped out the eggs with a sand shovel and rolled them like tiny bowling balls down the trench and kicked them into the ocean. It was a boy. No, a girl.

Hannah had patted the air and in her teacher voice told everyone to quiet down. She explained that a scattering of turtle eggs shells had been found along with fox prints. Will Brown had given the okay to excavate to see if the remaining eggs were intact.

Dutch's sister, Darla, the nest mom, was already kneeling in the sand. Hannah had assigned me plastic pail duty, and I hoped to God this time nothing human would get tossed into it.

"This nest was laid in a terrible spot," Darla told me. "Right on the waterline. Tourists spotted the female laying and called the hotline number they found with their cottage's rental info. We got there in time to see the mama make final pats and crawl back into the water. It was thrilling. If those tourists hadn't seen the mom or bothered to call, we probably wouldn't have found this nest. Of course, we had to move it. A hundred twenty-three eggs."

Hannah called, "Let's do it," and Darla and another volunteer got to it, scooping aside soft sand, then clawing down into wet, cement-like hard-pack. After ten minutes and not finding any eggs, Darla shifted and burrowed at an angle. Her digging mate attacked a different direction. Hannah stood over them, chin set hard, eyes focused on the hole. With hands on hips and head low, she stood like a stalking egret.

Darla looked up questioningly. "We couldn't have marked the wrong spot, could we?" Hannah shook her head. "I know the damn fox didn't get them all." Darla told her digging mate to go right and she'd go left. "Maybe somebody moved the stakes."

"Would somebody do that?" I asked.

"Who knows? The world's full of kooks." Darla said.

Bianca and Fala joined in, one above the nest, the other below. Fifteen minutes of groping in every direction ended when Hannah's voice broke through their concentration.

"Stop," she said, her tone, low and thick. The louder, "Stop!" The women sat back on their heels. "The nest is empty."

"Maybe it was a pack of foxes," a man suggested, stepping closer. "I'm one of the guys who called about the animal prints. You positive it wasn't foxes got 'em?"

"From the shell scraps we found, the fox ate maybe three eggs," Hannah said irritably. "He didn't put the rest in a basket and carry them home." It was the first time I heard her snap at a tourist. Hannah put both hands to her cheeks. A cold silence gripped the crowd. It was a good ten seconds before she said more calmly, "I appreciate your help, sir. The fox got only a few."

"Could they have hatched during the night?" I asked.

A chorus of "No-No-No" rose from the volunteers. "This nest is overdue," Fala said. "We've been checking it. We would have seen tiny tracks. A depression. And a lot of empty shells in the hole."

"Instead, we have nothing," Darla groaned. "No hatched shells, no unfertilized eggs, no pips, no live babies." She struggled to her feet. "I placed those eggs in this new hole myself," she repeated, as if insisting could force them to appear. She stood clumsily and Dutch caught her arm.

"We've been poached," Bianca declared, glaring at the crowd. "Again!" I recalled Bianca's insistence that London's killer did not live in Goose Inlet. But here she was, eyeballing her friends and neighbors, as if suspecting one or more of them had stolen sea turtle eggs from the Inlet beach.

Volunteers milled about like family at a wake, passing the lost egg count—one hundred twenty—around in funereal tones. At a nod from Hannah, Fala and Bianca shoved the displaced sand back into the huge hole. The crowd began to disburse. Dutch and Joop wandered a little way off and talked quietly. So unlike them.

LuAnn sat near the dune, alternately sifting sand through her fingers and pushing it into piles. I had to give her credit. Despite her depression, she showed up. Tonight's events offered nothing to cheer her. Darla walked over and said something, but LuAnn didn't look up.

Hannah stood near the filled hole, squeezing her forehead with her fingers. I put my arm around her waist. "A fox couldn't cover a ravaged nest to make it look normal," she said. "Only a human could do that."

In the twilight, I recognized Jason Stone standing several yards away, arms crossed. I didn't see the co-worker who'd argued with him at the Sloppy Parrot.

"I'll call Will tonight," Hannah mumbled. "He won't be happy."

"No one's happy." Fala brushed sand off her shorts. "And it's not our fault. We're not stealing the eggs."

Hannah's eyes narrowed. "Someone is stealing the eggs."

CHAPTER THIRTY-TWO

I stopped at Briny Bill's for two large cans of chunky tomatoes and a ring of Andouille sausage. At an outdoor market I filled a canvas tote with onions, okra, and red and yellow sweet peppers. I entered the seafood store next door and came out with two pounds of fresh-caught Carolina shrimp. Celery was in the refrigerator and spices in my kitchen cabinet. Forget anything? Mentally, I ran through the ingredients for jambalaya. No, had it all, plus a loaf of crusty bread to soak up the sauce.

I parked just as Hannah rode up to Lily Pad on her bike. From her basket, she took a brown bag holding what I hoped was a bottle of Prosecco to drink while we cooked and a bottle of Malbec to enjoy with dinner. I had invited Tanner, and Hannah said she'd bring someone. Hannah wasn't seeing anyone steadily. She'd gone through a series of male friends in Goose Inlet and the short-lived attachments were pure companionship. Hannah repeatedly told me she harbored no thoughts of marriage. She was comfortable sailing solo.

She dropped her bike in the grass. "Jambalaya!" she said in greeting, sounding much cheerier than I expected after finding Nest Five poached two days ago. One of the traits I admired in Hannah was resilience. "How can I help?"

I emptied my tote onto the kitchen counter. Oh, good, I'd remembered the jalapeno. Hannah worked on the cork and a discrete *pop* announced, "Prosecco!" I reached into the cabinet for two glasses. Pushed them and the shrimp toward Hannah.

"Pour then peel, please."

Hannah filled both glasses with the bubbly light wine, took a sip and pronounced it delicious. I began chopping vegetables. Hannah opened the bag of shrimp but immediately threw up her hands.

"We need music! What do you feel like?" She hurried to the living room and started pushing buttons to access Pandora on my small, flat screen TV. She was definitely pushing her happy button. I hoped she wouldn't overdo it. Too much fake joy meant emotions were teetering on a sharp edge and could collapse quickly into misery.

"Surprise me." I wiped an onion-induced tear off my cheek. Soon the Lovin' Spoonful announced what a lovely day it was for a daydream. "Perfect!" I called from the kitchen, wondering if that sixties group was still playing music. "Daydream" always reminded me of bright sunshine, a theme song for Goose Inlet.

Today had been a truly lovely day. First came what had become my daily, but never routine, walk on the beach, followed by a light lunch at the Sloppy Parrot with, of all people, LuAnn Sheetz. I'd bumped into her at the library, had asked about her mom and gotten a meek shrug.

"As best can be expected." LuAnn had refused to provide details, and I figured it wasn't my business to press and risk a breakdown.

Next came a lazy afternoon on the porch reading the latest Tami Hoag thriller, and then the run to the grocery and seafood market. Quiet. Calm. Serene. I was beginning to wonder about the bustle awaiting me at *Carolina* magazine. Could I handle it? Did I want to? My stomach fluttered. I was going to miss Goose Inlet, the beach. Hannah. Tanner.

"Tanner will be here at six." I dumped chopped vegetables into a large skillet and decided to ask a question I'd been holding back all summer. "Who are his parents?"

"What do you mean?"

"What nationality? Or nationalities. He looks like he's a combination of several." Tanner had never volunteered his heritage. "He has a yuppie name but doesn't look or act, I don't know—urban."

"Don't you think the mix picked all the best features?" Hannah asked, reaching for another shrimp.

"Definitely. He's a handsome guy. Honey-skinned. Gorgeous eyes. Glossy hair."

Hannah spoke over her shoulder. "Add 'stunning smile' and you'll be writing an ad for the perfect man."

I grinned wide. "Then let me add—and no beer belly." As I stirred the veggies, a fragrant aroma filled the kitchen. "So, which parts of the world do you think donated genes to Tanner's DNA?"

Hannah stopped peeling shrimp. "I don't think. I know. South America and the plain 'ol U.S. of A."

I turned from the stove. "Really? I was thinking Hungary and Iceland. Or maybe Hawaii and Samoa because of his water fetish."

Hannah began deveining the shrimp. "Nothing that exotic." She said she'd gotten the scoop through the grapevine, namely Dutch and Joop. How reliable could that be?

I wiped my hands on a kitchen towel. "Who did you say you invited?"

Hannah grinned. "I didn't say. It's a surprise."

"Oh, God, you're not bringing Dutch or Joop into this house, are you?"

Hannah busied herself wiping the counter and asked if I understood the meaning of *surprise*.

Well, I hope it's not LuAnn. Lunch had been pleasant. No rant about murderous, poaching Costa Ricans. No heart-rending tears over a lost boyfriend. I closed my eyes, guiltily recalling the many soggy, snot-filled tissues I'd tossed in the wastebasket the last three months. I added sliced sausage to the pan and browned it up, then poured in tomatoes, some chicken broth and a heaping tablespoon of Old Bay. LuAnn did mention she might have to move her mother from assisted living to a nursing home, but she hadn't flipped out over it. And she hadn't hauled out Randy's picture either. Still, sixty minutes with LuAnn Sheetz was enough. And I was probably going to hell for thinking that.

I measured out rice, added water, and put the pot on to boil before turning it down to simmer. I tasted the jambalaya sauce and added more garlic and onion powder. Tossed in a little crushed red pepper. There was a knock on the door and we both shouted, "Come in!"

"Ummm-m-m-m-m! Smells delicious." Tanner came into the kitchen wearing his hungry smile. Summer on the water had enhanced his skin's natural golden tone. His eyes, released from behind sunglasses, were milk chocolate. *He can't be just from the Americas.* In one hand Tanner carried a bottle of gin, in the other tonic. Behind him strode Erik Magnus.

I dropped my wooden spoon into the skillet and a splat of red sauce hit my chin. In slow motion my hand rose to wipe my face clean. My gaze slid to Hannah. My last personal interaction with Detective Magnus had been in the police station, and I'd left fuming.

"Surprise," she whispered.

Magnus set a hunk of cheese, a box of crackers, and a plastic tub of olives on the counter. "Surprise," he echoed, pointing. "Manchego. From Spain. Made with milk from Manchego sheep. Cervantes mentioned it in his novel. Have you read *Don Quixote*?" Before I could answer, he added, "The olives don't have pits."

"Good to know." I stirred the sauce. "And yes, I read *Don Quixote of La Mancha*. In ninth grade." It was six days since we'd found London's body and Detective Magnus had quizzed me on my "dislike" of the murdered man. I was still miffed.

"Prosecco anyone?" Hannah sang sweetly, although the bottle was nearly empty. "I should have gotten two of these."

I told her another was in the fridge and retrieved two more wine glasses. Magnus reached into the cabinet for a plate and arranged a semi-circle of wheat crackers around the cheese. He dumped olives into a small white bowl. I dug around in a drawer for a cheese cutter. "Make yourself at home," I sang, sweetly as Hannah, and handed him the cutter.

"Thanks," Magnus said. "And thanks for inviting me."

I stopped myself from clarifying that Hannah had invited him and won a smile from her when I voiced my pleasure that he could come. I herded everyone outside to enjoy the appetizer while the sauce simmered.

Hannah gave me a look that was a composite of *thank you* and *play nice*. I wondered if there was something going on between her and the detective. I hadn't noticed smiles or chats or pats on the fanny. Hannah had been consumed by baby sea turtles—both their appearance and absence—for the past five months. I hadn't seen her making eyes at any man, least of all Erik Magnus, who'd been obliged to show up at the worst of times. Maybe I'd missed something. No, my nosy nose would have scoped them out. So, this might be something very recent. Or, knowing Hannah, my friend was trying to nurture friendship between me and the detective. If that were true, she wouldn't want me bringing murder and toes and fleshy tattoos into the conversation.

"You like to kayak, Abby." Magnus said it as a statement rather than question. He handed me a smooth slice of cheese on a cracker.

"I've gone mostly with Tanner." My face heated up. I'd gotten over my silliness about paddling alone with him, so why the rosy cheeks?

"I have a couple boats," Magnus said. "We'll go out sometime."

I froze. My mouth couldn't even fall open. That did not sound like an invitation. I couldn't recall Aidan ever telling me to do anything, except not walk out in front of a car when I was yakking and not paying attention. My irritation with Detective Magnus ramped up a notch.

Hannah broke in with a light laugh. "Don't leave me out. I love Coal River. It's like floating in a primeval world. Do you like blackwater, Erik? Some people don't."

Tanner had explained blackwater as deep and slow moving through swamps and wetlands. Tannins leaching from decaying trees and other vegetation make it dark and acidic. "Like tea or coffee," he said. "Funny thing, the water is dark but transparent. In shallower depths, when you look down you see rocks and plants. Turtles and fish."

"Blackwater doesn't scare me," Magnus answered with a slow smile. "I've been on Jewel, Raven, and just about every other creek. Do you take tours out there?"

"The put-in at Jewel is a little rough," Tanner said. "I don't take newbies."

"Too rough for Abby?" Magnus asked.

The hair on my neck stood up stiff as a guard dog's. "I am not a newbie. I've kayaked for years on mountain lakes. And paddled here all summer." Tanner caught my eye. "At least a half-dozen times."

Magnus leaned back in his chair. "That many."

I stalked into the kitchen and pulled shrimp out of the refrigerator. Hannah came up behind me.

"Don't get huffy," she whispered. "Erik didn't mean you shouldn't come along." I folded shrimp into the sauce. "He didn't know you have experience."

I took out the crusty bread heating in the oven. First he declares we'll paddle together. Then he implies I'm inexperienced. Does that make sense? I fumed until the shrimp turned pink then spooned jambalaya into a large bowl. "I have no problem *not* paddling with Detective Erik."

I carried the meal outside. Tanner poured Malbec, and Erik decided he was in charge of filling everyone's bowl with hot seafood stew. Hannah passed bread and we dug in. I spooned up a shrimp, but my stomach felt tight as a fist. Why was I so upset? Calm down, Abby.

"This is delicious," Tanner said after a half dozen spoonsful. "Just the right amount of spicy."

"Do you ever use chicken?" Magnus asked. "My mama always made it with hot sausage and chicken. And, of course, shrimp."

I took a deep breath and decided to consider his question a request for information rather than criticism that my chicken-less jambalaya was deficient. "Sometimes. And I use different sausages. Not always Andouille. Depends on what I have in the fridge."

Dinner conversation continued with discussion about the most accessible kayak launches and progressed to stand-up paddling, fishing, and finally everything else that had to do with water, including storm runoff and depleted oyster beds. *Gracilaria*, an invasive grass crowding parts of the river, was especially scorned. Rumor said it came in with ballast water from a Russian freighter, but Tanner said he'd seen reports that suggested it arrived with shellfish imported to the Chesapeake Bay during some oyster restoration efforts.

After dinner, we sat on the porch with coffee and cognac. Tanner mentioned being in the Chamber office filling the information kiosk with business brochures and seeing Jason Stone walk out of the police station.

"He wasn't leaving your office, was he, Erik?" Tanner asked with a grin

The detective stared over the top of his cup and shook his head. "Must have come in about a parking ticket."

We were silent a moment, then Erik said, "I've heard the rumors. People are yapping that Alegria Villalobos, and by implication her husband, poached those nests." He leaned forward. "There's no proof of that. I'm not investigating the poaching, but have exchanged calls with Fish & Wildlife and Will Brown. Let me say emphatically: They are not investigating Jason Stone and his wife."

"I'm glad Will's talking to someone local," Hannah said, "Because he's not talking to me." She paused. "So, who are they investigating? Anyone?"

Erik shook his head. I couldn't decide if that meant, *No, they're not investigating anyone else, or Don't ask me, I can't tell you.*

Conversation had taken on a heavy tone. Everyone's forehead was creased, including mine. I was searching my memory bank for a lighthearted topic that would relax my guests when Hannah's phone, sitting on a metal outdoor table, began to rattle. When LuAnn's picture flashed on the screen, I knew the mood was about darken. Hannah listened briefly then clicked off.

"LuAnn's mother's been rushed to the hospital, and LuAnn's car won't start. Dammit! Do all bad things have to happen at once?" The three of us stared at her. "I rode here on my bike," she continued. "Erik, can you take me to her house? You," she pointed at me, "come with us." When I opened my mouth to protest, Hannah clapped her hands like the preschool teacher she was. "Pack a bag for LuAnn. She'll be stuck at the hospital for hours. I can't take time to do it. She'll be in a state and will insist on getting to the hospital ASAP. Erik and I will take her there and come back for the bag."

I turned so Hannah couldn't see my face. I hated that abbreviation—ASAP. It sounded much bossier than "as soon as possible." ASAP! I'd had an editor who said that. The same one who smiled when he was angry.

Our evening had crash landed. It would have been nice if LuAnn had called one of her close friends. The sympathetic ones patting her through those crying jags over Randy. Why call Hannah? They were both turtle people, but I hadn't noticed any buddy-buddy between them. Still, Hannah was friendly with everyone. And compassionate. Look how kind she'd been to me through the years.

Unlike me, Tanner and Erik seemed to take the disruption of our evening in stride. No protest from the detective over the commandeering of his vehicle. Hannah would probably have him turn on his Kojak light. Again, I wondered if there was something going on between them.

"I'll clean up the kitchen," Tanner said, already filling a storage container with leftover jambalaya.

"Thanks, Tanner." I touched his arm. He really was a sweet man. "I'll be back." I paused. "As soon as possible."

***

As Erik drove to LuAnn's house, I thought about my months in Goose Inlet. Am I healing? Am I less angry? With all there is to do here, do I take the time to grieve for Aidan? I closed my eyes. Yes, I do. But do I grieve enough? Yes. I mourn for my husband, but I do it alone. I cry in my bed. In my car. Riding my bike home from a turtle nest. Am I less wrathful, less resentful? Maybe not, but that's because I have no answers. I don't feel the fire lighting my fury will extinguish until I know why Aidan's lab exploded on the one Sunday he went in to check his work.

My phone dinged. Tillson's security guard Wade Ramsey: *Guys in suits meeting here with guys from customs.*

Guys in suits? I texted back: Do you mean Tillson management? Or the feds?

Wade: *Feds*

Feds meeting at Tillson with guys from customs. Custom agents from the port? I thought back to Jason Stone's contentious discussion with his co-worker. To Aidan being in Goose Inlet and maybe, if London had been telling the truth, talking to Stone. What the heck?

I must have said that aloud, because Hannah asked, "Are you talking to me?"

I uttered, "Uh, no," as my phone dinged again.

Wade: Customs tech guys looking at Dr. Finn's computer.

I remembered London saying Aidan closed his computer when he and Marc walked by. What the hell was Aidan up to?

***

LuAnn was pacing her front yard when we drove up in Magnus's car, roof light flashing. Hannah threw her arm around LuAnn's shoulders, hustled her into the vehicle, and they rocketed off to the hospital. I trudged into the house and rummaged in LuAnn's dresser for a clean shirt and underwear. Snagged a toothbrush and twisted tube of paste off the bathroom sink. In the kitchen I found a bottle of water and pack of peanut butter crackers. Tossed it all into a plastic bag I found on the pantry floor. LuAnn couldn't do this herself while waiting? Or hold off two minutes while Hannah did it? Ridiculous.

Setting the bag on the kitchen table for Hannah to find, I puffed my cheeks and exhaled, anticipating my walk home. LuAnn lived several blocks from the beach. It was a lengthy walk on a hot afternoon. At ten o'clock at night, a sulking silence cloaked the street.

I hadn't paid much attention to the kitchen when I'd walked through a week and a half ago. The dated appliances probably belonged to LuAnn's grandparents. Same with the living room. Old furniture. Old curtains. Old books stuck together with old dust. I strolled over to a bookcase. Ragged scrapbooks and photo albums jutted out from a bottom shelf. I perked up. If they're as old as everything else in this house, they might have pictures of early Goose Inlet natives. Maybe pictures of Joop and Dutch as kids. Maybe even of beach bum Erik before he morphed into a bossy detective.

Picking an album at random, I stared at labeled photos stuck in place with old-fashioned, white, triangle tabs. Here was LuAnn, age two, sitting in a water-filled hole, peeking out from under a sunhat, waving a plastic shovel. I flipped the pages and scanned photos, looking for names. There was a much younger Joop Dahl clutching a beer can, standing with five shirtless men around a charcoal grill. Four of them had cigarettes hanging from their lips and Sheetz for a last name. Little bare-chested kids romped in the background.

I stopped at a photo of a two-tiered, decorated cake. LuAnn, blond head boasting a princess crown, was the birthday girl. Her friends—labeled Darla, Bianca, and Fala—wore big grins and pointy party hats. LuAnn had been childhood friends with little girls destined to become nest mothers.

I sat down on the floor and pulled out another album. The folks pictured were older than LuAnn. Maybe even her grandparents' ages. I tried to figure out the time period from the clothes. Knee-length, one-piece bathing suits and heavy, twisted hairstyles. Thank goodness, clothes and hair and life were much simpler now. People wore what they wanted. Both women and men cut their hair short or even shaved their heads.

The third album fell open to the middle. There was Dutch dressed like Santa driving an old Pontiac in the Christmas parade. I wouldn't have recognized him if his name hadn't been written below the picture. And wow! There was LuAnn in a tight dress, high heels and big hair, microphone an inch from her lips, crooning a love song. At least it looked like a love song, the way her eyes cast sidelong at another member of the band. LuAnn had drawn a heart and an arrow pointing toward a dark-haired boy strumming a guitar. I pulled the photograph out of its paper fasteners. Dipped my head for a closer look and sucked in air.

Holy moly, there was nothing wrong with Bianca's memory. In my hand was an old image that left nothing to the imagination. LuAnn Sheetz was making goo-goo eyes at Marc Diamond.

CHAPTER THIRTY-THREE

LuAnn was loading a short kayak into the back of her Jeep when I drove up with my own boat strapped to the roof of my car. Yes, I bought one. Tanner had pointed out an end-of-summer sale at Explore Outdoors. And no, my fourteen-foot, thirty-five-pound, royal purple kayak was not an impulse buy, since the seed had been planted weeks earlier. Still, *sale* and *purple* pushed me over the edge. When Tanner said I could paddle all winter wearing waterproof pants, a lightweight jacket, and water shoes that covered my calves, I was sold. Maybe being a boat owner would knock me out of newbie status in Erik Magnus's eyes. Not that I cared. Much. Hannah was thrilled to learn I'd be at the beach on winter weekends.

It wasn't coincidence that I'd driven down LuAnn's street with my boat on my roof. I'd overheard her tell Fala at Aunt Biddy's that she was thinking of a solo paddle around noon to relax and clear her head. She needed a break from daily visits to the nursing home, where her mother had been taken to recover from a stroke. Spurred by the LuAnn-Marc connection, I'd decided to step out of my comfort zone and do a little snooping. Were they still in touch, I wondered? And considering the odd networking going on, namely the LuAnn-Marc-London-Tanner-Aidan link, was it outrageous to wonder if LuAnn had known Aidan? The thought tightened my stomach.

I coasted to the front of her house. "Hey! Going out on the water?"

LuAnn shoved her boat the last foot over the tailgate before turning around. The slightly cross-eyed look on her face reminded me of an owl. Had she been drinking this early in the day?

I smiled big. "Want company?"

"Actually, I want privacy."

I ignored the snub. "Come on. I haven't been out all week." A lie. "You can show me your favorite spot." LuAnn gripped the tailgate as if preparing to drop it and haul her boat back out. I walked over to her Jeep and offered my *relax, it's a sunshiny day* smile. The kind I used with nervous interviewees. "I have a new boat and I'm looking for new places to paddle. Where are you going?"

LuAnn's shoulders sagged. "Up the river. Maybe look for sharks' teeth." She squinted. "Ever been on the river?"

I shook my head. "But I'm eager to go." Ten thousand bull sharks be damned.

LuAnn stared a long moment, as if trying to make a decision much more difficult than whether or not to let me tag along. "Okay, then. Follow me."

I could understand LuAnn wanting privacy. The latest poached turtle nest, along with speculation about London's killer and Randy's disappearance, had been hot topics at Aunt Biddy's this morning. Even though they'd barely known him, customers expressed regrets over London's murder and inability of police to find his killer. And since nearly everyone in the diner had known Randy, LuAnn had been bombarded with expressions of sympathy. I could see why she needed a peaceful place to calm her body and soul.

We put in at River Green. Driving into the park, I was pleased to see that a thoughtful planner, most likely a woman, had installed restrooms. LuAnn surprised me by helping lift my boat off the roof carrier. We carted boats, paddles and gear down to the water.

"You don't have a lifejacket?" I asked, dropping my equipment at the launch site.

She pointed to a dirty brown rectangle stuffed behind the seat in her boat. "Carry one. Don't wear it." What good was that? Tanner had drummed "lifejackets are mandatory" into me and it made sense.

The tide was midpoint, so there was a decent amount of sandy beach from which to launch. LuAnn brightened as soon as she made her first strokes and asked if I wanted to see Tooth Isle, a spoil island. She pointed out a line of various-sized landmasses running north and south, saying, "That's why we find sharks' teeth. From the dredging."

"So there really are sharks in the river."

LuAnn gave a sidelong look. "Thousands of them." She pointed out Dram Island directly across from the boat launch. Tooth was just north, and we reached it in minutes. I looked for a smooth place to beach my boat. I wasn't about to scrape up the bottom on the carpet of stones that covered three-quarters of the landing zone. LuAnn had no such qualms and accelerated her paddling through the rough, whooshing up onto the debris-strewn beach. She hopped out and, head down, began wading in the shallows. Knowing high tide was coming, I pulled my boat far up near a blockade of rocks and trees. I took off my PFD, secured my paddle, and followed her.

LuAnn scrutinized the clear, shallow water cluttered with rocks the size of sports balls. Some were nubby baseballs, others smooth bowling balls, still others oddly shaped and covered with fossilized shells and barnacles. I thought some would be fun in a garden, and considered carrying a few back for Hannah. Five of the smaller rocks would fit comfortably in my boat without cramping leg room.

LuAnn reached into the shallows, snatched up something black, and stuffed it in her pocket. I almost had to beg her to show it to me. Finally, she pulled out an elongated, triangular-shaped, ebony bone with a pointed tip and, after a moment's hesitation, placed it in my hand. Interesting, but what's this fascination with sharks' teeth? People collected them by the bowlful. Measured them. Posted pictures of their latest acquisitions on social media. I tapped the pointy tip and handed it back. The sun hot on my back, I spent the next fifteen minutes following LuAnn around the island's perimeter, trying not to twist my ankles on slippery rocks, making small talk, and avoiding the words "poaching," "missing" and "dead." Eventually, it was time to stop tiptoeing around. I wanted information.

"Are you still in touch with Marc Diamond?"

LuAnn had been crossing a group of softball-sized rocks and at the mention of Marc slid off and landed on her hip among thick, partially submerged tree branches.

"Dammit!" She scowled at me, eyes glittering. Despite the brilliant Carolina sunshine, I'd never seen

LuAnn wear sunglasses. I took her elbow, but she wrenched her arm away. She tried to get up on her own but couldn't rise more than a couple inches. Her bottom was wedged in among thick tree roots and broken branches encircled her waist like brown belts. Slimy rocks and soggy sand added to her predicament.

"Let me help you." I pushed at the branches, hoping to dislodge them and give LuAnn more room to move. "Get your feet under you." LuAnn grimaced like a bearcat but grabbed my hand. With me pulling and her pushing with one free hand, we managed to get her up.

"Shit," LuAnn said. That seemed to cover it.

"Let's walk back to the boats and have lunch. Rest," I said, even though we hadn't done much. I paddled for hours with Tanner before taking a break.

Sitting on the bow of her boat, LuAnn gobbled a tuna sandwich in silence. I chewed my PB&J. "Why'd you get upset when I asked if you're still in touch with Marc?" I asked.

LuAnn worked the tuna around in her mouth. "How do you know about Marc?"

"My husband worked in the same lab with him."

LuAnn stuck her finger in her mouth and rubbed a back molar. "I mean, how do you know I knew Marc?"

"I saw a picture of you and him playing music." Let her think I saw the photo in someone else's album. "You said at Sardine that you sang with your brothers' band."

LuAnn took the shark's tooth out of her pocket and touched the point. "He played with us." LuAnn squinted at me. She definitely would benefit from a good pair of shades. Eyesight should not be taken lightly.

"Were you friends or just bandmates?" I asked.

She leaned over and drew a circle in the sand with the tooth. "Just bandmates. My brothers thought he played a mean guitar." She shrugged. "He was okay."

I took a long drink from my water bottle. It was new, insulated, and the water cool as a mountain stream. "Well, he gave up music for chemistry." I paused. "Did you know?"

LuAnn's lips were a straight line. She stood up, put her foot on the bow of her boat and shoved it into the water. "You want to cross the channel?"

I snapped to attention. "The shipping channel?"

Hannah had described crossing the shipping channel as a heads up activity requiring even more vigilance than crossing the ICW. She said some of the container ships were a thousand feet long and a hundred feet wide. I had never seen boats that size up close. I couldn't imagine paddling near one and looking up at the behemoth. When I told that to Hannah, my friend gaped, jaw rigid. "Never, ever get that close to a container ship," she'd said. "Wait until the coast is clear before crossing the channel. And then, you still haul ass."

LuAnn drifted in her boat, waiting, which kind of surprised me, since for most of our time together she'd acted as if I wasn't there. "Ready for a little adventure?" A slow smile spread across her face. She motioned me to follow.

When we reached the other side of Tooth Isle, I saw the great expanse of river that would allow a one-hundred-foot-wide boat to pass through with room to spare. The river was wide, but I could see islands on the channel's other side and the bank lined with trees.

"It's choppy," I said. A large yacht was leaving rollercoaster-like swells in its wake.

"There's another boat coming, but we can beat it across."

I looked left. A mammoth container ship lumbered upriver from the south. "That's a ship!"

"No problem. We can make it." LuAnn leaned forward, paddle raised. Hannah would not attempt this, I knew. Tanner would blow a gasket at the mere suggestion.

"I don't think we have enough time," I said above the call of sea gulls. "And it's windy here." My hair blew across my forehead. The current was pulling me south. I doubted I could maintain a straight line, the shortest distance, across the channel.

LuAnn looked back and smiled. Is she encouraging me? Or daring me? I shook my head so hard my sunglasses slipped down my nose. "Don't go, LuAnn. The ship's too close."

"Sweet Jesus, it's at least a half mile away."

I stared downriver. The ship was a lot closer than that. And it was much windier here than near the islands. And the current—

"So, you're not going?" LuAnn's expression had "chicken" written all over it.

Before I could answer, she struck out paddling. Instinctively, I paddled, too, but the container ship's bellowing horn—like a punch in the gut—nearly caused me to capsize my light boat, so high did I jump in my seat. I slapped my paddle in the water and back-paddled as fast as I could.

LuAnn never looked back. She struck out with more energy and strength than I thought she possessed, crossing the shipping channel with room to spare. From Tooth Isle, I watched the mammoth container ship motor past, my kayak bouncing in its wake. Somewhere on the western side, LuAnn tossed about, too.

I turned my boat around and headed back to the launch. Even though I wasn't an investigative reporter, as a journalist I cultivated a healthy suspicion about nearly everything. I took very little at face value, always wondering if what people said was what they really thought, and if their actions truly reflected their intentions. It was a trait I found useful for all stories, not only those meant to expose secrets.

Right now I entertained the suspicion that LuAnn Sheetz had tried purposely to put me in danger.

CHAPTER THIRTY-FOUR

The "big-haired skank from Greensboro" who gave Marc Diamond five children wore a peasant blouse, calf-length skirt and a pixie cut. Five minutes ago, Audra Diamond had put four kids on the school bus and her youngest into the back of her Lexus minivan and driven away. A half-hour earlier Marc himself had sauntered out of their home in one of Raleigh's older, but still nicer, neighborhoods, hopped into his Mercedes C-Class sedan, and backed out of his driveway.

Rattled by LuAnn's behavior the day before and unable to sleep, I'd jumped in my car before dawn and driven to Raleigh. The LuAnn-Marc connection fascinated me more now because of her violent reaction to my question about their possible ongoing involvement, and because it simmered on the edge of the London-Marc-Aiden connection. Last night, Wade Ramsey texted that Tillson had confiscated Marc's work computer as part of its investigation into the chemicals theft—did that mean Aidan was off the hook?—but Marc had not been suspended. The security guard also remembered overhearing Marc and London whispering Aidan's name, but he couldn't make out their conversation. I wondered if Tillson's investigators would be allowed to search Marc's home lab? With enough suspicion of wrongdoing, police could, with a warrant.

I was parked three houses away from the Diamond house, on the opposite side of the street, with a good view of its front and side doors. I waited another five minutes, nervous that one of them would return, having forgotten something. Or the cleaning lady would drive up. Or a nosy neighbor would pop out of the shrubbery. Finally, expelling a long breath, I approached the detached garage and peeked in the side door window. Dark. Quiet. Surprisingly, there was no deadbolt on the door, but when I turned the knob it was locked. Just a cheesy knob lock? With five kids in the house? I retrieved a credit card from my pocket and slid it up the side of the door, next to the frame. This always worked on TV. When the lock clicked open, I slipped into Marc Diamond's garage laboratory.

Prying was something private investigators and investigative reporters did. Since I was neither, the decision to embark on illegal snooping had not been easy. So, I was surprised that the little thrill curling up the back of my thighs was only mildly unsettling.

For a couple of weeks I'd been trying to fit puzzle pieces together and Marc Diamond seemed to be in the center of the board. Marc knew people. He worked in the lab where my husband had died violently. He knew someone who'd been murdered in Goose Inlet. And he knew or had known LuAnn Sheetz. Did LuAnn fit into the puzzle? Her refusal to answer my question about knowing modern-day Marc, then her dangerous dash across the river, had been, in my opinion, more than quirky behavior. These were the questions and thoughts that plagued me last night and put me where I stood right now. In Marc Diamond's private domain.

I pulled latex gloves and a small flashlight out of my cargo pocket. All those years watching crime shows paid off. The only thing I hadn't brought was a gun. I didn't own one. Seriously doubted I needed one. Absolutely didn't want one.

Someone had signed Aidan's name to the chemical inventory list. Aidan had suspected Marc of stealing Tillson chemicals, and I figured Marc was trying to hide his wrongdoing by casting suspicion on my husband. Aidan had popped into Marc's home lab, toting his unsigned lab book, and made him angry. Did Aidan identify bottles of chemicals that rightfully belonged to Tillson Pharmaceutical? Had he seen an experiment in progress? Figured out what Marc was cooking in his home lab and told management?

I shined the flashlight around the garage, across a wooden workbench, a small desk, a refrigerator, and over metal shelves holding rows of bottles. Holding the flashlight high, I read the labels. Lactic acid. Soybean oil. Chitosan. What the heck was that? A bunch of other bottles were labeled with chemical names I'd heard Aidan talk about throughout his chemistry career. Barium sulfate. Sodium chloride. Potassium bisulfate. I had no idea what Marc could make with those chemicals. No reactions were set up in beakers on the workbench. Even if there were, they would be meaningless to me. I flashed my light over another set of shelves holding beakers, test tubes and other pieces of equipment—one a scale—I'd seen during visits to Aidan's lab.

I waved my light across the desk surface. Pens, yellow legal pad, dirty food container, laptop, briefcase. Aidan never brought his company laptop home. Aidan's laptop, with its company secrets, stayed at work. So this must be Marc's personal computer. But why didn't he take his briefcase to work? I nibbled my lower lip and pushed the slide button on the case. Not surprisingly, the lock did not open. I flashed my light over a bulletin board. Periodic table. Taco Bell menu. List of phone numbers. My heart hiccupped when I saw LJ next to one. London James. I switched the light onto a piece of paper with two columns of dates, side by side, and read down the first list—May 9, May 16, June 2, June 5, July 24, July 26, August 1, August 3—and wondered what they signified. I read down the second list: July 15, July 22, July 28, July 31.

I held my light on the paper and thought back across the summer. The dates in column two were familiar. As well as I could remember, they were dates loggerhead nests had hatched on Goose Inlet beaches. I reread the lists, this time side by side.

May 9—July 15
May 16—July 22
June 2—July 28
June 5—July 31
July 24—August 3

August 3—the day after we found London James dead and the day we excavated Nest Five early because of suspected fox predation and found it empty.

July 26 and August 1 were scribbled in a column that had no corresponding dates. Thick black lines had been drawn through August 1. I almost missed August 8, written in faint black ink, as if the pen was drying up.

I tapped my chin. The dates were roughly two months apart. If my memory was correct and column two represented hatch dates, column one marked dates turtle nests were laid. Why would Marc Diamond have important dates for turtle nests pinned to his garage bulletin board? He wasn't a nest sitter. It would be ridiculous to drive nightly back and forth from Raleigh to sit at a turtle nest. I dug in my bag for a small notebook and pen, and scribbled down the dates. July 26 and August 1 would be Nests Six and Seven, not yet hatched. Why was August 1 scribbled out? And August 8? I hadn't heard about a nest being found two days ago.

A car door slammed. I flicked off the light. Sweat dribbled down the small of my back as I walked to the side door, knees shaking. My elbow knocked something off a table and it hit the floor dully. Another car door slammed. Pressing my face against the window, I saw Audra Diamond herding her child before her as she carried two fists-full of grocery bags to the back door. When she disappeared inside the house, I waved my flashlight at the floor. What had fallen? A recycling box? I set it back on the table.

After waiting five minutes for my heartbeat to slow, I gritted my teeth, eased out the door, and race-walked across the neighbor's lawn to my own vehicle. As I shifted into drive, I saw Audra exit the house and hurry her child back into the Lexus. I lay back on the headrest, breathed deeply, and watched her drive away. One of those on-the-go mothers with a toddler who napped in his car seat. I remembered those days and was thankful my kids were grown. That calming thought slipped away as I drove onto the highway, headed straight for Hannah's house.

CHAPTER THIRTY-FIVE

I'd spent the two-and-a-half-hour-drive back to Goose Inlet glancing at the scribbled dates lying on the car seat next to me. I'd memorized them in minutes, but still couldn't keep my eyes off them. Now I sat on Hannah's porch waiting for my friend to come home. I'd rewritten the dates in two straight columns and, alongside the second column, noted the results of the nest hatches.

"Hey! Nice surprise. What did you do today?" Hannah leaned her bike against the porch and climbed the steps.

I covered the notes with my hand and showed her the two columns. Hannah ticked off the lines on the page with her fingertip. "These are turtle dates."

I uncovered the notes. "The first nest hatched three live turtles and three toes." Hannah's smile faded. "The second nest hatched fifteen turtles and a piece of tattooed butt."

Hannah grimaced and sank into a chair. "Why are you rehashing this? It's Erik's job to find the mutilator and Will Brown's to help find the poacher."

"I'm investigating—like you so strongly suggested."

"You're going to write something?" Hannah's face brightened.

I did a combination head shake-hand waggle. "Don't know. Maybe. Not my area of expertise."

"Then what are you doing?" Hannah asked, her tone lowering.

I flipped the pages back to the one with the original chicken-scratched dates.

"Did you write these in the dark?" Hannah squinted at the cockeyed script.

I told her I copied them off Marc Diamond's bulletin board in his garage lab, reminding her that he was Aidan's lab partner and friends with London James. Hannah slapped her forehead. "You went *snooping* at his *home*?"

I snapped the notebook shut. "You wanted me to investigate. A large part of that involves going where I'm not supposed to go. And believe me, I didn't go easily. I was a nervous wreck."

Hannah crossed her legs and looked out over the dune. Finally, she asked, "Why would Marc know our turtle nesting and hatching dates?"

"Exactly. Why would Marc Diamond, who lives in Raleigh, who's not a member of the sea turtle project, who, I'm almost positive, hasn't seen one hatch or excavation this season, have the dates for all seven nests laid in Goose Inlet along with the correct dates for those that already hatched?"

Hannah put both hands to her temples and rubbed in small circles. "How'd he get them? They're not posted on our website."

"Someone here gave them to him."

She looked at me with disbelief. "Who would do that?"

I played with the spiral wire on my notebook. "My best guess is LuAnn Sheetz."

Hannah lurched as if poked with a cattle prod. "LuAnn! Does she even know—?"

"Yes! Marc is the guy LuAnn said was her teenage summer love, remember? She was crazy about him." I told her Bianca said the same thing and that I saw an old photo of LuAnn and Marc singing together. I related how weird and evasive LuAnn acted when I asked her if she was still in touch with Marc and how she charged across the shipping channel in her kayak with a container ship coming to get away from me. Hannah sucked in her breath. Her mouth made a small o. I knew that would get her.

But her words disappointed me. "Give LuAnn a break. It was years ago. She probably doesn't remember him." She laughed. "Or maybe wants to forget him. Maybe he dumped her—summer love, puppy love. He's history. I get that." Still, she tapped my notebook. "What are you getting at?"

"The list was next to shelves cluttered with bottles of chemicals and lab equipment. One of those bottles had a funny name—Carosan?" I should have written the names down. "I'm going to ask LuAnn about it."

"Ask if she gave the dates of our turtle nests to her old boyfriend? That's ludicrous. Turtle people know better than that. LuAnn knows better. Stop harassing her."

"I'm not harassing her!"

"Sounds like it to me. Where's your proof? All you know is that LuAnn Sheetz knew Marc Diamond as a kid in Goose Inlet. Big damn deal. " Hannah put her feet up on the porch railing, but they bumped together nervously. "He came here all the time? Then a lot of people knew him."

I ran my tongue over my teeth. Hannah had something there. LuAnn's brothers had known Marc. Bianca and her friends had known him or known of him. Dutch and Joop might have known his relatives and seen him at barbeques, oyster roasts, or just playing on the beach. Shoot, Erik Magnus might have played ball and surfed with Marc Diamond. My certainty about LuAnn deflated.

"With all LuAnn's going through. Randy missing and most likely dead. Her mother old, sick, poor. I can't believe you're trying to pin a crime on her." I didn't respond. "You think LuAnn is involved with the turtle nest poaching, right?" I remained quiet. "You think she stole eggs from three nests and what? Gave them to this Marc guy? Why?"

I shrugged. "I think she's involved. Somehow."

Hannah stormed off the porch. "Let it go!" she shouted from inside the house.

***

Two days later, I walked along the beach, still troubled by Hannah's refusal to share my suspicion of LuAnn. They were turtle volunteers, but not bosom buddies. LuAnn had called Hannah during her mom crisis, but I couldn't complain because I'd discovered the LuAnn-Marc connection after being dragged into the drama. Hannah thought my imagination was working overtime. I was quite certain I was on to something.

I enjoyed one last lungful of musky ocean air and was on the first step of the access near Lily Pad, when a body hurtled past, knocking me against the wooden railing. "Hey! Watch—" The body did not stop. No lips opened in apology. I stared after the person, a woman, who stumbled through the sand, nearly falling twice before reaching the hard-pack exposed by the receding tide. She flopped down on her knees in shallow water, soaking her flowered shorts, and lowered her face into her hands. Although the wind and waves masked the sound, I knew by the way her shoulders shook that she was crying. Bawling. My irritation at being nearly run through by a human spear subsided.

I walked back to the shoreline where great gasps and snorts masked audible sobbing. The poor thing seemed to struggle for breath. I leaned over and placed a hand on her shoulder. At my touch, the woman's head whipped around, and I looked into the beet red, slippery wet face of LuAnn Sheetz. She'd butchered her hair into a buzz cut, which might be why I hadn't recognized her.

"LuAnn, what happened?" I knelt in the sand. "Why are you crying?"

LuAnn opened her mouth wide as a whale's and yowled. Beach walkers stopped in their tracks. Some began a cautious approach.

"Can I help you? Come back to Lily Pad. We can talk."

LuAnn dropped her head to her knees, and I took the opportunity to touch a little water to her face. "To cool you down. Try to catch your breath." LuAnn tried to twist away, but I held her head and gently dabbed more water. The wailing slipped to a whimper.

"She's calming down," I said to several people who'd gathered behind us. "I'll stay with her." They nodded and drifted away.

I sat down in the shallows. "Tell me why you're crying."

LuAnn scooped up wet sand and plopped it on her knees. She let the waves wash it off then scooped on some more. Dug out shells with a finger and tossed them weakly into the surf.

"Something terrible happened," I said. LuAnn didn't look injured. She had energy to run and cry. "Maybe I can help you."

She hung her head and mumbled something that ended in "…ide."

I leaned closer. "I missed that. Can you lift your head?"

LuAnn straightened her spine. Turned to face me. "My mother died." Then her spine collapsed. Her shoulders shook but now her weeping was nearly silent.

I put an arm around her. "I'm so sorry for you."

My opinion of and feelings for LuAnn had flip-flopped throughout the summer. I sympathized with her efforts to help her mother that were affecting her financially and emotionally. And I certainly shared her agony over her missing boyfriend, Randy. But her vicious, baseless attack on Alegria Villalobos still angered me. Then I thought about my own lost mother, both parents in fact, and of course my dead husband, so my sympathy rose again. When I looked at the broken woman tucked in the crook of my arm, I tried to forget that I'd accused her of giving Goose Inlet nesting dates to Marc Diamond.

"I know you loved your mom. You worried about her."

"She was sick. But I thought she'd last longer than this." LuAnn swallowed great gulps of air. "Now everything I did was for nothing." She shook convulsively, like the sides of a tent in a windstorm.

I hugged her. "That's not true. Not for nothing. You got her the best care you could. You found her a good place to live. You made her life more comfortable." I dropped my tone to one I hoped was soothing. "I *know* what you did to get her in a good place."

LuAnn's head whipped around and her torso stiffened. She glared at me as if I'd cursed her. "And it was all for nothing," she said through gritted teeth. "Nothing!"

I knew better than to contradict someone as distraught as LuAnn was right now. I let my arm slip off her shoulder. We sat a while, she rocking in time with the ebb and flow of gentle waves washing the beach. After a while, I caught her staring at me from the corner of her eye. When I looked back, she held my gaze a beat before looking away.

"I want to go out on the water," she said flatly.

"Now?" It was getting on toward twilight. "It's late, but I'll go with you tomorrow morning." Earlier, I'd checked the tides, wind and precipitation, just in case I felt like paddling. I'd even thought of going out myself, just to have the time to think quietly on this Marc Diamond business. But if LuAnn wanted—needed—company, I was willing.

She clawed her fingers through the sand. "Mom's being cremated tomorrow morning."

"Then tomorrow's not a good day."

She squared her shoulders. "Tomorrow's fine."

"Don't you have arrangements to make?"

"For what?" LuAnn's eyes narrowed, as if my question was unreasonable.

"A wake? Her funeral?" I said gently, so as not to trigger another meltdown.

She shook her head. "There won't be any of that. All Mom's friends are dead. And my brothers? They haven't done squat to help out. Why should I throw money away on a going away party when they can get drunk and blubber their guilty regrets in the corner bar?"

I had no answer for that.

LuAnn looked me in the eye. "I need to be on the water."

I nodded, knowing the comforting effect water of any kind—ocean, creek, river, lake—had on me. "I'll pack us a special lunch and something fancier than water," I said. "You pick the launch. Anyplace you want to go. Meet at your house at ten?" LuAnn dipped her head. I gave her a gentle squeeze and offered to walk her home, but she wanted to stay on the beach.

"See you tomorrow." I headed for the steps. When I looked back, LuAnn had lain down flat near the shoreline. Luckily, the tide was going out.

CHAPTER THIRTY-SIX

"I want to paddle Raven Creek," LuAnn announced as soon as I pulled into her driveway. Before I could reply, she added, "You're not afraid of blackwater, are you?" One corner of LuAnn's mouth inched upward.

I was undecided about blackwater or dark water, as Tanner also called it. I'd been on Coal River with him and Hannah and had been both mystified by its beauty and distressed by its solitude. I'd felt peaceful and lonely at the same time.

"If you're afraid," LuAnn continued, leaning against her Jeep, arms crossed, "we can do something easy. Like the back bays."

So she was feisty the day after her mother died. The reservoir of tears gone dry. I stretched my face in a confident smile. "I'm bored with the bays," I lied. "Never been on Raven Creek." She said it was across the river and would take about forty minutes to get there.

"Let's go." I put my car in reverse. "I'll follow. Don't lose me."

LuAnn looked over her shoulder as she opened her car door. "Oh, I won't lose you."

Less than an hour later, we turned off the highway, drove down a dirt road, then another dirt road, then into a rutted, rock-strewn clearing that ended at a boat launch.

"We got a lot a water," LuAnn said, walking down to where a short, narrow dock dipped its near end below the surface. "I don't think I've ever seen Raven Creek this high."

We were silent as we brought down our boats and gear. A sharp edge seemed to separate me from LuAnn, which shouldn't have been there, considering our intimate encounter on the beach the evening before.

LuAnn stuffed her dirty lifejacket behind her seat. I had packed our lunch into a small, soft-sided cooler: cold salmon, cucumbers and tomatoes, peanut butter brownies, and a Mason jar of merlot. Tanner never brought alcohol on the boat, but I didn't think a glass each would numb our ability to paddle. Rather, I hoped the wine would mellow LuAnn, should she slip into one of her crying spells. I tucked the cooler in my front hatch along with a drybag that held a change of clothes, a light vinyl jacket, sunscreen, bug spray, Band-Aids, and my phone. LuAnn dropped a bag into her hatch. I assumed it contained pretty much the same supplies. She stepped into her boat and struck out to the right. I was right behind her.

So far, August had been spectacular, weather-wise. Perpetual Carolina blue skies with temps in the mid-eighties and humidity below the gasping line. At the moment, the wind wasn't moving on Raven Creek, and I felt a closeness, a heaviness press down on me. I dragged my hand through warm water. Splashed a little on my arms. To the right, a wide reflection of trees, a few already hinting at light yellow and red, splattered the dark water, making the visual as deep as it was tall. A sudden breeze sailed through the swamp forest and set the reflection shimmering, which I found strangely disorienting. My kayak seemed to tip side to side, but it was an illusion. The feeling I had experienced on Coal River returned. An odd combination of apprehension and elation. As sudden as the breeze, came the pain of missing Aidan, and the lonesomeness of Raven Creek reminded me of the solitary life I now led.

We passed a wide expanse of spatterdock. Yellow flowers stuck up from a thick mat of heart-shaped leaves. "There's a snake," LuAnn called over her shoulder.

I paddled close to the patch. "Don't see it."

"About two o'clock.

A long, black snake was stretched on top of the leaves, sunning itself. "Rat snake?" I asked.

LuAnn shrugged indifferently. "Cottonmouth, maybe. They like water." I grimaced. Cottonmouth equaled bite and venom. "Rat snakes don't hang around water," she said.

Okay, time to exit. I stroked firmly and was startled when my paddle caught in the long spatterdock stems. My boat tipped far enough that my elbow dipped in the creek. It didn't take long to extricate myself but the surprise of getting snatched and held by the stout stems made my heart skip.

Like Coal River, Raven Creek appeared a throwback to a primeval era. It wound through swamp forest, past bald cypress, hickory trees and swamp tupelo. The cypress were especially otherworldly, their bulbous bottoms sunk in red, tannin-rich water, surrounded by cypress knees that poked up in clusters like gnome villages. Tanner had told me that a group of ancient bald cypress, documented back to something as outrageous as 364 AD, inhabited an area not far from here. I'd asked him to take me there, but he'd acted as if it were a privilege for an initiated cult. It was the only time Tanner had annoyed me.

LuAnn pointed out a pawpaw tree and said her granddaddy had one in his yard and it was the stinkiest tree on the planet. The fruit tasted like banana custard and he loved. LuAnn said it was too damn sweet for her and there was something in the leaves that kept bugs from eating them. Only one kind of butterfly, one with zebra stripes, ate from the pawpaw, according to LuAnn's grandad.

I stared into the forest, marveling at its diversity and intensity. When I turned back, LuAnn was staring at me with as much interest as I'd had observing the dwarf palmettos. "What?"

"Nothing."

"Hungry? Ready for lunch?" It was only late morning.

"Uh uh." LuAnn lowered her gaze but her eyelids rose again slowly like drawn up window shades. Her head pivoted ninety degrees, kind of like an owl marking its prey. "We'll go that way. I want to show you something."

We paddled in silence except for the occasional bird twitter. I breathed in the earthy smell of old trees, decaying leaves, sunshine on my skin. The water was so black it reflected vignettes from each bank like a mirror. Everywhere I looked, the beauty of Raven Creek was doubled. It wasn't hard to follow the main waterway but a few times I thought we could turn right or left only to find a dead end. In a few places trees had fallen across one part of the creek, making our choice of direction simple. LuAnn paddled confidently, and I noticed she was keeping to the right whenever a choice needed to be made. She seemed to know Raven Creek quite well.

We took our boats through a short, narrow stretch, branches crowding in from the sides and overhead. Coming out of the pass, LuAnn did not maintain her pattern of keeping to the right. This was the first left turn we'd taken, so I looked back to mark the place, since we'd be facing it from the opposite direction on the return trip. I was searching for a landmark—a crooked branch, a fallen tree near the water—when I spied a flash of red. Cardinal? Red maple snapped by the wind? Another kayaker? We hadn't encountered other paddlers so far. I drifted briefly to see if someone would come around the bend, but no one did, so I stroked after LuAnn.

When she pulled over to another patch of spatterdock and suggested lunch, a squirrel sitting on a fallen tree several yards away complained but held its ground. I immediately looked for snakes and was rewarded with another black, this one coiled, head up, looking ticked off that two boats had invaded its privacy. Unlike the squirrel, it chose to exit directly toward me, but I managed to slice through the water, once, twice, and get out of the way. I really didn't think it would slither into my boat, but why chance it.

I turned at the sound of LuAnn's snicker. "He slipped into the water just off your stern." I grimaced. "Relax. It could have been a gator."

Tanner had revealed that in North Carolina, if there was water, there were alligators. Earlier in the summer The Gator Man, a wiry octogenarian, had been summoned to capture a six-foot critter residents spotted ambling down the middle of a street in their upscale neighborhood. The only water around was a skimpy stream that, on the evening news, looked more like a drainage ditch. Alligators were common on golf courses, and residents who lived near water hazards knew to keep their cats indoors and their dogs leashed.

"Alligators hide in spatterdock? Seriously?" Then why choose a popular gator lounge for a lunch counter?

"Sure. There's one right there."

I could have auditioned for a remake of "The Exorcist," the way my head spun. "Where?" My shaky voice stretched it into a two-syllable word.

LuAnn snorted and pointed to a wide, flat log near the bank. With lightning speed, the log lunged. I heard a loud *SNAP*, and the squirrel that had settled on a clutch of downed branches disappeared. The log sunk underwater. I stared, afraid to move. Gradually, the log reappeared and big eyeballs looked across the spatterdock leaves.

LuAnn pulled close to my boat, removed the front cargo cover, and pulled out my lunch bag. "We can spread food atop the decks."

I gasped, face twisted in disbelief. "Are you crazy? You're gonna wave food in front of an alligator?"

"Relax. He just ate." She rigged her paddle under her deck ties.

Not wanting to act the total coward, I looked across the creek. "How about we poke our boats between those cypress trees? Besides the gator, the sun's pretty hot here." Or we can paddle a half mile up-creek and leave this bumpy boy alone.

As if she didn't hear, LuAnn opened the bag and arranged containers of salmon and vegetables on the top of her boat. She raised the jar of wine. For a split second, I thought she was going to offer a toast: "To gators!" Or even, "To Mom!"

"There he goes." LuAnn pointed with her thumb at the alligator swimming smoothly to the opposite side of the creek. "Thing to remember about gators is, when they see big boats like ours, they think Big Predator."

I wrinkled my nose. "Who told you that?"

"Some guy I paddled with once."

Once? Because he ended up gator bait?

LuAnn pointed across the creek with her chin. The alligator had nosed into the cypress where I'd suggested lunching, so maybe LuAnn was a gator whisperer.

"I don't usually bring liquor along," I said, taking the jar from her, "but this is one of my last paddles of the season. I'll be going home soon."

Head down, it sounded like LuAnn mumbled, "Yeah, you will."

I reached for the lunch bag. "I didn't catch that."

"Nothing." LuAnn broke off a chunk of salmon with her fingers and stuffed it in her mouth.

I found two forks in the bag, handed one to LuAnn, and made a conscious decision not to let snakes and alligators, or LuAnn Sheetz, dim my appreciation of this dazzling, primitive swamp.

"Be leaving in a couple weeks. Only have a short time left in paradise." I watched LuAnn spear a cucumber then a tomato and cram both into her mouth. Her eyes drilled into me as she chewed. A tingle climbed my spine.

"What's up? What are you thinking?" I felt compelled to ask, even though I disliked that question, feeling a person's thoughts should be her own.

"Nothing."

I bit the inside of my cheek. That was her third "nothing."

"Are you feeling better today?" I asked, pouring wine into two cups.

When she looked up sharply, I added, my voice sympathetic. "You don't seem so terribly sad like you did yesterday." I had avoided talking about her mother's death, fearing another nervous collapse. "You had a right to be sad, of course. You still do. But you were right to come out on the water. Especially Raven Creek. It's soothing, don't you think?"

She didn't answer. Just drank down her wine and poured what remained in the jar into her cup. I wondered if bringing the liquor was a mistake. It wasn't a lot of wine. I'd filled the cups half way, expecting we'd each have another half, but LuAnn had commandeered the rest. She emptied the cup and wiped her mouth on her shoulder.

I glanced back the way we'd come, thinking it might be time to head home, and saw another flash of red.

"That's the second time I've seen something behind us." I pointed back up the creek. "Just a glimpse, but both times, something red. I haven't heard voices."

LuAnn slouched in her seat, apparently uninterested. Might have a little buzz. Content to drift among the spatterdock and nap with the wildlife.

I packed away the food containers and used cups and stuffed the bag between my feet. "Maybe we should head home."

LuAnn didn't reply. Her boat drifted away with her lollygagging inside. Her paddle had worked its way out from under the deck ties and one half reached out over the side like an oar. Did she doze off? The thought wasn't out of my head before LuAnn's paddle slipped into the creek.

"LuAnn! Hey! LuAnn!"

She jolted, rocking her boat.

"Grab your paddle. In the water." When she didn't react, I maneuvered close and snatched it up. Handed it back. "You lose this and you'll literally be up a creek without a paddle." I laughed but I wasn't happy. "It might be a good idea to get a leash." I raised my paddle so she could see it secured to my boat by a length of braided nylon.

LuAnn splashed some water on the back of her neck. "Can't afford it."

That's odd. With her mother gone, she won't be supplementing nursing home bills and should anticipate extra money. Unless there was a huge backlog of medical debt. The thought made me shudder. My parents had been well off enough to take care of their own expenses, including medical bills and, eventually, their burials. Not everyone was so lucky.

Snakes, gators and LuAnn's inability, or refusal, to offer companionship finally took the shine off my day. I said I was heading back and this time led the way. The return trip would be as visually stimulating as the trek out, and I almost wished it wouldn't end. If I were paddling with Tanner or Hannah, or even Erik Magnus, it could have gone on forever. But LuAnn was too much. I'd felt sympathy for her last evening and even a little panicked at the woman's hysteria, but her behavior today gave me goosebumps. I was also annoyed by my foolishness, sticking around spatterdock with food on my bow. Good grief, Abby! I should have taken my lunch and gone somewhere safer. Then a thought struck. I'd taken a risk! Maybe I should be praising my courage instead of condemning my carelessness. Somewhere in the back of my mind, a piece of me argued there was a difference between a safe risk and a stupid one.

I tossed a glance over my shoulder and saw that LuAnn lagged behind half the length of a football field. Maybe she was as tired of me as I was of her. I was nearly through a section of narrow, brush-crowded creek when I heard a scream. Back-paddling quickly through the passage, I twisted and saw LuAnn, arms flailing, kick her way out of her kayak. My first thought was that she was not wearing a lifejacket. I turned my boat and paddled back, stressing over what to do when I got there.

"Grab your boat! Grab your paddle!" I shouted the directions Tanner had taught me. LuAnn did neither. "What happened?" I called, still several yards away.

LuAnn's reply was lost in a large gulp of blackwater. Raven Creek was slow moving, so all the seeds, leaves and colorful scum floating on top, which made pretty patterns when seen from inside a boat, became a mouthful of rank, fibrous yuk when swallowed by a person thrashing about in the creek. A person like LuAnn, who was trying to get as far away from her boat as possible. Her paddle floated within reach, but she made no attempt to retrieve it, so I stroked over, pulled it up and secured it under the ties on my bow. I'd made two strokes toward LuAnn when she plunged in my direction, panic marking her face in stark relief. Fear gushed through me, one fear paramount. If she grabs my boat, she'll tip me over. And there's a gator in the water. My head swiveled as if on a spindle. Is that what she's rushing away from?

"Where's your lifejacket?" I screamed. Of course, she hadn't grabbed it from behind her seat on her wild exit. My inflatable belt pack was snug around my waist, but that didn't mean I wanted to end up in the drink.

LuAnn splashed closer, jerking her head side to side and behind, as if searching for something she was afraid to find. Her overturned kayak drifted away with the current.

I held up one hand. "Don't grab my boat!" Alligator fear swam through my system, along with a flash image of me whacking LuAnn with my paddle if she tried to climb up. Would I really do that?

"Slow down. Tread water. I won't let you drown." Probably shouldn't have used that word. I tried to speak calmly, even though the two sides of my brain were in a quandary. The right side told me to stretch out my paddle for LuAnn to grab. The left side saw LuAnn whirling toward me like an Everglades fan boat, and insisted I raise that paddle in the air in self-defense. I glanced at the staggered line of cypress trees growing at water's edge. They were plentiful and clustered, but there really wasn't any land to stand on. At least not here. LuAnn could have clung to one long enough, however, to regain her equilibrium.

"Calm down. You can hold onto my boat, but don't tip me over." What would we do, dumped in the creek, boats floating away? "Slow. Down."

When LuAnn grabbed the side of my boat and tilted it, water poured into the cockpit. I lurched to the opposite side to right the vessel and instinctively cracked LuAnn's knuckles with my fist. She yowled, but I pounded until she let go. I was far from ready to test my wet entry skills. I'd bought tight-fitting swim shorts and had practiced the ladder entry with Tanner several times, getting as far atop the boat as the cockpit before slipping off. Getting in line with Earth's gravity was no easy task.

"Don't tip me! Hold lightly. That's all you have to do." I wanted to look for the squirrel-gobbling gator but was afraid to take my eyes off the panicked woman gripping the gunwale.

LuAnn pulled down on the side of the boat again. Water rushed in, and the thought spurted through my mind that LuAnn Sheetz was purposely trying to dump me out of my boat. I pitched to the opposite side, inhaled mightily, brought up my paddle intent on slamming her on the head. Abby! Keep your senses. LuAnn's panicked. Don't be a brute. I exhaled a gasp.

"Take it easy," I said, trying to calm the tremor in my voice. "I'll help you."

LuAnn came up out of the water as if doing a chin-up on the side of my kayak. She bared her teeth and hissed. That hiss pierced my skin, squirmed through my body, and curled around my heart. I raised my paddle. Before I could bring it down, LuAnn sank below the surface and, still gripping my boat, shot back up as if on springs. She straightened her arms, my boat tipped ninety degrees, and water rushed in like a flash flood. I plummeted sideways, my cheek slapped the water, and I sank below the surface. Jerking like a mad woman, I twisted my torso, and came up loaded for bear. LuAnn had disappeared. An instinct more primal than any fear I'd felt before pulled my gaze across the black, shiny water to the opposite bank. Two bulging eyes poked up from beneath the spatterdock. A long, bumpy snout appeared and a second later the gator began a slow glide across the creek, its two eyes rolling like glass balls over the smooth surface.

CHAPTER THIRTY-SEVEN

"Goddammit!" I gagged on a mouthful of blackwater and reached for my capsized boat which had not yet drifted away. I grasped my leashed paddle, and clumsily slapped one end on the water. The slap, softer than a bird's chirp, did not impress Ally Gator, who slid steadily along,

Keeping my eyes on the creature, I pulled the boat in front of me, unexpectedly tugging along LuAnn, who gripped the cockpit underwater. At the sight of her, my brain pulsed with a barrage of expressions, most of them profane, and instincts, most of them violent. I fought a nearly uncontrollable urge to hold her head underwater. But I couldn't waste energy on rage against this witless human. I had to keep the boat between me and the gator. Which was only a half-decent plan, since the beast could easily dive underwater and come up beneath me. Still, with no other options, I positioned myself behind the boat, keeping one eye on LuAnn, the other on the sharp-toothed creature slithering toward us. Which one was more dangerous?

"What are we going to do?" she whimpered.

I fixed her with a loathsome scowl. Since the gator didn't appear to fear my boat as a predator, I soon might be swimming in that great blackwater creek in the sky. If I was lucky, he'd grab LuAnn first and be satisfied.

"Keep the boat in front of us and don't thrash around," I growled. That's all I could think of. Those tactics were, in fact, useless because, when I looked again, I didn't see the beast. Did it dive down? Instinctively— and pointlessly—I pulled up my legs. My heartbeat kicked up to allegro, and my breathing slipped into a chilling imitation of a squeaky piccolo.

"Shit!"

"What?" LuAnn stared at me wide-eyed.

"Where's the gator?"

LuAnn's head jerked side to side. She began pushing and pulling the boat, making ripples on the water.

"Stay still!" I hissed.

The swamp forest was soundless. I didn't hear a bird twitter or a turtle plop. The breeze had calmed, and a heavy stillness pressed down like wet canvas. I looked across the top of the boat toward the tree-crowded creek side. I looked behind me. The sun threw spots of bright light through the trees onto the water. It was into one of these bright spots that the gator's eyes popped up. I clamped my teeth onto my tongue to keep from screaming. The reptile had surfaced about twenty yards away. On our side of the boat.

LuAnn shrieked, thrust the boat from her, and began thrashing toward the stand of bald cypress a good fifty feet away. The force of her push caused my hand to slip off the boat. As I lunged to grab it back, I lost my hold on my paddle, and, leashed as it was to the boat, it floated out of reach.

"Idiot!" I was left treading water in the middle of the creek, alone, heart crashing against my ribs.

LuAnn's shrieking and thrashing appeared to give the gator pause. It floated in place, not moving toward or away from me. Now what? Swim to the boat? Swim to the cypress? The breeze picked up, rustling tree leaves, and moving bright sun spots around on the water like a spotlight seeking an actor on stage. For a moment I lost track of the gator and held my breath until I located it again, eyes and snout pointed in my direction.

I hadn't pulled the cord on my inflatable vest. The PFD was still fanny pack-size around my waist as I treaded water. My boat had nosed into the spatterdock on the near side of the creek and wallowed there like a tipped cow. Where was LuAnn? Had she scampered up a tupelo? Was she grinning down at me? Mission complete. For I was convinced, LuAnn Sheetz had deliberately dumped me out of my kayak. Intent on drowning me. Now, she'd have the added entertainment of seeing me pulled underwater by an alligator. Tomorrow's lunch.

But why? Why would LuAnn try to eliminate me? My attitude toward her had been passable. Not buddy-buddy, cozy-cozy, but decent. I'd bounced between irritation and sympathy, depending on what shot out of her mouth. I'd done nothing to hurt her. So why this bizarre display of violent intent? Did Hannah reveal that I suspected her of giving the nest dates to Marc Diamond? If I wasn't, at this very moment, in a stare-down with a big jawed, sharp-toothed crocodilian, I'd ask her.

The water rippled and my heart became a kettle drum. Boom! Boom! Boom! The gator moved toward me. And then it dove.

Every nerve, every muscle, every instinct jerked into action. I swam wildly in the direction that made most sense to me at the moment—to my boat. There might be another gator hiding in the spatterdock, or a family of water snakes eager to wriggle over me, but that was only speculation. The gator I faced in the middle of the creek was real and every primal directive I possessed said *get away from it.*

My first challenge was to flip the boat right side up, which I should have done as soon as I fell out. Thankfully this was the easiest part of a self-rescue. I pushed the kayak out of the spatterdock, gripped the gunwale, and brought my arm up strong and fast. The boat landed on its bottom with a loud splat. Now came the hard part.

I got behind the stern and fumbled for the deck lines, cracking my knuckles on the hard surface. My arms trembled and my hands, missing the lines, slipped into the water. I reached again and my fingers finally hooked the tight, black strings. Somewhere in my deepest consciousness I heard Tanner's voice. "Now relax." *Relax?* My brain screamed at this ridiculous instruction.

I issued my own order. Get in the goddam boat!

I glanced around for the alligator. Didn't see it. I took a deep breath and, as I expelled it, pushed the stern down. I tried to get my chest up onto the boat but my PFD was in the way and I slipped off. I pushed down again, harder, deeper, and this time got my chest into position. My legs dangled in the water, and I let them float up behind me. *Calm down. Breathe.* Tanner again. I swallowed around a lump that, stupidly, formed in my throat. No time to cry, Abigail. Hold it together. Get in the boat. Move!

I clenched my teeth. Bucking and pulling, the skin on my thighs stretching painfully, I tried to drag myself forward but my PFD caught on the back of my seat, just as it had during practice. Should I turn it around to the back, or—

I struggled to balance while wiggling one hand down to my waist and felt my right thigh start to cramp. The boat tipped side to side and I started to slide but let my legs hang over the sides—much as that distressed me—to maintain balance. More wiggling, more straining, finally I unhooked the belt pack and, with much cursing, pushed it out from under me into the water. I was still atop the boat. Miracles do happen.

Okay, Abby, get your ass in the seat. I reached across the cockpit and pulled forward, keeping my head down, trying to balance my body, the boat—trying to keep Earth's gravity in mind— until my chest hung over the opening. I was halfway there and let out a sob. Idiot! Why hadn't I practiced this maneuver every single day? Please, Universe! Are you listening? I need to get in my boat. Make it happen. Enough. Pay attention. My chest was over the cockpit, but it was too early to pull my legs up. Exhausted, I gasped for breath. Forced myself not to look for the gator, which might be close enough to nibble my toes.

After two deep breaths, I wriggled forward, inch by painful inch, until my pelvis was over the cockpit. Almost there. One more deep breath.

Please, please, please, please, please.

Holding onto the bow, I simultaneously sat up, lifted both legs, and dropped my butt into the wide opening. Steadied the boat. Scooted back. Steadied the boat. Brought in one leg. Steadied the boat. Brought in the second leg. Steadied the boat.

I was in. *Voi*-freakin'-*la*.

CHAPTER THIRTY-EIGHT

Before I could take a breath, congratulate myself, and thank Tanner Banks, planet Earth, and Mother Universe for their patience and instruction, I felt a bump-bump-bump-bump, almost as if I'd slid the boat down a dry, rocky streambed. I looked to my left. The gator surfaced, opened its mouth wide, and snapped up my brand new PFD. The beast had swum directly beneath me. The show over, the gator moseyed up Raven Creek, probably glad to be done with me.

I don't know how many minutes I stared at the bottom of my boat, breathing quietly, marveling at my miraculous self-rescue, and wondering, reluctantly, what had happened to LuAnn. LuAnn? It didn't take more than two seconds to decide I didn't give a rat's ass where LuAnn Sheetz was. I pulled up my paddle—thank you, leash—and stroked to the middle of the creek. I was heading back to the launch. Crazy LuAnn could figure out her next move. After her vicious attack, to say nothing of her stupidity, I felt no obligation to assist her.

An eerie squeal broke through the swamp's stillness. And there was LuAnn, balanced on a tiny hummock of mud and leaves, her overturned boat lodged in a nest of cypress knees ten feet away. It looked like she could have hopped from tree to tree to reach it, but she remained rooted to her hummock.

"Sorry to disappoint you," I said just loud enough for her to hear.

She didn't respond but stared at some point behind me. I back-paddled five strokes and my heart shot clear into my brain, or so it felt, when I bumped into something. Whipping my head around, I was relieved to see it was another kayaker. Tack Stanley wore a red bandana. He looked at LuAnn perched on the hummock.

"Lose your boat, darlin'?" His gaze drifted over the stand of cypress knees. "Y'all fall in?" The sun blinked off his eyes like off a lighthouse signal lamp.

I couldn't keep the disgust out of my voice. "She *jumped* out of her boat. Then she *dumped* me out of mine." I glared at LuAnn, daring her to deny it. My suspicion that she'd given Marc Diamond the turtle nesting dates and might even be the poacher stoked my fury. Maybe she and Marc knew I'd snooped around his garage lab and found those dates. Diamond might have security cameras on his property and especially inside his, probably illegal, home lab. I hadn't given a thought to cameras when I broke in. If they were involved in a high-stakes poaching scheme and knew I was on to them, was it absurd to believe LuAnn tried to silence me? Permanently?

"A snake fell out of a tree!" LuAnn exclaimed. "Right on me!" She pointed at her boat. "Is it still in there?"

A snake? Tack paddled over to LuAnn's boat and flipped it over.

"If a snake fell in there, wouldn't it swim out when the boat capsized?" I asked sarcastically. "I'm pretty sure cottonmouths swim underwater." No one answered me. Stanley leaned over the side of the boat and jerk back quickly. He broke a branch off a low hanging tree and poked around until it appeared he'd secured something. Then quick as a lick he reached down with his other arm, lifted out a long, black rope, and flung it across the creek. The snake flew through the air like the loop on a lariat until it smacked down on the water. I watched it wriggle away, probably wondering what the hell had happened.

"Okeydokey." Tack clapped his hands at a job well done. He maneuvered LuAnn's boat near her hummock. "Hop in." He steadied the craft and LuAnn climbed aboard. She sat motionless, wet, slimy, buzzed hair slick with creek scum, until Tack found her paddle wedged in a clutch of scrub. It must have slipped out from under my bungees when my boat capsized. LuAnn yanked the paddle from his hand and, without a "Thank you" or even a "Kiss my hairy butt" set off in the direction of the boat launch.

Good riddance.

Letting her get several yards head start, I drifted and eyed this man who'd appeared out of nowhere. "I saw a flash of red a couple times while we were going up the creek. That was you." I nodded at his bandanna. "You're Tack Stanley. My friend Tanner Banks knows you from the Parrot."

"Yeah, that's me." He laughed. "Sure, I know ol' Tanner. The cornhole king."

"I saw you at the Parrot and once or twice at a turtle nest. You work at the port with the husband of one of our volunteers."

Grin slightly faded, he skipped a couple beats before saying, "Yeah, Ol' Jase. Jason Stone." He ran his fingers through the water. "I get out in my boat when I can." He waved his hand toward some trees already speckled with autumn orange. "Pretty out here."

I wondered how close he'd been when Mr. Gator challenged my presence in his creek. "We both fell in the water. You hear us yelling?"

He shook his head. Stroked the water lazily. "Maybe the wind was blowing the other way." He drank from his water bottle. "Heard a couple shrieks. Thought it was birds." Stanley said he saw us first as he rounded the bend. "Saw you climb into your boat. That's not easy."

I paddled gently to keep my boat in place. Two flashes of red. He might deny it, but I was sure he'd been behind us. And he hadn't heard us shouting and flogging about in the water? Didn't see us till he rounded the bend? Bullshit.

Stanley paddle closer and grasped the side of my kayak, making me catch my breath. "You say she dumped you out?"

A wave of nausea roiled through me, as I recalled LuAnn's hiss and the cold gleam in her eyes. Her clench-teethed grin. Her death grip on my gunwale. I fought the urge to pry his fingers off my boat.

"She tipped you?" he asked again.

"Seemed that way. When it happened."

"I can get her being scared. Panicked. There was a snake in her boat," he offered. "Just like she said. Hell, I'd be—"

I pushed off and watched Stanley's fingers slip off the side. "I'm going back."

"Sure 'nough. Me, too."

With Stanley paddling beside me, I went through another roller-coaster of emotions concerning LuAnn Sheetz. Okay, she panicked. I most likely would have done the same thing. Maybe. Part of me—the small part that considered ignoring her bared-teeth sneer, her murderous hiss—wanted to cut LuAnn some slack. She'd been under stress all summer with Randy missing. For Pete's sake, her mother had died just yesterday and was probably getting turned to ash at this very moment. With a surge of guilt, I regretted intending to club LuAnn with the paddle. Felt bad about bashing her knuckles with my fist. My anger toward LuAnn subsided somewhat. My suspicion of her did not.

And I wasn't one hundred percent comfortable with Ol' Tack. The way sound traveled over water, I found it difficult—near impossible—to believe he'd been out of hearing range. Especially since, as soon as the drama ended, he was within bumping distance. If he'd shown up a few minutes earlier, he could have frightened the alligator away. I relived how my heart hammered when the creature dove underwater. What if I hadn't gotten back in my boat? I might be dead right now.

I'd taken a big risk swimming for my boat, but it would have been riskier floating in the middle of the creek, unprotected, and hoping the gator would swim away. Maybe risk wasn't involved at all. Only choice. And luck.

The boat launch came into view. LuAnn's kayak touched shore and she struggled out, favoring one arm. I wanted her to cram her kayak into the back of her Jeep and take off, but she stood on the pebbled beach, cradling her right hand. I slid to shore and felt the bottom of my boat scrape across a carpet of stones. Shit! If I had better control of my emotions and not been thinking about keeping LuAnn at arm's length, I would have spotted a smoother place to land. I hopped out, floated my boat to a sandy patch, and pulled it out of the water. Stanley's boat slid beside mine. LuAnn's feet pounded the ground as she stalked toward us.

"What the hell!" she shouted. "You almost broke my hand." She thrust out a set of swollen, purple knuckles.

Tack made quieting motions. "You scared Abby."

I turned toward him quickly. He knew my name.

"Scared *her*? I had a goddamn snake in my boat."

"And you didn't have your lifejacket on," I shouted back, enraged by this second, now verbal, attack. "If you did you wouldn't have acted like an idiot in the water." Maybe. "You wouldn't have thrashed around and attracted that alligator!" Maybe. "And why the hell did you dump me overboard, then push my boat away?"

We'd been in a life or death dilemma on Raven Creek. The crisis had sickened my system, but I couldn't decide if the cause was nausea or rage. Fear or fury. Did PTSD set in so quickly?

"I had to get out of the water!" LuAnn screamed. "That goddam gator was waiting for me!"

"For you!" Who knows if the gator would have taken interest if she hadn't raised a ruckus? Maybe it would have ignored us. Maybe not.

LuAnn dragged her boat one-handed across the rocky beach, oblivious to the damage being done to its underside. The sympathy I'd let sneak in earlier dissolved. I didn't buy her act that she was only trying to save herself.

The look in her eye had said something different. Just as it did now.

Tack pulled a cigarette out of his shirt pocket. "And I thought I'd just be out enjoying a peaceful time on the water."

I broke down my paddle and looked around for my PFD, remembering with an icy shiver that it had gone down a gator's belly. My body started to react big time. Now that my arms weren't busy paddling a boat, they shook from shoulders to fingertips. My legs felt like jelly. Yet, strangely, the gator seemed less dangerous than my companions. I watched Stanley puff the last smidge of tar out of his cigarette, my suspicion increasing that he hadn't been paddling Raven Creek by coincidence. And it wasn't chance that LuAnn and I had paddled Raven Creek. No, today LuAnn had chosen Raven Creek.

I dropped my gear in the trunk and drove the car close to shore, but instead of loading the boat, I sat a minute. When Jason Stone's name had been mentioned, Stanley's grin slipped and he changed the subject. Were they still at odds after the argument I'd witnessed at the Sloppy Parrot?

I watched LuAnn leaning against her Jeep and pictured Marc Diamond's list of nesting and hatching dates. Marc was LuAnn's childhood friend, and I suspected, as much as Hannah refused to entertain the idea, that he'd gotten the lists from her, a long-time sea turtle volunteer who should have known better. For whatever reason, money most likely, LuAnn had poached Goose Inlet's eggs and given them to Marc, who was doing something to them in his lab. Packing them for distribution or shipment? LuAnn could do that herself.

She also could sell them herself to people who craved a turtle egg omelet or needed a boost in bed. A black market operation. She didn't need Marc. But he had the lists, and I was convinced they were in cahoots.

I peered through the car window at Stanley removing gear from his boat. The shipping port, like the airport, was a hot spot for smuggling. Had Stanley and Stone argued about smuggling sea turtle eggs? Since LuAnn had accused Alegria, Stone's wife, of poaching, it was ludicrous to consider them a team.

My phone dinged. Wade Ramsey: *Forgot to tell you. One day I heard Dr. Diamond tell his lunch buddy he caught Dr. Finn looking at websites on his computer.*

I texted back: *On whose computer? Aidan's or Marc's?*

Wade: *Dr. Diamond's*

So Aidan was checking out Marc's computer and London was checking out Aidan's. Spies all around.

"Hey!" Stanley stood calf deep in water behind my boat, waving to get my attention. "I'll take the stern."

I grabbed the bow, and we hoisted the boat onto the roof. "Thanks," I said, opening the trunk to retrieve my tie-downs.

"Before you jokers take off, someone has to load my boat," LuAnn said, tossing Stanley her car key. She stood sour-faced while he loaded the kayak then dumped her bag and useless lifejacket in the back seat. Like the snake, her filthy PFD had managed to stay in the boat.

"Can you drive?" he asked, gesturing toward LuAnn's swollen hand. Her head jerk must have meant yes, because she got in her car and sped away, the Jeep's tires shooting stones through a dusty fog.

Stanley packed his boat into the back of a big black SUV. He climbed into the front seat and stuck his head out of the window. "Nice job out-swimming that gator."

My heart hit my rib cage, reminding me that I was alive. I made final tugs on the straps securing my boat. My arms began to tremble again, and I slid my hand along the car to the driver's side. Stanley cranked the ignition but appeared to be waiting for me. Was it him, the gator, or LuAnn that knocked me the most off balance?

Nice job out-swimming that gator. It had been a snap decision to strike out for my boat. Big risks need to be analyzed before they're taken. But I hadn't done that. I'd blasted off like the Olympic swimmer I wasn't. Yet what was the alternative? To float in the middle of the creek with an alligator churning the water below me?

I headed down the dirt road, pondering Wade's texts. Stanley followed me to the highway, across the bridge, and stayed on my tail until he took the turnoff for the port.

My first visit to primordial Raven Creek had been a mixed bag of joy, confusion and terror. I'd ended up in a heavenly oasis with a mysterious man and a dangerous woman. Perhaps more dangerous than the reptile I'd outmaneuvered. I'd harbored reservations about LuAnn Sheetz. At the moment, not even the snake in her boat overrode my misgivings.

CHAPTER THIRTY-NINE

My sentiments did not quiet during the ride home. LuAnn's glare, bared teeth, and that *hiss* relayed through my head all the way to Goose Inlet. I pulled into Lily Pad's driveway, charged into the cottage, and poured three fingers of Jack Daniels. Then I stood, filthy and stinking, beside the blue cotton sofa, and analyzed the ordeal one more time. LuAnn would try to hurt me, even kill me, only if she considered me her enemy. I suspected her of colluding with Marc, maybe even poaching the nests herself. But I hadn't accused her to her face. The only time I'd mentioned Marc, she'd paddled recklessly across the path of a monster container ship. To get away from me, she'd put herself in danger. Today was different. LuAnn had used the snake as an excuse to grab my boat and dump me out.

Should I drive to the Inlet PD and charge LuAnn Sheetz with attempted murder? With only a snake and a gator as witnesses, Detective Magnus would laugh me out of his office. Inscrutable Tack Stanley would claim not to have seen a thing.

I polished off the whiskey, peeled off my putrid clothes, and took a hotter than hell shower. Vigorous scrubbing scoured blackwater muck from my skin, but three shampoos could not cleanse my head of confusion. Finally, I got on my bike and pedaled to Hannah's. I found her pulling pesky pennyweed in her front garden. In rushed, jagged phrases I told her what had happened on Raven Creek. The dump out. The gator. My shockingly successful self-rescue.

Hannah wrapped me in a strong hug. "Abby, how awful. I'm so glad you're safe."

"Me, too." I wiggled out of her grasp. "So what should I do about LuAnn? Tell Detective Magnus?"

Hannah looked at me sadly. "I don't think LuAnn did it on purpose. There was a snake in her boat."

"I know! But you didn't see her eyes or hear the hiss that shot out of her mouth when she tipped me over."

LuAnn had seemed casual about the two reptiles sunning themselves atop the spatterdock. Casual, too, about the alligator crossing Raven Creek. Of course, she'd been sheltered inside her kayak and not spilled suddenly into blackwater. Incorrect. LuAnn hadn't been spilled. She'd catapulted out of her boat. Still, I had to admit a snake snoozing ten feet away was not as alarming as one writhing in your lap. But I was still furious.

"You think she used the snake as an excuse to hurt you?"

"Absolutely. She might even have brought the damn thing with her!"

Hannah grimaced. "For what reason?"

"She gave Marc Diamond the Inlet's nesting dates and either she or he stole our eggs. And she knows I know." I wasn't positive of that, but what else could turn her vicious?

"You *think* you know." Hannah knelt down and slung her rake into the dirt, lifting up a white mesh of thin roots. "You're slandering a faithful turtle volunteer and I don't like it."

"Hannah! I had to outmuscle a freakin' alligator! And you're saying I insulted poor, sweet LuAnn."

She leaned back on her heels and rubbed her forehead. "I don't—you must have been scared—"

"Shitless."

She pulled off her gardening gloves. "You had a frightening experience, but it's over. No need to be overly dramatic."

"Dramatic? If Tanner hadn't insisted I learn how to get back in my kayak, I'd be *dead* right now." It was pure terror-charged luck that I'd maneuvered my quivering frame across the boat and sunk my ass into the cockpit. Pure luck the gator had snacked on squirrel and maybe wasn't hungry enough to pursue a floundering human who must have been spraying fear pheromones like teargas at a riot.

Hannah stood up, slapping sand from her shorts. "Then call the cops. Tell Erik that LuAnn Sheetz tried to kill you." Her tight voice oozed an annoying amount of incredulity.

I glared at her a good five seconds before flopping down on the porch's bottom step. I was fighting with my best friend. But a best friend should be supportive and I wasn't getting that. Hannah was putting her faith in her turtle volunteer instead of me. We'd known each other half our lives.

"Big help the detective would be," I said. "He hasn't solved a crime all summer. Randy's body hasn't been found. London's killer is still on the loose."

"The killer must not have left any clues." Hannah said.

"So damn frustrating." The three fingers of whiskey had done nothing to settle my nerves or improve my mood.

"Sarcasm?" Hannah waved her rake at me. "Shame on you, Abby."

"Yeah, shame on me. And shame on you. You don't care that LuAnn threw me for gator bait." I stomped to my bike and peddled like an Olympic cyclist back to Lily Pad.

Once again I charged into the house but this time pulled the tray of apricot slush out of the freezer and filled a large tumbler. I was working on a Big Headache. When I turned around Hannah stood in the kitchen.

"You don't like Erik, do you?" she asked.

I scraped the slush—a concoction of tea, orange juice and flavored brandy—into a second glass. "I have nothing against Erik. Right now I'm concentrating all my whacky meanness on LuAnn Sheetz." My comment about the detective was meant to get back at Hannah for defending LuAnn. Childish and whiskey induced.

Hannah sipped her drink. "I wish he'd find out who owned the body parts buried under the nests. It's been a month."

"DNA testing takes a lot longer in real life than it does on TV."

A twinkle sparkled in Hannah's eye. "And anyway, how much evidence could he get from three toes and a tattoo?"

I tried not to smile. As my mother used to say, mutilation was no laughing matter.

"Friends again?" Hannah asked.

"Friends always, my dear." Nothing to gain by browbeating Hannah into agreeing with me about Ms. Sheetz. I knew what had happened on Raven Creek and that's all I needed.

***

We were on our second glass of slush, and while my heartbeat had slowed, my mind was a tempest. Did LuAnn try to kill me? Was she the poacher? Who killed London James? Did I like or dislike Detective Magnus and did it matter? Did LuAnn try to kill me? Why was Aidan's computer confiscated? Why did Stone lie? Was the Tillson explosion an accident? Did LuAnn try to kill me? Would Randy Boone's body be found? Since the gator ate my PFD, could I replace it at an Explore Outdoors end-of-year sale? Did LuAnn try to kill me?

I tried to block Raven Creek from my thoughts, but the link between LuAnn and Marc Diamond persisted. What was Marc doing in his private lab that involved sea turtle eggs? Aidan never told me which chemicals he thought Marc had pilfered. I'd looked at those bottles and drawn a blank. But Aidan would have known. Marc had been angry with Aidan for coming to his private lab. And he'd been angry with me.

CHAPTER FORTY

Late that afternoon, I sat on Lily Pad's porch watching the sun shine through the rain. It was a phenomenon I liked to pretend happened only on the coast. I rearranged pillows on the wicker chaise and stretched out, contemplating a day that had begun in joyful brilliance but had taken a frightfully dark turn.

"Hey, Abby." Erik Magnus stood by the porch in baggy swim trunks, surfboard tucked under an arm. A thin, T-shirt stuck to his chest. His black hair, usually tamed in a short ponytail, hung in wet ringlets.

I sat up, better to see over the railing. "An old beach bum told me dinnertime wasn't a good time to play in the water. Sharks like to eat then, too."

"Was that old beach bum my Uncle Dutch? If so, it's one of the few truths that ever came out of his mouth."

"But you're ignoring it." I looked up at the sky. "I guess you didn't notice the rain either." It had been drizzling for a good half hour.

"It's only water." Magnus shook his head and droplets flew off his hair like from a salad spinner. "Why do people race out of the ocean when it starts raining?"

"Might have something to do with lightning. Have time for a beer?" Anticipating the affirmative, I headed inside.

"Always have time for a beer," he confirmed as the porch door slammed. I returned with two Bass ales. "Did you see lightning?" he asked, dropping into a chair.

I mouthed, "No."

We took a couple swallows before Erik asked how I'd spent my day. "I'm not being nosy, just making conversation." When I didn't answer right away, he added, "Peaceful, I hope."

I took another sip. "Today I paddled Raven Creek. LuAnn Sheetz dumped me out of my boat. On purpose."

He grinned. "What'd you do to make her mad?"

I gazed at him steadily. "Nothing."

He rubbed his chin, which boasted just the right amount of stubble. It took a good ten seconds for him to ask, "Why do you think she did that, Abby?"

I pressed the cool bottle to my temple. A steady tick there had annoyed me since my chat with Hannah. "The look in her eye." I described LuAnn's frantic thrashing, chinning up and tipping the boat, chucking me out. The alligator gliding toward me, diving underwater. My fear-charged clamber onto the back of my kayak. My lucky—lucky-lucky—self-rescue. And finally, Tack Stanley's sudden appearance on the creek. At the mention of Stanley's name, a slight furrow dug between Erik's brows.

"Do you know him?" I asked.

"I've seen him around."

I scooted to the edge of my chair. "I have this creepy feeling he was following us."

Magnus screwed up his mouth. "LuAnn tried to drown you. Stanley stalked you."

"Paranoid?"

He shrugged and offered, "Coincidence?"

Someone smart or clever or witty had once said there was no such thing as coincidence.

"I have this notion—Hannah hates it—that LuAnn Sheetz poached our turtle eggs." The detective's eyes flickered with what I hoped was interest. "I don't have proof, just things, circumstances, sort of point to her. Well, not *point*, but include her somehow."

Do I admit a B&E to a cop? I dashed inside the house and came out with a bag of Cheetos, the crunchy kind, and two more ales.

"Why do you think LuAnn's the poacher?" the detective asked.

"She needs money." I ripped open the bag. "Or needed it before her mother died. Maybe still needs it for hospital and nursing home bills. I tested my theory on Hannah, but she thinks LuAnn's a saint." I passed him the bag.

Erik reached in and came out with a paw full of twisted orange sticks. "Did you accuse LuAnn to her face?"

"No!" I munched a Cheeto. "I saw a list of dates on a bulletin board in Marc Diamond's garage. He has a home laboratory set up there. The dates marked when nests were laid and hatched in Goose Inlet." I waited for the detective to ask why I was in Diamond's garage.

Magnus stopped with his beer halfway to his mouth and stared at me. I noticed his eyes were a deep green. A rich avocado that bottled up all of nature's verdant pigment.

"Marc was my husband's lab partner. Do you know him?"

269

Erik's large body shifted. "Knew him as a kid. Haven't seen him in decades."

"Well, Marc and LuAnn knew each other, too, as kids, and kept in touch. She admitted it to me. I think they're our turtle egg poachers. I think LuAnn gave Marc the nesting and hatch dates. And he's doing something funky in his trashy garage lab."

We sat silently for about a minute. "You saw the dates, and that's why you think LuAnn dumped you out? Tried to kill you?"

Those words "tried to kill you" stabbed like a knife. *Dumped you out* was mild. *Kill you* was a whole 'nother ball game.

"Maybe Marc had a security camera and caught me on video—"

"So you were in there illegally?" The detective's body stiffened.

I waggled my hands, screwed up my face, and decided to push on. "Maybe he told LuAnn. That's a pretty good incentive for her to say I fell out of my kayak into Raven Creek and an alligator swallowed me up." I could hear Marc issuing the order: *LuAnn, Aidan's wife's on to us. Snuff out Abby Finn.* Was I right or did I watch too many crime shows?

I took a slow breath. "Hannah said I overreacted. Do you?"

Without taking his eyes off me, Erik brushed orange dust off his hands, then leaned his forearms on his thighs. "I can't say, Abby. I wasn't there. You shouldn't have been either." He leaned back and drained his beer. "But I'll keep what happened to you in mind."

I smiled gratefully. It was more interest than I'd gotten from Hannah. I asked if he had leads on London's killer. He was working on it, couldn't talk about it. I asked if he thought there was a connection between the poaching, the toes and the tattoo.

Magnus linked his hands behind his head. "It would be a freaky coincidence if there wasn't." There it was again—coincidence.

I said it sounded to me like a warning, but who would, or could, leave them beneath the nests except the poacher. And who was the poacher warning and why? I followed Eric's gaze to a line of pelicans coursing the sky. "Do you have any leads at all?"

He winked. "Working on it." He seemed deep in thought and after a pause, pointed his beer bottle at me. "Are you sure you didn't accuse LuAnn of poaching the turtle eggs?"

"Of course I'm sure! Never said a word to her. I only suggested it to Hannah, strongly, and now to you."

"How did you end up on Raven Creek with her in the first place? I thought you paddled with Tanner Banks." His tone deepened with the last sentence. Erik brought the Cheetos bag to his mouth and began blowing it up, like a kid who intended to pop it.

I sat back on the chaise and told about seeing LuAnn bawling her eyes out on the beach right after her mother died. "In the middle of sobbing, she blurts that she 'did it all for nothing'. All she did to help her mother was for nothing because she died. I tried to comfort her. Told her I knew what she did. Working extra hours, the doctor appointments, monitoring her meds. She shouldn't feel guilty. She did all she could. LuAnn looked at me strangely—"

"How strangely?"

I paused. "Deeply. Intently. But she looked strange all over. Her face was tomato red and bloated from crying. She'd even wacked off her hair." LuAnn's mottled complexion was still fresh in my mind. "Said she wanted to be on the water. I got that. It's peaceful. Restorative. So I offered to go with her. She picked Raven Creek. I'd never been, so I was all for it. We paddled, ate lunch, then suddenly—drama! Who shows up? A snake and a gator."

Erik popped the snack bag. Orange crumbs shot through the air and floated to the floor. "You told her *you knew what she did?*"

I began to nod, but sucked in a deep breath and felt my eyes widen. Holy moly. I'd said her actions weren't in vain because she made her mother's last few months bearable. But maybe LuAnn heard something different.

"I meant that she took good care of her mom. Helped with prescription costs. Moved her to a good nursing home after her stroke." I covered my mouth with my hand. "Honestly, that's what I meant. Did she think I *knew* she was the poacher?" I did suspect LuAnn, but would not have consciously accused her to her face.

Magnus stared at Cheetos debris on the porch floor and at the tiny birds pecking at the crumbs. Then in an action I was beginning to think of as familiar, he stared across the dune at the ocean. "So, you're trying to be nice, and LuAnn purposely dumps you out of your boat." He stood quickly, jogged down the steps, and picked up his surfboard.

"Are you going to be the first person to take me seriously?"

Before he could answer, I thrust both hands in my hair and raked my scalp. "Well, shoot, why believe me? I only have accusations. No real proof." I knew the look in LuAnn eyes had been menacing. But—dammit—there was no denying the snake.

Erik rested one foot on the bottom step. "You think she had blood in her eye?"

"When I see her bared teeth and hear that hiss, yes." I collected the empty bottles. "But I waver."

There had been a snake.

CHAPTER FORTY-ONE

I rolled around in my bed all night either condemning or vindicating LuAnn Sheetz. At midnight she was a puzzle whose pieces needed sorting. By six a.m., she was an assassin who'd tried to terminate me. When I put her alongside Marc Diamond, a man suspected of chemical theft and in possession of lists he had no reason to own, there was no way I was going to "let it go," as Hannah insisted. At seven a.m., I pulled on an old pair of capris and an even older T-shirt, stuffed my bag with a flashlight, notebook, pens, phone, and a bottle of water, jumped in my car and headed for the Triangle.

A half-hour into the trip, my inner angel tried to shame me over breaking the law again. I ignored her, pointing out that Detective Magnus hadn't made a stink about it. Then she claimed luck had been on my side with the first B&E. What if this time Audra Diamond needed something in the garage? Or Marc took a personal day, or had been suspended, and popped into the garage while I was inside snooping? My hands slipped on the steering wheel, reminding me of my fumbling fingers grasping for my boat's deck lines. I'd been terrified of an alligator. How dangerous was Marc Diamond? I wiped first my left hand, then the right, on my pants. The car radio became just noise, so I switched it off. My foot slipped off the accelerator. Get a grip! You are no longer timid Abby Finn. Yesterday you took a big risk and won. So, inner angel—worry wart—shut the hell up. I turned the car radio back on, way past my comfort level, and let the noise push away my misgivings.

***

I waited halfway up the street, until—hallelujah—Marc left for work. Audra put the kids on the bus and strapped her youngest into his car seat for the first of what would likely be many sorties into Triangle traffic. My worrying angel silenced, I let a credit card do its duty on the side door lock. I was thrilled at the ease of entry but gave Marc a huge demerit under the heading "Parents, Children & Safety." Inside Diamond's lab cave, flashlight in hand, I scanned the ceiling, corners and behind furniture and cabinets for security cameras. Finding none, I began searching for his briefcase, hoping this wouldn't be the day he took it to work.

I beamed the light across the desk. No briefcase. No laptop. No loose papers or printouts. No notebook, such as every chemist kept to track experiments, lay open. Or closed. I searched the drawers, even the tiny ones. I scanned the flashlight across the shelves of chemicals and dug out my notebook and pen. Lactic acid, I wrote. Barium sulfate. Potassium bisulfate. I carefully spelled each name, knowing there was a big difference between sulfates and sulfites. Sodium chloride. Soybean oil. That seemed like an odd fit with the rest of these bottles. Chitosan. I'd definitely look that one up.

I pulled out my phone and photographed Marc's lists of sea turtle nesting and hatching dates and then took a photo of the desk and bulletin board together. I wished there was an identifier to put in the picture. Like a mug that said I Love Marc. The coffee-stained cup on the desk said World's Best Chemist.

Continuing my search for the briefcase, I passed a tool bench where it appeared Marc had run chemical reactions. I noted the hot plate and scale. More bottles of chemicals. A glass beaker with connected tubing, a stopper in the top, and a small amount of residue in the bottom. A tool Aidan had called a spatula, but didn't look like a kitchen tool, lay alongside the beaker. It had a long handle, a small spoon on one end and a flat scraper-like piece of metal on the opposite end. I hadn't noticed a sink during my first visit, but saw one now cluttered with dirty glassware—and not the kind I'd drink from.

The refrigerator kicked on, making me jump. When I flashed my light on the handle, I saw it was fitted with a lock. Maybe he keeps really dangerous chemicals in there, away from his kids, who might try the easy credit card trick to enter dad's secret space. I glanced at the chemicals lining the wall shelves. If he's concerned, then why not secure all the chemicals? Bad, bad parenting. Might call DSS on my way out. I inspected the refrigerator lock. It wasn't a simple padlock to open with a key, and it wasn't a combination lock. It was an elaborate gizmo, a James Bond kind of thing. Must need a pin code or a fingerprint. Or maybe an eyeball scan. Now that's crazy, Abby. The refrigerator partially blocked an alcove that appeared to be a personal landfill, cluttered as it was with empty bottles, faded newspapers, sloppy paint cans, smelly fast food containers, collapsing boxes of moldy books, and even a twisted tricycle.

It was hot inside the garage and I began to sweat. Come on, Marc, where'd you hide the damn briefcase? I felt around the refrigerator and there, in back, crammed between it and the bench, I found a standard business case with two combination locks. Calling on luck, I set it on the bench and pressed the buttons. Luck didn't open it. If there was a key lock, I could jam a knife or screwdriver into the hole and pop it. I sucked in my lower lip and considered stealing the case. Breaking and entering to snoop was bad enough, taking someone's private property—especially when I had no idea what the case contained—was another. I decided to try picking the locks.

In old movies an expert safe-cracker would spit on his fingers, rub them together, hold his ear close to the lock, tell the other bad guys in the gang to shut the hell up, then deftly touch and listen until he opened the safe. I knew that wasn't going to work for me, so I brought up YouTube on my phone, typed in "how to open a briefcase without the combination" and, yahoo, a screen full of videos appeared. Most proposed that the lock could be opened by finding small black marks on the right side of certain numbers. Even in the video close-ups, I couldn't see the marks. I couldn't see them on Marc's briefcase locks either.

One video claimed the lock could be opened by starting at zero on the far right, rolling back to zero in that same space, then scrolling to "one" in the middle row to make "ten." From there, you rolled out eleven, twelve and on to twenty. Or something like that. I speculated this rolling could go on to nine hundred ninety-nine. And then you had to do the other side. I didn't have time to figure it out.

I rummaged in a drawer for something sharp. I'd just have to jam my way in. Or slam the locks with a hammer. Did I care if Marc knew his briefcase had been vandalized and the contents, if incriminating, compromised? Is banging the hell out of it less criminal than stealing it? Maybe I should just steal it. The longer I fumbled with the locks, the faster my heart beat, and the slicker my curiosity juices flowed.

Desperate, I poked around in the long desk drawer and—thank you, Universe!—found a magnifying glass. I held the glass above the combination numbers and scrolled one, two, three. Beside number five I saw a faint black mark. This could work. I set the number. In the middle spot I saw a black dot next to number eight. Let's go with that. I found a black mark by number two in the left slot, held my breath, slid the lock. Click! I felt like I'd swallowed half a bottle of champagne. I worked the same magic with the left lock. Click! I lifted the lid.

The briefcase was stuffed with papers depicting charts, graphs and tables. When I read the all-caps heading on top of the first chart, my toes curled. SEA TURTLE EGGS. I shuffled through the pages. The same heading appeared on each one. On the first page, below the title, was the subhead: Coating eggs with chitosan minimizes shell tearing and improves quality of eggs. Below the subhead was an experiment abstract.

My breath escaped in a raw hiss, which to my annoyance bore a striking resemblance to LuAnn's vocalization on Raven Creek. I recognized the fury. I walked to the table near the door and peered into the recycling box that had fallen to the floor on my first visit. Cardboard egg cartons. At least four dozen. My fists clenched. I returned to the briefcase and reread SEA TURTLE EGGS at the top of the first page. And stared at the locked refrigerator.

My skin prickled like a bad sunburn. I pulled my phone out of my bag and photographed each page in the briefcase, playing back each shot to make sure it was readable. I photographed the bottles of chemicals individually and as a group, making sure the ones of chitosan, lactic acid and soybean oil were crystal clear. I captured the stacks of cardboard egg cartons. Lastly, I photographed the refrigerator and a close-up of the state-of-the-art lock.

"I got you, Marc Diamond. Turtle egg poacher."

A car door slammed. I shut the briefcase and stuffed it back between the refrigerator and bench. Footsteps approached the garage. Damn! And my B&E had been going so well. A key fit into the side door lock. I sucked in my stomach and squeezed past the refrigerator into the dark, cluttered alcove, feeling blindly for a wall. I positioned myself as far away from the alcove opening as I could get and turned my face into my shoulder. What the hell was I doing here? I held my breath as someone— could it be anyone other than Marc?—shuffled across the garage floor. After a series of beeps, the refrigerator door opened. Objects were moved about. What sounded like a paper bag was shaken open. In less than a minute the door closed and footsteps exited the garage.

Again, a car door slammed. I tiptoed to the side door and opened it a crack. Took a quick look, slipped out, walked behind the garage, turned the corner, and inched toward the front of the house. Overgrown azalea bushes formed an L-shaped fence between Diamond's property and his neighbor's and blocked my view of the driveway.

"How's the price of eggs in China?" I heard Marc ask.

"Better every day," came the reply.

Marc snorted. "I laughed when the boss insisted on a secret code, but I guess he was right. You're the guy."

"I'm the guy."

"Well, tell the boss I did it." I could hear the smile in Diamond's voice. "These are perfect."

"Good."

I couldn't make out the other quieter voice, except that it was male. I wanted to stick my nose outside the shrubbery, peek around the corner, but feared coming face to face with the bad guys.

"How many?" the man asked.

"Eight dozen," Diamond replied. I steeled my nerves, parted the branches, and poked my head forward just enough to peer around the corner. Marc held a large shopping bag, but blocked my view of the other man.

"They're not in a cooler?" The quiet voice registered surprise.

"Don't need one. That's the point. What the experiments were about," Marc said. "Finding something to coat the eggs so they survive transport at room temperature. These eggs are good for five to seven weeks. At five weeks, these babies will come off the boat as fresh as the day their mama laid them."

Goose bumps climbed my arms and waddled across my shoulders. Eyes on the men, I rummaged in my bag for my phone, hoping to stick it out far enough to video without being seen. Shoot, I didn't leave it in the garage, did I? Will the mic pick up their conversation this far away? Dammit, find the phone.

"I'll take them to the boss," the man said. There was a pause. "You sure they're good? You don't want to disappoint him."

"Disappoint him? Christ, what do you think I am? An undergrad?" Marc slapped his hand against something metal—the car hood?—and made me jump. "Just tell him I want the next payment. Got a nice vacation planned. I gave up a lot of family time for this project. My wife's on my ass. And not in a good way."

The men moved, and I jerked back. Footsteps traveled down the driveway. Spreading the bushes apart a bit farther this time, I had a good view of Marc's front property. I had to bite my tongue to keep from squealing. Carrying the bag and crossing the street to a blue pickup truck was Jason Stone.

Jason Stone, who worked at the port. The American with the Costa Rican wife just made all the nasty rumors come true. Those volunteers who gossiped about Alegria Villalobos poaching turtle eggs would be insufferable. I rubbed my temples. Had Aidan somehow fit into this scheme as London suggested? And what about LuAnn? At three a.m. today I'd convinced myself she was camouflaging her involvement in the poaching scheme by pointing fingers at Alegria and yammering about a "village of wolves." I'd been dead wrong.

The mayhem on Raven Creek flashed before me. The damn snake had fallen into LuAnn's boat. She'd panicked, and lost all thought of the danger we'd both be in if she dumped me into a gator's creek. I swallowed a groan. My sick stomach was beginning to be a common ailment. One thing was certain. I had caught the turtle egg poachers red handed. That creep Marc Diamond? Fine. But did he have to gang up with Alegria's husband?

I found my phone in my jacket pocket and, somewhat reluctantly, pointed it at Stone in his blue pickup and clicked.

The door to the Diamond house closed and the pickup's engine started almost simultaneously. Still concealed by large bushy shrubs, I watched Stone drive down the street. I was about to run to my car when a large, black SUV rolled past the house. I squinted, trying to make out the driver, and recognized Tack Stanley. His presence on Raven Creek I might accept as coincidence, but not his appearance at Marc's house. I'd been right. Stanley was suspicious of Stone's activities at the port, perhaps had accused him of misdeeds, which led to their argument at the Sloppy Parrot. His suspicion caused him to follow Stone today. Now he would report his coworker to port authorities for smuggling sea turtle eggs.

Jason Stone gave Marc those nest and hatch dates. Alegria probably shared the dates innocently, while telling her husband about her experiences on the beach. That's what I hoped. I shredded leaves off the shrub and let them sift through my fingers. I recalled Stone walking hand in hand with his daughter. Pilar loved baby sea turtles. So did Benito in his boy's way. Learning their father was a poacher and a smuggler would crush the children.

CHAPTER FORTY-TWO

"Well, you're right," I began the second Hannah collapsed into a chair on her front porch. Summer vacation was nearly over, and Hannah was in the last throes of preparation for the next Montessori school year. I handed her a full glass of wine.

She rubbed the back of her neck. "Today was orientation. We broke it up with games and music, so there was shouting and cheering and—you can imagine." Hannah rolled her head to loosen her muscles. "What am I right about?"

I smiled generously. "LuAnn is not the poacher."

"I never thought she was."

"Or she still could be. Maybe. But I'm not positive. Either way."

Hannah raised a hand to her forehead. "You're not helping my headache." She looked at me with half-lowered lids. "LuAnn isn't, but she might be, but you're not sure. You sound like one of my preschoolers." She held out a hand, inviting explanation.

"There's no doubt she knew Marc Diamond as a kid. But LuAnn didn't give Marc the list of nest dates."

Hannah kicked off her shoes, crossed one leg over the other, and rubbed her foot. "You're serious about Marc," she said. It was witness to her fatigue that she didn't ask who did give him the lists. I was relieved, in no hurry to bring down storm clouds on Alegria's family.

"Serious as a shark attack. I snuck back into his crappy lab and took pictures."

Hannah came to life. "You broke in *again*!"

I snatched my phone off the wicker table, pulled up the first photo, and handed her the device.

Hannah scrolled through a few pictures. "I can't read it. Too small."

I retrieved a folder from under my chair and pulled out the stack of pages I'd printed. "I just wanted you to know I took these pictures myself with my phone." I handed her the pages. "These will be easy to understand."

When Hannah read the heading on the first page her eyes widened. She placed her finger at the subhead—Coating eggs with chitosan minimizes tearing of shells and improves quality of eggs—and ran it alongside the abstract. Her face contorted. The abstract talked about the benefits of coating sea turtle eggs with a chitosan-lactic acid mixture. Hannah looked like she'd been injected with that very acid. Still, she read page after page, tracing the graphs and running her fingers up and down the tables.

"Marc Diamond did this?" she whispered, dropping the pages on her lap.

"He's been running experiments for months. Some with chitosan and lactic acid. Others with chitosan and soybean oil. They both served his purpose."

Hannah hugged her stomach. "What is chitosan anyway?"

I laughed humorlessly. "Something we live with daily but never think about." I pointed to my laptop. "Chitosan comes from shrimp and crab shells. It has all kinds of uses. I was surprised."

"Like what?" Hannah asked. She brought her wine glass to her lips with a shaky hand.

I ticked off on my fingers. "It's used to treat seeds in agriculture. To help plants fight fungal infections." I pointed to Hannah's glass. "Winemakers use it to help prevent spoilage. It's in polyurethane paint coating. It's used with bandages to reduce bleeding. It's an antibacterial agent. It can deliver drugs through skin." I was out of breath.

Hannah brought her hands together as if praying. "And now we have a new use for chitosan. Preserving sea turtle eggs."

I shook my head. "Not really preserving. Diamond's coating the shells to make them stronger. The research I found online was done for the chicken egg industry, basically to increase shelf life. If coated with a mixture of chitosan and lactic acid, chicken eggs last up to five weeks at room temperature. And consumers can't tell the difference."

"They test for taste?" Hannah squeezed her chin.

I pointed to the pile of papers. "One of those abstracts talks about sensory evaluation. It doesn't say if consumers looked at the eggs or smelled them or tasted them."

"I wonder if Diamond tasted the turtle eggs," Hannah said. She leaned on the chair arm and set her chin in her hand. "From chicken eggs to sea turtle eggs. Diamond coated them with chitosan to see how long they last."

"And now that he's perfected the technique, he's smuggling them out of the country." I rocked back and forth in my chair. "It's a federal crime to harm protected sea turtles or steal their eggs, but we know turtle eggs bring big bucks in other parts of the world. Maybe three hundred dollars for an egg that promises to make the eater's pecker stand up."

Hannah had spelled it out for me weeks ago, saying sea turtle egg smuggling was more profitable than drug dealing in Costa Rica. I dreaded telling Hannah of Stone's involvement.

"Marc Diamond is working with smugglers," I said.

"He's a poacher, too," Hannah added through clenched teeth.

I shook my head. "He's too far away to do the poaching. Someone close to the beach brought him eggs to experiment on. Marc did the lab work. Making the eggs travel-ready."

I stared out across Hannah's front yard, across the dune, and let my gaze rest on the quiet ocean, which today was a surprising Bahama green. Pelicans began to feed, soaring above the smooth water then crashing headfirst into the drink like downed combat planes. Something nagged at me. I had the feeling that things were off, although I couldn't pinpoint what the things were or exactly what off meant. I looked back over the list of nesting dates. The last nest to be poached was Nest Five, laid June 7 and excavated a week ago after volunteers noticed a fox had gotten in. Nest Five was empty. Cleaned out, but no one blamed the fox. Nest Six wasn't due to hatch until late September; Nest Seven in early October.

Hannah drummed her fingers on her knee. "You've nailed Marc Diamond. We still have to pinpoint the poacher." When I didn't respond, she reached over and nudged my arm. "Is there something else?"

It was time to come out with it. "Today I saw Marc with a shopping bag full of turtle eggs."

"Oh, my God!" The words themselves were exclamatory, but Hannah's voice was a dull whisper. She slouched in the chair, head sunk into her shoulders.

"Where did he get them?" I asked.

"From Nest Five," Hannah blurted. "It was empty, nothing—"

I waved away her comments. "That's impossible. A poacher wants fresh eggs. If someone poached those eggs the night they were laid, June 7, gave them to Marc that night or early the next morning to coat with his chitosan compound, they'd be long gone. Shipped within a couple days. This is mid-August. Where'd the eggs I saw today come from?"

Hannah sat perfectly still, understanding blooming across her face. "It couldn't be Nest Six either. It was laid July 26." Hannah had all nesting dates imprinted on her brain. "If that nest's been poached, they're long gone, too."

"Same with Nest Seven," I prompted.

"Laid August 1. Still too early."

"By now, Marc's perfected his coating solution. He's getting fresh eggs, treating them, and sending them out lickety-split, so they remain fresh till they get where they're going."

We sat silently for a while. Finally, our eyes met.

"There was an eighth nest," Hannah whispered. "Laid recently."

"Like yesterday. Or the day before."

"We never found it."

"Somebody found it."

"Not the turtle patrol."

I shook my head. "Not the patrol. The poacher."

Hannah looked at me with wide, hollow eyes. "A mama laid a nest, maybe at the waterline, and her tracks were washed away." She squeezed her upper arms. "Or maybe she laid way down at the south end of the beach. And no one noticed the tracks."

"Somebody noticed. Somebody found that nest and didn't report it to you," I said. "That person poached the eggs and gave them to Diamond."

"Someone watched the beach. Someone with experience. An Inlet native, maybe. A member of one of the old families." Her tone was heavy, as if filtered through sludge. "Or someone in our turtle project."

I ran my hands over my face. It was going to get worse. I was going to need that whole bottle of wine.

"I just didn't see Marc Diamond holding a bag of eggs today, Hannah. He handed that bag to someone."

She tensed, mouth agape. "And you recognized the person." She set her feet directly beneath her, as if ready to pounce. "Who was it?"

I gazed into my friend's eyes, anticipating her reaction. "Jason Stone. Marc gave the eggs to Alegria's husband."

CHAPTER FORTY-THREE

I prowled the porch waiting for Hannah to pick up her phone and call Will Brown.

"I saw him," I insisted, when Hannah continued to stare at me in disbelief. "I saw Stone take the bag from Diamond. And I know sea turtle eggs were in the bag."

Hannah's face showed an infuriating degree of doubt. I threw my arm in the direction of Raleigh. "You read the tables and charts with the words SEA TURTLE EGGS printed on them. I saw egg cartons in Diamond's lab, and they're the exact brand sold at Briny Bill's that the project uses to transport eggs when you move a nest. Someone here took those cartons and used them when they poached our eggs and took them to Marc."

"And you think that person was Jason Stone?" Hannah asked. "He's not a member of the turtle project. He doesn't know how to remove eggs from a nest without damaging them. Or how to cover them up. He doesn't have access to our supplies. And, for Pete's sake, many stores besides Briny Bill's carry that brand of eggs."

I ground my teeth. "Okay. I'll give you that. But an active volunteer must have helped him. Maybe LuAnn,"

I added maliciously, reverting to my original theory. "She poached the eggs and gave them to Marc. He coated them and gave them to Stone to smuggle out of the port."

"You're still trying to blame LuAnn because she tipped your kayak."

She sounded disgusted, but I was furious. Mad at myself for not calling Will Brown myself the first day I saw the lists. "But if you won't accept LuAnn or Stone as the poacher," I said, "there's another person on the possibility list."

"Me?" Hannah's arched brows prompted my quick reply.

"Alegria."

"Oh, my God." Hannah's mouth turned down and she spun away.

"I know—*everybody blames the Costa Ricans*. That doesn't mean she's innocent. Stone could have forced his wife to poach. I don't want it to be true anymore than you do. But I saw him take a bag of sea turtle eggs from Diamond and I know he works at the port and, dammit, he's the smuggler."

Hannah turned partially back to me, her face dark, her lips pressed together so tightly they looked welded.

"Okay, forget calling Will," I blurted. "He'll find out eventually."

"You're going to squeal?" She sounded like a ten-year-old playground bully. "You're going to hurt that family on a whim?"

Whim? I didn't want to hurt anybody, but the truth was burning a hole in my tongue. I could not understand Hannah's obstinacy. The eggs in the bag were her poached loggerhead eggs. I'd identified the villains. At least two of them. This was not the time to be politically correct.

Hannah faced me. "What do you mean he'll find out eventually?"

"After Stone drove away, I saw a guy named Tack Stanley follow him. Stanley works with him at the port."

"You think he's in on it, too?"

I shook my head. "Just the opposite. I saw Stone and Stanley arguing at the Sloppy Parrot. Now I'm thinking Stanley was warning him against doing something stupid. Now he has proof. He'll tell his superiors. They'll catch Jason Stone."

My thoughts drifted to Stanley's *coincidental* appearance on Raven Creek. He was probably an undercover officer for Fish & Wildlife or NOAA. Maybe he'd tied LuAnn, Stone and Diamond together and was following her, scoping her out.

My thoughts tumbled back to Hannah. Why was she reluctant to accept Jason Stone as the smuggler? She was head of the sea turtle project, lived and breathed it year round. She'd been physically ill over the poaching. Now I handed her the culprit and she's squirrely about turning him in?

"I know this hurts, Hannah. I like Alegria and her kids. I don't know her husband, but he seemed like a nice family man. He acted interested around the nests." Now I knew why. "I don't want it to be him. But it is him."

We went into the house. Hannah pushed into a corner of the sofa, and threw an afghan over her knees. She looked so beaten, that, despite my irritation, I gathered her in my arms.

"Don't turn him in," I said softly. "I'm sure Stanley will do it." The guy's jaw was set like rock candy when he drove off in his SUV.

Ten minutes later, Hannah speed dialed Will Brown.

***

"Send me copies of everything you have," Will said. "Graphs. Charts. Photos. Those nest and hatch dates. Did you get a picture of Diamond handing over the eggs?"

I hadn't. Just the back of Jason Stone walking down Marc's driveway with a shopping bag.

Will had taken down Diamond and Stone's names without comment. I left LuAnn out, since I only had proof she was terrified of snakes, not that she was a turtle egg poacher. Will said he'd update the enforcement departments at the state division of marine fisheries and the NC Wildlife Resources Commission. The poacher police would find the third villain now that they had the smugglers almost in hand.

To my surprise, Will took his time with me on the phone. He said I might be interviewed by the agencies and to keep my eyes and ears open. He praised my courage and persistence. He didn't comment on my B&Es. A private citizen didn't need a warrant to prowl someone's property. Only nerve and a blind eye to the law. But, hey, it was for a good cause.

Before hanging up, Will gave me his direct number. I put him on speed dial. Number eight for the mysterious last nest whose eggs had been poached, coated, and smuggled by now to parts unknown, each stamped with one-to-three hundred dollar price tags.

Despite my argument with Hannah, I felt great. Nearly euphoric. I'd done something difficult, outside my MO. I'd taken risks and they'd paid off big time. A gang of crooks was nearly caught and I was proud of my contribution.

CHAPTER FORTY-FOUR

That evening, I walked along the beach at ebb tide, rolling through the address book in my head, trying to pinpoint an egg thief. I suspected all members of the sea turtle project. Sad to say, I didn't trust any of them. Volunteers like Bianca and Fala were most suspect because they knew how to find a nest, uncover it, remove the eggs, and cover it up so it looked unmolested.

Dutch and Joop were high on the list for being older natives from a poaching culture and at that stage of life where they thought they could do and say anything they liked. I had shrugged off their turtle noshing stories, but I knew old habits and deep-rooted ethos died hard. After their gleeful harangue in Aunt Biddy's diner, Joop had sent me a recipe for Sea Turtle Eggs. I'd read it out of morbid curiosity and was relieved to find it called for breakfast sausage, cheese, jalapeno peppers and "your favorite BBQ rub." The "eggs" sounded like tasty finger food, but, Holy Heaven, why name them after an endangered species?

I dragged my thoughts back to possible suspects. At least I'd pinned down the smuggler, hard as it had been to convince Hannah. I wanted to think my friend resisted because she didn't want to jump on the let's-all-hate-the-Costa-Rican-poachers bandwagon. But—and here I let myself go to a dark place—was Hannah protecting Alegria because they were accomplices in the smuggling ring? Nausea flowed through me like lava. I gulped sea air and forced myself to free-associate. Would Hannah gain anything by poaching? She was a dedicated environmentalist who carried a sack in her kayak to hold the trash she collected on the water —beer bottles, pop cans, dirty diapers, milk jugs, cigarette packs, the ubiquitous plastic bags—and took the junk home to recycle. She lived simply. Cast a small footprint on the earth. She enjoyed her job, lived comfortably, and never bemoaned lacking a large bank account. I truly could not see Hannah, a woman I'd known and loved for twenty years, performing a criminal act that went against all she stood for. And she had, finally, called Will Brown.

I rubbed my head with my fingernails, sending a tingling sensation skittering across my scalp. Tanner seemed content with his kayak tour business. His boats were seaworthy and equipped for safety, but not top of the line. He never talked about upgrading his fleet. He lived modestly and didn't travel, at least not in summer. He was a naturalist as well as an environmentalist. He enjoyed sitting at turtle nests but didn't feel obligated to sit at them all. He had other interests—hiking, paddle boarding, surfing—which didn't require a trust fund to enjoy.

The key word was money. Maybe Stone did need money to buy Alegria legal papers. Or maybe placid Pilar needed an expensive operation. By now, he had smuggled the coated sea turtle eggs aboard a ship sailing for South America or Asia. He had a partner to hide the eggs and protect them from discovery. At their final destination, someone would purchase those smuggled turtle eggs and sell them for a hell of a lot of cash. So, stepping down the ladder, how much money did Stone make per egg? How much did Diamond make? And how much did the poacher get? In most business chains, the person at the bottom of the ladder—think farmer—made the least. Still, Marc had said something about using his cut for a vacation. Well, there were vacations and there were *vacations*. A person could rent a cabin at a Greensboro campground for $52 a night or plunk down $52,000 a night at the Royal Penthouse Suite in Hotel President Wilson in Geneva, Switzerland. I knew the spread, having once done research on affordable vs. flagrantly out-of-my-reach escapes for *Carolina*.

So, who in Goose Inlet needed money and would turn to criminal acts to gain it?

I was pumping my legs on a boardwalk swing and pondering that question when Detective Magnus, in khakis and polo shirt, walked up.

"I heard you broke into a garage and rummaged through someone's private property." He leaned against the railing, arms crossed. "Your *second* B&E."

"Are you here to arrest me?" I squinted into what was left of the sun.

He patted his hip. "Didn't bring my cuffs."

I wiped imaginary sweat off my forehead. "Have Diamond and Stone been arrested?" The detective watched an elderly man pushing his wheelchair-bound wife down the boardwalk. "Come on, share! I'm the one who got the goods on those guys."

"Illegally."

I shook my head. "It would be illegal for you to do it without a search warrant. But not for me." Magnus's eyebrows shot up. I stretched my legs and pushed to get the swing moving again. "I didn't steal anything. Didn't take his briefcase or make off with anything in the room—lists, charts, bottles of chemicals."

"Only their images."

I kept pumping. "And it helped, right? Will Brown was pleased. And Marc isn't pressing charges against me, or you'd have brought your handcuffs."

A smile broke across Magnus's face. "I doubt Diamond thought of pressing charges. He was shaking like a rattle when Raleigh PD picked him up for questioning."

"That was fast!" But I stopped pumping. "Just *questioning*? They didn't charge him? I got proof. Marc coated stolen sea turtle eggs and Stone smuggled them out of the port." I paused. "Or aren't my photos admissible in court?"

Magnus sat down beside me. "Your photos indicate Diamond might have experimented with coating sea turtle eggs. And we don't know for certain those were sea turtle eggs in the bag Diamond gave Stone. Or what Stone did with the eggs." He paused. "You helped, Abby. The police will use what you gave them to—"

"Trick Marc into confessing?" Like on Law & Order.

Magnus shrugged a shoulder.

"And Stone?"

The detective shaded his eyes and looked out across the water. "Quite a few sailboats out there."

"Use Tack Stanley to get to Stone," I suggested. "Tack followed him from Diamond's house. I bet right to the port and saw him smuggle—"

"Stop." Magnus held up a hand.

"Tack's been on to Stone for a while. I saw them talking a couple times—and arguing." Magnus blew small puffs of air through pursed lips. "Maybe Stanley's a Fish & Wildlife cop," I continued, "sent to investigate poaching on our beach." Magnus gave me a squinty look. "You'd know if he was, right? Would you tell me if you did?"

"Most likely no," he said, with enough heat to translate into *absolutely not*. Magnus drummed his fingers on the seat.

"How soon do you think they'll get a confession?"

He shrugged. "Jurisdiction is tricky. Hard to settle on where the real crime occurred."

The eggs were poached from a nest in one location, tampered with in another, and sent on their way in a third. My spirits drooped. "Do you know if Diamond gave up the poacher?"

Magnus leaned back to watch a line of feeding pelicans rise into the sky.

I poked his shoulder. "You know but you won't tell me."

"It's an ongoing investigation, darlin'," Magnus said, emphasizing his North Carolina drawl. At my grimace, he sighed. "Customs suspected something was going on at the port for a while. And I tell you this because there's always something going on at the port—smuggling, attempted smuggling. The airport, too."

"I wondered about that. With shelf life being the issue, wouldn't it be quicker to smuggle sea turtle eggs out by airplane?"

"Seems logical." He threw an arm over the back of the swing. "Last summer cigarette smugglers got busted big time at the airport. Maybe these egg smugglers don't want to risk it. Or they have better contacts at the port."

"Like Jason Stone!" I stared at the side of Erik's face until he returned the look. "I took a picture of him with a bag of eggs, for Pete's sake. When will *he* be arrested?" Magnus shrugged. "You know, but you won't tell me."

"I shouldn't have told you Diamond was picked up."

We sat quietly for a while. Officer Kane strolled by and Magnus asked if she had a full day of paddle board lessons scheduled for her day off. She did. She was saving money for a trip to Spain. She was going to hike some ancient pilgrims' trail. Not all eight hundred miles of it. Just a hundred. She sauntered off, calling a warning to kids climbing on the dunes.

Swimmers and sunbathers clambered up from the beach and made their way down the boardwalk, chairs, blankets, and carryalls bumping against their legs. Dinnertime. Gulls laughed and swooped behind a little boy carrying a bag of popcorn. Magnus kept the swing moving at a lazy tempo and seemed in no hurry to leave.

"I'm wondering if my husband's death had something to do with the poaching," I said quietly, after the crowd had passed.

His feet stopped the swing with a jerk. "Why do you think that?"

I swallowed hard. "Things that happened. Aidan's name signed for chemicals he didn't use. London

James saying Aidan acted suspiciously at work. Aidan's computer was searched and poaching sites were found. Federal investigators were at Tillson Pharmaceutical. And customs cops. At first I thought my husband had done something wrong. But now I think he knew Diamond was working on something illegal. Maybe Aidan was researching about poaching and smuggling sea turtle eggs because he suspected Marc."

The detective pushed off the swing and walked to the steps that led down to the beach, rubbing his chin.

"I ran into Aidan's research director," I continued. "He said he couldn't talk about the cause of the explosion that killed my husband or *anything else going on with the investigation*."

Magnus's lips parted, but he closed his mouth firmly.

"I think Aidan figured out what Marc was doing when he visited his home lab," I said. "Or maybe he caught Marc doing something shady at work. An experiment unrelated to work. I don't know. I—" Heat ignited behind my eyes, the burn turning to tears. I forced out the words. "Did Marc Diamond cause the explosion that killed my husband?"

To my surprise, Detective Magnus sat down and put his arm around my shoulder. I felt his warmth through my T-shirt. "I can't answer your questions, Abby," he said softly. "The explosion and its possible connection to *anything else* is under investigation by agencies far above Goose Inlet PD." He squeezed my shoulder once, gently. "I know a little more than you, but not much. And what I know, I can't share."

CHAPTER FORTY-FIVE

My last days in Goose Inlet were tranquil. I kayaked with Tanner and each time practiced wet entry. Practice was short, only fifteen minutes, which was all my heart, lungs, and thighs could handle. I'd purposely fall out of my boat and work on scrambling back in, making progress on the speed of entry. The center of gravity and I were coming to terms. It was a miracle I'd escaped the alligator's jaws on Raven Creek. I couldn't trust miracles, so perfecting a variety of reentry techniques was high on my survival list.

I also paddled with Hannah, who managed to squeeze a morning out of school preparations. She was pensive while we roamed the back bays, our conversation limited and a bit stilted. Dark shadows bruised her eyes, and I wondered if she was losing sleep. Heartbroken as she was over the loss of so many baby sea turtles, she appeared crushed by the identification of the villains. Or at least one of them.

The turtle project finished patrolling at the end of August, without finding more nests. No new babies would replace the ones lost. Will Brown had told Hannah and me to keep my discovery of Diamond and Stone's alleged criminal activity a secret while authorities continued their investigation. Hannah refused to badger Will for updates and squeezed a promise out of me to leave him alone and let him do his job. I didn't see Jason Stone nor his family on the beach. Didn't know if he'd been arrested or had skipped town.

Now that the smugglers were, in my mind, identified, the Goose Inlet poacher who had hung around all summer like a poltergeist morphed into something corporeal. A person. A person to be branded a criminal.

***

Hannah sank into her chair. "Two hundred and thirty-six eggs! That's not even adding in what we lost in Nest Two, the one we moved and never got an accurate count on. The total poached has to be over three hundred." She gritted her teeth. "Who did it?"

I wasn't going to rile Hannah by uttering LuAnn's name, so I deflected. "We have two nests left."

"Most likely they've been trashed."

The certainty and harshness of her tone surprised me. "Hannah, don't torment yourself. Be positive, like you tell me."

"We won't know till the end of September or early October, if they hatch on time." She refilled our coffee cups. "Even if all the eggs hatch, I'll worry all winter about next season and someone stealing eggs again. We have to catch this person."

"And we will. The poacher is no longer a phantom," I said. "Finding Marc's research, witnessing him hand off sea turtle eggs to Stone changed that. The poacher is real and will be caught."

***

After dark, I sat on Lily Pad's front porch trying to anticipate my return to Chapel Hill and *Carolina* magazine, but dwelling instead on the bizarre highlights of my summer at the beach. A poacher, a murderer, and a mutilator—ingredients for one sickening stew—were running loose in Goose Inlet. Would the stewpot spill and reveal its fixings before I left?

Would Randy Boone's body turn up, putting LuAnn's distress at least partially to rest? Would Detective Magnus catch London's killer? Would he discover who buried three toes and a chunk of tattooed butt under two turtle nests? Would he identify the victim?

I winced at how my life had become peppered with violence. The trauma streak had begun with Aidan being blown away. The pain of his loss mushroomed inside me when I least expected it. Had I truly recovered enough from my husband's death to perform my editorial function? I wasn't one hundred percent positive I wanted to return to the Triangle, where we had lived and loved. Where we'd worked and raised our children. I had friends in Goose Inlet. I had friends and children in the Triangle. But I didn't have Aidan.

I struggled to escape the melancholy that pinned me low. Be positive, Abs, like you told Hannah. Despite the drama, I'd enjoyed falling asleep to hushing waves. Walking the beach at low tide. Thrilling to an orange-gold sunrise over an awakening ocean. Digging my toes in the sand and my mind into a good novel, while sunshine tanned me to a honey brown. I would miss cooking with Hannah. Tanner would continue his unobtrusive paddles through the silent marsh without my companionship. Be positive? I was already missing Lily Pad. Shoot, I was going to miss Dutch and Joop.

CHAPTER FORTY-SIX

On my last Saturday in Goose Inlet, the sky outside my bedroom window was a cloudless Carolina blue. The sun's brilliance, however, did not warm me. I'd awoken with the memory of Marc Diamond asking how I was holding up. The lump in my throat was so big I had to sit up to swallow it. With a hand on my heart, I forgave Aidan everything. Those evening meetings and absences from the lab? Well, he'd been spying on Diamond or meeting with police. A girlfriend? A mistress? I was disgusted with myself for thinking he had loved me so little. And I'd considered divorce! My eyes bulged with tears. I wiped them on the bedsheet. Out they rolled again.

I was charged with nervous energy, a mixture of anxiety, distress and mounting fury. I'd spilled the beans to Will Brown, yet nothing public was known about the smuggling. Was Diamond in jail? Yesterday I saw Stone playing volleyball with Tack Stanley and Tanner at the Sloppy Parrot. My anger could have blasted a hole in the large tent covering the outdoor seating area. Stone was partnered with Diamond in a federal crime and still hanging around a bar playing ball. I had convinced myself Aidan had known what his lab mate was up to, and Marc had silenced him. Stone was Marc's accomplice and just as guilty. Why weren't the police doing something?

The turmoil that kind-hearted friends had managed to ease over the summer again roiled within me, to the point where I doubted I could resume my duties at *Carolina*. Or wanted to. So here I was, wallowing in bed on my last Saturday in Goose Inlet, emotionally back at square one.

I had to straighten out. If I didn't return after this sabbatical, I wouldn't have a job. At least not at *Carolina*. I had to return to Chapel Hill on schedule, so I focused on a reentry plan. I'd take a week to reorient to life in the city, air out the house and replenish the refrigerator, inspect my neglected gardens. I'd buy new work clothes. One bright spot, I'd shed ten pounds walking the beach and could count on a smaller jeans size. I'd have Derek and Kate over for dinner and not mention murder. I'd stop at the office and see what projects were in the works. I shouldn't be entirely ignorant of the magazine's direction after a long absence.

Convinced, Abby? I rolled onto my side and looked out the window at my neighbor's fence. Several boards were missing. If I was honest, everything I'd just itemized, except for seeing my children, was drudgery. Should I stay in Goose Inlet? I could sell the Chapel Hill house and buy a beach cottage. Maybe Lily Pad, if the owner could be convinced to sell. No, I must return and earn a living. And I want to work. I got up, soaked a washcloth with cold water, and held it to my eyes. Get a grip, girl. Get in line with Earth's gravity. I took a huge breath and shuddered on exhale. The best way to regain balance was to enjoy one last paddle before heading home.

Unfortunately, I didn't have a partner. Hannah was directing an in-house teaching seminar. Tanner was at a nature conference. Bianca was visiting family in Charlotte. LuAnn was off my friends list. Although I'd never kayaked alone, if I didn't want to waste a beautiful day I had to do it. Take another risk? No fear. I was getting good at it.

The Inlet was hosting a regatta, and the Intracoastal would be bow to stern motor craft, not conducive to paddling, so I scratched the ICW and its connecting bays. As much as I loved the blackwater creeks, my body froze at the memory of LuAnn's bared-teeth grin. Snakes, gators—a creek was a stomach sinker. That left the river. It was blackwater, too, but not closed in by trees and reptile-harboring vegetation. If I stayed between the boat launch and Dram Island, stayed out of the marsh bordering the river—maybe ventured to Tooth Isle to hunt sharks' teeth—I could enjoy a peaceful paddle away from the shipping channel.

I drove to River Green and unloaded boat and gear. Assembled the paddle and clipped on a new PFD. Smacked my forehead with my palm, reopened the hatch and searched my drybag. Shoot! No phone. Would I dare venture onto the water alone without it? Get real, Abby. Cell phones have been around twenty, twenty-five years? And people circled the globe in boats for thousands of years. Don't miss out on this sunshiny morning because of ICPD—irrational cell phone dependence.

I paddled straight to Tooth Isle. A few sharks' teeth in a shallow dish on my office desk would be a quiet reminder of this extended vacation. A half hour combing the rocky shallows, however, produced no treasure. It took concentration to find sharks' teeth. A person had to have the Eye.

Sunshine bounced off the water making it sparkle like glitter-strewn satin. I was about to move on when something thin and black caught my attention. I fingered it in the water and giggled. Between thumb and index finger, I held a fossilized bull shark's tooth. It was black, with a rough base angled upward. I laid it across my fingers. Nearly two inches long—a prize. The smooth tooth was slightly curved, about a half-inch wide near the base and tapering to about a quarter inch. I pressed the pointed tip into my thumb and imagined feeling three hundred pricks from a bull shark bite. I tucked the tooth into my shorts pocket. I wouldn't have enough teeth to fill a dish, but my work desk would serve as a pedestal for at least one treasure.

I was on the shipping channel side of the island. The air was steamy, and the wind had deserted me. Ah, to walk into chest high water and cool off. When I thought about the ten thousand bull sharks Joop insisted patrolled the river, I opted to squat at the shoreline and toss handfuls of water on my chest and back.

Paddling to Dram Island, I saw a man in a jon boat puttering near the sea grass north of the boat launch, where someone was unloading a small green craft. The jon boat owner wore a wide-brimmed hat and sunglasses and was probably looking for a place to drop a fishing line. Another kayaker was just visible heading south, and I selfishly hoped the person wouldn't beach on Dram. I wanted the island to myself. Everyone was out today.

I slid my sunglasses down my nose to view the brilliant blue sky. Couldn't blame them.

It was high tide and thick spartina blocked any attempt to land on Dram's eastern shore. I paddled back to the channel side and maneuvered onto a rocky beach. Carrying my drybag and water bottle, I followed a path to the island's interior. I expected the trail to be littered with beer cans, soda bottles, and cigarette packs, but it was clean. Then I remembered that a group of environmentalists dedicated to the river had used their boats to cart away dozens of bags of garbage, twisted lawn chairs, crushed coolers, broken fishing reels, old tires, torn sneakers, and even a vintage icebox. TV news had reported it as an annual cleanup.

Black flies buzzed around my ears, but mosquitos held off their attack. I fought my way through a tangle of shrubs and vines, their leaves dry and shriveled after the blistering summer. I was beginning to despair of finding an open spot to eat lunch when I broke into a small clearing. In the center was a circle of large stones littered with charred scraps of wood. A lawn chair, its sparse webbing shredded with age, lay folded on the ground as if awaiting burial. A bottle of Wild Turkey and two empty cans from a six-pack of beer rested on a configuration of large rocks that, with some imagination, could be construed as a table. Attempting to pop the top off the third can was LuAnn Sheetz.

Had LuAnn been the kayaker paddling south? If yes, she'd beached in a hurry and guzzled two beers with gusto. I turned, ready to scoot, but the noise coming from LuAnn stopped me. This time the waterworks weren't loud howls but soft eek-eeks like tweets from a tiny bird. What gave LuAnn's weeping away was the sunlight reflecting off the shiny tears cascading down her cheeks. My entry into the clearing had not been quiet, but LuAnn did not seem to notice. All her concentration was focused on the can in her hand. Even though she doggedly pinched the flip top, her fingers slipped off each time her shoulders jerked forward with a squeaky sob.

LuAnn Sheetz. Who was this woman? Mourning girlfriend? Dedicated daughter? Kayak-tipping attempted murderer? I couldn't decide whether to help or run. When LuAnn looked up, the words that gushed from her mouth nearly knocked me to the ground.

"I stole the turtle eggs," she blubbered. "And I killed him."

"You killed Randy?" It was the first "him" that popped into my head.

LuAnn flung the full beer can at me, missing my shoulder by inches. Pretty good aim for someone who'd slugged down twenty-four ounces of ale. Plus whiskey.

"Not Randy, asshole!"

I flipped out my arms. *Then who?*

"That evil shit London James!"

My thoughts tumbled a series of somersaults, landing where I thought most appropriate. "He caught you poaching."

"He made me poach!"

London James knew Marc Diamond knew LuAnn Sheetz. I'd been right all along.

LuAnn threw back her head and shouted at the sky. "I didn't want to!" She sucked in a great gulp of air. "I did at first—for the money. But then—I couldn't do it anymore. So he killed Randy and cut him up—" Air burst from LuAnn's lungs like a blast from the Hindenburg.

"London killed Randy?" I dropped my drybag on the ground. "Why?"

LuAnn's face turned into a muddled mask of fear and fury. "To scare the shit out of me! Why else?"

The warning. When I'd asked Detective Magnus why someone would bury body parts beneath turtle nests, he'd asked, "What does it look like to you?" And I'd said, "A warning."

"He did it to make me keep poaching. I didn't want to." LuAnn pried away another can from the plastic ring. This time she jammed her finger under the tab, yanked it up, slammed the beer can onto her mouth, and sucked it like a teat.

Poor Randy! Killed and mutilated—for his sake, I hoped in that order—because his girlfriend backed out of a poaching ring. London James was not an odd city slicker, but a merciless killer. It sickened and terrified me to realize that brutal gang tactics had jumped from Costa Rica to Goose Inlet.

I ventured a step forward. "LuAnn, I am truly sorry about Randy. But how did you get tangled up in this?" I'd been about to take another step, but LuAnn's dark glare stopped me. Still, I needed an answer. "Marc, your old boyfriend—"

LuAnn threw the empty can on the ground and stomped on it. "He was never my boyfriend."

"But he wanted you to steal the turtle eggs."

LuAnn sunk onto the sand. "We kept in touch. Christmas cards. I wrote a note on the last one. Told him about all the money it took taking care of Mama." She ran a hand around her face. "He wrote something about having a side business. Was gonna make a lot of money." She grabbed the Wild Turkey. Her arm turned to jelly, she dropped the bottle, but managed to wobble its base into the sand. With a little fumbling, she opened another beer. When LuAnn passes out, I'll get my phone—Dammit!

"Next thing I know, this—this—James guy—was knocking on my door. Said he was Marc's friend, and they were gonna help me out. Help my mom." She hiccupped loudly. "They were gonna ship turtle eggs to Hong Kong or someplace. Marc put something on them so they wouldn't bust up or rot—I don't know." Good for five weeks. No refrigeration required.

"Asked if I wanted in on a good thing." LuAnn scrubbed at her buzzed hair. "All I had to do was get them the eggs." She wiped her nose on her bare arm. "They were gonna make big bucks selling eggs to somebody at the port."

Jason Stone. But when Stone had taken the bag from Diamond, he'd mentioned "the boss." Who was that? Not London. He was dead. Had I mentioned a boss to Will Brown when I gave him evidence against the smugglers?

"That guy was gonna sell them to a guy in China." LuAnn pulled on her beer. "Someplace like that."

And the guy in China could afford to pay a lot because he was going to charge his customer—some bozo with a limp weenie—three hundred bucks for one turtle egg. Marc had said he gave Jason eight dozen eggs. That batch alone meant—I closed my eyes—almost thirty thousand dollars for the seller in China.

"And then Randy came home." LuAnn fumbled with the Wild Turkey, swallowed, and gasped. "Randy was all for it. He wanted a new boat. Said I could put Mama in a nicer place."

"Randy talked you into it."

LuAnn shrugged.

"How many turtle eggs did you steal?"

The poacher hung her head. "I dunno. Eight, nine hundred. Maybe more."

"Nine hundred!" I nearly stopped breathing. Two hundred seventy-four baby loggerheads had hatched. LuAnn was claiming to have poached nearly four times that. I wanted to strangle her. Hannah's estimate of stolen eggs was two hundred-thirty six. Even adding another hundred from Nest Two didn't reach LuAnn's estimate. A painful thought hit me. She was counting eggs stolen from the nests still buried. Nests Six and Seven. And Nest Eight, the secret one she found and didn't reveal to the turtle project. I clenched my fists. Those four nests could have yielded at least four hundred hatchlings. But that still didn't add up to—

"Did you find other nests and poach them? I know you found what would have been Nest Eight."

"Nest Eight! Shit, girl. I found lots of nests and never told nobody. Why you think I was tired all the time? I poached 'em and drove 'em to Raleigh."

LuAnn Sheetz had killed nine hundred baby loggerhead turtles at a price tag of roughly three hundred thousand dollars. And at the price of one dead and mutilated Randy Boone. And a drowned and dead London James. If LuAnn had wanted out of the scheme, why had she chosen to kill the man instead of turn him in?

The poacher tipped the Wild Turkey to her lips, swallowed twice, and collapsed on the ground. My smart gene told me to spin on my heel and hoof it back to my boat, get off Dram Island, but that nosy gene glued me to the perimeter of the clearing. When she propped up on one elbow, I thought if she could talk, I wanted the whole story.

"You poached the first two nests," I prompted. LuAnn winced. "But you stopped. The next two nests hatched perfectly."

She didn't answer. Had she passed out with her eyes open?

"Is that why London killed Randy? To make you—"

LuAnn lifted the whiskey bottle and I ducked, but she didn't throw it, or drink. "We felt awful," she repeated dully. "Had second thoughts even before we poached those first two. Left three eggs in the first. Fifteen in the second." She let out a low groan. "Just to give a few of them a chance."

"Why didn't London take those eggs when he hid Randy's—pieces?" I asked.

"How the hell should I know?" LuAnn shouted. "Some sick joke, maybe. Throwing me a bone." She moaned as if physically injured. "I wanted out! I was a turtle volunteer since it started. I'm a nest mom every year."

Not next year, honey.

"I couldn't do it. Randy couldn't either. Said his old boat was good enough. We couldn't kill those babies. The money couldn't make up for it."

"So you left the next two nests alone."

LuAnn's mouth worked like she was ready to spit. "London kept *pushing* and *pushing*. But we said no."

"Why didn't you tell the cops?"

Her jaw dropped. "We poached, moron! I couldn't go to jail. Who'd look after Mama?" She popped the top on the last beer can. "We thought London would go away if we ignored him." A deep burp rumbled up from her belly. "But he didn't."

I stepped a little closer and said softly, "When you saw the body parts in the nests, you knew they belonged to Randy."

LuAnn bent her head almost to the sand, weeping low and ragged. "Randy went missing a week before the first nest hatched," she said. "I knew London was talking to me." I could hear the gargle of sobs rumbling in her throat. She suddenly sat up straight. "That bastard laughed about it. Said they—him and Marc—lured Randy out on the water and snuffed him." She crushed the beer can in her hand. "Chopped his toes off. Cut out a piece of him." Face contorted, LuAnn clutched her knees and rocked.

"They scared you back into poaching. Nest Five was cleaned out."

"Fox got three," she mumbled, like that let her off the hook.

Her head popped up. "Scared me, you said?" LuAnn's face turned from boozy red to purulent purple. "They shocked the ever-lovin' shit out of me! I got that same tattoo they took off Randy. I didn't want my ass cut up. So, yeah, I cleaned out all the eggs from Nest Five. Over a hundred. That nest was *empty* at excavation."

I recalled LuAnn's behavior at the nests. I'd thought she was grieving for Randy, and she was, but not because he was missing. She knew he was dead.

"I hated myself," LuAnn said, her tone deep and raspy. "For hurting Hannah. For killing the turtles." She rocked side to side, mumbling into her knees. "For letting Marc talk me into it. Getting Randy killed."

"So you killed London," I said quietly, wishing I had a phone to record her confession.

LuAnn lifted her head. "He made me poach Nest Six. And was after me to steal from Seven the night after it was laid. But I had enough. Randy was dead, too many turtles were lost, and I didn't want to live if they were gonna keep making me do evil. Go ahead and kill me. Carve me up. I didn't care. I told London to go poach it himself, he wanted those eggs so bad. He said he would but I'd regret making him do it."

She told how she watched London come out of his house carrying a bag of egg cartons, followed him to the nest, and watched him start digging. When the night patrol officers motored down the beach, he ran behind a dune, and flattened himself in deep sand.

"Scared him good," she said, "'cause he picked up his stuff and left. I followed him to that long bridge by the condos." She slouched, head down, as if dozing.

"Why'd he go there?" I asked loudly. "His house is—"

LuAnn's head popped up. "How the hell should I know?" She gripped her stubby hair. "Taking a walk? Hiding from the cops? He had his shovel. I was scared he'd go back after the eggs." She took a slug of whiskey. Don't pass out, LuAnn. Finish your story.

"I walked up on the bridge and said he better not do it or I'd turn him in. He told me keep poaching or he'd turn me in. I said I'd send cops to Marc's lab and they'd end up the bad guys. The cops would let me off." She said London chased her to the condo garden, knocked her on the ground, and slapped her.

"He put his hands around my neck." She squirmed. "My eyes popped. Tongue—" she stuck it out once, twice, and clutched her throat. "I felt 'round for something to club him with. That garden has rocks and shells. My hand found a conch and I slammed it on his head. I think the pointy part hit him." LuAnn tipped her head back, eyes closed, smug smile on her lips. "He conked out."

I waited. "You dragged him to the bridge and pushed him off, into the cove."

"No!" Her head snapped back. "He stumbled his own self back. Fell down. Laid there a while. Rolled off, fell in the water."

I considered whether or not to believe her. My own experience with LuAnn Sheetz in a fit of temper or panic had been horrific. Bianca had seen London stumbling around on the bridge but had gone back inside her condo before he fell off. Or LuAnn pushed him.

"You didn't go for help."

She answered with another *ain't you stupid* look. "Glad to be rid of him. I took his stuff and scrammed." The bottle bobbled as she took a long, slow sip of Wild Turkey. "Glad it's over."

Over? Lady, you are a freakin' liar. I took two steps into the circle. "I know for a fact you poached a nest a few days ago and gave the eggs to Marc. Long after London died."

LuAnn cocked her head but didn't ask how I knew this. I made no attempt to suppress the disgust in my voice. I did squelch the urge to run up and kick her. "Why continue? Did Marc bully you?"

LuAnn dropped her face in her hands. Was she trying to remember, organize her lies, or had she fallen asleep? A trembling voice made its way between her fingers. "I started getting phone calls."

She told how a man threatened to turn her in to Fish & Wildlife and to the police for murder. "It wasn't Marc. I didn't recognize the voice. But he scared me bad." LuAnn's arms trembled. "Scared me more than London did. I don't know who he was."

I knew who he was. Jason Stone. As if my knowledge could materialize into a tangible threat, Alegria Villalobos's husband stepped into the clearing from a gap in the shrubbery.

CHAPTER FORTY-SEVEN

LuAnn exhaled a boozy gasp. At the sight of the gun strapped to Stone's hip, every muscle in my body stiffened. Did he know I was the one who turned him in? And did that matter now? He'd probably heard LuAnn blab the whole story. We were evidence against him. My eyes roamed from Stone to LuAnn and back, but they were my only body parts moving.

There was more rustling in the scrub and Tack Stanley stepped into the clearing from the other side, wearing a wide-brimmed hat and sunglasses. The man puttering in a jon boat along the riverbank. For several seconds no one spoke.

"Who—are you?" LuAnn asked around a woozy hiccup, obviously too drunk to remember him from Raven Creek.

"I'm the guy's gonna clean up this mess," Stanley said, smiling.

"He's okay. He works at the port," I told her, guessing the man was a port cop, any sort of cop. Stone stood across the clearing, jaw set, muscles tense, his eyes riveted on Stanley.

Tank took a step into the clearing and motioned to LuAnn and me. "Come here. Quick!"

"No!" Stone shouted. "Stay where you are," but I hurried to Tank's side. LuAnn stumbled over on wobbly legs. Stone advanced into the clearing, hand on his holster.

"I'm with U.S. Customs," Tank declared. "I've been following this man."

"I know. I saw you at Marc Diamond's house," I whispered. LuAnn and I were on either side of him now.

Tank's grin slipped. "You should leave investigating to the police." His tone was as serious as Detective Magnus's.

"Step away from him," Stone ordered. "He's not an agent." He slipped his gun out of its holster. The relief I'd felt at Tank's appearance turned to dread.

"Leave these girls alone, Jase. It's over." Tank nodded toward the shipping channel. "I brought the Coast Guard."

Smart. He'd been watching LuAnn, saw Stone put his green boat in the water to follow her—most likely to eliminate a dangerous loose end—and called the Guard before tracking them. And here I was, thrown into the mix, because of the need for one last paddle and a quiet, solitary lunch.

My heart, already beating several speeds faster than normal, ratcheted up to flight range when Stone began to creep across the clearing, gun leveled. On the other side of Tank, LuAnn was struggling to keep her balance, feet spread apart, arms waving out to the sides. The only body parts under control were her eyes, which were fixed and narrowed on Stone. She must have figured out he was the man who took over for London James and forced her to poach that last nest.

Tank's hand moved slowly toward the small of his back. Another weapon? Well, he was a customs agent. Still, two guns meant disaster. My legs twitched with the urge to run. Stone stepped closer. I caught movement in the corner of my eye. With a growl, LuAnn charged forward and grabbed Stone around the knees in a diving tackle. They hit the ground, and his head bounced like a basketball, eyes rolling back in his head. I ran forward and saw the edge of a rock sticking out of the sand. I pulled the gun from his slackened fist.

Tank strode up behind me. "Give me that." I handed him the pistol, turned, and ran down the path toward the shore. I was getting the hell out of there. The customs agent could handle the poacher and the smuggler. I wasn't losing a minute getting to that Coast Guard boat. I'd paddle out, flag them down. They'd send agents to help their fellow officer.

A pistol shot rang out. I flinched and stumbled. Shit! Regaining my feet, I charged down the path, burst through the trees, and nearly collided with my boat. I dragged it to the water and was picking up my paddle when I was hit from behind and knocked to the ground. Goddam that LuAnn! I twisted onto my back and brought my legs up, ready to heave the woman off, but it was Tack Stanley's fist that grazed my head as I jerked to the side, so shocked I couldn't scream.

I kicked instinctively at his stomach and rolled away. Small, sharp stones bit into my skin. Stanley? I scrambled to my feet and grabbed my paddle, but he yanked it from my hands. Had I gotten it wrong? My mind spun like a waterspout, but one fear, one realization, floated to the top. There was no Coast Guard boat.

Stanley leaped and knocked me backwards into the water. His gray eyes glittered like knives. I punched his nose with my head, more by accident than intent, and when his grip relaxed, twisted from his hands. He fell back, clutching his face. Blood oozed between his fingers and trickled in pink swirls across his mouth and down his chin. I tried to pick up a rock, but it was slimy with moss and dropped back into the water with a sickening plop. My eyes scoured the shoreline for a piece of driftwood. I stuck my hand in my pocket as Stanley lunged. He grabbed the back of my head, wrapped his fingers in my hair and slapped me across the face. What might have been the Milky Way floated before my eyes. My hand came out of my pocket as I flailed with his next blow. His hands closed around my throat. I grabbed the front of his shirt and pulled myself close, jabbing at his face.

"Aw! Bitch!" He let go with one hand and grabbed his cheek. He pulled me close again, and as he did my hand came up and slashed across his eye.

His scream made the veins in my neck vibrate. He rolled on the ground, gripping his eye with both hands. Blood squirted between his fingers like from a pierced hose.

I thrust the shark's tooth into my pocket, jumped in my boat, and struck out across the river toward its west bank. With luck, a big boat would pick me up and race full speed to the Coast Guard station. The Guard would bring agents and officers and EMTs to help Jason Stone.

I'd gotten it all wrong, and it was suddenly all clear. Jason Stone was the customs agent working undercover. He had not threatened me, he'd warned me not to rush to Stanley. The pistol shot rang again in my head, but I did not want to think about Alegria's husband injured. Or dying.

The wind picked up and blew from the west, making the river choppy. The tide was going out, and I felt my boat being pulled south. I looked to the right. A powerboat had passed and was out of shouting distance. A small motorboat raced by, its bow smacking the water like a beaver's tail. I waved my arms, but its occupants were too busy hanging on for dear life to notice. I paused, paddle raised. With no boats around, I might have to hide on one of the small islands near the west bank. That meant crossing the shipping channel.

The sound of a motor buzzed behind me. Thank God! I turned, ready to shout for help. Instead of a rescuer, I saw Stanley, a bandana tied around his head, gunning toward me in his jon boat. My nerves sprang like forage fish. With the same instinct for survival, I threw myself into a blind drive across the river. I hunched forward, stomach muscles crunched, head low, pulling at the water, twisting right then left, trying to maintain a straight line against the tug of the tide, the push of the wind, the drag of the current. In my mad dash from Dram Island, I'd forgotten my new lifejacket. All Stanley had to do was ram my boat, knock me into the water, and run me over. Even wearing the PFD, I would be helpless prey.

The first loud, low blast sounded like something buried underground, struggling to dig its way out. I ignored it and continued to punch the water. It seemed an impossible task—motor vs. paddle—but I couldn't give up. My body worked hard but so did my mind. The story fell into place. Aidan had given Stone information about Marc Diamond on the beach last January. Figuring Aidan was on to him, Diamond, who knew a thousand ways to rig an explosion in the lab, had killed him.

I was nearly halfway across the river when a second blast, closer this time, broke through my thoughts. Without stopping, I glanced around. Salt water stung and clouded my eyes. I didn't see any boats in the near distance, but could hear the predator bearing down from behind. I continued to paddle like a machine, eyes on the far bank.

The third blast forced me to look south. When I did, all the organs in my body seemed to change place. I was smack in the middle of the shipping lane, and a massive dark green container ship was steaming north. Behind me, the motor on Stanley's boat hummed like a giant wasp. To my left, the ship showed no sign of— what, stopping, turning, slowing down? There was no way any of those actions could happen. Not in the short distance between us.

My astonishment had not caused me to stop paddling. It only made my heart pump harder, faster, increasing my power. I hated formal exercise, but all those hours at the gym, the miles walked, the weights lifted, were paying off.

I plowed straight ahead. It was the only direction to go. Turning would take an impossible amount of time and keep me in the path of the ship. Plus, I'd hand myself back to Stanley. The bad guy. The man at the port who saw the turtle eggs tucked in a safe place and transported far away. The man who gave the order to kill Aidan. The boss.

My heart throbbed and my lungs ached as if they'd been stomped, but I pushed forward, driving my paddle into the water. Left. Right. Just haul ass, Hannah had said. Pretend you're crossing the ICW and a big, bad yacht was bearing down, running full tilt across my path.

A fourth blast sounded in my ear and a monster shadow blocked the sun. Had I passed in front of the bow? I refused to look and strained harder. My arms were on fire. My heart seemed to press against my chest. What if the ship sucked me down? What if it hit and knocked me into the water? Ran over me. And if by a miracle the ship didn't obliterate me, I'd be floating in the river with Joop's ten thousand bull sharks.

A wave hit me from behind and washed over the back of the boat. This was good. It meant I'd passed the bow and was being tossed by the ship's wake. In rough seas, Tanner had said, keep one end of the paddle in the water. The paddle was in the water, but the wave still spun me ninety degrees. A second one hit broadside. The kayak tipped right, then left, and water poured into the cockpit. I dropped my paddle flat on the water to steady myself, and with one hand clutched the gunwale as the boat bobbed like an apple in a washtub. I was still in my boat, but ass deep in water.

A fifth horn blast pulled my attention north. The ship lumbered up river like a colossal prehistoric sea monster. I knew the harbor pilot was reporting my stupid dash across his path to the Coast Guard. No, not stupid. Risky.

I was still caught in the ship's wake, but managed to maneuver the bow into the waves for a rollercoaster ride. Water flew up from inside the boat to splash my face, but it was cooling and slowed my heartbeat to a skittish patter. I was stiff with salt from the briny river.

The kayak's rocking horse motion finally stopped, and I slumped against the back of the seat. The ship had passed. I hadn't gotten hit or dumped or drowned—or eaten.

My spirit soared when I looked back across the channel. The Coast Guard and a fire rescue boat had Stanley pinned between them. Maybe Stone had come to and used a phone. I prayed Alegria's husband, Pilar and Benito's father, was alive.

My boat floated dangerously low in the water. I tried to bale with my hands, but most of the water fell back in before I could pitch it over the side. I should paddle to an island. Turn the kayak over to drain it. What I really needed was a giant sponge. Should have bought a pump.

My heart leaped again at the sound of a horn. The Coast Guard boat pulled away from the fireboat and headed toward me.

CHAPTER FORTY-EIGHT

"I'm thinking veal piccata." It was the afternoon before I left Goose Inlet, and Hannah had promised me one last food orgy at Guido's. Instead, she pulled into a parking space a block from the Chubby Fish.

"Change your mind? Not up for Italian?" I scanned the street even though I knew this stretch did not offer an eatery.

"Come on." Hannah undid her seatbelt. I followed, wondering what my friend was up to.

When Hannah opened the door to the Chubby Fish, I stopped dead. "They don't serve food here."

"They do today." She grabbed my arm and pulled me through the doorway.

I had never been inside the Chubby Fish. The fact that it was Dutch and Joop's favorite hangout was enough reason to give the place a wide berth. It was dark inside and the half-dozen customers sitting at the small bar turned to stare. I didn't recognize any of them. Hannah waved to the bartender and led me through a warren of tiny rooms crowded with scarred chairs and tables, lumpy sofas, and cockeyed lamps. I noticed two tall boat chairs leaning against a far wall, not attached to the floor. A small, black wood stove didn't appear connected to the outside. Old license plates and the names of possibly every customer who'd tossed back a beer at the Fish decorated the dark plank walls.

Hannah tugged on a warped door until it squeaked open. I pulled back. "Where are we going? I've never been—"

"I know! This is the one encounter lacking in your Goose Inlet experience. But we're going to fix that today." Hannah placed her hand on my back and pushed me across the threshold.

I was surprised when my shoes touched deep sand and sunshine pricked my eyes. I was back outside. Before me spread a sea of umbrella tables, Adirondack chairs, covered wooden swings and picnic tables. A chorus of "Surprise!" knocked me back.

Collected in the sandy, fenced-in lot were dozens of volunteers from the sea turtle project. Fala and Bianca blew kisses as they placed bowls and platters on a long wooden table. Jill stopped unwrapping paper plates to wave. The aroma of roasting meat wafted past. I looked through the crowd and saw Tanner and Erik wielding long forks at a wide grill. Both men offered beer bottle salutes.

I waved back and tried to speak but my throat tightened. Was this a going away party? I hadn't really become friends with many people during my summer in Goose Inlet. I'd chatted with volunteers at the nests but hadn't done much in the way of friendly things like lunches or walks or paddles with anyone but Hannah, Tanner and, once or twice, Bianca or Fala. And that was my fault. I'd spent a lot of solitary time thinking about my lost husband and what my life would be without him. And then I'd gotten angered by poaching, and emboldened by B&Es, and dumped in blackwater, and finally chased by a murderous smuggler across a container ship-patrolled river.

Still, it appeared the crowd of smiling faces was here to celebrate. It became clear I was the guest of honor when Joop and Dutch elbowed their way through the pack and scared the bejesus out of me by lifting me onto their bony shoulders. My face must have registered alarm because Erik dropped his grilling tool, hurried over, and lifted me down.

"Christ, Dutch! Don't damage her before the party even starts." He stooped and stared. "Look, you made her cry."

"No! He didn't. I mean, yes, you all made me cry—I'm happy. Happy to see everyone." My words crawled clumsily around the lump in my throat. "I didn't expect—Hannah, you are one sneaky—darling—woman." I threw my arms around my beaming friend. Dutch and Joop inched closer. I hugged them, too, then gripped Erik's arm with both hands.

"You knew all along Jason Stone was a customs agent?" I whispered to him.

"Contrary to what you see on TV, law enforcement agencies do communicate," the detective replied with a wink.

I opened my mouth but before I could utter a witty reply, Tanner embraced me. "Happy going away party. And congratulations!"

"For what?"

The answer came from a series of well-wishers who squeezed, hugged, kissed, patted, and thanked me for catching the villains who stole our sea turtle eggs and for finding the murderer and mutilators. I denied any contribution to the capture, but was shouted down by people who not only lauded my bold actions but also encouraged me to stay in Goose Inlet.

"You really should rethink this move away from the beach," Bianca said. "Chapel Hill has nothing on the Inlet. You belong here."

"Hey! Who's tending the grill?" someone shouted from across the sandlot. "These sausages look just about delicious!" Tanner and Erik strode back to their post.

"You need a beer." Dutch and Joop grabbed my arms and led me back inside the Chubby Fish and into a refrigerated room. I staggered at the sight of floor to ceiling shelves covering every inch of wall space and stacked with cases and six packs of beer, and not the ordinary kind. Clutching my arms to ward off the chill, I scanned the shelf to my left, then perused the one on my right.

I'd never heard of ninety percent of these varieties. "How can I possibly pick?"

"Well, don't pick your old favorite," Joop warned. "You come to the Fish, you pick something special."

"Something weird you never had before," Dutch added. His twisted beard stuck out like an ice pick. He pointed to one bottle. "That one has real gold in it."

I chose a bottle of Duck-Rabbit Milk Stout and hurried out of the frigid room. Before I could dig money out of my pocket, Dutch yelled, "Put whatever she wants on my tab." I shook my head at the bartender, but he waved me away.

On our return to the sandlot, we ran into the Stone family weaving through the bar to the picnic area. Pilar held her mother's hand. Benito bounced from lumpy sofa to scruffy chair, laughing at the stuffed pig and Mickey Mouse chess set.

"It's good to see you, Jason," I said. "How do you feel?" We sat down at a picnic table. The sun shone brightly, but a mild September breeze kept the air comfortable.

He rubbed the back of his head. "Still have a lump, but it doesn't hurt as much."

I had so much to say but didn't know where to start, so I began with, "Thank you."

He laughed. "For what? I got tackled by a drunk woman and knocked out. The other agents won't let me live this down." His smile faded. "You were left on your own with a murderer. I'm ashamed and can't apologize enough."

I touched his hand. "Don't feel that way. It was a freaky thing. All that soft sand—"

"And my head finds a rock." He smiled faintly and lifted Pilar onto his lap.

Tanner handed Jason a Sam Adams and clapped him on the shoulder. "You're both heroes," he said. "Together you caught the poacher and smuggler. And that's what this party is about as much as a going away bash. It's a big thank you from the turtle people."

My face began to burn. "Again—I didn't catch anybody."

"But you witnessed LuAnn admitting her guilt. And no denying you weakened Tack Stanley," Jason said.

Joop leaned into my shoulder. "Do you always carry a shark's tooth in your pocket?" he asked, confidentially, perhaps considering doing the same.

"That was the first shark's tooth I ever found!" I took a sip of beer. "Honest!"

"Ma, I'm hungry." Benito shook his mother's arm.

"There's ribs, chicken, hot dogs, hamburgers, hot sausage," Tanner said. "And some great looking salads." Alegria followed the children to the grill. A pang of guilt stabbed mercilessly as I remembered falling into the trap of *blame the Costa Rican.*

I finished my beer and before I set the bottle down Joop placed another called Duck Duck Gooze—that's right *Gooze*—in front of me. "I better get some food in me."

The words were barely out of my mouth when Erik set two platters piled with grilled meats on the table. Hannah and the turtle moms set out bowls of potato, macaroni and bean salads. Jill passed paper plates and utensils. Someone plunked down a delicious looking plate of roasted vegetables and toasted grains.

"Jason, two things I need to know," I said, wiping BBQ sauce off my lips. "One, did you know LuAnn was the poacher before you found us on Dram Island? And two, what was that gunshot?"

"I never thought the poacher was LuAnn," Joop said through a mouthful of chicken. "Not in a million years." His eyebrows shot toward his hairline. "And killing that James guy? Not the LuAnn I knew."

"Well, people can surprise us," Fala said sadly. "But you didn't give the man a chance to answer."

Jason paused spooning potato salad. "I got interested in LuAnn after my wife told me about her money problems and her extreme moodiness at the nests. I kept an eye on her."

"And Tack Stanley?" Jill asked. "You were on to him?"

"There was always something shady about Tack. Other agents suspected he was into smuggling, but we didn't know what or how big. I got friendly with him. Let him think I needed money to get my wife into the country legally—"

"See, I told you!" Dutch blurted.

"It wasn't true, you fool!" Bianca spit back.

Jason chuckled good-naturedly. "Eventually I let him recruit me into the smuggling ring. That argument you saw at the Sloppy Parrot," he said to me. "I pretended I wanted out. Let him think he had power over me. Played him pretty good." He smiled, and I recognized the mischievous grin I'd seen on Benito.

I spread spicy mustard on my burger. "I feel like an idiot. Was totally wrong about you. I believed Stanley when he said he was the customs agent. Then he attacked me." I stared into Jason Stone's eyes. "Please accept *my* huge apology."

He shrugged. "No way you could have known what was going on, Abby. But it turned out well. You're safe." He winked. "And, may I add, pretty damn brave."

A collective groan convulsed the group. I knew the story of my escape across the river had circled the Inlet several times.

"You say brave," Dutch said to Jason. "I say foolish." To my surprise, he sounded like a worried grandfather.

"Hey, I had to get away from that guy and the best way was to put a container ship between us." I might have used up a lifetime of luck, but if the ship hadn't come lumbering by, Stanley would have caught me.

As everyone concentrated on their food, I thought about LuAnn in jail. The DA did not believe her story that London James had fallen into the water unassisted. So far she'd had no visitors. Her family and childhood friends were embarrassed. Turtle people considered her a traitor and were too angry to sympathize with either her money or dead boyfriend excuses. Some even speculated that LuAnn had dragged Randy into the scheme and gotten him killed, making her a murderer twice.

Ironically, Hannah was the only volunteer with a smidgen of sympathy for LuAnn. She felt LuAnn's concern for her mother pushed her over the edge. Hannah was confident the volunteers' ire would lighten in time.

Joop cleared his throat. "I want to hear about the gunshot on Dram."

"Oh, right." Jason put down his fork. "In her statement LuAnn said Stanley threatened her but she was vague about how. When he turned around to chase Abby, LuAnn whopped him with the whiskey bottle but she was too drunk to be effective. I guess she'd expended all her energy tackling me," he added, to a chorus of grumbles. "The bottle grazed his ear. Stanley dropped the gun and it went off. That's the shot you heard."

Jason picked up a sausage sandwich loaded with grilled peppers and onions. After one bite, he put it down, paused, and then reached for my hand. "I feel terrible about your husband, Abby," he said softly. "Our investigation began with his suspicions about Diamond. I couldn't admit to you that I'd met him on the beach." His voice gained strength. "He helped us a lot. He was a good man."

"Thank you." A familiar tightness gripped my chest. "Aidan tried to help. Turned out he just got in the way."

Jason opened his mouth to say something but stopped.

I had received an explanation, abbreviated certainly, from the authorities. After Aidan told his research director he was pretty sure Diamond was stealing chemicals from the storage room, he saw Marc browsing endangered species and poaching websites on his work computer enough times to make him curious. He looked up those sites himself, and probably closed them abruptly when London walked in the room. At his police questioning, Diamond said he knew Aidan was snooping around his work computer and his home lab. After Tack Stanley's arrest, Diamond blurted the whole scheme to law enforcement, admitting he'd lured Aidan to the laboratory and killed him with a rigged explosion. He said Stanley made him do it. Both men were in jail, and I hoped they rotted there.

"Aidan helped us, Abby," Jason said, after a short pause. "This was not a small time operation. Not confined to Goose Inlet and those four people. A lot of money was involved and those guys weren't going to lose it."

"Were they in cahoots with the smugglers in Costa Rica?" Dutch asked, oblivious to Hannah's dagger looks.

"I can't talk about that part of the investigation," Jason replied. "But poaching doesn't happen only in Central America. Authorities just caught a ring of poachers in Juno Beach, Florida. We catch poachers along the coasts of Georgia and Alabama."

People shuttled food around on their plates, perhaps thinking, like me, about the great loss and damage done to endangered animals.

"If there's an opportunity, some will take it," Hannah said. "And, sadly, there are many opportunities to poach and many opportunities to sell sea turtle eggs."

Pilar and Benito, who'd been listening quietly, finished their hot dogs and ran off to play. Erik Magnus took their place.

"LuAnn said London and Marc killed Randy," I said, recalling the poacher's rant on Dram Island. "Is that true, Erik?"

"I guess she would assume that," he said, "since she didn't know about Stanley. He stayed in the background till London was gone. I can't say more than that."

Joop pulled his chair closer to the table. "Whoever did it, how'd they keep Randy's toes and butt from turning to mush in the sand?"

Bianca groaned. "For heaven's sake, Joop. You're going to bring that up at the table?"

"Maybe they coated them with the same stuff Diamond made for the eggs," Hannah said.

"The toes were red for Christ's sake," Dutch growled. "What's up with that?"

"Smugglers' sick humor?" Tanner offered. "Blood red to make it even creepier for LuAnn, as if that were possible."

"Too much weird shit going on around here," Dutch grumbled. "I'm thinking of moving. Buying a farm. Raisin' some goats like my buddy Unger Rice. There's money in goats these days."

"Another hair-brained idea," Bianca grumbled.

Dutch ignored her and slid over until his shoulder touched mine. "But let me say one thing, sweetheart. You were pretty clever to filet that dude's eyeball with a shark's tooth."

CHAPTER FORTY-NINE

I stored my bike and kayak at Hannah's house and promised to return to Goose Inlet between Christmas and New Year's, when *Carolina* traditionally shut down. Derek would be snowboarding in Wyoming and Kate was going to New York City with friends.

I was eager to return to work and even do a little investigative reporting. I had a couple of B&Es under my belt and had survived two risky choices that could have taken my life. Most importantly, I'd helped catch my husband's killer. So, yeah, I could tackle an IR story.

"Goodbye, sweet friend." Hannah held me snuggly in Lily Pad's driveway.

My eyes moistened. "You've been so kind to me. Thank you."

She hugged tighter. "You are welcome, but I'm still thanking you and your nosy gene."

I slid behind the steering wheel. "I'll see you in three months," I called, backing out of Lily Pad's driveway.

I drove slowly down Pinfish Lane thinking about birth, growth and change. I'd come to Goose Inlet angry and sorrowful. After learning that Aidan had been instructed not to share information with me or his coworkers, I'd thanked Mother Universe that I hadn't threatened him with divorce over my silly suspicions. Anger had melted into regret. I had finally crawled out of my hole. Just like the turtle hatchlings, I was embarking on a new experience. They scrambled to the sea to grow and procreate. I headed toward a new life as a single, widowed woman. Unlike a nest of turtle hatchlings, I was traveling alone. Aidan would never again cuddle me. Or find the TV remote. He would never take me to a Mother's Day brunch. I stopped the car on the shoulder and closed my eyes. I miss you, dear man, my protector, my companion. And I'll always, always love you.

As I drove past the beach access I saw Tanner Banks tossing a Frisbee to his neighbor's son. Erik Magnus lay on his surfboard, paddling out to deep water. Beyond him, a pelican dove headfirst into the ocean. Seagulls camped on the boardwalk railing stretched their necks and laughed. I inhaled sea air slowly and exhaled reluctantly. Then I turned away from the beach and headed home.

Acknowledgements

As with my previous books, I am most indebted to my writers' group, the Sea Quills. Nancy Gadzuk, Sheila Boneham, Charlene Pollano, and Teri Meadowcroft offered skillful criticism and constant encouragement. After tossing around several titles, Sheila came up with the perfect one.

Patricia Petro, Gail Smyth, and Sherry Anderson were early readers. Thanks also to Pat for designing my website, www.georgiamullen.com. Gail read specifically for accuracy of all things "sea turtle." She also took me patrolling the beach for mama turtle tracks one stormy morning. Nancy Busovne answered various turtle questions and if there are errors in the text they are mine, and not the fault of these two dedicated turtle volunteers.

Research biologist Byron Toothman with the North Carolina Coastal Reserve and National Estuarine Research Reserve was helpful identifying the invasive marsh grass that has become problematic along the East Coast.

Thanks go to Andre Blouin for passing along the historical anecdotes about early 20th century attitudes and behavior toward sea turtles and their eggs.

Chief medical examiner Dr. Darinka Mileusnic-Polchan, led me to forensic anthropologist Dr. Murray K. Marks who explained decomposition of human tissue in sandy, watery conditions. I obviously fudged a bit by applying red goo to the human parts to make them last longer.

Dr. Kenneth Mattes, a friend and retired chemist, deserves huge thanks for giving me the idea of coating eggs to preserve freshness, which jump started *The Loggerhead Murders'* plot.

Made in the USA
Middletown, DE
02 March 2020

85650695R00205